Royally (RE) ARRANGED

EMMA ST. CLAIR

AUTHOR'S NOTE

While there are perfectly lovely ACTUAL countries with royals, I have created fictional countries for this book. Much of what people know of royals comes from Great Britain, but royalty and peerage and titles work differently in other countries. To that end, my fictional countries each have their own laws governing their people and their monarchies. I imagine these countries sort of shoved into the nooks and crannies of Europe. You know, like Liechtenstein.

(Be honest: do YOU know where Liechtenstein is??? Gold star if you do!)

Though my characters may have other national languages, the book is written in English. In my head, I hear them speaking in British English, which comes from my British friends, a semester I spent in London in college, and watching *Ted Lasso*. (He's here, he's there, he's every**where!)

So, when you imagine my characters speaking or run across some phrases that sound a little different to my readers in the United States, it's because in my mind, they're all speaking (what I know of) British English. Ex: people get things sorted, whereas in the US, people get things sorted *out*. They also might do things WHILST instead of WHILE doing something else.

Oi! Thanks for suspending your belief a little to enter my fictional world. Are you ready? Let's go!

THE FAIRY TALE: ONCE UPON A TIME

THE KING of Viore

"Daddy! Tell me a story."

I'll never tire of being called *Daddy*. Or being the father of this sweet girl, with her bird's nest of brown hair—her mother's—and impish smile—mine.

"If you want a story, you'll have to scoot over, my little Ava-bird."

She giggles, her face such a perfect, beautiful imitation of her mother that I can't help but smile. She wiggles over about half a centimeter, and I flop down on her, careful to keep most of my weight off.

The giggles turn to full-on laughter, and even as I'm shushing her, Serafina pokes her head in the room with a deep sigh, one hand grazing the swell of her pregnant belly.

"She'll never fall asleep like this. You wind her up," she says, but her eyes are warm on the two of us as I tuck Ava under my arm.

"Then we need you to join us, Queen No-Fun." I pull Ava closer and pat the space on her other side.

"Come on, Mummy! Dad's going to tell a story."

Serafina's eyes soften as she looks at me, and even after all these years, her gaze still has the ability to make my heart thump wildly. After a pause, where she pretends she's actually considering it and where Ava and I make puppy-dog eyes at her, Serafina snuggles up on Ava's other side. Her hand finds mine, and we share a secret smile over our daughter's dark hair, fluffed out over the pillow. Ava rests her hand on her mother's belly, already protective of the little one who will be joining us in a few months.

"Daddy," Ava begs. "The story!"

After kissing her forehead, I wink at Serafina and begin.

"Once upon a time, there was a princess. She was the fairest, most beautiful maiden in all the land, but she fancied herself in love with a prince who was an idiot."

"Hey!" Serafina interrupts, with a sharp finger poke to my shoulder.

"Daddy, we don't say idiot. Mum says it's not a nice word."

"It isn't nice, you're right. But in this case, it's true."

"He wasn't an idiot," Serafina argues. "He was just—" She pauses, scrunching up her nose. "Fine. Maybe he was. But a different word, please?"

I hold up my free hand. "May I tell my story, please?"

Serafina huffs, but settles in again as Ava yawns.

"As I was saying, the man she fell in love with was a *fool* because he didn't love her back. He couldn't see how wonderful and beautiful and amazing she was. Someone really should have thrown him in a moat."

"A moat filled with crocodiles?" Ava asks.

I kiss her temple. "Filled with dragons."

"Dragons don't live in moats," Serafina says.

"Dragons don't exist, Mummy," Ava corrects. "And anyway, it's Dad's story."

I chuckle. "And in my story, they not only exist, but they breathe fire and live in moats *and* eat princes who can't see the perfect woman right in front of them."

Blowing out a breath and shaking her head, the perfect woman in front of me urges me on. "What happened next?"

"Did the dragons eat the stupid prince?"

"Don't say stupid, Ava."

I run a hand over Ava's hair. "The dragons unfortunately did NOT eat the *foolish* prince, even if he deserved it. But there was a handsome, brave knight"—Serafina squeezes my fingers—"who fell in love with the princess the moment they met. Head over heels, love at first sight."

"And they lived happily ever after?" Ava asks through a yawn.

Serafina's gaze is heavy on mine, but as I squeeze her hand, I look my daughter straight in the eyes. "Not so fast, Ava-bird. Happily-ever-afters, the *real* kind, almost never happen easily or without a few dragons getting in the way."

"I thought dragons weren't real?"

"Metaphorical dragons."

"What's meta-forkful?"

Serafina hides her laughter under a fake coughing fit.

"Never mind. The point is, without a journey, without some struggle, a few challenges, and some metaphorical dragons—which Mummy will explain to you later—the happily-ever-after wouldn't be so sweet."

Ava stirs impatiently, even as her eyes grow droopy. "Daddy, what happened next? Just tell the story!"

"Yes, just tell the story," Serafina echoes. "I can't wait to hear this."

3

"This story begins the week of a very important ball," I begin. And as my daughter fights sleep, curled against my chest, I begin to tell the story of how I wooed and won the woman gazing at me from the other side of the bed, my very own happily-ever-after.

FROM THE ROYAL POST
SEPTEMBER

DEAR CALLUM,

Hey! It's me, Fi! Did you figure that out yet? I'm leaving the return address off the envelope in hopes that this letter might surprise you, but you probably know my handwriting by now. Years of writing will do that. Also, who else writes you letters but me?

Actually, now I'm wondering—*does* anyone else write you? Besides fan mail to His Royal Highness Prince Callum of Elsinore. That doesn't count.

Oh! I got my dozenth (is that a word?) wedding proposal this week—this one from an eight-year-old French boy named Harry. Though he has adorable freckles, the thirteen-year age gap seems a bit much. Plus, I think he's in it for the wrong reasons. Namely, I think he's after the title.

Prince Harry does have a nice ring to it!

I'm rubbish at starting letters. Clearly. How are you? Maybe I should have led with that!

I just miss you. I miss US.

Is that weird to say? US? I'll be honest—I'm writing this letter after a glass of wine. So, maybe I'm a little looser than usual?

I'm looking forward to seeing you when all is said and done! I'll finish my exams and jump on a plane straightaway for Elsinore. I feel in some ways like I've been looking forward to the Centennial Ball my whole life. Or, what comes after. The next chapter.

I know we don't ever speak of, well, IT. Not the creepy clown book or film. You know, the IT you and I don't talk about.

Why DON'T we talk about it, by the way? We really should have.

But so you know, I can't wait to see you, Callum. To be with you.

No more letters, no more hedging around the future. Just US. (And a whole lot of obligations and expectations, but that comes with the territory, right?)

Wow, the wine is really hitting me. I just giggled! You'd be having quite a laugh at my expense right now. Remember when you gave me too many mai tais last summer? I thought Mum was going to toss you off the yacht.

But it's nice to let loose a little. I know you've always said I should be a little less—how did you put it? Rigid? Stuffy?

It was quite rude, for the record. Don't worry, I forgive you.

Anyway. I probably wouldn't have earned the Ice Princess nickname if I'd figured out how to be looser and less rigid. Or, at least, a better balance.

I've been struggling the last few years with balance and with the weight of it all—the personal, the national. Duty versus choice. The responsibility toward the greater good over what I want. Being myself. Being who everyone expects me to be.

I wouldn't complain like this to anyone else, but I know you get it. You have the same pressures. Not as many as Phillip does—I know you're thankful to be the spare not the heir, as much as you joke about it.

But in a little over a year's time, I'll be the flipping QUEEN. Viore isn't as large as Elsinore, but it's still a lot to manage. A whole country!

I don't want to scare you off, though! Just ruling a small European country in the twenty-first century. No biggie! Do not panic!

Not that you—I mean … Well. Let's just say WHOEVER rules alongside me as king will have a lot of work, but not so much more than, say, you have right now as the Prince of Elsinore.

And WHOEVER this king is, he'll have me. A partner. A friend. A lover.

(I just giggled again! Why do I always hear the word *lover* in my head in this deep, husky voice? LOVER. It sounds so dirty! This is definitely the wine talking now!)

The point is: I don't want to do this alone. But I'm happy to do it together with someone who is on my side, my team. A particular SOMEONE who knows me better than anyone else in the world …

Wink, wink.

Wow … the wine is hitting me a little hard. It was just one glass, I promise!

(Maybe a glass and a fourth. Fine. A glass and a half. I could totally walk a straight line or touch my fingers to my nose. That's what the authorities always have people doing in movies. Is that a real thing? I wouldn't know. I've never

7

had too much to drink or learned to drive, so it's kind of a non-issue. Do you ever think how weird our "normal" lives are?)

I'm starting to think writing you now was a bad idea. I just hiccuped! Definitely a bad idea.

I wish you were here, Callum.

You always make everything better.

Ah! There I go again.

This letter is not from the Ice Princess. More like the Emo Princess or the Glass-and-a-Half-of-Wine Princess. You're the only one I let see this side of me. Or a part of this side of me. I haven't told you everything or let you see all of me ... yet.

Maybe one day I will.

Maybe, Callum, one day, I'll spill all my dirty—and not so dirty, because let's be honest, I'm pretty innocent—secrets to you.

One day, you'll know it all.

Write me back! And I promise next time I'll send you a totally sober, no-wine-at-all letter.

Unless you prefer this, and then I'll ONLY write to you after at least one glass of wine. Your choice!

I miss you.

Love,

Your Fi

———

October

Dear Callum,

Hello! I hope you're doing well. Classes have started, and

my coursework is keeping me quite busy. Socioeconomics and geology are no joke!

Anyway, I wanted to reach out about a letter you may have received which I MAY have written under the influence of a glass (and a half) of wine. Don't laugh—I know I'm a lightweight. Maybe you didn't get my letter—that wouldn't be a bad thing. I'm mostly hoping it got lost in the post.

Honestly, I don't remember the contents of the letter exactly, but in CASE you got it and in CASE I overstepped or got weird or awkward, I wanted to apologize. When I didn't hear from you, I assumed the worst. I tend to do that, as you know—overanalyze and worry unnecessarily. That is, when I'm not being overly optimistic and seeing the world through rose-colored glasses, like my father always says I do. Not sure how it's possible to do both, but what can I say—I'm talented.

I hope you're well! Look forward to speaking with you soon. New Year's can't come quickly enough!

Your friend,
Serafina

———

February

Dear Callum,

It's been a while, and you're way overdue for a letter. I feel like the last time we really spoke was … I don't know—last summer in the Maldives? That seems like ages ago!

This is the longest stretch we've gone without speaking since we were nine. Maybe we should both get over our aversion to texting?

I really don't mean to make you feel guilty for not writing! But I have to ask—are you okay?

You're probably just busy. I know I am! I'm sure you have a lot of obligations now that you're done with the royal guard. Based solely off the tabloids, your social calendar seems quite full! You know I don't believe the stories—all rubbish—but going from the pictures, you sure have had a string of gorgeous dates.

I have to say I'm quite the wallflower in comparison. My last social event was the New Year's Gala (I was so disappointed you couldn't make it!) and my date was nothing like the women you've been seeing.

Lewis is a prince (of Valdonia, which is smaller than either of our countries!), mid-forties and looks nearly sixty. He smelled of sardines (or maybe it was cod?), had wandering hands, and I think I could braid his ear hair.

Not that I want to! Disgusting. I'd like to stop thinking of ear hair at all right now and forevermore.

(Are you still picturing ear hair? I am. *Shudder.*)

Anyway, I'm not doing much in the way of being social, as I've got weekly calls with Mum and Dad to prepare me for my impending coronation. Mum's training includes a lot about charitable causes, while Dad is walking me through the minefield of the royal haters and issues he says I should know about but are really more for the man who will be my king. Not even a little sexist. *eyeroll*

In addition, my last year of uni is quite a lot more work than I anticipated. For now, my life is simply overwhelming.

I don't mean to spend this whole letter complaining! I hope you're well. I really do miss you!

I'm still planning to attend the Centennial Ball and the preceding events. If you don't have time to write before then,

I'll probably coordinate with someone at the palace. I'm sure we'll have plenty of time to catch up then. At least, I hope!

Looking forward to seeing you!

Yours,

Fi

CHAPTER ONE

Serafina

Is duty still considered duty when it's something you *want* to do?

This is the question I'm pondering as I watch Prince Callum thoroughly trounce his opponent in tennis. Specifically, I'm watching Callum's firm, athletic bum as he trounces his opponent in tennis. His thighs too. Hard not to ogle those when they look good enough to eat. Almost like two meaty Christmas hams.

Duty looks delicious.

In case you're the judgy sort, thinking I'm just objectifying the poor man, he's my fiancé. Well. *Almost* my fiancé. And I have waited my whole life for this man without so much as a kiss goodnight from him, so you'll forgive me if my mind is a little focused on his physical attributes.

He's also my best friend, so this isn't a crush or just physical attraction. I'm not *that* shallow! But a girl can admire her fiancé, can't she?

"You've got a little drool there."

From beside me, the incredibly irritating and decidedly devilish Duke of Weldon swipes a fingertip across my lower lip. I swat him away, feeling my cheeks heat. Callum may be my best friend and almost fiancé, but I don't want to get caught ogling him.

"Keep your hands to yourself," I hiss to Rafe. "I don't want to even know where they've been."

"Let me know if you change your mind about that."

His grin is pure wickedness. It makes me shudder. Not in a good way.

I don't miss the way my personal protection officer, a hulk of a man Kat and I simply refer to as The Dane, gives me a look from his spot at the end of our row. I give him a slight headshake. Rafe is an annoyance. Not an actual threat. Unfortunately. I'd love nothing more than to watch The Dane pick Rafe up over his head and toss him out of the match.

But I can handle Rafe. "Why don't you crawl back under whatever rock or woman you crawled out from under?"

His dark chuckle matches his dark eyes and even darker hair. Honestly, Prince of Darkness would be a more fitting title for the duke. One might think that there would be more sympathy and compassion for Rafe. After all, he was orphaned when he was only eight, losing both his parents in a car accident. Tragic, really. He was left in the care of his uncle, the Baron de Silva, a smarmy snake of a man who always seems to be plotting something with a too-wide smile. He's never hidden his disdain for the King and Queen of Elsinore, apparently stemming from some land dispute years before I was born.

Rafe must have learned at his uncle's feet. I've never seen

him look anything but smug. He doesn't walk; he saunters. Every smile, every chuckle, every comment is useful, intended toward some purpose—that purpose usually involving a woman.

And duty? He's allergic to the very idea.

He's the very antithesis of me, the opposite of Callum who is the hero to Rafe's bad boy. It makes total sense that Callum and Rafe have always been rivals. Which means Rafe is my rival too.

I'm not sure what his game is today. He's been flirting with me, which is a first. Normally he seems to either ignore me or treat me with cool detachment while flirting the pants off any woman who has, well, pants. Or a dress. Basically, anyone with a pulse.

Today though, he's like one of those gnats humming irritatingly near my ear. I'd like to squash him.

"I promise my hands are clean, and I haven't been under any rocks or women. Just so we're clear, Princess."

Kat leans her head around me to bat her lashes at Rafe. "Does that mean you're actually single for once?"

He winks, and I roll my eyes. "Very much."

"Let me know if you want to change that."

"We'll see, Kitty Kat."

"Both of you, hush!" I lean closer to Kat, whispering, "Don't encourage him. Never feed the strays."

"But he's so pretty," she whines, smoothing a hand over her short, dark bob. "And you know how I feel about bad boys."

"The same way you feel about *all* men?"

Despite our different personalities, Kat is my best—and other than Callum, *only*—friend. She acts as my sole source of personal information about men as she tends to enjoy them. A *lot*. It's not my style, but after watching her parents divorce bitterly after surviving twenty-seven years of marriage, three kids, and emigrating from Korea, I think it's Kat's way of guarding herself against feeling anything too deeply.

She's excellent at guarding—I would know. She's acted as my unofficial bodyguard almost since the moment we met. Five feet two inches of Kat fury is surprisingly effective at keeping people at bay. Kat all but adopted me my first year in uni when she was the resident assistant.

I adopted her right back, and hope when she finishes law school, she'll join me in Elsinore as part of our legal team.

"Yes, but the bad ones are so good," Kat says.

We can agree to disagree. Tall, dark, and roguish isn't my type. I return my focus to Callum down below, who is exactly and *only* my type: golden hair, a crooked smile complete with dimple, and eyes the blue of the Mediterranean. My childhood best friend. My soon-to-be fiancé. I can hardly wait but am going to be a ball of tightly wound nerves until things are official.

Interrupting my romantic thoughts, my stomach growls loudly, and Rafe chuckles again. "I'm going to grab a bite. Can I bring you something?"

Tempted, I glance at Rafe, but some pretty socialite-type further down the row seems to have caught his eye with a flirty wave. It's no wonder he's known as the Royal Rogue.

"So much for being single," I mutter to Kat.

I wave Rafe off, glad when his presence isn't overshadowing the moment. Why is he even here if he's going to miss the end of the match?

I am starving, to be honest. I've been too nervous to eat much for the last few days. First, I had to pass my last set of final exams at uni—check! Now, I'm here in Elsinore to publicly announce my engagement to Prince Callum—almost check!

We need to iron out the actual details of the engagement, but have almost a week before the Centennial Ball to do so. It will be strange to actually discuss this out loud.

Ever since our parents made this arrangement when Callum and I were just children, it's been very hush-hush. The kind of thing where I could tell you, but then I'd have to kill you.

It's an unspoken rule about something unspoken. Callum and I have never even discussed it, though in one of my last letters to him (penned after imbibing in a little wine), I came close to mentioning it out loud. I can't quite remember what I wrote, but from the bits I can piece together, I know it wasn't very subtle.

When Callum never wrote back, I sent a quick apology letter, and when he didn't respond to that either, I've done my best not to panic and obsess.

Did he even get the letter? Was it too forward or did he smile while reading at how ridiculous I was?

Is he looking forward to this as much as I am? Will it be strange to flip the switch from lifelong friendship to something more? Did he already pick out the ring or will we do that together? Is he planning to officially ask for my hand in private or with a grand gesture?

Kat has listened to me obsess over these questions—and more—all year as the date grew closer and closer. Finishing my coursework provided a necessary distraction, but the questions and worries have been pinging around in my brain like a bunch of rubber balls.

It's been worse this year since Callum's letters have trickled to a stop. I've missed my best and oldest friend but knew it was just a matter of time. Now that I'm finally done with uni, I can't wait to start the rest of my life with this man. We'll have all the time in the world to catch up.

Kat fans herself with her hand. Her hair brushes over her cheeks, looking effortlessly chic as always. My light brown hair is rather wild, falling in unruly waves down my back. Without Kat's help, I would probably pin it up in a ponytail every day. I jokingly tell her often that if the lawyer thing doesn't work out, she could be a hairstylist.

Leaning close, Kat says, "Your *betrothed* looks particularly delectable in short shorts. I've never been so thankful for the invention of tennis. Specifically, tennis shorts."

You and me both.

I grin. "Yes. My *betrothed* does look delicious, doesn't he?"

I'd certainly like to take a bite out of Prince Callum. A love bite, obviously. I'm not a zombie or vampire, for heaven's sake. I'm a *princess*.

Though at the moment, my thoughts do not in any way match the prim and proper image I've cultivated and maintained my whole life. No one would ever suspect that Serafina the Ice Princess (the nickname given to me by the press) is all hot and bothered watching her secret, soon-to-be-official fiancé.

Callum could inspire the most innocent thoughts to take a turn to the wild side. He's *that* attractive. More than that, Callum is a genuinely great guy. Kind and funny—the sort of man you could be yourself around. Or, at least, I always could.

He and Kat might be the only ones who have truly seen behind my Ice Princess facade, who know that I'm not a closed-off, snobbish royal. They know I'm much more Anna than Elsa, even if I tend to publicly give off very frozen vibes. He didn't ever mind my awkward years, and he always laughed at my lame jokes. Our friendship has always been so easy, so safe.

But in his tennis shorts, his personality is not what's on full display. I'll ogle his personality later.

Kat's bad influence is probably the reason half these thoughts are floating through my head. For years, I've listened to her go on about the men she's dated and the wild, free life she's embraced. I'm grateful for my lot in life—at least, most days—but I do sometimes live vicariously through her.

I have yet to taste so much as Prince Callum's lips on mine. Something I plan to remedy posthaste. The few kisses I've had over the years have been disappointing and made me feel like I was cheating. It's hard to date around when I knew one day, I would be Callum's. I've always felt like *his*.

And though he seems to have dated half of Europe this year, I'm choosing to believe he probably feels the same. They were simply ... placeholders. Dates to events he had to attend. That's all.

Callum wins the point after a particularly long volley and people politely clap in that reserved way they do for tennis matches. Except for the woman behind me who has been giggling obnoxiously this whole time. She lets out a loud whoop and then whistles, a piercing sound that I'm sure has dogs howling three countries away.

She's got an American accent, and I'm not sure how she ended up in the royal box. Maybe she won a contest? When I give her a subtle glance all I can make out is bright blonde curls and some kind of horrendous red and white ensemble. Tacky.

I try to block out the grating sound of her laugh and focus on this moment, the one I've been waiting for. Not literally this *exact* moment. I'm sure Callum isn't planning to get down on one knee in the red clay before his next serve, or even after he wins the final point. He doesn't even know I'm here. I thought I'd surprise him, arriving a few days earlier than planned for the ball. I've missed him so much this year.

Callum dives to save a ball right on the line, sending it over the net with just enough spin that his opponent can't return it. Only one more point and it's game, set, match.

A riot of butterflies takes flight in my stomach—or maybe that's the hunger pains? I can't tell the difference at this point. As soon as Callum wins, I can make my way down to surprise and congratulate him. Maybe boldly, with a kiss? The thought makes me giddy. Soon, all the waiting, all the loneliness, all the missing him will be worth it.

Before he serves, Callum wipes the sweat from his brow with a small towel.

"That towel would go for a million euros," Kat says. "Think you could snag it for me? It would help make a dent in paying off my student loans."

I elbow her. "Absolutely not."

Not because that would be wrong, but because if anyone's keeping that hand towel, it's *me*. I'm also secretly working out how to pay off Kat's student loans without her knowing. She's ridiculously stubborn when it comes to letting me help her with anything, so I have to be sneaky.

Callum bounces the ball a few times before his serve and then pauses to glance at the crowd. My heart swells as his gaze finds mine. A wide grin takes over his handsome face, making the dimple appear in his right cheek.

For years, I've been fascinated with that dimple. One more thing I've been waiting for—to trace it with my finger, to kiss it. Maybe lick it?

Giggles and whispers behind me have Kat turning around

to glare at the American. Kat mutters something under her breath that could make a sailor blush.

"Is she talking about us?" I whisper.

Kat rolls her eyes. "No. About your *betrothed.*"

Jealousy flares hot in me, not for the first time. I haven't been able to avoid seeing the tabloid photos of Callum with other women, especially this past year. I've thought of them as necessary evils, the way Mum and Dad arranged for the potbellied Duke of Valdonia to be my date when Callum couldn't come to the New Year's Gala. Elsinore had their own celebration, so I understood. Mostly. If Callum had called or written to me himself rather than politely declining by way of his press secretary, I might not have been hurt at all.

It didn't help that the Valdonian prince, whose limp hands kept trying to rove over my body, isn't quite on par with the women Callum has been seen with. Like the leggy Swiss supermodel or that second-rate actress with the ridiculously massive fake breasts. I swear, you could hang coats on those things!

The jealousy I've felt from afar is nothing compared to the molten liquid fire igniting every inch of me right now as the woman whispers "Callum" on a sigh. It's ridiculous, really. This loud American isn't my competition. I've already won, and it's simply time to collect my much-coveted prize: the prince who has owned my heart since childhood.

Speaking of winning, Callum's opponent hits a ball wide, and I find myself getting to my feet along with the rest of the stadium, clapping. I'm eager to get down to the court and greet Callum properly. I can't stop the spread of a smile over my cheeks.

The American giggler bumps into us on the stairs and this time, I barely restrain Kat.

"Don't make a scene," I hiss between gritted teeth.

"But you know I love making scenes. I'm quite accomplished at it."

"And usually I don't mind. You know how I do love your scenes—they're glorious. But not here. Not. Today."

Kat sighs, and we continue down the stairs. "Not all problems are best solved by ignoring them."

As though to prove how wrong she is, I ignore her comment. My tolerance for ignoring is unusually high. It has to be.

I've learned to ignore digs from the paparazzi about my weight (no matter whether I'm up or down on the scale), my (lack of) dating life, and Prince Callum's overactive one this year. I've perfected smiling primly while deflecting questions about marriage, my coronation in a year's time, and the growing criticism for the monarchy.

Smile and nod. Ignore, ignore, ignore. It's served me well thus far.

But all the years of decorum lessons disappear in a cloud of dust as I reach the court, waving and grinning like a fool. "Callum!"

His eyes meet mine, and my confident steps falter. Callum looks … surprised. Which can't be right. Wasn't he just smiling up at me?

His expression quickly shifts, replaced by a grin that's decidedly casual. No dimple in sight.

"Mayday, mayday," Kat mutters, letting me know that whatever this strangeness is, unfortunately, I'm not imagining it.

My stomach drops, feeling like an ocean trench, dark and fathomless. I force myself to keep walking toward Callum.

"Fi," he says, striding forward to meet me.

The sound of his nickname on my lips dispels some of the

strangeness, and I close the distance between us. His smile settles into the handsome, warm look I'm familiar with, dimple on full display.

Things are fine. We are fine. It's just been a long time. Soon, you'll settle back into your friendship—and more. No need to panic.

Then he holds out a hand for me to shake. We stand there for a moment, frozen. His hand, outstretched formally. My arms, open wide for a hug.

It's awkward, and the panic I just tried to shove down is suddenly climbing up my throat again. Along with—*oh, don't you dare!*—hot tears of rejection, which sting the backs of my eyes.

Keep it together, Serafina. It doesn't mean anything. We're in public, and displays of affection are best kept behind closed doors.

It's because of my stupid letter, I bet. I wish I could remember exactly what I said, and how hard I hinted at our arrangement. It was too bold, too honest. Callum is the kind of man who wants to wear the proverbial pants, something that at times has worried me. Did I overstep by hinting at what we've avoided discussing all these years?

"Sorry," Callum says. "I'm quite sweaty."

"Of course." We shake hands, and it feels … wrong. Stiff. Formal. Unfamiliar. "Great match!" I say. "Quite a show."

"Yes. Quite a show," Kat says, letting her eyes rove over Callum's torso. I swear she's about to squeeze his biceps when a shrill voice interrupts the moment.

A shrill *American* voice. I can't seem to escape this dreadful woman seated behind me.

"Callie!"

Callie??

Callum's warm smile widens as his eyes shift somewhere behind me. And then, in a flash of blonde curls and—*dear*

Lord, is that gingham?—the obnoxious woman from behind me launches herself into his arms.

The arms that were, apparently, too sweaty for me.

I watch as Callum swings her around, the tablecloth she appears to be wearing fanning out behind her. She's tiny and gorgeous and perfect, like a miniature doll. I manage to find my royal smile, the one that's practiced enough to fool almost anyone.

"You should have let me have a go at her," Kat whispers to me.

"Shut up. It's nothing. Probably just—"

Whatever words were on my tongue disappear as the fluffy blonde tablecloth-wearer presses her lips to Callum's mouth.

I hear a loud cracking as a big piece of the iceberg that is now my heart breaks off and floats away. Gone. Dead. Irrecoverable.

Callum carefully sets the woman down before glancing at me with what appears to be guilt. Maybe a little regret. Not quite enough emotion compared to the utter devastation inside me, but it's something.

The woman wraps an arm around Callum's waist like a tentacle. She places her other hand possessively on his chest, stroking him.

I'm going to be sick.

She is stroking Prince Callum's chest. My Prince Callum.

Except he doesn't really appear to be mine, does he?

I've never touched him so casually, so proprietarily. I think back to when we were children, so rough and tumble together, hardly knowing where one of us ended and the other began. Back then, everything between us was easy as we climbed trees in the royal garden, snuck into the servants' quarters in his palace, and explored that closed-off turret

24

rumored to be haunted.

The memories leave me feeling hollow, and I can't drag my eyes away from the sight of this woman's polished nails, staking a claim on what—who—I always assumed was mine.

She turns her big brown eyes to me and blinks, another giggle escaping. "Oh! I'm sorry! How rude of me. I'm Brit. Callie's girlfriend."

Whatever was left of my heart shatters until it's all just tiny pieces of ice, bobbing and floating in an arctic sea.

"Girlfriend." It's as though I've never said the word before. It feels funny on my lips.

I have never been anyone's girlfriend. Because I was waiting for this man. The one looking at me with apologetic eyes. But not *so* apologetic, because he doesn't shove Brit away and wrap me up in his arms instead.

If anything, he pulls her closer. I stare at his hand on her waist. It looks far too large, too powerful for this small, shrill woman. I saw plenty of photographs this year of Callum with his hands on other women. It stung, but I assumed it meant nothing. Now, with a painful sinking sensation, I realize those women might have been *more*.

That's the moment when the paparazzi swarm out of nowhere like the insects they are. Photographers shouldn't be on the court at all, but that doesn't seem to be stopping them. Callum's security team steps forward, blocking them as best they can. The photogs are snapping pictures and shouting questions and practically shoving me and Kat out of the way to capture shots of Prince Callum of Elsinore and his new American *girlfriend*.

"Prince Callum—are you officially off the market?"

"How and when did you two meet?"

"Are you in love?"

Yes, Prince Callum, do tell.

The Dane is suddenly a solid wall behind me, ushering us toward the exit. Kat takes my arm and we quickly walk away from the throngs of reporters.

"You're going to be fine," she assures me, and I think I nod, though I don't believe it. Not for a second.

We pass Rafe as we're almost to the private exit where a car waits to take us to the palace.

"Trouble in paradise?"

I glare, and his smirk disappears, morphing into something more like concern.

"Hey, are you okay?"

The concern in his eyes seems genuine, but there's a lipstick smudge on his cheek the same color as Brit's tablecloth dress.

I snort and pass right by without pausing. Rafe seems to be the only one who watches our quick exit, and we disappear into the black car as though we were never there at all.

CHAPTER TWO

Rafe

I slip through the line waiting to purchase merchandise and behind a large group in order to lose the boozy socialite following me. Who knew years of learning to disappear would come in handy trying to escape a woman? Other women are the last complication I need right now. I have enough complications on my own and only one woman I'm interested in.

Unfortunately, that one woman has zero interest in me.

Finding an empty balcony area near the back of the sports complex, I walk to the edge of the balcony and grip the railing, staring out at the Elsinorian mountain ranges. Just beyond those ridges is my duchy, consisting of farmlands and a few small towns nestled in a little valley.

Well, what *should be* my duchy. Since my parents' deaths, Uncle has kept me under his control one way or another. Right now, by way of a legal conservatorship due to "mental instability." Because of his reach, I cannot so much as get a judge to consider my case.

But if I do one favor for him this week—*one simple thing*, he said, which means anything but simple and probably more along the lines of nefarious—he promised to dissolve the conservatorship. I want to be out from under his thumb, but my stomach twists thinking about what he might have me do.

And, knowing this, Uncle dangled the one thing in front of me he knew I couldn't say no to.

His smile had been slow and wicked when he said, "The rumor is your princess is getting engaged this week to Prince Callum."

My princess. I wish.

And though I knew it would be exquisite torture to witness this, I couldn't *not* be here. I'm the furthest thing from an optimist, but a tiny sliver of me must be. Because I am holding on to the hope that by some miraculous chance, I could convince Seraf to consider me instead.

The only problem is that the things in my toolbox either won't impress Serafina, or they can't compare to what she could have with Callum.

I'm a duke; he's a prince.

I have land and money; he has more.

I've loved her from afar; he's been her best friend since childhood.

While I have no illusions that my good looks are admired by many, the same can be said of Callum. I'd bet his fan club is bigger. As for our reputations … I'm known as the Royal Rogue. He's the Golden Boy.

There is really no contest here. No choice. Plus, I saw the way she looked at Callum down on the court, the way she's always looked at him.

With LOVE.

"Did you really think you could compete with him?" I say the words out loud, needing to hear them.

"Oh, there's no competition," a voice purrs, and as a hand slides up my neck, I turn to see the woman I thought I'd shaken.

Before I can step back, she grips my shirt and moves in for a kiss, like a casual hook-up right here in the open is totally on the table.

Not so long ago for me, it might have been.

I manage to turn my head, and her lips only brush my cheek. With firm hands—but not so tight a grip as to leave bruises—I take hold of her shoulders and move her back.

"I'm sorry," I say in my most cool, even tone. "I'm taken."

Her eyes widen. She laughs then, and it's crueler than any insult she could have lobbed my way. "Don't tell me you're in a *relationship.*"

She says the word like she wouldn't touch it with a ten-foot pole. Or maybe it's not the general idea of a relationship, but specifically ME in a relationship.

"You?"

The one word makes her meaning all too clear: she cannot imagine me in a relationship. I wonder how she'd laugh if I told her who holds my heart in her hands.

"Sorry," she says, covering her mouth and stepping away until my hands drop, fisting at my sides. "It's just ... you don't seem like the type to settle down. Ever."

"Things change."

"But people don't. At least, that's what they say."

"Maybe *they* are wrong."

"Maybe," she says, but her eyes regain that flirty look, and before I can stop her, she shoves a cocktail napkin into my shirt pocket, presumably with her number on it.

I guess she gets points for preparedness as well as boldness. Too bad those aren't the qualities I'm looking for in a woman.

Kindness, gentleness, a brilliant mind, and a heart that inspires me to more—that's what I've got my sights set on. Even if it's not a realistic goal.

Go big or go home, right?

I catch the eye of a security guard standing just inside the building. I may not be a prince or princess with my own personal protection detail, but they know who I am. The guard steps in between us.

The woman holds up both hands, then gives me a saucy wink as she walks away, hips swaying. Before she's even out of sight, I ball up the napkin and toss it in the nearest bin.

The guard eyes me, then glances back at her retreating form. "Must be a pretty special woman, to have you turning down offers like that."

I give him a wry grin, even as I start to head back to the stands.

"You have no idea," I tell the man, shaking my head as he fishes in the trash for the woman's number scrawled carelessly on a napkin.

That used to be me. But I want—and want to *be*—more. If only I can show that to Seraf … before Callum proposes and I lose my chance.

My phone buzzes in my pocket, and I glance down at the screen. All it takes is two sentences to fill me with dread.

I unlock the phone, reading the message again, then once more, trying to understand the unexpected and unwelcome words on the screen. His favor is not at all what I would have imagined. Ever.

The sound of cheering tells me the match has ended, and I make my way through the crowds streaming toward the exit. With a shaking hand, I slide the phone back into my pocket, Uncle's words searing through me.

The stands are nearly empty, and as I make my way down to the court, swarms of paparazzi flood out as the ineffectual security guards try to push them back.

Seraf's safety is my first thought, but she slips away, Kat beside her and the big body of her protection officer shielding her. They head right for me, or more like the exit behind me.

"Trouble in paradise?"

I want to take the words back the moment I say them. Her expression is one I've never seen, and one I've never wanted to see on her. Hurt, mixed with a bitterness that doesn't look like Seraf at all.

"Hey, are you okay?"

She makes a small noise, and when I reach out to touch her arm, her PPO knocks my arm away with a warning glare. They disappear into a black car waiting at the other end of the short tunnel.

What just happened?

I turn back to the courts, where the security guards are finally able to control the paparazzi, herding them toward another exit. As they move, I see Callum's personal protection officer moving him toward a separate exit.

Only he's not alone.

Callum has his arm thrown over the shoulders of a petite blonde woman wrapped up in … is that a checkered flag? No —it's a dress. A travesty of fashion, but definitely a dress.

And as I watch, she tilts her head up and Callum places a quick kiss on her lips.

Shock moves through me, limb by limb. Callum has a girlfriend?

My first thought maybe should be celebration. With the perfect prince out of the way, I might stand an actual chance with Seraf. But the image of pain on her face flashes before me. I can't be happy about it, because she must be crushed, especially if she was expecting a proposal this week.

Callum is an idiot.

I mean, I've thought that for years, but this confirms it. How could he choose someone—anyone—over Seraf?

As quickly as I can, I locate my driver and have him get us back to the palace. I may not be the person Seraf would turn to for comfort, but I'm going to do my best to mend her broken heart.

Not because I want to take advantage of it. That would be wrong, on so many levels. This has to be all about Seraf and what she needs.

The mental reassurance seems necessary to untangle my conflicted emotions. Because the selfish part of me wants Serafina any way I can get her. I don't want to be that man, putting myself and my desires first. It needs to be about her and only her.

Pulling out my phone, the tangle of confused emotions knots even tighter in my chest. I can't do what Uncle is asking, as tempting as it is.

I would finally wrest his control from my life, once and for all.

More than that, I *want* what he's asking me to do. So badly I feel the burn rising in my throat, stinging in my eyes. It's all I want.

But because this is coming from him, I'm now in an impossible position. I stare down at my phone, wishing I could chuck it out the window and have all my problems disappear.

Uncle: Here's part one of my favor. I need you to steal Princess Serafina from Callum. Have fun.

CHAPTER THREE

Serafina

"I don't understand what's happening," I say, addressing the King and Queen of Elsinore. Better known as James and Suzette, aka Callum's parents.

I'm pleased with how even my voice is. How calm I seem. Hands primly folded in my lap. Legs crossed at the ankles as I perch on the edge of an antique sofa having a very civilized conversation hiding the complete riot of anxiety and emotion happening inside me.

I appear completely cool and collected—the Ice Princess, indeed.

Thanks to Kat's pep talk and some 500-euro de-puffing miracle eye cream, no one would know that I sobbed the entire way to the Elsinorian palace. Or that a maid took my dress to be cleaned, holding it between a thumb and forefinger because I used it as my tissue. Hopefully, she'll just take it to the incinerator straightaway to be burned.

I never want to see it again—the dress I was wearing when I had my heart well and truly broken. Now, I'm in a fresh dress, seated in one of several formal parlors in the palace, watching the king and queen fall apart.

"What's happening is that our son is being careless with his future and the future of his nation."

Right. Because beyond emotions, this arrangement is about strengthening the ties between our kingdoms. Elsinore is often referred to as the Silicon Valley of Europe. They invested early and heavily in tech. Viore's copper mines produce about eighty percent of the resources needed for everything from circuit boards to sockets, and a relationship was forged.

But it's never felt like it was about that ... not just business. Not just about our nations. Until this moment. The realization makes my skin feel itchy, as though I'm wearing a rough burlap sack rather than a silky dress.

Callum's mother knocks back another vodka. At this rate, she's moments away from melting into an 80-proof puddle. The king raises an eyebrow but says nothing as she pours herself a fresh glass. He sips his whiskey before giving me a sad smile.

Without comment, the queen removes the glass from his hand and encourages him to sit with a squeeze of his shoulder. He harrumphs but doesn't argue. Now that I'm looking, his complexion looks a little sallow, and sweat beads on his forehead. Is he sick or just stressed?

Suzette hands him a crystal glass of water, but he sets it on the table nearby with a heavy *thunk*.

"If only you'd said you were coming. I mean, so soon. We expected you in a few days' time," the king says.

The queen clears her throat, as though she can see me

wilting at the implication that I've overstepped by showing up a few days early.

"Of course, we're glad you're here. The doors are always open to you and your family," he adds.

"No matter what, we're family," Queen Suzette says.

Right. Just not in the way I'd thought. I can sense the desperation in both of them, the need for reassurance that whatever Callum's doing, it won't affect the official trade relationship between us. I hate that they're even entertaining the thought.

"Coming early was supposed to be a surprise," I say, my voice breaking just the tiniest bit. "And why should a few days matter? We've known of this arrangement our whole lives."

Haven't we? I'm suddenly struck by the realization that I always assumed we both knew. *What if ...* My stomach ties itself into a tiny, painful knot.

"Wait—Callum *did* know of the arrangement, didn't he?"

The king and queen exchange a look, and the knot in my stomach tightens into a noose. Forget posture. Forget calm and cool. I am officially uncollected. With a groan, I slump back on the sofa and cover my face with my hands.

"He didn't know? How did he *not* know?"

And how did I not know that he didn't know? I'm not a princess; I'm the royal fool, the very picture of embarrassment.

I smell the alcohol before the queen even takes her seat next to me, patting my hand. "You know Callum, dear. He's always enjoyed being the spare, letting Phillip bear the weight of responsibility. Not that Phillip minded."

That's an understatement. I've never met someone so stiff and responsible as Phillip. Whereas Callum is all easy smiles and laughter. A proper prince, but with a more laid-back approach to life. But he's always fulfilled his duties, unlike Rafe, who seems to use his title and position to open doors to a hedonistic, self-centered lifestyle. Maybe that's why it's news to me that Callum's parents didn't mention this arrangement to him years ago.

"So, you simply didn't tell him? What did you think was going to happen?"

Maybe I shouldn't be so shrill, so sharp, so demanding with the king and queen of a country, but titles aside, James and Suzette have always been like family to me.

"We thought we'd ease him into the idea," King James says.

This makes me feel like the consolation to the consolation prize. Callum needed to be *eased into* hearing that he'd have to marry me. I drop my hands and look at Queen Suzette.

"What happened? How long has he known?"

They exchange a glance again. "Since last fall," Suzette says.

When the realization hits me, I'm stunned into immobility, like my muscles have all hardened into something like stone. My letter. My stupid, wine-addled letter, the one I wrote after our last joint trip to Maldives, when Callum and I spent the last night talking late on the beach. There was a moment of hesitation when I swear we almost kissed. Now I don't trust the memory.

But it was that almost-maybe-kiss (and the wine) that had me writing things I normally wouldn't have addressed. Like hinting at our arrangement.

It takes another moment for me to process that all of this is my fault.

No. I take that back. A lot of fault rests with our parents and how they handled this. But the way Callum found out is all on me.

"It was my letter, then? Is that how Callum found out?"

Her lips purse, and she nods, giving me a pitying look. "You said enough to get him asking questions, and he came to us."

Did the king and queen READ MY LETTER?

I squeeze my eyes shut and count silently. It's silly, but that's how one of my earliest governesses taught me to soothe myself, to keep my emotions in check: count the caterpillars. If I'm feeling particularly stressed or upset, it can take up to ten caterpillars. My governess always joked that after ten, they'd turn into butterflies.

One caterpillar. Two caterpillars. Three caterpillars. Four caterpillars.

Four. I can breathe more steadily again at four. Not so bad, all things considered.

"So, Callum got my letter, confronted you, and then ..." I can fill in the blanks myself, but the king jumps in.

"And enter the parade of trollops."

I glare, and the queen does too.

"*James.* Don't blame the women. Our son was just as much of a ... of a ..." She searches for an appropriate word, and comes up empty.

I can think of several, and count another two caterpillars to keep the words locked up where they belong.

I try to wrap my head around all of this information. According to my parents, they have been discussing this arrangement with Callum's parents for years. Literally, twenty-one of them.

From what I understood, we were keeping it under wraps until I finished university. We would announce our engagement at the Centennial Ball and marry by the end of the summer, just before my coronation. Mum is already planning the wedding.

37

In my mind, Callum knew, just as I did. He was holding back, waiting for the right time, just as I was. I assumed I would show up this week, reconnect with Callum, and we would privately discuss everything before going public next week.

This now sounds utterly preposterous. All of it. Why did I believe it? Probably because it's what I *wanted* to believe. An arranged marriage that was more, one that was based on love.

"And now he's dating this American," I say flatly.

"It's all very new." The queen blinks and then bursts into tears. Loud, ugly, un-queen-like tears. Wrapping her arms around me, she sobs loudly, sounding like a barking seal.

I've always been close with Suzette and James, but not *this* kind of close. I pat her back, because what else do you do when a queen wants to cry on your shoulder? And I do mean *on* my shoulder. I can feel the tears—*oh, please let those be tears and not snot*—on my neck.

Also, shouldn't I be the one crying? I'm the one whose heart has been broken. I'm the one who's been made a fool of.

The king clears his throat. "The one advantage we have is that the press has no idea."

"About that," I say with a wince. Suzette cries even harder. I want to join her, but I refrain, taking deep breaths until the sting of tears subsides. I don't need anyone else witnessing my personal misery.

I spent the ride to the palace reading headlines through the blur of my tears. The paparazzi are fast. I can say that much for them.

Prince Callum Is Officially Off the Market!

A Royal Fairy Tale! Callum Chooses a Commoner!

American Abroad Absconds with Crown Prince Callum!

They also love their alliteration.

In a few of the photographs, I spotted me and Kat in the background. Truly, I'm lucky the paparazzi were so focused on Callum that they didn't notice me. Otherwise, my shaky smile and clear heartbreak would be plastered on just as many websites. I'm grateful at least for that.

The king mutters a curse under his breath and grabs the whole bottle of whiskey, filling his glass to the top. So this is how the King and Queen of Elsinore fall apart behind closed doors—swimming in a sea of liquor. My parents are more the door-slamming, silent-treatment variety.

Me? I'm more of the lock-everything-in-a-vault-and-throw-away-the-key kind of person. Really and truly, I can't even be mad at the Ice Princess moniker because that's what I show the world. No one ever sees—publicly, anyway—when I'm hurting. It's served me well.

Hasn't it?

I mean, if I hadn't written Callum a letter under the influence of a glass (and a half) of wine, if I had just kept myself controlled, we wouldn't be here.

No, that's not true. He would have found out some other way and reacted the same.

Maybe if I'd been less rigid and we'd spoken about this years ago, it would have been different. Or if I'd told Callum about my feelings, that this wasn't just about some arrangement, but about him, about *us* … would it have made a difference?

I'll never know now.

The smell of vodka seems to be wafting off the queen's skin like a spring breeze near a distillery. Or maybe the scent is coming from her tears. It wouldn't surprise me if they're pure alcohol. I can only hope that what went down isn't going to come back up at some point. It would be rather embarrassing to have not one, but two, dresses needing to go to the cleaners my very first day at Elsinore.

At least there are servants who can clean up after that sort of thing. Our court in Viore is much smaller. We get by with far fewer staff and far less formality. I wouldn't be shocked if a servant walked into this parlor, introducing herself as the Drunk Handler. Probably with a fancier name, like the Sick Specialist or the Hurl Handmaiden.

Is there also a royal Hair-Holder assigned to that duty after a night of overindulgence?

I feel the burn of loss eat through me as I realize that this is the kind of thing I'd joke about with Callum once upon a time. He and I never shied away from talking about the reality behind the royalty. As close as Kat is, there are things that only Callum has been able to know and understand. To complain about my pampered life to someone who isn't also just as pampered would be inappropriate and inconsiderate.

"I'm so sorry, Serafina." The queen sits up, stroking my cheek. Her own cheeks are streaked with vodka tears, her eyes red. Thankfully, her nose seems quite dry.

So, just tears on my shoulder, then. One small relief in this hell of a day.

"Where does this leave us? I mean, what's next? What do I do?"

I try not to wring my hands. I'd definitely like to wring something.

"You wait. This will all blow over," the king says. "Boys will have their fun."

Both the queen and I bristle at this remark. If she were less inebriated, the queen looks like she'd be across the room, leaving a handprint on his cheek rather than gaping at him like a fish.

He clears his throat, looking chastised. "I mean, of

course, this will pass. Our arrangement still stands. We'll get it sorted."

"By the ball next week?" I ask, incredulous. Because as far as I'm concerned, the press will have a field day with such a quick turnaround. I can imagine the headlines now.

Princess Serafina Settles as Callum's Sloppy Seconds.

Secret Baby? Sudden Royal Engagement Begs the Question.

Catfight! Serafina Sends American Packing in a Royal Love Triangle.

If Callum and I get engaged now, on the original schedule, it would only look fake. And that's the one thing I've never wanted or never felt. Arrangement or no, it's always been *real* between us.

But of course it hasn't. I have to face the truth: I've been in love with my best friend for years, under the assumption he felt the same way. Quite the wrong assumption to make.

A pit seems to open in my stomach, matching the one that has yawned open in my life where solid ground used to be. Everything I thought I knew, everything I've been counting on has disappeared.

The king makes a very un-king-like snort. "He'll come to his senses soon enough."

"Who will come to his senses?"

That deep voice, gravelly and low, slides through me, leaving heat in its wake, despite my icy heart. I turn to see Callum in the doorway.

With *her*.

Miss America, still draped in her red-checked excuse for a dress. Now that I'm seeing her for the second time, with a little less shock, her dress isn't really so horrible—if you're into picnic-wear as fashion, that is. Because it's much more of a picnic blanket hugging her curves—which, despite her petite frame, are what Kat would call *banging*—than a tablecloth.

I hate her. Before I even saw her and knew that she'd stolen Callum, I disliked her incessant giggling and general obnoxious demeanor behind me at the tennis match. But the hate sprang into being the moment she called him *Callie.* Don't even get me started on that nickname, but it's the sheer fact that she gave him a nickname at all.

Now, seeing her in the palace, her fingers entwined with his, new hate springs forth like a second head. I'm a mythical creature, sprouting new heads of hatred. Some of it should direct itself toward Callum, not just Brit. But she's an easier target.

There is a pause as awkward as it is long before Callum strides into the room like he belongs there—which, of course, he does—with Miss America. The confident tilt of her chin makes it seem as though she too belongs. Which she definitely doesn't. I almost feel a little sorry for her, knowing that she's walking into a hostile, alcohol-soaked room.

Yes, we will *get this sorted.*

Though it may not be pretty. Because there's no way Callum's parents will let this American—

"It's lovely to meet you, Brit," the queen says, standing and smoothing down her dress with a pleasant smile. "We've heard so much about you."

Wait—what?!

I can't sprout any more heads, die any more, or feel my icy heart shatter again. Except that clearly I can, as I watch the king and queen politely—and even warmly—greet Brit, who makes a bumbling, giggling show of curtsying in her ridiculous outfit.

It's so awkward that it's actually endearing. The king even laughs. Callum beams at Brit like she's a show pony who has just performed a successful trick. Not once has he even met my eyes since he walked into the room.

More heads spring forth. More heartache. More death.

In a room full of royals, people I once considered family, the man I still love, *I* am the outsider.

CHAPTER FOUR

Serafina

Kat is my only link to sanity at this point, and the only reason I haven't run screaming from the palace. That and the fear that I'll bump into Callum or *her* making my hasty getaway. Really, I don't want to see the king and queen either. I'm over the entire Elsinorian royal family.

Okay, maybe not Callum's older brother, Phillip, or his younger sisters, Juliet and Henrietta. Though if Callum's parents were so quick to turn against me in favor of Brit, his siblings will likely do the same. It feels like I've lost Callum and the family I always considered second to my own.

Part of me knows that greeting her warmly was the polite thing to do. The *royal* thing. But I'm in too much pain to care *why* they welcomed her. I'm still feeling abandoned and betrayed and like I'm standing across enemy lines.

I've lost everything to *her*.

I can't bring myself to use her name. It's a little trick I've picked up from true crime shows. Serial killers don't use names so they don't have to humanize their victims. If I refuse to use *her* name, she doesn't have to be human. Or real.

Or adorably perfect. Which she is. Annoying, yes, but she's like a golden retriever—so bright and friendly and not pretentious that it's hard to hate her. Even though I'm trying very hard.

If I met her under different circumstances, maybe I'd even appreciate her warmth and exuberance. Heaven knows, those aren't words anyone would use to describe me.

Is that what Callum wants? Someone warmer than the Ice Princess?

My big regret in all this, one that seems so glaringly obvious now, is the lack of communication and honesty. Maybe discussing the arrangement would have been awkward. Maybe confessing my feelings for Callum wouldn't have made a difference in the long run.

I simply always assumed he and I were on the same page. In actuality, it's more like I'm reading a book and he's watching the film adaptation.

"We just need a plan," Kat keeps muttering. She's actually punching a fist into her hand, like we are in some kind of heist movie, plotting in our secret hideout, not just hiding out in my lavish suite.

"High marks for drama," I tell her. "But we're leaving. Just as soon as I can manage to climb out of this bed and my depression."

Kat whirls on me, pointing a finger. "No! You will not leave. You will not give up. This is your prince we're talking about here. *Your* prince. Not hers. 'Callie'?" Kat makes a disgusted noise. "That's not happening."

Except that it is. They already have a couple name: *Britum*.

Terrible, but aren't all couple names? Polls show approval ratings through the roof. People are voting to *ship them*, whatever that means, on Twitter.

I'd like to ship her somewhere. Without a return address.

I wave my hands. "It's happening. It's happened. It's done. And I'm not going to stay here, having to pretend everything is fine. I can't do it, Kat."

Kat mutters something and unzips her bag, rooting through it for something.

I fall back among the pillows again. Oh, but these pillows are so much better than those in Viore. Maybe I'll stuff one of the pillows in my bag before I go. I may not get the prince, but I can certainly abscond with his pillows.

"Don't bother unpacking," I tell Kat. "I've already messaged the pilot and they're going to turn the jet around as soon as they've refueled."

"Nope." Kat sits down next to me and pulls me to a seated position. Her heavy makeup only serves to make her look fiercer. More like a warrior than a lawyer, though really the two aren't so far off from one another. "We are not giving up. We are not backing down. There is no retreat. This is *war*."

"This is not war. And if it were, I've already lost. This is me, waving my white flag."

Kat snatches the tissue I'm waving and crosses the room to throw it in the bin.

While the idea of losing Callum hurts deeper than I can admit, I can't fight for a man who doesn't want me back. The thought of staying here through the Centennial Ball, as planned, having to see him with *her*, up close and personal day after day, is more than I can bear.

Just *how* personal are they? I shudder at the image that keeps replaying in my mind of their kiss. Callum looked

47

surprised by it, but probably more like surprised that she did it in front of the crowds. It was impulsive. Passionate. Uninhibited.

More things I am not.

Things I'll never be.

A few sharp knocks at the door pull me out of my downward spiral.

"I'll get it," Kat says cheerfully, bounding over to the door. "Maybe it's *Callum*." She drops her voice to a whisper, winking at me before throwing open the door. "And who might you be—the royal librarian?"

I smile softly, knowing only one person who might fit that description. "Let him in, Kat."

With a dramatic flourish, she opens the door wide. Claudius is ridiculously tall—having-to-stoop-through-the-doorway tall—with deep olive skin and short-cropped black hair. His glasses are small and wire-rimmed, and he absolutely looks the part of a royal librarian. But a very attractive librarian. He has a clipboard in one hand. When was the last time I saw a clipboard?

I manage to drag myself out of bed. "Claudius! How lovely to see you."

He tries to bow, but I grab him in a hug that's made awkward by the way he stiffens, the clipboard jamming into my ribs. "Your Royal Highness."

Over the years, Claudius has become one of my favorite people in Elsinore. I'm not sure what his official title is, only that he's the glue holding things together. And right now, if there's anything I need, it's being put back together.

Claudius clears his throat and straightens his tie. He's the kind of man who dresses to the nines and keeps his intensity level at a ten. Forget the palace pillows; I want to take Claudius home with me.

With his level of organization and strict professionalism, he could probably solve all my problems in a heartbeat. He can also be quite fun to tease.

My heart sinks as I realize ... considering his position in the palace here, Claudius probably knows all about my current predicament. How embarrassing.

As though following the train of my thoughts, Claudius gives me a rare smile. "It's wonderful to see you again. Looking lovely, as always."

Kat is circling Claudius like a great white eyeing a ... whatever smaller fish the great white eats. He's trying and failing to ignore her, his dark eyes flicking her way, then back to me. Kat hasn't traveled to Elsinore with me before, so the two of them haven't met. This should be fun.

"Claudius, this is my lady-in-waiting, Kat."

Kat glares at the fake title, one she hates that I like to pull out when she's being particularly difficult.

"It's a pleasure to make your acquaintance, Lady Kat."

"Just Kat will do," she says, and I smile because Claudius will never call her anything but Lady Kat, just as he never calls me anything but Your Royal Highness or Princess Serafina. I've also tried to get him to stop bowing to me, but to no avail.

Turning his attention back to me, Claudius gestures to the formal sitting area on one side of my suite. "Shall we? I have this week's itinerary for us to discuss."

Though she's still eyeing him as though searching for a chink in his uptight armor, Kat joins me on the sofa. Claudius glances to me, then to Kat.

I wave a hand. "She's fine. Kat should know the schedule of events as well."

"Good, good. I did make a few extra copies."

Of course he did. I grin as Kat snatches the paper from

his outstretched hand, looking down on it suspiciously. I'm not sure what has her so riled up about Claudius. My best guess? The handsome face accompanying all this type A behavior.

"When you're ready, Your Royal Highness."

"Go ahead, Claudius."

I follow along with the itinerary he's prepared, which is, as with all things Claudius, exacting and full of relevant and concise details. The Centennial Ball is in six days. Leading up to it, there are a series of events ranging in formality, including the Working Day, a yearly event where the royals of Elsinore spend time in the nearest village personally assisting with families in need.

There are several dinners, and my stomach falls when I see that tonight, there's a more formal one with dancing. Kat notices my wilting expression and begins fanning me with a book.

"Oh dear me, Princess! You! Jeeves!"

Claudius almost drops his clipboard. "Me?"

"Yes, Jeeves, you."

"It's Claudius."

"That's what I meant." She snaps her fingers. "Fetch us some smelling salts."

I give Kat a light shove, but I'm laughing now, especially with the pinched look on Claudius's face. "Ignore her. I'm quite all right. Go on about the schedule."

"I believe that's everything. I'll be checking in daily to make sure you have everything you need and providing any updates or adjustments to the schedule."

"Excellent."

Claudius shifts and looks like he's about to head for the door, then pauses. "Please let me know if I can help in any way, Your Royal Highness. Any way at all."

"Can you smuggle me out of here?"

I'm teasing, but Claudius nods sharply. "If that's what you need, then I could make those arrangements, yes."

Kat finally looks impressed rather than suspicious. "Can you get me the latest flavor of Riesling chocolate biscuits?"

I roll my eyes. Kat has talked of nothing else but these biscuits for months. I'm not sure what's so special about them, other than the fact that they're impossible to get. Even for me, and I did try for her.

"The limited edition salted cocoa and espresso flavor?"

"That's the one."

I give him an apologetic look. "Kat, Claudius can't—"

"I'll see what I can do." Claudius pulls out his phone, types in a quick note, and then, with a formal bow, is gone.

Kat stares at the closed door. "What a strange little man."

"He's wonderful."

"Are you sure he's not some animatronic robot-cyborg thing that Phillip invented?"

I laugh. "I'm pretty sure Elsinore isn't looking into building cyborgs."

"Doesn't mean Phillip isn't. A nerdy engineering genius, right? Maybe Claudius is a prototype?"

"Kat, I've known Claudius for years, and he isn't any kind of robot."

"Time will tell. Anyway, I'll see how he does with the biscuits. Now. I'm taking a bath. Then we'll reconvene for strategy."

I ignore the strategy comment because it's not happening. And Kat is heading for my bathroom, not the door to the hallway, leading to her bedroom and bathroom.

"You're taking a bath in my bathroom?"

"Have you seen your tub? I could fit a circus troupe in there."

"That's … a disturbing image."

She laughs. "Don't worry. It's just me for now. Unless you find some handsome servant or courtier hanging about who can join me."

"I'm not inviting some man in here so you can do whatever in *my* bathtub."

"Fine." Kat pulls her earbuds and phone from her purse and strides toward the bathroom.

This feels entirely too much like settling in. "Maybe you should wait. The plane—"

"Won't be ready for a few hours. I'm sure they had to refuel when they returned to Viore. Plus, we're not leaving. Not without a prince. Calm down. Take a nap. Eat a cookie." She closes the door to the bathroom firmly, point made.

I'd love to have a cookie right now. Or a whole batch of them. I still haven't eaten, and my stomach feels like it's folding in on itself. Or maybe that's just the feeling of heartbreak?

There's a knock at the door, and my pulse leaps, immediately imagining Callum on the other side. I straighten my dress and fluff my hair. *Just in case.*

But standing on the other side of the door is the antithesis of Callum, and I stifle my urge to slam the door on Rafe.

CHAPTER FIVE

Serafina

"Hello, Princess."

The way he always addresses me is somewhere between a lover's caress and the hiss of a snake. It's not a title when he says *princess*, but a nickname. I can feel it.

"Duke."

He smiles. I frown.

His dark eyes rove over me, that ever-present smirk on his annoyingly full lips. He may be Callum's opposite, but objectively speaking, both have good looks that should be unlawful.

With olive skin and regal bone structure, a chiseled jaw with stubble that always looks perfectly drawn on, and the kind of smile that makes women all over the world—literally —weak at the knees, Rafe is dangerously attractive.

I once saw a woman faint when he smiled at her during a

diplomat's dinner in France. I think in romance novels as well as the eighteenth century, this was known as a swoon.

His dark eyes always hold a spark of amusement and are framed with dark lashes to match his dark, wavy hair. I know better than to look directly into those eyes. That's how he gets you, this devilish rogue of a royal.

Except I realize that's what I'm doing now, falling into the depths of his brown eyes. And I've been doing so for several long moments without speaking.

"Yes?"

The eye contact has clearly shorted out the part of my brain responsible for coherent speech, and I focus on his eyebrows, which are thick, but groomed. Not overly so, and I almost wish they were, so I could focus on some flaw.

"I come bearing gifts," he says.

I've been so distracted by the man himself I didn't notice he's got a wheeled silver cart filled with food and drink. *Rafe brought me food?* My stomach clenches with anticipation and I'm thankful it doesn't make any noise.

I block the door, though my first impulse is to drag the cart inside and shove him back out. "Are you moonlighting as a butler?"

Rafe takes a deep bow, his brown eyes twinkling with mischief. "At your service, Princess." When I don't move out of the way, he straightens up, sighing and running a hand through his hair. "Let me in, Seraf."

Seraf. The name draws forth a strange reaction in me. My parents and Kat sometimes call me Sera, and Callum's nickname for me is Fi. But no one has ever called me Seraf. Hearing Rafe do so now has me closing the door another inch.

"Oh, are we on nickname terms now? I didn't realize."

Rafe continues to stare me down, looking as though he

knows a secret I don't. The lipstick on his cheek from the socialite at the tennis match is gone, and his hair is rumpled from running his hand through it.

"We didn't order food."

"But I bet you haven't eaten since at least breakfast, if at all, based on the way your stomach was growling at the match. It sounded like a dragon ready to feast on a whole village."

"Is it poisoned? Laced with GHB?"

His eyes narrow. "Of course not. Now, step aside."

I'm not sure why I do. Probably the food. Yes, most definitely the food. I almost jerk the cart out of his hands, but manage to control myself as he pushes it inside.

From his post in the hall, The Dane gives me a look and I nod. His expression doesn't shift, but I swear I read the judgement in his eyes. Good thing his job is protection, not giving advice.

The reality of Rafe inside my suite fills me with nerves. He stops the cart near the small table by the window and then wanders, his eyes drinking in the room with undisguised interest. I should warn him that Kat's in the bathroom, or maybe warn Kat, but he doesn't go near the door.

Rafe seems particularly interested in my things, which aren't many. He looks over the open, empty suitcase and the books and journal I've stacked on the large antique desk by the window.

"What are you doing?" I ask with a nervous laugh. I find that I'm wringing my hands and force them into fists at my sides.

"Getting to see the princess behind the curtain." He runs a hand along the zipper on my leather suitcase.

Sweat begins beading along my spine and lower back. I wipe a hand across my forehead.

Rafe and I have never been alone in a room, I realize. Especially never a bedroom. I'm suddenly aware of the rumpled comforter from where I threw myself down earlier, and the pillows which clearly have the imprint of my head on them.

Unlike the cloistered, structured life I've lived as the crown princess, Rafe has all the benefits of a title with none of the restrictions. And he has taken every advantage of both his wealth and freedom to indulge himself in every way he can.

Lavish trips. Ridiculous purchases like yachts, cars, and even a small German castle. And, of course, the one that sticks out the most in my mind, *women*.

It's this last one that has me feeling so self-conscious as he strides over to the wardrobe, opening it to look through the dresses one of the servants has already hung up. When his fingers trace the bodice of a dress inside, I swear, I feel his touch ghosting down my rib cage.

I walk over and close the wardrobe, having to stand so close to him that I can smell his cologne. Spicy and dark— just like the man himself.

Undeterred, he moves from the wardrobe to the desk, riffling through my papers and flipping the pages of the book I've been reading. It's a romance, and I feel a blush spreading up from my neck to my cheeks, even though the cover is of a beach scene, not some half-nude couple.

I snatch the book from his hands and set it down again, shoving it and my journal to the other side of the desk. "Thank you, Rafe. You can leave the tray and, um, slink back to wherever you came from."

"I could," he says. Instead, he wanders over to the bed and flops down, kicking off his dark dress shoes as he does so.

I'm not sure why, but the sight of Rafe in his white button-down shirt, dark pants, and socked feet, his head on the same pillow where mine rested minutes ago has me fumbling with words.

"What are you doing?" I demand.

He stretches, with a lazy, catlike grin and puts his hands behind his head. "Don't mind me, Princess. Just eat. Please."

I want to argue, or at least to get Rafe off my bed before he makes it smell like him or infects it with whatever diseases he might be carrying, but hunger wins out. Underneath the silver domed lid, the cart has an array of cheeses, sliced meats, and fruits as well as pastries and breads. I'd like to pull a chair up and just dig in, but I force myself to make a plate with reasonably sized portions.

I take a seat at the desk, but this means my back is to Rafe. I swear, I can feel the man's eyes burning into me. Clearing my throat, I turn my chair and balance the plate on my knees. Better to face your enemy, right?

I almost groan as I tuck into a bite of some kind of sharp cheese.

"Eating sliced cheese with a fork, Princess?"

"How do you eat *your* cheese, Rafe? Do tell." I take another bite, holding back a moan. I hadn't quite realized the extent of my hunger. It's all I can do not to shovel the contents of my plate into my mouth.

His grin widens. "I like to use my hands."

Is he … using some kind of double entendre? Just the thought makes my cheeks heat again. My blush is one thing I've never been able to keep tight control over.

Tears? I can hold them back. Stress? I have breathing techniques. Dislike or distaste? I can hide behind a mask of politeness. But my blush cannot be tamed. Stupid uncontrollable capillaries! Or is it veins?

"I'm not a beast like you," I snap, keeping my chin tucked to hide my red cheeks.

"That's quite true, Princess. You're the picture of perfection."

There's something different in his tone. It forces me to glance up, and I'm unnerved to find his gaze trained on me, a soft smile on his face. I clear my throat and go back to my plate.

Why does Rafe make me so uncomfortable? Not just now —*always*. But especially now, when it feels like I have the full force of his attention fixed on me. It's like having the full heat and light of the sun beaming directly at me.

I think back to the first time I remember meeting Rafe. It was years ago, and I had come to attend a lacrosse scrimmage to watch Callum play. He and Callum almost came to blows after Rafe winked at me, which made my cheeks turn into twin tomatoes.

Not much has changed—Callum and Rafe still hate each other and I'm still reduced to blushing like a kid.

He seems to make a sport of goading Callum and twisting me around so I never know which way is up. He teases and flirts and almost never says what he means, to me or anyone else.

Rafe belongs in Wonderland—a cat in a tree, spouting riddles with an impossibly wide grin.

Then there's the matter of the company Rafe keeps. Being as inexperienced and naive as I am, I can't help but feel self-conscious around a man who is intimately familiar with so many women. At least, if the tabloids are to be believed.

My stomach twists. If I believe what they've said about Rafe in the past, has Callum's behavior over this past year really been so different?

How must I seem to a man like Rafe? Or even to Callum?

I feel, suddenly, like a child. I'm sure watching a woman eat cheese with a fork doesn't rank high on the list of activities Rafe usually does in the bedroom.

"Are you feeling okay?" Rafe asks in that same gentle tone.

I have to squeeze my eyes shut against the tears. I can take his teasing but right now, I can't take kindness.

Think of the lipstick on his cheek earlier after the match. That helps, even if just a little. But then I see the spread of food before me. Rafe—of all the people in this palace—noticed my hunger and brought me food. This simple gesture melts a tiny bit of my shattered, icy heart.

Maybe Rafe isn't quite the man I assume him to be. Or maybe he is, but he also has another side, one that I'm just starting to see.

Or perhaps this is all part of some game to get under Callum's skin.

"Why are you acting so nice?"

"Who said I'm not nice?"

"*Nice* is never a word I'd associate with you," I tell him, taking a small bite of a tiny sandwich triangle.

"But you just called me nice," he points out.

"I said you were *acting* nice."

"Ah. You think this is an act?"

Wiping my mouth, I change tactics. "Why aren't you bringing that other woman food?"

"Who?"

"The woman from the match. Or have you already moved on from her?"

Rafe's easy smile halts, sliding into a strangely serious expression. "There is no *her*."

"I beg to differ. I saw her smiling at you. I saw you after the match, shirt untucked and her lipstick on your cheek.

Why deny it? I thought you loved flaunting your hook-ups."

"That wasn't a hook-up. The woman followed me, tried to kiss me, and I brushed her off. Hence the lipstick on my cheek."

This shouldn't make me feel relieved, but somehow it does. "Hm."

"Don't believe me?"

"Should I?"

"Yes. You should." The conversation has become tense enough that it's palpable in the room. But Rafe blinks and that sly smile returns. "I do like that you're jealous."

"I'm not jealous."

"Possessive?"

"Not that either."

Rafe studies me. "But it does bother you—the idea that I might have hooked up with a woman at the tennis match and now am here, bringing you food?"

My gut reaction is to deny it. But I am bothered, and the only reason I can think of is that I'm transferring my twisted-up feelings for Callum to Rafe.

I'm jealous and hurt that Callum has been dating other women. I'm crushed that he's with Brit when I thought we'd be getting engaged this week.

And now, it's making me behave strangely with Rafe.

I heave out a sigh. "I'm sorry. I think I'm just … taking out my feelings on you. It doesn't matter what you do or with whom. And thank you for the food."

"I couldn't stand thinking about you, hungry and heartbroken."

I set my fork down, swallowing despite the way the food seems determined to lodge itself in my throat. In a move as smooth as a panther, Rafe leaps up and pours me a glass of water from a silver pitcher on the cart. I take it from his hands, careful to keep my fingers from brushing his.

"I'm sorry," he says. "I shouldn't have said anything."

You shouldn't have noticed, I think, but I guess I was being obvious. Rafe's knowledge—but even more, his kindness—has me feeling raw and exposed.

When the glass is safely in my hands, he settles back in my bed. I try not to look at him there, lest that image take up permanent residence in my brain.

"Thank you," I say, setting the glass down on the desk. The condensation will form a ring on the antique wood, so I locate a silver coaster and set my glass on top.

"Does it get boring, always doing what you're supposed to do?" Rafe's tone has regained its usual smug satisfaction.

"Does it get tiresome being so selfish and pretending like you have no responsibilities at all?"

I'm not usually so snappish. I don't like the impact Rafe has on me. It's even worse since my emotions are so volatile right now.

My cheeks flush again, this time with anger. Our eyes lock. A lesser man, or maybe a man who cared, might have been burnt to a crisp from my gaze. But Rafe only returns fire with fire.

A loud, echoing and off-key singing voice through the bathroom door breaks our staring contest and the tension.

"Sewing machines of love! Machines of love! Sewing machines!" Kat half sings, half shouts in a very off-key voice.

I burst out laughing, one hand over my mouth. Rafe's laughter joins mine, and I look up to see he's standing, slipping on his shoes.

"Leaving so soon?"

I'm torn between relief and a surprising surge of disappointment.

Rafe tilts his head toward the bathroom door, where Kat is still singing the wrong lyrics to the Tears for Fears song. "Sounds like you've got company."

I want to say something, anything, to make him stay as he crosses the room. But why would I want him to stay? We aren't friends. We're hardly acquaintances. Just two royals running in opposite directions in the same circles.

"Thank you," I say quickly as Rafe opens the door.

How many times have I had to thank him in the last few minutes?

He pauses in the doorway but doesn't turn back. Instead, he keeps one hand on the doorknob and lifts the other, running it roughly through his hair.

"For what it's worth, I'm sorry. You deserve better, Seraf. Callum, as always, is being an idiot."

Rafe's pity makes me feel filthy, as though his words landed on my skin like a layer of dust, cloying and thick. "He's not the only idiot," I snap.

"I agree, Princess. He isn't. But at least I'm aware of what I am, and what I'm not." Rafe gives me a tight smile, then like a shadow, he slips away.

The bathroom door opens almost simultaneously, and Kat steps out, wearing only a towel. She pulls out her earbuds and heads straight for the food.

"Wow! This looks fabulous. Thanks for ordering."

It's on the tip of my tongue to tell her about Rafe, but I don't. "You know the song is actually called 'Sowing THE SEEDS of Love,' right?"

Kat answers around a full bite of croissant. "Mm-hm. But I prefer thinking of it as a song about love between two textile workers. They've been working alongside one another for months, the attraction building slowly as they sew … whatever people sew. It's quite romantic, don't you think?"

Romantic? I have no idea what the word means anymore. I manage a smile. "Sure. I can almost imagine it now."

And the thing is, I *can* imagine it. She may have made up a story and lyrics to a song, but those fictional people working in the textile mill have more of a chance at love than I do.

CHAPTER SIX

Serafina

My phone has been ringing for the last hour, and I've been dutifully ignoring it until Kat left to take a nap before dinner. Lying back in my bed, which smells distractingly like a certain duke I'd rather not think about, my fingers hover over my phone screen.

The last thing I want is to discuss my current circumstances with my parents. But I know that if I don't check in, Mum and Dad are likely to declare a state of emergency or send someone from Viore for proof of life. Surely, they've seen the news. She and Callum's mum are close, so maybe they've already talked.

Preparing myself for the humiliation ahead, I ring Mum back. I'm greeted with a string of creative curses that would make Kat laugh.

"Mum?"

"Serafina?" There's a shuffling sound, then her voice goes distant. "Oh fresh *heel*."

Yes—*heel*. That's the normal sort of cursing Mum does. A turn of word and phrase to keep her mouth from the gutter, as she likes to say. It's silly, as we all know what she means, but every so often I've picked up on the habit as well. It's always made Callum laugh.

Mum sounds more breathless than usual, almost as though she's running. I know she'd never run unless chased, which can only mean one thing: she's got the dogs.

"Are you walking the terrors? Because we have people for that."

We may not have drunk handlers on the Viore palace staff, but dog walkers, absolutely. Mum has three. One for each terror.

The terrors are three Jack Russell terriers. But *terror* truly is the best word to describe them. For all the schooling and tutoring and training my parents forced me to go through, they couldn't be bothered to do the same for the royal dogs.

What behaviors were adorable when they were puppies are horrific now that they're grown dogs. At least they're all under thirty pounds. Though Chesterfield might have surpassed that. His girth had widened significantly the last time I saw him. It wouldn't shock me in the least to hear that he had eaten Eustace and Leonidas.

"Yes. Well, I could use the exercise. Apparently." Mum's voice is edged with bitterness under the breathlessness.

"You're not overweight, Mum."

"No. But I do have cankles. The press were spot on about that. *Leo! Down, girl!*" More panting and muttered curses. "How are you holding up, dear?"

Right. For half a second, I hadn't thought about Callum.

"As well as could be expected, I suppose."

She sighs, knowing me too well to believe anything but the truth. "I am so, so sorry. I'm not even speaking to Suzette at the moment."

The breath leaves my lungs. "You've spoken to the queen?"

"We've exchanged words and unpleasantries."

I see one of Rafe's dark hairs on my pillow and hold it between two fingers. I should let it drop to the floor, but instead, I set it on the white marble top of my bedside table where it stands out like a thin slash of ink. "Did you know about this?" I ask.

"About the American? No. Quite a nasty shock all around, it seems."

This should reassure me but instead I find myself shoving down a sense of panic. Because Mum's answer was oddly specific, and I can tell she's hedging around something she'd rather not say.

She continues in that same breathless voice. "Not that I knew you were planning to go straight from university to Elsinore. I found out only after your father told me where the jet had gone."

I don't have the emotional bandwidth to feel her guilt trip for not sharing my plans. Plus, I'm still hung up on the idea that she does know *something* she hasn't told me.

"You didn't know about his girlfriend." *Oh, that word hurts to say.* "What *did* you know, Mum?" My voice sounds like the rattle of a newspaper, flimsy and soft.

Her sigh this time is deeper, bone-weary. "I knew that Callum wasn't pleased about the arrangement."

Kill me now.

Someone, please, have the decency to run a sword through me or put poison in my coffee. Maybe drop an anvil on my head or a piano, like in one of those old cartoons. I

67

wish the Elsinorian palace had a moat filled with crocodiles and a turret from which I could dive straight in.

"He didn't want to marry me?" Tears threaten to choke my voice. I threaten to choke *them*, and they back down. For now.

"Oh, sweetie. It's not about you, per se. Callum objected to the idea of an arranged marriage. He wants the freedom to make his own choice."

Choice.

I hate the word. It's a luxury most royals don't have. Other than those like Rafe, who have a title and money but no real power to wield, no throne overshadowing everything else. Money and power are like cages, or glass domes. Never have I felt this suffocating pressure as much as I do now.

In a way, I understand it. Maybe I even envy Callum a little. Phillip is the heir and Callum the spare—he *can* exercise some freedom. Why should Callum have to be pinned down by such an arrangement? He decided to fight for his choice, to stand firm. I can respect that.

Except standing firm means that he's pressing the heel of his boot right into my heart.

"I see. So, you've known about this for some time."

"We didn't want to worry you."

A memo somewhere along the way would have been appreciated. A text. An email. A carrier pigeon. Any hint at all that the man I grew up thinking I'd marry had no actual interest in doing so.

Or maybe that's what he was telling me when he stopped writing. Or when he paraded all those gorgeous women on his arm this last year. It was his quiet—no, his *cowardly*—way of telling me plans had changed.

Finally, an emotion aside from sorrow rises up in me. I'm angry. Maybe even furious.

"I'm sure it will all work out. Callum will realize what's at stake."

I hate the way this is being discussed, through clinical, objective eyes, as though this whole thing really is just a business deal, a transaction of some kind. I never objected to an arranged marriage, because I thought it was *real*. It wasn't simply a marriage of convenience but a relationship with love at its center. Love and friendship.

Even if Callum *comes to his senses,* as his father said, or *realizes what's at stake,* as Mum just said, I can't imagine marrying him. Not like this. Not when I have feelings and he has none.

I would always wonder ... am I really his choice?

"Chesterfield! Stop humping Eustace. That's your brother! Have you no shame?"

The fact that I don't laugh at Mum's reprimand to the terrors illustrates the dark depths to which I've sunk.

"Look, Sera. I know this isn't ideal."

"Which part?" *Being humiliated or heartbroken?*

There is a moment of silence on the line. I bite my lip. I've never actually expressed to my parents how I feel about Callum or the arrangement, though I'm sure they suspect. Only Kat knows how completely smitten I've been. How I've been waiting for Callum, in more ways than one, my whole life.

"It will be over soon." Her voice is one part sympathy and one part get-over-yourself. Mum never was one for comfort. I really should have called Dad.

"I know. I'm flying home to Viore with Kat as soon as the plane returns."

Mum's voice is sharp as a blade. "No, I'm afraid you aren't, darling. This fling with the American will be over soon. You're staying right where you are. Standing your ground. Fighting for what's yours. Fulfilling our part of the arrangement."

"Mum—"

"You have two weeks. That should be enough time."

I frown, glancing at the itinerary from Claudius, ending with the ball. "Two weeks? The ball is in less than a week. When Callum was supposed to, you know, propose."

"The plan has gone to heel in a breadbasket." She pauses, then laughs. "That's very punny! Heel and a breadbasket. Get it?"

I am not amused by her pun. *"Mother."*

"Eustace! Don't pee on that! Look, dear. You've got two weeks to work things out with Callum. After that, well—we don't need to worry about that because I know you'll do what needs to be done."

Her words flit around in my head, never quite settling down where I can piece them together. But I get the distinct suspicion that when I do understand, I won't like it.

"So, why the specificity. Why two weeks?"

"The *contract*. Don't be a dullard, dear."

"What contract?"

"*The* contract. The one we drew up with Callum's parents ages ago. The one they don't seem to want to uphold. Callum has two more weeks to propose or our arrangement expires."

My stomach is an elevator whose cable has been cut, plummeting to the basement from the penthouse. They actually wrote and signed a contract? I thought it was more of a casually spoken arrangement, not the legally binding kind. This makes everything feel so much worse.

Unease prickles along my skin, and for a moment, I completely empathize with Callum feeling the need to get out from under all these obligations. They stink much more heavily of duty, even to me, now that I know actual paper-work was drawn up and signed.

Mind you, it was drawn up and signed without *me*. Anger rises up again, and I lean into the emotion, grateful for a reprieve from the ache.

"You wrote up a legal document? With lawyers and everything?"

Mum scoffs. "Of course we wrote up an actual contract. We've talked about it for years. You've seen it."

"I have *not* seen it. And I did not know. You talked about an *arrangement* but I had no idea it was a legitimate, legal contract. Something so formal."

"Well. Now you know. And you have two weeks to get Callum on board."

"What happens if I can't?"

"You will."

"And if I don't? What happens? What else haven't you told me?"

She's silent, the only sound muffled barking in the background. I squeeze my eyes closed and put a pillow over my face.

"Mum, please. You've kept enough from me, don't you think?"

There is a much longer pause. One my mind fills with horrors that I suspect are not too far from the truth. "If Callum doesn't change his mind, we'll have to go for the backup plan."

My voice was as icy as my dead and frozen wasteland of a heart. "Meaning?"

"Valdonia."

I squeeze my eyes closed, remembering the smell of the Valdonian prince—that dead-fish-washed-up-on-shore odor—

and the feel of his cool, limp hands sliding down toward my butt as we danced at the New Year's Gala.

Understanding washes over me with all the subtlety of a cold shower. He wasn't a placeholder, some royal figure to be my date at an event. He was my parents' backup plan all along.

"No," I say. "I'd rather not marry and take my chances with the vote."

"Absolutely not. There is too much at stake to risk it with all those flogging royal haters. This is your duty. You know this, darling. You've always known it."

I have. But it was always an afterthought. Because I had Callum. Now, I feel like a carton of yogurt sitting on the shelf, watching my own expiration date approach.

"There has to be someone else." Anyone else, really.

"I can send you the dossier if you'd like."

I'm going to vomit. "You have a dossier? Of … eligible bachelors?"

"That makes it sound like some tawdry reality show. No. It's a short list of appropriate potential partners. Allies with whom a partnership would be ideal."

Way to squeeze any iota of romance out of the whole thing. I might prefer a reality show, to be honest. At least then, the idea of attraction would be on the table, or at least in the dining room near the table. Mum makes this all sound so transactional.

I suppose I need to come to grips with the fact that not only am I losing Callum, but losing my chance to marry for love. Period.

"Mum. There must be another way. Not Valdonia."

"You know how difficult this is. It can't just be anyone with a title."

Technically, it *can*. But as Mum launches into the process

she and Dad went through to create the dossier of eligible matches, I can't help thinking how I'd love to exchange strong words with the founders of Viore who wrote up the charter.

I imagine a bunch of stodgy, old men sitting around smoking pipes or whatever people smoked in the 1600s. I can see them roaring with laughter as they drew up this document with such a specific set of parameters.

Why the specificity? Why must the reigning king and queen retire when they reach fifty-five? Why must the heir marry someone with a title before this time?

And why has no one questioned this or tried to have it updated or fixed with more modern addendums? I swear, if I get through this and take the throne, updating some of these things will be top of my to-do list.

Every country with a monarchy has its own governing rules and lines of succession. Some make more sense than others. I've always liked that in Viore, the heir's spouse is on equal footing. Mum wasn't considered a *queen consort* as she would be in England. She is the queen to my father's king. They rule together, taking on different roles, but with equal say.

"I hate to point this out," Mum begins.

I already know where she's going with this and how much she actually *loves* pointing this out.

"But we would have had more time if you hadn't chosen to go to university, getting an unnecessary education."

Attending university is the one thing I've really fought them on. And it wasn't, contrary to what they believe, because I wanted some "normal experience" or to "get something out of my system." I've been studying subjects specifically to help me serve the people of Viore. Geology has given me a better understanding of our own resources (specifically copper and silicon) and socioeconomics so I can have a firm grasp on existing and proposed policies.

French literature was just for fun, to give me a break from all the other, more serious things. Nothing like a little Flaubert or Baudelaire to lighten things up.

(Sorry, a little nerdy humor there. There is nothing light about French lit.)

Mum is still droning on. "The point is, our time is short. We have two months before your wedding. And there *will be* a wedding. The date is set. It's only the groom who's in question."

I want to scream and rail against her words, against the idea that the man I'm going to marry is so interchangeable. Shouldn't she care more? Shouldn't she wish for my happiness? Or, at least, not wish an older, handsy lecher on me?

The idea of the Valdonian prince coming anywhere near me again brings with it a knee-jerk nausea I have to fight down.

"But *Valdonia*? He's so much older." And so fishy, so handsy.

So ear hairy.

"You could learn to love him. As I did with your father."

Mum and Dad never talked much about their courtship, but I do know that in romance terms, theirs was more of an arranged marriage, friends to lovers, slow burn sort of thing. They do love one another, but theirs isn't the sort of relationship I wanted to emulate.

Silly me for thinking I could have more.

"If the idea is so distasteful to you, then you only have one choice. Pull up your knickers, as they say, and get Callum on board. It should be no trouble at all. I've seen the American. What was she wearing? A tablecloth?"

A faint smile finds its way to my lips, thin as a ghost. "A picnic blanket."

"Yes! A picnic blanket. That's exactly what it looked like. Now, hop to it because—*oof!*"

There are a series of small yips and a short scream from Mum. I hear a thud and then the sound goes a little faint, as though the phone has been dropped onto the grass. There's a splash, followed by muffled shouting and then the line goes dead. From the sound of it, the terrors have managed to trip her up or knock her into one of the garden fountains.

Good dogs.

I set the phone down carefully on the nightstand, feeling like I might break at any moment. Not my heart. That's already shattered. But whatever is left of my dignity and my sanity.

Am I really okay with the idea of trying to steal Callum from Brit? With my almost total lack of relationship experience, I wouldn't even know where to begin.

But Valdonia …

There's a knock at the door to my suite. I consider not answering. I don't want to talk to Kat. I don't want tea or any other service the staff might be offering. But then there's another rap on the door, and I realize that I *know* this knock.

It's Callum.

I rise, my legs feeling a little shaky, and don't bother so much as glancing in the ornate mirror I pass. Hopefully the ridiculously expensive eye cream is still doing its job. With one last, measured breath, I open the door to look on the face of the man I've loved since he was a boy.

I've accepted my lot in life, but this arrangement was never just about duty.

It was always about *him.*

Callum's hands are jammed into his pockets, and his eyes

look sad and maybe a little sheepish. His hair flops over his forehead in an adorably messy way. A part of me wants to reach up and brush it out of his eyes. A bigger, more logical part of me resists.

Giving me a rueful smile, Callum says, "Can we talk?"

CHAPTER SEVEN

Serafina

For initiating this little talk, Callum sure is being quiet. I follow him toward the gardens, easily my favorite place at the palace. Does he remember that? Is that why he chose this location?

My heart—the stupid, stubborn organ that refuses to die —feels like it's being squeezed by a fist. Because of the phone call with Mum, the pressure is even greater.

Because: Valdonia.

I trail my hand along the top of the hedges. When my family visited Elsinore during my childhood, Callum and I made secret trails through them, wedging our bodies in and breaking off branches so we could crawl and sit up inside.

We played spy, a game that felt indulgent knowing neither of us would have the ability to choose such an occupation. I yearn for the feeling of those days, crawling and stooping inside a canopy of green, chasing Callum's laughter, emerging with leaves in our hair. So easy, so carefree.

So long ago.

As Callum and I pass a thick set of hedges, I can spot the entrance to one of our trails. It's overgrown, but not as much as I'd expect after all these years. Has someone kept them up and taken care of them? The thought fills me with a conflicting tangle of emotions.

I steal a glance at Callum, trying to be discreet. I'm almost as nervous as I was earlier when I let Rafe into my room. It's surprising that two very different men can produce such a similar reaction in me. This man that I thought I knew so well suddenly looks and feels like a stranger.

Is his hair longer? Did he always have that little bump in his nose? I'm certain he's taller. Definitely broader. I think he even smells different. I fight the urge to lean closer and breathe him in.

We make our way with a sort of forced casualness down the gravel path, as though the impending conversation isn't hanging between us, hanging over us, blowing through the air like tiny particles of pollen.

We stop near a bench just where the gardens transition into a manicured lawn. A series of stone terraces extend like wide steps down, punctuated by a few fountains and water features. The last little waterfall empties into a large pond, which used to be home to vicious swans that Callum and I teased. Scanning the water, I don't see any sign of them, which is both a relief and another sad nostalgic moment. Swans are beautiful but nasty birds to start with, and after all our teasing, the swans here were lethal.

Surely, those specific swans are long dead. How long is a swan's lifespan, anyway?

Thinking about them, seeing the trails through the

hedges, I wish Callum had chosen a different location for our walk. I feel like I'm being haunted by the ghost of childhood crushes—fine, CRUSH, *singular*—past.

"Why don't we sit?" Callum suggests gesturing to the stone bench. He takes a seat and pats the spot next to him, looking expectantly at me with those big blue eyes.

There was a time—and, sure, maybe it was less than twenty-four hours ago—when I'd do just about anything Callum asked if he looked at me that way. Or ... if he looked at me *any* way.

Now, a part of me wants to stand with my hands clasped in front of me, as though waiting for a verdict, a final judgment.

Another part of me wants to turn and run. I'm so incredibly, intensely embarrassed by all of this. My tipsy-wine letter, which set this current trajectory in motion. The reality that there is a literal, legal contract I'm just finding out about. My total misreading of my relationship with Callum.

If I were some random Serafina, just a typical woman, I would run. I'd leave this garden, leave the palace, leave the country. But I'm not. I'm royal. The future of the monarchy, the future of my country, hinges on me staying, on me somehow winning Callum over.

Or ... Valdonia.

I sit.

"Well, this is awkward," he says with a chuckle, dragging a hand through his hair.

It is. Things were never awkward between us. Always easy, always comfortable. This loss, too, is a tiny assault on my heart, an aftershock of the main break. I suspect it won't be the last one.

I do my best to arrange my expression into something like wry amusement. "I don't know what you're talking about.

79

It's just like old times." I bump his shoulder with mine, though it literally pains me to do so.

But it does make some of the tension evaporate. At least on his end. He laughs, the sound familiar and warm. I have to stop cataloging all these moments as though they're lasts: our last walk through the garden, his last laugh at something I've said, our last conversation.

Callum smiles. "I've missed you, Fi."

Have you? I barely bite back the question and the bitterness that would for sure have colored my tone.

I lick my lips, which feel parchment paper dry, before speaking. "I wondered if something was wrong this year."

Understatement.

I continue, "You know, when we fell out of touch."

Aka when you stopped writing to me.

"Things seemed—*you* seemed … different."

As in, dating half of Europe. The half with breasts and legs and gleaming white teeth and recognizable first names.

"I didn't quite know what to say after I read your letter. Everything in my life started to feel … stifling. Being a working royal, my parents, and dealing with Phillip …"

Phillip? I'm not sure how Callum's older brother fits into this, but okay.

"… and the idea of a marriage contract everyone but me seemed to be aware of."

I don't correct him, explaining that I didn't know about the legal document part. It seems like splitting hairs at this point. My big takeaway is that I'm a part of what's stifling.

"I stopped writing to you this year because I was embarrassed. Humiliated."

"And you think I wasn't? That I'm *not*?"

"I wish you'd written that letter sooner."

I wish I'd never written it at all. Though maybe Callum is right; we should have been honest sooner.

You're still not being honest now, a little voice tells me. It sounds like Kat.

My lips feel cemented shut. I'm not about to confess my feelings now. Or admit that my parents have a dossier on other potential husbands for me, plus a backup plan if I can't manage to change Callum's mind in the next two weeks.

This feels like such an impossible task. And if it weren't for the impending wedding hanging over my head like a guillotine, I wouldn't try. I would walk away from Callum now.

"Knowing my parents had secretly planned to marry me off didn't go over well, as I'm sure you've guessed by now. Even to you. *Especially* to you."

Especially to me. "Right. Because I'm ..."

I trail off, swallowing down the string of words that come to mind. It's the worst kind of guessing game. Fill in the blank with an adjective that essentially means: not good enough.

Callum covers my hand with his, briefly, then pulls away. "That came out wrong. I just mean because we're such good friends. You're like family to me."

Ouch. At least I know very clearly where I stand with him. He didn't come out and call me his sister, but he might as well have. This bench might as well be inscribed with, *Abandon hope, all ye who sit here.*

"I know you'd do anything for your country," he continues. "You've always done what your parents asked of you."

This also hurts. Somehow even more than what he said about me being like a sister. Because it's true. I've always done what my parents asked. Going to university is the only thing I've fought for, and I've been dealing with their

81

disparaging comments the whole time, as though they're trying to reinforce my poor decision.

"I want *more*," Callum says.

More choice? More than simply doing a duty?

More than *me*?

Callum sighs heavily. "It was a silly dream of our parents. I mean, what did they think? We'd grow up together, fall in love, and then go along with their plans for us?"

I did. I did exactly that. Down to this moment, where I'm sitting on a garden bench, thinking of the growing likelihood that I'll end up with the hairy-eared, fish-cologned Valdonian prince. Or ... I could do what Mum said. I could stand my ground and win Callum back.

But *win him back* isn't quite the right wording. It seems I never had Callum to begin with.

He's got a girlfriend.

And he doesn't want you.

But maybe if he could only see me the way I've always seen him: as a best friend who could be more. We could be so perfect together. Maybe if Callum could look past the duty aspect of it all, he would see what I do ... but then there's the matter of Brit.

As though summoned by my thoughts, she emerges from a path down the hill from us. If she glanced up, we'd be visible, but she turns and heads for the pond. She's changed out of her tablecloth dress and has on what resembles a patchwork quilt. Seriously, it's as though she stole the finished product from a quilting bee and draped it over herself. It's so hideous I almost laugh.

Callum has turned slightly to face me, one leg up on the bench, so his back is to Brit. "You're smiling funny," Callum says. "Are you okay?"

Can't he see that I'm the furthest thing from okay? I'm

SO not okay that even the concept of *okay* looks like a tiny speck on the horizon, a tiny island or maybe a mirage. Maybe I don't know this man beside me as well as I did the boy I grew up with. That boy could read all the secrets on my face.

Even Rafe, a man I hardly know or care to know, noticed when I was hungry and brought me a tray of food. Rafe also recognized my heartbreak. But Callum is fooled by the thinnest veil, one I'm barely maintaining.

How can Callum miss so much?

Oh, right. Because he doesn't care. He wants more than me.

"Earth to Fi."

Callum takes my hand, and I wish he hadn't. There's still a part of me, despite everything, that longs for his touch, for him. But his fingertips are cool against my skin, and they don't light a single spark of excitement or desire. I'm made of the same stone as the bench where we're sitting.

He doesn't entwine our fingers or trace patterns on my hand with his thumb. It's friendly—platonic, not romantic. I stare down at my slim, pale hand in his masculine, tanned one wishing I felt something, wishing he did.

I give myself a count of exactly three caterpillars, and then I pull my hand away. "Sorry." My cheeks are stained with humiliation. "Jet lag."

"It's only a two-hour flight."

"Right." I pull my hand away and smooth down my skirt.

Brit catches my eye down below. Is she ... *dancing?* She spins on the lawn, grinning up at the sky. The quilt dress tangles around her ankles so she almost trips, righting herself at the very last moment.

"Are you and Brit serious, then?"

Callum gives his head a slight shake. "We're ... getting to know one another."

"Like you got to know that actress? Or the model? Or the heiresses?"

Didn't he just ask for honesty? He looks like he regrets it.

With a sheepish grin, he tugs a hand through his hair. "Yeah, I guess hearing my parents were trying to marry me off pushed me in the opposite direction."

"It would seem."

Callum laughs, misreading my bitterness for teasing sarcasm. He must also not have noticed the way I'm white-knuckling the bench.

"I'm glad we talked this out," he says. "I feel better."

"I'm glad one of us does."

The words did not have permission to leave my mouth, especially not in such a bitter tone, but they still did. Callum's expression shifts from placid and easy to shock and something even worse—pity.

"Fi—did you actually consider going along with this? For real?"

I shrug. "I did. Though I didn't know it was an actual contract. I thought it was an informal arrangement our parents joked about that had roots in reality. I assumed you were on board as well. I arrived in Elsinore expecting an imminent proposal. I guess you know what they say about assuming."

My joke falls flat. It's as though Callum didn't even hear it. He shakes his head, brows furrowed.

"You were going to go along with it? *Marrying* me?"

I wish I could peel back the last few minutes of conversation and say, "Just kidding!" Or pretend we're on some kind of prank camera show. I couldn't feel more like a fool unless I were wearing a jester's cap and one of those weird uni-suit jumper things they always wear in the cartoons.

"But … why?" He asks the question with such disbelief, such horror that my cheeks flame.

I could tell him the full truth—that I love him. It's what Kat and my mum would have me do. But it definitely doesn't feel right. I'm not sure if it's because the situation has changed or because my feelings have. I'm suddenly seeing everything with new eyes.

Callum shakes his head. "Actually, I get it. I know you. Of course—you'd do it for duty."

Or for love.

But can it be love when it's lopsided? Unrequited? I'm beginning to think it's been nothing more than a crush—a stupidly large, impossibly childish crush. I may not be able to fully confess all my feelings, but I don't want to stay silent.

I glance down, where Brit approaches a congregation of birds in the grass. She has a bright smile and holds out a hand, as though she expects the birds to alight on her fingertips. Does she think she's some kind of cartoon princess?

The birds, clearly realists, take off in a rush, as though Brit is a carrier for the avian flu. One manages to leave a hefty deposit on the shoulder of her quilt dress. She is like the comic relief to balance out my heartache.

"Not just for duty," I say quietly.

At first, I don't think Callum hears me. But then, with measured slowness, he turns toward me.

"Fi …"

His voice is raw, and I don't even get a chance to wonder what he's about to say—*Fi … are you saying you love me? Fi … I've always secretly loved you too. Fi … you're completely mental*—because his voice is lost to the rushing in my ears as Brit kneels by the edge of the pond.

The pond that used to have the swans.

"Oh, *blogger*," I say, standing as my eyes search the pond for any sign of the evil white birds.

They're gone. Surely, they're gone. If they're not …

"What is it?"

"Callum." I grab his arm just as the swans emerge out of nowhere, making a beeline for Brit in what is most definitely a choreographed attack. "The swans!"

Brit sees the fast-approaching swans at the same time I do. Her smile is so innocent. So very sweet. I can almost hear her saying, "Pretty bird, pretty bird."

Callum and I begin dashing together down the hill, like we are the official royal swan rescue team.

The team that's too late.

Because in a flurry of feathers and screams and quilt squares, the swans attack.

THE PREVIOUS AUGUST - THE MALDIVES

Serafina

Hiccup.

Whatever they say about liquid courage, I think they're lying. One mai tai (yes, I'm a lightweight) has me feeling no braver than I did before. Only a lot more hicccupy.

Callum and I are sitting hip to hip, nestled in the sand, watching the last sunset of our vacation together with our families. This is our tradition, sneaking away from his siblings as well as our parents who have a tendency to hit the bottle hard the last night in celebration.

Callum may have been somewhat distracted today by the two heiresses in their Brazilian bikinis, but who's he here with now? That's right—ME.

And this year, on the last vacation before next year when I'm to be married to Callum, I'm finally going to tell him how I feel about him. We've never spoken about it, not any part of it and it feels like we just need to finally address the elephant in the—

Hic.

Callum laughs, and nudges my shoulder. I almost tip over right there in the sand, but he wraps a solid arm around my back, keeping me upright.

I could get used to this.

I will get used to this.

In about a year's time, Callum will be—

Hic.

"Have you tried holding your breath and swallowing three times?" Callum asks.

I give him a faux glare. "I can't. It makes me feel as though I'm going to perish from asphyxiation."

He laughs again, blue eyes twinkling like the—

Hic.

"Anyway." I wave a dismissive hand, willing the stupid muscle spasms inspired by the first alcoholic drink I've had since last year's trip to subside. "You were saying?"

"Right."

I fully expect Callum's hand to drop from my shoulder, but it doesn't, and as he starts going on about whatever he was saying about duty and his role and frustrations with his parents—*I swear I was really listening before he put his arm around me!*—I'm debating about whether I can relax into his embrace.

It would be so easy to simply lean into him. But any movement feels as though it would break the spell. Callum might pull back and put the usual distance between us?

My internal debate rages while I stay completely immobile, afraid to lose the warm weight of his arm, when Callum says, "Don't you think?"

"Yes. Of course. Wait—sorry. What?"

He shakes his head but is smiling. "You're right not to listen. I'm just babbling about impossibilities."

"No—I'm here. I'm"—*hic*—"listening. Anything important to you is important to me."

If I'm not imagining it, his arm tightens a fraction of a millimeter—or whatever unit of measurement would be used to measure the strength of someone's arm giving you a squeeze.

"It all feels so heavy sometimes, you know? The expectations. I can't imagine how much more it must weigh on Phillip. He seems built for it, though. Sturdy, responsible Phillip."

I don't say what thought runs through my mind—that even sturdy and responsible people sometimes crack under pressure. In fact, sometimes it's the ones you don't expect.

I also don't point out that I'm in a similar position as Phillip. And while Callum's brother has time, I have just over a year before this all becomes real to me. I swallow, suddenly feeling every ounce of that weight Callum just mentioned.

"Sometimes I hate it," I whisper. "We never get a choice. But then, I feel badly when I consider that there are people born all over the world, even in my own kingdom, who have nothing. Literally, nothing. Or are in situations so horrific—"

"Fi, you can't change that."

His voice is gentle, but it does nothing to quell the passion I feel rising in me, the one I feel every time I start to think about poverty, of abuse, of so many situations that I don't have to deal with just because I was born Her Royal Highness Princess Serafina of Viore. The unfairness of it all only makes me more desperate to serve my people well. To make a difference.

"That's the thing. I can't change the station they were born into any more than I can change my own. But I can use what I've been given—that same weighty responsibility—to bring about change. It may be difficult sometimes to swallow all the parts of this life I may not want, but I have the privilege to do good. And I will."

"You're such a good person, Fi," Callum says, warming my heart. "You were definitely born to do this."

"It's so nice to know we're not a duty, you and me." That's not quite a confession or acknowledging our arrangement, but it's close, right? It feels like a tiny bite of bravery.

"Agreed. You've never felt like duty to me."

My pulse races and my body heats. He didn't quite come out and say it, but that's something, right? I'm not duty to Callum. I'm—

Hic.

Callum squeezes my shoulder, laughing. "Fi, just try the swallowing thing."

"You try it! It's hard to swallow three times while holding your breath. I don't have enough saliva!"

I give Callum a shove, and he pulls me tighter. *I'll take it!* My heart, which should really send some kind of signal to my diaphragm to hold it together, begins a complicated Irish dance in my chest.

"Here. Watch how it's done."

Callum pulls back slightly so he can tip his face down toward mine. My heart now feels like a whole troupe of Irish dancers are going mad in there, wearing the clogs and everything. With exaggerated slowness, Callum clamps his mouth shut and swallows, then holds up a finger from his free hand.

One.

Now I'm holding my breath too. Did the sun dip below the horizon finally? Because my vision feels like it's darkening as Callum's throat bobs with the motion once, then again. He holds up a second finger.

Two.

I bite my lip, eyes moving from his throat to his mouth as

he makes the motion of swallowing a third time, holding up that last finger before hitting me with the full force of his smug grin.

Three.

My gaze doesn't move from his mouth, so full, lips so tempting in that crooked grin. Which, while I'm watching, fades into something more serious.

"Fi?"

I glance up, my gaze colliding with his, knowing my desire is probably written all over my face. Definitely in my hot cheeks, but my eyes too. They feel … like lusty eyes.

No—that's not quite right. Lust isn't the word for what I feel for Callum, despite the haze of desire that's washed over me like the swell of a wave. There is the deep connection of our friendship, solid beneath the more fluttery feelings of desire, the ones making my fingertips tingle and my lips feel like they're practically begging to touch his.

"Fi?" he asks again. "Are you okay? You look—"

Hic.

I want to rip my diaphragm out of my chest and toss it into the palm trees behind us. What was he going to say? His mouth closes, his brows furrowing now, and the moment feels like it's slipping away.

"I look—*what?*"

Say it! Tell me I look beautiful in the fading sun's glow. Tell me I look like everything you've dreamed of. Tell me I look like your future happiness. Tell me I look like yours. Go ahead, acknowledge the lovesick look on my face, the desire, the burning need to—

Hic.

"FLIPPING HEEL!" I shout.

Callum's arm disappears from around my shoulders as he falls back to the sand, laughing long and loud, one hand over his stomach.

"I love when you do that, Fi."

It's not the compliment I wanted, but I scoop up every single nice thing Callum ever tells me, saving them for the long months we spend apart with only our letters to sustain me.

"You're so—"

I spin, crouching over him in the sand and finding those ticklish spots right on the sides of his rib cage. "Don't you dare say innocent!"

"I wasn't—Fi! Stop!" His laughter deepens as he tries to fight me off, but the man is ridiculously ticklish and I refuse to let up.

"Never!"

My tickling intensifies until he grabs my wrists in his strong hand and suddenly I'm flipped over on my back with Callum poised over me in the sand.

My mood instantly shifts. He's breathing heavy, smiling, his hair falling over his eyes as he gazes down on me. Desire hangs heavy over me, and I can't drag my eyes away from Callum's lips. We're so close. This is one of those perfect scenes for a movie. He could just lean in, closing the distance, or I could—

Hic.

Words my mother would definitely not approve of fly through my head as Callum releases his grip on my wrists, pulling me back up so we're back where we started, hip to hip, separated by a few inches that feel like the whole sea.

"I thought maybe I scared the hiccups out of you," he says as we both stare out to the sea. The sun has dipped below the horizon line, leaving the dregs of sunset behind, muted gold and pink leading into the deep velvet of the night sky directly above.

It's not too late. The moment has passed, but I can still tell him. I can bring up the arrangement, tell Callum that it's what I've always wanted, that he's who I've always wanted, and then—

Hic.

Nothing kills a mood—or my bravery—like a case of the stupid hiccups. Callum groans and hops to his feet.

"Come on, then. Sun's down. Time to go see what fun and trouble the parents have gotten into and if my sisters have managed to sneak into the rum yet."

He uses a strong hand to pull me up, and my stomach bottoms out with disappointment when he lets go, starting to amble back through the trees to the private villas nestled further inland.

"You coming?"

Everything in me is screaming to speak, to tell Callum to wait. To shove aside all pretense, all of my proper princess behavior and just lay out my real, true feelings in a way I only have to Kat. And compared to her oversharing, my true feelings are almost insignificant.

I can do this. I imagine Kat in front of me, giving my cheeks a good slap before shoving me toward Callum, telling me, *Get him, tiger! He's yours!*

Taking a gulp of air, I swallow and scramble after Callum through the trees.

"Wait up!" I call, breathless, and he pauses, just a dark silhouette against the lights from the villas behind him. Even as a dark shape, Callum is so large and striking that it's hard to breathe.

When I reach him, I pause, trembling with the need to let go of the truths I've kept curled around my heart for so many years now. The words rise in my throat and I fist my shirt in my hands, trying to ground myself in the moment.

"Callum—" I start, just as he says, "Hey!"

My mouth clamps shut.

"You've lost the hiccups! Finally!" He pats me on the back twice, like a footballer wishing someone a good game on the pitch. Before his hand leaves me, he urges me forward through the dark, toward the clearing ahead.

"I guess I have," I say, feeling a twist in my gut that might be partly alcohol-induced or might be the knowledge of my cowardice sinking in deep.

And by the time we reach the glowing lights and loud laughter and voices of our families in the main villa, it's hard to remember that I had the hiccups at all.

CHAPTER EIGHT

Serafina

If you want to know why I am currently wearing a dress made from what looks like a set of curtains, blame the swans —the blogging, flipping swans from the depths of heel. In case you were wondering, swans apparently have a lifespan of twenty to thirty years, a need for vengeance, and a thirst for human blood.

"You can still change your mind," Kat says, her tone indicating that I *should* change my mind. She can't hide her look of horror as she eyes my dress made of drapes. She, meanwhile, looks dead sexy in a silky black dress with a low V in the front and a sheer back.

"No. I can't," I say, gritting my teeth. "I promised her."

The *her*, of course, being Miss America, aka Brit, aka one half of the new power couple that is Britum.

Why did I make this particular promise? Because that's

the kind of thing you do when you're comforting a bleeding, hysterical woman attacked by the very swans you tormented as a child. Forget elephants—swans are the ones with a long memory. They never forget. Or forgive.

Callum practically had to beat them off with a fallen tree branch, but they only scattered when the royal guard, hearing the commotion, came down and fired some shots in the air.

This led to more members of the guard rushing out, an alert being sent that the palace was under attack, and blog headlines within the hour about domestic terrorism and an assassination attempt.

When I offered to do anything to help—anything at all—while Brit was being checked out by the royal physician, I did not mean *this*. But how could I have known that she would ask me to wear the latest design in her aptly titled American Homeland line?

Yes. Brit is the designer of the very dresses I made fun of, which explains a LOT.

I was correct in my assessment that the dress she wore to the tennis match was made out of a picnic blanket. The one shredded in the swan attack was, in fact, a quilt.

These terrible choices were *intentional*. While waiting to get her stitches, Brit explained that her whole line is based on folk Americana.

"A nod to my homeland," she said, then bowed her head as though giving the United States a moment of silence. "I've got something simply perfect for you," she promised.

What does it say about me that *simply perfect* means curtains? Only Maria von Trapp would approve. The material is thick, a mossy green inlaid with gold filigree. Combined with my pale skin, the overall look I'm sporting is sort of like moldy white bread.

I also look like I'm expecting. Even the uncomfortable one-piece shapewear that's a corset style up top and bicycle shorts on the bottom does nothing. The weighty fabric hangs over the empire waist—belted with a gold cord used to hold back curtains, naturally—making it appear as though I've got a bun I'm trying very hard to hide in the oven.

Brit really might be an evil genius. She steals the prince, suffers two black eyes and twelve stitches in a swan attack, and then gets a princess to promote her dreadful line of dresses—all while potentially starting new royal baby rumors.

Well played, Brit. Simply brilliant.

Kat giggles. "I don't even have words."

"That's a first."

"Should I take a photograph for Instagram?"

"I'm sure this truly macabre ensemble will be catalogued enough by the press tonight."

As this is the first in a number of dinners and smaller events Claudius told us about this afternoon—which feels like ages ago—there will be official photographers present. Tomorrow I'll be breaking the internet with my drapery dress.

Kat presses her hands together, pleading. "Can I take a photo for me? I'll use it to ward off depression. Whenever I'm feeling down, I'll have this to look at. Also, it would be great for memes."

"No memes."

"Yay!" Kat whips out her phone with glee.

I can't blame her. I look utterly ridiculous, draped in curtains so heavy that it's hard to move faster than a shuffle. Dancing tonight will be near impossible.

There is a crisp knock at the door. It's Claudius, standing

with an expression I've never seen him wear. His eyes have a mirthful glint, as though he's holding back a big smile. As Kat lets him in, he keeps both hands behind his back. She tries to peek, and he angles his body so she can't see.

"You're surprisingly agile for being such a stiff," Kat complains, trying to duck past his right shoulder.

The whole thing is comical. Adorable even.

With a huff, Kat gives up. Breathing heavy, she puts her hands on her hips and resorts to glaring.

"Your Royal Highness," Claudius says to me, managing to still keep whatever he has hidden while bowing. "And Lady Kat."

She rolls her eyes. "Just Kat."

Claudius ignores her. "Pardon my intrusion. When I didn't find Lady Kat in her room, I assumed she might be here."

"You were looking for me?" Kat asks.

With the tiniest tilt of his lips, Claudius pulls out what he was hiding behind his back. It's a box of biscuits, the very kind Kat mentioned earlier today.

There is a brief pause, in which Kat looks completely stunned, and then she snatches the box from his hands, staring at it, then at Claudius. "You found them!"

"I did. I've had the rest delivered to your room."

"The rest?"

The sliver of his smile grows. "I told them to be sure you had a clear path to the bed between the boxes."

Kat's mouth falls open, and for the first time since I've known her, she seems at a loss for what to say. I want to laugh, but this moment is more than comical. I have a feeling I'm watching some key turning point in a battle.

Kat must sense this as well, because her whole body stiffens, and she takes a step back. "Thank you, Claudius. How very ... enterprising of you."

If he's affected by her chilly thanks, Claudius doesn't show it. He looks totally triumphant. Smug, even. I mean, in a very restrained Claudius kind of way. I love it.

Moving to the door, he turns back with one hand on the knob. His gaze barely slides over me before landing on Kat.

"And if I may say so, you both look quite lovely this evening. Any man who finds himself in your presence should consider himself lucky."

With another quick bow, Claudius is gone.

Kat stares down at the box of biscuits in her hand like she doesn't know if she's going to tear into it and stuff her face or toss it into the fireplace and light a match.

"Still think Claudius is a robot?" I ask.

"I think he's a sorcerer," she mutters.

With a quick shake of her head, she sets the biscuits carefully down on a side table and turns back to me. "Do you want me to put your hair up? Or shall we keep it down?" Kat fluffs my hair, which she curled earlier in loose waves.

I choose to ignore her abrupt subject change. For now. I'm sure if I push or tease her about Claudius, it will only make her more resistant to him. Which is the very last thing I want. I might not have ever imagined it, but he's exactly the kind of man Kat needs.

"It really doesn't matter what you do with my hair. It's not going to get any better," I tell her.

"Perhaps Callum likes curtains?" Kat suggests. "He'll at least appreciate you doing something sacrificial for Brit."

Will Callum notice? Do I *want* him to? After our earlier conversation in the garden, I'm wondering if he's ever really *seen* me.

Yet ... I'm still supposed to fight for him. I must. The

99

contract still exists. So does my quickly approaching deadline. In two months, I must marry *someone*, or risk losing the monarchy. It's a gamble I can't make. Which means I NEED to get Callum to see me. To want me.

At the least, to say *yes* to me.

"Any luck on that contract?" I ask.

Kat sits at my desk, picking up her tablet to look at the documents my parents sent. First, they gave us the actual contract they set up with Callum's parents. I still can't believe such a thing exists. I didn't even want to look at it. The second document is much older—a scanned copy of the Viore charter which outlines the requirements for monarchs.

The third is the dossier, which I wouldn't let Kat open. Maybe later I'll look. MAYBE. Hopefully there will be no need.

"I'm afraid there are no loopholes, plot holes, knot holes, or blow holes," Kat says. "No holes of any kind. It's like a solid piece of iron, forged in the depths of Mordor."

"A little less drama and a little more using that law degree, please. Every contract has a weakness."

"Did you learn that by watching American legal dramas?" Kat gives me a pointed look.

"No."

Yes.

She scrolls through the document again, making a few notes on a piece of paper beside her. Though I know my bestie is quite sharp, it's another thing to see her in serious work mode. She's been poring over both documents since her nap, plied with endless cups of coffee and promises of an introduction to the viscount she thinks is cute.

"So, to sum up ..." I start.

"To sum up, you're royally screwed," Kat says. "Pun

intended. If Callum doesn't agree to marry you in two weeks, this contract between your families is void."

"Are there any other contingencies or stipulations?"

"Thankfully, no. It doesn't impact any other agreements between Elsinore and Viore. But as far as the charter ... if you're not married to someone titled by your father's birthday—"

"A wedding in two months, which my mother has already begun planning."

"Right. Then the Council of the People have the right to call for a vote to abolish the monarchy and establish a republic."

"And with the current feelings toward my parents as well as concerns about my age, it seems pretty clear how that would go. What kind of title counts? Do they have a list?"

Kat gives me a sly look. "Does that mean you're ready to look at the dossier? Find your own backup plan?"

"*No.*" If my parents have already gone through whatever list they've put together, I'll have to fight them tooth and nail to choose anyone other than the Valdonian prince. But still— it would be nice to have my own backup plan. "I'd just like to know all the angles."

"Fine. According to your illustrious ancestors, you may marry anyone raised to peerage in any nation. From a prince or duke all the way down to a baron. Or whatever's at the bottom. It gets confusing since the titles vary by country. Point being: pick a title, any title."

Not according to my parents, whose standards apparently left only the Prince of Valdonia.

"Honestly, though. I'm surprised your families made this arrangement, considering how close Callum is in the line of succession."

She's right, and honestly, I hadn't thought too deeply

about it. "Something would have to happen to King James and then to Phillip, before he had any heirs. It's unlikely."

But not impossible. It would wreak havoc on both our kingdoms if Callum and I married and then something did happen to James and Phillip. I'm sure my parents and Callum's considered this and thought it worth the risk.

Kat claps her hands, startling me out of thinking through worst-case scenarios. "Think fast, Princess. Yes or no: do you want to marry Callum?"

"What?"

"*What* isn't an answer."

"I don't understand the question. Of course I want to marry Callum."

Don't I?

"Does it even matter?" I ask. "Do I have a choice? It's Callum or … Valdonia." I shudder.

"It does matter. And you do have a choice. We could open the dossier and pick someone else. Stand your ground with your parents. It's about time. You'll have to in a few months, anyway," Kat says. "I mean, if you don't want to just be their puppet. You're going to have to activate that backbone I know you possess."

"I know."

I suspect my parents are going to have a hard time handing over the reins. But I don't plan to be walked over.

Kat gives me an uncharacteristically serious look. *Oh boy.*

"There is another option. You could always *not* marry, win over the people, and prevent such a vote." As though sensing my protest rising in my throat, Kat holds up a hand. "No offense to your parents, but we can both agree they haven't been helping the cause."

My parents are not horrible people or bad rulers. They're simply … detached. They don't seem to consult or care about the people and they often make decisions without announcing them. And when it comes to modernizing anything, they simply refuse. This goes for updating our mining practices or even considering the idea of opening up the palace for tours, two things I feel quite strongly about.

"What no one knows—and what they *should* know—is that you have been taking your role seriously. You've listened to the demands of the people and align with them much more than your parents do. But no one knows that. Not your parents. Not your people. They see you as the Ice Princess—cool and detached just like your mum and dad. But that's not you."

"No. It certainly isn't."

"It's time for you to shine," Kat says. "To come out of your ice castle and show the people who you are. You're more than the cool and collected Ice Princess the press has made you out to be. You have fire. And I know it burns strong for the things and people you care about." Kat clears her throat, then gives me a pointed look. "That means speaking the truth to your parents, to the people of Viore, and to Callum."

Kat's words strike a nerve. Okay—a LOT of nerves. Even if she is making great points, they are needle-sharp and pricking me uncomfortably. Which is why I respond with a light tone and a joke.

"And tonight, who I am is the princess wearing curtains."

Kat crosses the room, takes my hand, and gives it a quick squeeze. "We'll get this sorted. One way or another. I promise."

"You can't promise that, unfortunately. But I appreciate the sentiment all the same."

Regaining her usual fiery look, Kat says. "But nothing is

impossible. Especially with my help. Tonight is the start of our plan to win over Callum."

Our plan?

She takes me by the shoulders and gives me a little shake. "Other than the dress, you look gorgeous. Are you ready?"

Definitely not.

She continues without waiting for my answer. "Now, normally, I'm not one for chasing taken men. But until Callum walks down the aisle with Brit, it's not finished."

"I guess? It still feels ... wrong."

"They can't be serious when it's so new. And when she's so ... her. Anyway. When you were talking earlier, I'm guessing you didn't tell Callum how you feel?"

"No."

"Did you grab him by the lapels and kiss him into next week?" She grins wickedly.

"Definitely no! I wouldn't anyway, but especially not when he's got a girlfriend! He also might have told me he sees me as a sister."

"Did he actually say that?"

"He said I'm like family."

Kat shakes her head. "Not the same. We still have hope. Maybe all he needs is something to help him see you, really *see* you. He just needs something to make him look."

"This dress will certainly catch his eye."

Kat gives me an assessing look. "Maybe we could pull the front down a bit, let your glorious ladies breathe ..."

I cross my arms over my chest. "My ladies are staying exactly where they are."

"Fine. No ladies. You two have history. There's something deeper there. Focus on that. He's known Brit—what? A few weeks? It's not really *stealing* him if they're not in love. You claimed him first."

"Sort of."

That's the whole crux of the issue, honestly. I didn't claim him. I was never honest with him, even today.

But maybe Kat's right. Maybe it's not too late? I'm still finding it hard to get excited about this idea. Even when I remember Valdonia.

She continues, her voice gaining momentum. "You have to let him know that he has a choice—that this is more than simply duty. Let him know that you *love* him."

The words feel … off. I've always thought I loved Callum. We've been good friends, and I can't remember a time when his smile didn't make my heart race, when I didn't glow under his attention. Friends plus attraction equals love. Right?

Or maybe love is not so simple.

It's definitely not bossy or pushy. It doesn't start cat fights or form a wedge between two people in a relationship.

Love isn't selfish. And if Callum doesn't want to be forced into marriage with me, I should let him go.

Shouldn't I? Isn't that love?

This whole situation makes me feel totally lost. I've never been in a relationship. I don't know how to work through things, much less how to fight for them. All my life, fire and passion have been things I've been told to keep nicely tended to in the right fireplace, not let it out all over the rug. Who knows what else could get burned?

And I can't make more of a fool of myself than I already have. Chasing a man who has made his choice. The thought makes my heart hurt, and it has already been hurt enough.

Callum's knock sounds at the door. As though bent on ignoring common sense and rational thought, my heart leaps at the cage of my ribs. It's an errant dog who needs to be trained not to jump up on the furniture. *Down, girl! Heel!*

Kat opens the door, and Callum steps through. He looks amazing in a black suit with the royal blue and gold military regalia of Elsinore. His smile falters when he sees me. He blinks much too fast as his gaze moves from the bottom of my dress upward.

Right. For half a second, I forgot I was wearing drapes.

"I told you not to wear it," Kat mutters from somewhere behind me. I resist the urge to kick her shin.

"Is that ..." His voice trails off, and he bites his lip, barely constraining a smile.

I brush past him to do a tiny runway walk, almost tripping over the large gold tassels along the hem. I spin, striking my best model pose, which is probably rubbish. Kat gives me a slow clap.

"Who am I wearing? This dress is from the American Homeland line created by up-and-coming designer Brit Malloy."

Did she have to be so literal with her designs though? I swear these curtains were probably stolen from a manor somewhere. Hopefully not the palace. Although, that might be enough to get her kicked out or deported. I should ask Kat about the penalties for stealing palace furnishings. That also might alter my plans to steal a pillow.

"Well?" I flutter my eyelashes at Callum, doing my best to pretend like it's all going to be okay. Like we're who we've always been. Like I don't have an agenda, which is to change his mind about the arrangement.

A wide smile settles over his face, slowly, like the most gorgeous sunrise. His dimple appears, completing the effect. Then he tosses his head back and laughs.

"Brilliant! You're the best, Fi. Brit will simply be delighted. You know I don't understand a lick of fashion, but it must be the height of it if you've agreed to wear it."

Behind him, Kat snorts and shuts the door of our suite a little too loudly. Callum holds out his arms to us both. Kat loops a hand through his left, but I hesitate, fingering the rope belt of my dress.

"You don't have to ..."

"It's my pleasure," Callum says.

I find his eyes. "But isn't Brit coming?"

"Mum thought it might be better if she sat this one out. Given the state of her face." He grimaces. "She's starting to get two black eyes. Plus the stitches in her arm."

I hate the ugly part of me that's glad she won't be here tonight. But I can't imagine the kind of speculation that would come from Brit attending this event looking like she'd been punched. It's already been a busy news day with Britum and then rumors of an assassination attempt.

"Come on, then, Sera," Kat says, giving me a look.

"Right."

I settle my palm on the crook of Callum's elbow. Even through his suit jacket, I feel the heat of him. But I can't stop thinking of Brit. I need to stop thinking about her, if I'm going to go about stealing—*winning*, not stealing—her boyfriend.

As he leads us down to the main floor of the palace, I let Kat's words run through my head. My Mum's words. Callum's words.

But where are MY words?

If I had a choice—just for the sake of argument—what would my choice be?

Honestly, in this moment, I'm too confused to say.

All these thoughts only add to the nausea rolling around in my stomach.

"Are you all right?" Callum's breath tickles my ear as he

bends close to speak. I can feel the effects of it along every nerve ending in my body.

Am I all right? No.

But I will be.

Valdonia. The word is like a whisper, like a curse, and I tighten my hand on Callum's arm, smiling up at him as though I haven't a care in the world.

CHAPTER NINE

Serafina

Near the top of the grand staircase, we separate. The royal family will make a grand entrance a little later. Kat takes a back staircase, leaving me to make an entrance all by myself … in curtains.

Humiliation can take many forms. One is when the man you thought you'd be getting engaged to turns up with a girl-friend. Another is being photographed at an official royal event while wearing *this*.

I descend the staircase carefully as the shutters click, praying I don't trip on the heavy material or the tassels. The practiced smile I've employed for years comes in handy, so at least I don't look like I'm completely miserable and horrifi-cally embarrassed by my ensemble. Which, to be clear, I most certainly am.

Fake it till you make it, right? I'm not sure what I'm making though.

These are approved professional photographers, not paparazzi, taking respectful photographs. Thankfully, at the king's request, there are no interviews, but I can see the questions in their eyes.

I shuffle to the Blue and Gold Room, which is the smallest of three ballrooms inside the palace. Claudius informed us there will be around seventy-five guests tonight, mostly Elsinorian royalty and society. Most of the visiting dignitaries and royals will arrive in a few days, like my parents. The room is already half full by the time I arrive, and my eyes scan the room until they settle on Kat, who gives me a little wave.

I make my way to her, soaking in the details of the room. As the name would suggest, the room is decorated in rich blues and golds, except for the floor, which is a gleaming white marble. A string quartet plays soft music from a low stage. Long tables with white tablecloths frame the room, all decorated with crystal vases full of cornflowers, the national flower of Elsinore. Soft light emanates from a large crystal chandelier with its lights dimmed.

Everything looks beautiful, and I wish I could enjoy the festivities rather than feeling slightly ill. I make note of large topiaries around the room, maybe a good option if I *actually* become sick. Always good to have a vomit strategy as well as an exit strategy. Too few people plan for this.

"How was your grand entrance?" Kat asks, a devilish glint in her eyes.

"I didn't trip over myself, which I'll consider a win. Where can I procure a glass of wine?"

I figure wine started this by giving me the courage—or stupidity, I still haven't decided—to send the letter, so I might as well come full circle.

Kat looks surprised but snags two champagne flutes from

a tray as a server dressed in all black passes by. He eyes Kat, and she winks, sending him scurrying away. She hands a glass to me.

"Don't go too fast. You need to keep your wits about you. Remember, you've got a prince to win."

I roll my eyes and take a quick swallow, then a small sip. The last thing I need is hiccups.

"Now. About Operation Ditch the Bi—"

"We're not calling it that," I hiss, stopping Kat before she can finish. I may want Callum, but I won't stoop to being petty.

"Fine. Plan Purloin the Prince?"

"No." I glare. "Please refrain from names with cursing or any form of the word *loins*."

Kat covers her mouth to stifle her laughter. I'm still glaring when a deep, silky voice lifts the hair on the back of my neck, the way a dog's hackles might rise at the sign of danger.

"Sounds like I'm missing a scintillating conversation. What's this about loins?"

I wonder if Rafe can be summoned magically by the use of certain words. I should start keeping a list. *Loins* goes right at the top. Shouldn't be so hard to avoid in the future.

Only now it's like an earworm: *loins, loins, loins.*

GAH!

"Rafe," I say through gritted teeth meant to emulate a smile. "How lovely to see you."

With hair as dark and shiny as a raven's feather and eyes like sinful dark chocolate, Rafe de Silva is danger personified. Or, as Kat would likely say, sexy personified.

His presence unsettles me even more than usual after his visit to my room this afternoon. Are we … friends now? That term feels wrong, but I wouldn't say we're enemies the way we've always been. At the very least, we've called a strange truce.

"Even lovelier to see you," Rafe says, taking my hand. Without breaking eye contact, he presses his lips to my knuckles.

The kiss should be innocent and polite, but those two words don't apply to Rafe. Instead, he makes the brush of his mouth over my hand feel like we're rounding second base.

Er—first base? I don't understand baseball, nor do I have experience with *any* of the bases beyond simple kisses. Whatever the case, this doesn't feel like the kind of greeting that should be happening anywhere with an open door. Even Kat begins fanning herself.

I yank my hand back and wipe his kiss off on my dress as quickly as I can, wishing I could wipe the blush from my cheeks as easily.

"What were you saying when I walked up? Something about loins?" he asks.

Kat giggles.

Loins, loins, loins.

Shut up, Serafina!

"We were discussing dinner," I say.

"I thought we were having seafood. In any case, it sounds delicious." Rafe takes a sip of his champagne, his dark eyes still searing me.

"Stop doing that," I demand.

"Doing what?"

His grin tells me he knows exactly what, but he turns and gives Kat a smile that looks a lot more tame than the one he gave me. "Kitty Kat. Looking sleek and gorgeous this evening."

She preens under his praise, and my irritation grows. Rafe is like one of those itchy tags on the inside hem of a shirt, itchy and impossible to ignore. The best solution, obviously, is to cut it out. I'm not sure what kind of sharp blade will best rid me of Rafe.

He turns from Kat to give my dress a slow perusal. I feel even more exposed than I did walking down the grand staircase in front of the photographers. Wearing this thing is like having my own personal sauna. I swear the temperature underneath the fabric has risen ten degrees since Rafe has been standing here.

"What a unique dress," he says to me, and his slow perusal makes me shiver. His fingers brush the material near my waist, and I bat his hand away. "Are these the drapes from the drawing room? Or perhaps the library?"

He's teasing, but it feels friendly and flirty somehow, not cutting. Still, I want to slap the smirk off his devilish face. Emphasis on devil.

"This dress is couture," I tell Rafe, lifting my chin.

I'm not sure what technically constitutes couture, but considering it's a one-of-a-kind dress that seamstresses measured just for me earlier, I think it counts.

"Any designer I know?" Rafe asks. "Perhaps one of Stella's? Or Giorgio's? Carolina's?"

Of course, Rafe is the kind of man who can name-drop designers. I perhaps should be more familiar, but I've let Kat act as my personal stylist for the past few years. She loves fashion, and I'd rather have one less thing to think about. I'm sure Rafe is wearing one of those names he mentioned now. To me, men's fashion is rather boring, but even so, Rafe wears the heel out of a suit. Not that I would ever tell him that. His ego would probably achieve liftoff and blast into space.

"She's up and coming," I say.

"Will you be wearing something similar to the ball?"

"*No.*"

"Actually," Kat starts, and I don't like the look in her eye, "Sera has a dress, but not a date to the ball."

Rafe arches an eyebrow. "Is that so?"

"I don't need a date," I say through gritted teeth, narrowing my eyes at Kat.

Kat's eyes narrow right back. "You *do* need a date."

She's clearly trying to convey something with her expression, but the only thing she's conveying are crazy eyes.

"Why don't we see if we can find the viscount?" It's phrased as a question, but my pointed look is more of a demand.

Rafe *tsks*. "Princess! Are you planning to slum it with a viscount now that your prince is taken?"

Oh, this man!

Earlier in my room, I could have sworn that I saw a little bit of softness in Rafe. I must have been imagining it, because there are only rough edges to this man right now, and he's rubbing against me like sandpaper.

Maybe he's just trying to get a rise out of me. Well, consider me unleavened bread. Totally flat. No rise at all.

"Who, me? Of course not. I'm not looking for anyone right now." *Lie.* "I simply promised to introduce Kat to the Viscount of Denbury, and I wanted to make sure she didn't fall for your particular brand of charm first."

Rafe's smug look turns positively insufferable. "You think I'm charming, Princess?"

"I didn't say that. I said you have a particular *brand* of charm."

"What about you, Kitty Kat? Do you like my *brand*?"

Rafe unbuttons his suit jacket, then spreads his arms wide, spinning in a slow circle. He even lifts his jacket with his back to us, and I wish I could say my eyes didn't drop to his backside.

Look away from the devil's bum!

I elbow Kat, who is still staring.

"Ouch!" she says, rubbing her side and giving me a narrow-eyed glare. "You looked too!"

"Shut up!" I hiss.

"Well?" Rafe asks, buttoning his jacket and looking far too pleased with himself.

"Pass," I say.

Rafe gives an exaggerated sigh. "Kitty Kat, put in a good word for me with Princess here, would you? She seems to think I'm some kind of devil."

"Oh, I know you're some kind of devil," Kat says. "Just a handsome one."

"Too bad. Well, then, if I'm not wanted, I think I'll make my presence known elsewhere."

Translation: find more willing females.

Kat sighs, and we both watch his retreating form. As if he knows, Rafe flips the back of the jacket up, showing off his bum again. I scoff, but Kat giggles as he turns his head just enough to throw a wink our way.

I shake my head. "I feel like I need to take another shower."

Kat gives me a wicked smile. "So the duke *does* have an effect on you!"

"Not that kind of effect! I don't mean a cold shower! I meant to clean off from his slimy presence."

I never did tell her how he stopped by my room. The whole thing seems like a dream, honestly—the playboy duke going out of his way to do something thoughtful for me. I'm not sure why I kept it to myself, but I'm certainly not going to tell her now.

"I don't know," Kat muses. "Rafe seems different. And he definitely seems interested in you. He's got a title. Maybe we should consider—"

"No."

Kat sighs. "Still stuck on plan Steal the Crown—"

"If you say Jewels, I'll have you forcibly removed and shipped straight back to London."

"I'm just saying … you're at a point where you should keep all viable options open."

"You're considering *Rafe* as a viable option?"

"He has a title. And a very nice—"

A trumpet blows from somewhere—probably from a speaker, as I don't see an actual trumpeter anywhere—and the entire room quiets, turning toward the double doors. My stomach tightens with a sudden onslaught of nerves.

The royal family has arrived.

CHAPTER TEN

Serafina

A herald standing by the door introduces the royal family one by one, as we all stand by, bowing and clapping politely.

First, there are the king and queen, looking much less alcohol-soaked than they did the last time I saw them. Not that I'm surprised. In public, they're never anything but completely poised and perfectly royal.

The queen gives me a tight smile, which I return in kind. I'm not sure of where I stand with them, or where they are with my parents. I expect all of this to hit the fan when my parents arrive, unless I can sort it out first.

The king and queen are followed by Phillip. Where Callum is sunshine and smiles, the crown prince is serious to the point of being sour. I'm not sure I've ever heard Phillip laugh. I must have witnessed a smile or two over the years, but for the life of me, I can't picture it. He's a tech genius, and I always feel like he's designing microchips in his mind.

It's easy to imagine him ruling responsibly over Elsinore, but he lacks all the warmth and personality that his parents and siblings have. He'll be respected, but I wonder if he'll be *liked*. This is only evidenced more as Callum is announced and the whole mood of the room seems to shift.

He strides into the room smiling, and somehow looking even more handsome than he did when I left him upstairs not ten minutes ago. His blue eyes sparkle, his white teeth gleam, and light seems to exude from him. It's almost as if he has a permanently attached Instagram filter. It's no wonder the press call him Golden Boy.

When he catches my eye, he winks, and I feel a simultaneous lifting and sinking sensation. *Am I really doing this? Am I going to actually throw my hat in whatever ring people throw hats into and be a contender?*

I press my hand to my stomach as though that could quiet its churning. Callum's two younger sisters are announced next and walk in together, hands clasped. Henrietta, aka Henri, and Juliet are more like Callum, but with wild streaks neither of their brothers possess. Despite being outspoken, Henri has a fairly good head on her shoulders, while Juliet is more like a lovely, wild horse. They look and act almost like twins, despite the year between them, and are each other's best friends. They'll need to find a matching set of brothers to marry someday.

At sixteen and seventeen now, they're stunning young women and the picture of poise. I still remember them begging me to braid their hair while they talked my ear off about boys and school. They find me in the crowd and give me matching expressions of pity.

They met Brit, then, I suppose. I sigh, and Kat leans closer.

"You've got this," she whispers. "Tonight, Brit is out of

the picture. Be your charming self. Make Callum see why you're his perfect match. Not because of duty, but because you belong together."

I turn to Kat, needing to see the expression on her face, needing someone else's backbone to help me find my own.

"Do you really believe that? You think we belong together?"

Kat tilts her head, giving me a funny look. "It doesn't matter. Don't you think so?"

The clear answer is *of course I do*, but I say nothing, instead turning my attention to the servant who has appeared to lead us to our tables. I'm tempted to clutch Kat like she's the last life preserver on a sinking ship, but instead smile and take my seat at the head table while she finds her place across the room.

I'm sandwiched between Callum and the ancient and very deaf queen mother, with Rafe straight across from me. How did he earn a seat at the head table? As though reading my thoughts, he winks. This will be fun.

The servants bring out small bowls filled with what's supposed to be soup but looks more like a carrot or pumpkin massacre. Aside from curry, I make it a point to avoid bright orange foods. Ignoring the soup, I nibble on the crusty piece of bread on the side.

Callum leans close, and his proximity makes my head feel woozy, though I'm almost as aware of Rafe, whose gaze is fixed on me across the table.

"Carrots—your favorite," Callum says.

"You remember?"

"Of course. Hard to forget the time your mum forced you to eat them and they came back up."

Not helping my upset stomach. I set down my bread.

"Lovely topic for dinner conversation," Rafe says, and he

must have bat hearing, because Callum was practically whispering in my ear.

"I don't think we were including you in it," Callum says, and his mother frowns.

Over the years, the sense of unfriendly competition between these two has only gained momentum. Callum has always complained to me about Rafe, warning me away in no uncertain terms. But I wonder if there's more to their history than Callum has shared with me.

"Serafina, do tell us about your studies," the queen says, and I'm grateful for the question, which breaks up the tension.

"We're thinking of allowing the girls to go to uni," the king adds. "We'd trust your judgment as to whether it's a proper place for a princess, Serafina."

Henri and Juliet look at me with bright, pleading eyes. I can tell they're clutching one another's hands under the table. Probably because they've constantly pushed the boundaries from birth, the girls have been kept under a fairly tight set of constrictions.

Setting them loose at university might be the start of a Royals Gone Wild franchise. But given my current set of restrictions, I'm all for all the choices.

"Yes," Rafe says, "do tell us how you liked uni. You must have been a good girl, as I didn't read much about you in the tabloids."

"Unlike some others at this table," I fire back, realizing only after the words have left my mouth that they don't just apply to Rafe but Callum as well. Beside me, Callum clears his throat and takes a sip of wine.

Rafe's smile widens. "Quite true. I think the Golden Boy has finally eclipsed me for the number of headlines and front pages he's had this year."

Oh boy.

Callum's hand tightens around his spoon, and just when I think the metal is going to bend under his grip, the servers return, smoothly taking our bowls.

"There's going to be an eclipse?" the queen mother asks at full volume. "Don't stare straight at the sun. You'll go blind."

She pats my hand, and I give her a small smile. "I'll keep that in mind." Turning back to the king and queen, I continue. "I mostly kept to my studies. I've never been one for the typical social life, so I can't speak to that. But I quite enjoyed the independence and loved my coursework. I also met some great friends."

Only one in actuality, but Kat's personality is big enough to count for a handful of friends.

The truth is most people thought of me as stuck up and wrote me off without ever giving me a chance. Even the few times I allowed Kat to drag me out to events, people either didn't talk to me because I'm a princess, or only talked to me because I was a princess. I don't think Henri and Juliet would have the same problem.

"Remind me what you studied," the king says.

"Geology and socioeconomics. With a concentration in French literature."

"That's quite a course load," the queen says.

"You're quite impressive, Princess," Rafe says, and Callum glares.

"She is." Callum puts an arm over the back of my chair, and I find myself stiffening and wanting to lean away.

I feel like I'm under a microscope, with a crowd of scientists jostling each other for a chance to take a look. Except the queen mother, who has blissfully fallen asleep and is snoring softly.

"We'll have to discuss more with you later," the queen says, giving her daughters a look like she knows exactly how they would behave at university.

"So, Cal," Rafe says, lounging back in his chair like a proper scoundrel. "I was under the impression you would be Serafina's date to the ball. But I hear you've got yourself a new American bird."

Callum bristles. He hates being called Cal. Apparently, he doesn't mind Callie, which in my estimation is far worse.

"You sure seem to be apprised of the royal gossip," Callum says, his tone sharper than I've heard it before.

"You know what they say. The walls have eyes."

"Ears!" the queen mother shouts, startling me. I guess her first-course nap is over. "The walls have ears!" She leans closer to me. "My Gerald had ears like an elf. Pointed at the top and everything. Not an attractive look. Nothing like that young blond one from the Tolkien movies."

"Nana!" Callum says, looking horrified.

"What? I'm a widow in my twilight years. I can admire an elf if I want to."

Rafe wipes his mouth, hiding his smile behind the napkin. "I think you mean Legolas," he suggests. "Played by Orlando Bloom."

The queen mother beams at Rafe. "That's the one. He makes an ugly pirate though."

"Can't argue with you there," Rafe says.

The servers bring out small plates of escargot with butter. I swear, it's as though someone has purposefully planned a meal full of things I hate.

"Still don't eat snails?" Callum asks, taking my plate and setting it on top of his empty one. This is old hat for us. His parents are escargot aficionados, which means this isn't the first meal where Callum has eaten my share for me.

"I'm afraid not. My palate is still a little simpler—carbs and dessert."

Which means that I'm practically starving by the time dessert is served, as the main course was some kind of ceviche. Call me mad, but I don't trust meats "cooked" by dousing them in lemon juice.

All through dinner, I'm all too aware of Callum's presence beside me, his warmth and familiar steadiness. Every so often, he leans close to whisper comments or bring up a memory or private jokes. It's almost like old times, except I can't stop thinking about the pressure I'm under. And I can't escape Rafe's gaze, which counteracts Callum's steadiness by making me feel unsettled. Thankfully the tension between him and Callum eases as we move through the meal.

Still, I'm overwhelmed. I'd like nothing more than to escape to my room for an early bedtime. But not before dessert. Never run before dessert. When—*if*—I'm queen, perhaps I'll make this my motto.

I take a bite of tiramisu, barely holding back a groan. Creamy, delicious, rich—it's the kind of food that would have me tempted to lick my plate if I weren't surrounded by people. I do my best to pace myself, but it's a challenge.

"You're welcome to have mine as well, Princess." Rafe's eyes twinkle as he holds out his plate.

I look down and realize that mine is empty, save for a smear of chocolate. How disappointing.

"Oh, I couldn't. You should enjoy it yourself," I tell Rafe.

"I insist," Rafe says. "I can see how much you're enjoying it."

Leaning across the table, Rafe switches my empty plate with his untouched dessert. His fingers graze mine as he does so, and the way his smile lifts tells me it was intentional.

Callum bristles and practically growls beside me, and I find myself irritated with all his bluster. Why should he be irritated if Rafe shares a dessert with me?

"Thank you," I tell Rafe.

"My pleasure."

"So, Rafe, how have things been since you left the royal guard?" Callum asks, and Juliet drops her fork.

I don't know much about the situation, but two years ago, right after entering the Elsinorian royal guard at the same time Callum did, Rafe was discharged. The papers reported medical reasons, but there were also ugly rumors about his uncle covering up for desertion.

Rafe's lips press into a thin line, and a frown ghosts across his face. He recovers a moment later and finds his smirk again.

"I've been fine. And I'm sure the royal guard was just fine without me. After all, they had *you*."

"So, what have you been doing with your free time, then?"

Rafe takes a long swallow of water, as though giving himself time to measure out his words. It's obvious Callum is goading him, and Rafe is trying to maintain his cool. "Not much free time when I have a duchy to keep and maintain."

Rafe has a fairly substantial duchy, inherited when his parents died, and kept under his uncle's control until he was eighteen. I believe it includes a few small towns and a valley which grows barley, wheat, and rapeseed.

He's young to control so much, and my heart aches at the reminder that Rafe lost his family when he was so young. He doesn't have anything close to what's repre-sented at this table—loving parents and siblings. Just his uncle, a man who seems hard, cold, and conniving. I've only seen the baron with Rafe a handful of times over the years, but there was never any warmth between them, no kindness.

The servants collect our dessert plates, and the music swells as the king and queen take to the dance floor, performing a graceful waltz. I watch them, noting the tightness in Suzette's posture and the tiredness around James's eyes. But there is still love in their eyes. I've seen them together for years and know it's more than a front.

Did they marry for love? Or was theirs an arrangement where love grew from necessity, from friendship, from duty?

I long for what they have, what my parents have. Maybe I won't get to have the storybook love. But it doesn't really matter how love begins, only that it's given room to grow. Right?

If only I could convince Callum.

As the song ends, James smiles broadly and gestures to the room. "Please, everyone—join us if you'd like. Or enjoy a glass of port on the terrace." Servants swing open the doors along one wall and move around the room with trays holding small glasses of dark port.

Callum stands and extends his hand to me, a smile tugging at his lips. "May I claim a dance?"

Despite my clumsiness, dancing is a chance to be in Callum's arms, perfect for my plan—though the plan is the last thing I want to be thinking about.

I stand. "Of course."

Rafe calls, "Save me a dance as well, Seraf. If you'll have me."

Before I can answer, Callum practically drags me to the floor like some kind of caveman. I almost trip over the fringe at the bottom of the curtains.

"Slow down," I protest.

"Sorry," Callum grumbles, pulling me into his arms.

I'm grateful for his strong lead as well as the years of training. I may not be graceful, especially in this dress, but I can at least follow. I seem unable to come up with anything to say, though. I can't stop thinking about Valdonia. Or Brit. Being in Callum's arms feels wrong.

After a few minutes, Callum breaks the silence. "You should be careful of Rafe. He's up to something. He and that uncle of his."

"You've been warning me off Rafe for years. Honestly, I'm beginning to take offense."

"Right, well. He's very charming, and I'd hate to see him get his hooks into someone like you."

I raise a brow. "Someone like me?"

"Someone sweet and kind and good."

I know those are all compliments, but somehow, they don't seem that way. They are the same kinds of words one might use to describe one's sisters. Or the elderly woman living in the flat next door.

"I can handle myself, Callum."

"Can you?" His brow furrows a little. "I don't mean anything by it, only, I know you haven't dated much."

A fresh, hot wave of emotion seems to billow through me, getting trapped under the material of my dress creating a sauna-like situation. Maybe that was Brit's goal—to make me sweat to death in her ugly dress.

Kat dances by, moving much quicker than the music requires, practically dragging the viscount with her. By the hungry look in his eyes, I don't think he minds. But she's looking at me, not him, and I can read the signal on her face.

Right. I'm supposed to be winning over Callum, not getting frustrated with him.

"I'll be careful," I tell him.

Callum seems just as relieved to move on to other topics.

"You look lovely tonight," he says, but before I can respond to the compliment, he continues. "Though you seem a bit sad around the eyes."

Yes, well, I have you to thank for it.

"I think I'm still recovering from exams."

"You?" His eyes twinkle. "If you haven't changed, you were probably prepared for them three months ago. Congrats, by the way. I understand you graduated with honors."

"Thank you."

For a moment, we dance in silence. Then Callum speaks in a low voice, one that has my stomach tightening.

"Ever wish things were different?" he asks. "That we didn't have all of these duties and restrictions? That we were just Callum and Fi, a typical guy and girl without all these things hanging over us?"

I study his face, so handsome, so familiar. I swallow, trying to clear whatever emotion is trapped there. "All the time."

Except, I realize even as I'm answering, I don't wish that. As much as I resent some of the requirements—especially the ones that feel particularly arbitrary—and my current predicament, I look forward to serving my country. I was born to do it, and I'm thrilled to do so. It's an honor, and I wouldn't wish it away.

Not even for Callum, I realize.

"Me too," he says, and I could clarify my answer, but I don't.

The song slows, and we move from more formal steps to simple swaying, which is a relief. I smooth my hand over Callum's shoulder, feeling the muscles underneath, remembering the scar that runs just above his collarbone. While body surfing on one of our family trips, a wave knocked him to the ocean floor and a broken shell sliced him. I held my hand over the bleeding wound—right there—until we were able to get it stitched up.

A little over a day ago, my thoughts were consumed with Callum, wanting to be this close to him. Closer, even.

Why am I suddenly feeling like my own skin is too tight? Why doesn't it feel the way I thought it would to have him hold me close?

Callum's fingertips begin to slide along my hip, the slightest movement, but it has the subtlety of a blowtorch. I'm hot all over, and not in the good way. It's panic, or maybe I'm on the verge of heatstroke in this completely unbreathable fabric.

I try to think Ice Princess thoughts and regulate my body temperature. I should want this. I should want *him*—or is it that I *need* him?

Is there a difference?

Does it even matter?

Valdonia, Valdonia, Valdonia.

Brit, Brit, Brit.

Shoving thoughts of Brit away, I take a breath and lift my chin to look at Callum. His eyes hold warmth and affection. Not the heat that the viscount had looking at Kat. But something steady and true. Not sisterly, I think.

Surely, this is *something*. I'm not imagining the connection between us, borne of childhood friendship and blooming into something more. Kat is right—we have history.

He also has a girlfriend.

A heaviness settles in my chest.

I try to shove Brit out of my mind, but it's like closing a door on someone set on coming in, sticking their foot in the crack. Callum's thumb grazes my cheek, and our eyes lock.

My heart thuds in my chest, but it's as much with dread as it is anticipation. This just feels … wrong.

I shiver as his thumb continues to coast along my skin, over the apple of my cheek and landing near the edge of my jaw.

It is a classic *I'm about to kiss you* move. The kind immortalized in so many movies, where both leads have their lips parted (check), their gazes bouncing from eyes to lips (check, check), and enough tension charging the air to power a power grid (check, check, check!). Kat moves into view, giving me a thumbs-up.

Callum is going to kiss me!

Callum is going to kiss me—while his girlfriend is somewhere inside these palace walls, recovering from a swan attack.

I desperately try to push thoughts of Brit aside, but I can't. No matter how much I want Callum.

I *do* want him, right? Because whilst a part of me feels like this is the culmination of all my hopes and dreams, another larger, louder voice is shouting like some kind of law officer: *Lower your weapons and step away from the prince!*

"Fi." My name on Callum's lips is like a gravelly, desperate plea.

I've wanted to hear him say my name like that for so long.

But not anymore. Not when he has a girlfriend.

I can't. It's not who I am.

And if this is who Callum is, maybe I don't want him either.

I pull away and take a big step back just as a most unwelcome, most *American* voice makes me grateful I did.

"Callie?"

Despite the trapped heat underneath this dress, my skin is icy cold the moment Callum lets me go.

"Brit—you're here."

His hand, the one that was just touching my face, now curves around her elbow.

Callum looks guilty as all heel.

And Brit looks … well, like she fought a swan and lost.

Despite her attempts at makeup, there is no hiding her swollen eyes and the darkening bruises around them. White silk gloves hide the bandage over her stitches. And her dress —well, let's just say it doesn't hide much else.

A lacy material the same white as her gloves, it looks like she poured herself into it. With lacy cutouts around the waist, a deep vee at the neck and a slit up one leg, there is more skin on display than material.

So far, she's worn a tablecloth and put me into curtains. Which would make this … a torn napkin?

No—a doily! She's totally a doily!

My triumph at figuring it out fizzles out as I realize she is *Callum's* doily. And I came very close to kissing him.

I feel simply ill.

"I thought you were going to rest," Callum says.

Brit shrugs, blinking up at him with long lashes that, up close, look very real. "Do I look awful?" she asks.

She's not just fishing for compliments. There's a raw vulnerability there, making my heart soften toward her. I want to dislike her. Why does she have to be so disarmingly sincere?

"Of course not. It would take more than a vengeful swan to diminish your beauty," he assures her.

Callum's arm goes from her elbow to her shoulders, drawing her in closer. He presses a kiss to the top of her coiffed hair.

I try to slip away, but Brit stops me, reaching out her good arm to take my hand. Her eyes glow with pleasure as she looks at my dress. I'm not sure what she sees that I don't, but I still look like I'm wearing a maternity dress made of curtains.

"I cannot thank you enough for wearing my dress, Princess Serafina," she gushes, giving me a small curtsy.

Callum grins. "No need to be so formal. It's just Fi."

"Serafina will do." My tone is a little prim, so I locate my formal smile and fight to find something positive. "And it's an honor to wear an original design of yours."

There—that was nice and neutral. Positive, even, and in a warm tone.

Callum gives me an approving smile, which reminds me of the private smiles he gave me earlier. *Ugh.* How quickly can I make it to an exit?

Before I can do so, a hand curls around my waist, pulling me snugly against a solid body. Rafe grins down at me.

"Mind if I steal the princess for a dance?"

I'm not sure who he's asking, since Callum has already let me go.

When I look like I'm going to argue, Rafe adds, "Don't make me beg." He leans closer, until his warm breath is a spring breeze moving over me. "Though I'm not above begging when it's something—or someone—I really want."

Under normal circumstances, I would shove him off and tell him to go find someone else to charm. But I am tilting like a three-legged chair and desperately need steadying. Rafe's body is a solid presence against mine, his hand on my waist somehow reassuring.

I find myself relaxing against him, batting my eyes up at him in my best attempt at flirty eyes. "We can't have the Duke of Weldon stoop to begging, now can we?"

Rafe looks delighted by my response and wastes no time twirling me away. One glimpse at Callum's face shows a look which, if I didn't know better, resembles jealousy.

"I'm not sure how you manage to be so light on your feet in that dress, but I applaud you, Princess." Rafe's tone is teasing and light, and it's exactly what I need at the moment.

"It must be your lead, because I'm rubbish at dancing, especially in this dress. But all my formal training has led to this pinnacle moment, it seems."

Rafe tosses his head back and laughs fully, not missing a step. I find my eyes drawn to his neck and the light shadow of stubble below his chin where his throat bobs. When his eyes meet mine again, they practically glow, like the sun shining through some kind of amber crystal.

"I think a compliment was buried in there somewhere, which I'll take. You really are a vision, despite the monstrosity of a dress. I heard Brit mention the design was hers. Let me guess: you agreed to wear it because you felt guilty about the swans?"

"How did you know?"

"I know you better than you think, Princess. Tell me, did you train them to attack?" His smile turns teasing.

I narrow my eyes. "No. I most certainly did not."

"Don't be offended! It would be brilliant strategy if you were trying to win him over."

"I'm not—"

"Aren't you?" The teasing leaves his voice, and his gaze turns assessing.

I glance over at Brit and Callum dancing. He may have her in his arms, but his eyes are fixed on me. Or … is he simply glaring at Rafe?

"I don't know what I'm doing," I confess.

"For the record, Callum is a fool. He has no idea what he's missing out on."

Letting go of my hand, Rafe cups my cheek and *oh my stars!* How does any woman's resolve not crumple under the weight of his attention! It's heady and intense, to the point where I swear I can almost see it drifting off him like magic dust. His warm eyes are somewhere between chocolate and caramel. Both are delicious.

Maybe later I'll regret it, but for now, just for a moment, I let myself fall just a little bit under Rafe's spell. His words and his touch are a balm, soothing the sting of rejection and humiliation I've been feeling since the tennis match.

Rafe's fingertip moves dangerously close to the corner of my mouth, and my breath hitches even before his words hit me.

"Seraf, I would *never* take you for granted. It would be simply impossible."

I laugh nervously. "Did you hit the wine too hard at dinner, Rafe?"

His eyes darken. "No. A man would have to be daft to miss the treasure you are."

Rafe trails his finger over my face, as though he needs to touch every place Callum just did, to stake his own claim. I realize we're still standing in the middle of the room, not dancing, not even swaying. His intensity keeps me pinned in place. I can't look away from his eyes, which means I also can't stop thinking about chocolate. Rafe and chocolate—that sounds like a delicious and deadly combination.

"You don't look like you believe me, Seraf," he says.

"I just … maybe I just see myself a little more realistically than you seem to."

"What does that mean?" His jaw tightens.

Callum's words from earlier echo in my mind. *Someone like you.*

"I just know I'm not everyone's cup of tea. I come with a lot of strings and requirements. And it's not like I've been fighting off suitors."

"You want a dose of reality?"

Rafe pulls me close so suddenly that I have trouble breathing for a moment. His spell drags me a little deeper as his lips graze my ear.

"You are gorgeous. Brilliant. A truly good woman. And if given the opportunity, I could make you completely forget Callum in a matter of minutes. But I want more than mere minutes. I want hours and days."

No one has ever spoken to me this way. I didn't know words could have such a visceral impact. The bold suggestiveness of Rafe's comments flood me with raw, flaming heat and an electric buzz that makes black dots appear in front of my eyes.

"A lifetime," he whispers. "Maybe a lifetime would be enough."

This is Rafe, I remind myself. The Royal Rogue. I'm probably not the first or last to hear this little speech from his lips.

And I almost bought it.

The spell breaks. I stiffen and pull back. "Do those kinds of lines work on other women?"

Rafe drags a hand through his inky hair, one side of his smile tipping up, though his smile is more sardonic than happy. "On everyone but you."

I poke a finger into his chest. "And that's why you're after me, isn't it? Because I'm the only one who has ever told you no."

He glances away. "I do love a good chase."

"Well, I don't like the chase at all," I say, my voice hardly more than a whisper. Rafe may be chasing me, but I'm chasing Callum. And I hate the feeling.

My emotions are so close to the surface. If I'm not careful, tears will be spilling down my cheeks in moments. This is the last place I need to let go, and the last person I can let go in front of.

I grip him, turning my head into his shoulder, beginning to sway again. I need movement, something that feels normal for the moment.

"I don't want a chase. No games," I tell Rafe's shoulder, blinking back my tears. "I want to be adored. Cherished. I want someone I can trust. I want a chance at love, even if it has to grow from friendship or from duty first. I've always wanted Callum. But it's time to admit that he doesn't want me back."

"If you were mine"—Rafe's arms tighten around me—"I would treasure you. I would adore you. I would cherish you the way you deserve."

The words make my heart tremor, and yet they also cause the first tear to escape. I feel the path it traces over my cheek, past my chin, and down my neck.

Callum's warning from earlier rings in my ears. What am I doing, listening to Rafe's words, falling for his charm?

There's no way that the playboy Duke of Weldon truly sees me as some kind of treasure. More like a conquest, or a prize to be won. This is all part of some game he's playing, a way of getting at Callum.

"Treasure?" I scoff, taking a big step back from Rafe and the spell he's casting with his words, his eyes, and the seeming sincerity in his voice. "I guess you'd know, wouldn't you? Having pillaged your way through so many *treasures*. A different one every week over the years."

My words are sharper than perhaps they should be, and I'm not sure the anger burning in my chest is even because of Rafe. He's simply the one standing closest to me, the one who had the misfortune to push me past my careful control.

"That may have been true of me in the past. But tell me,

Princess, who stole more headlines this past year—me or Callum?"

His words are a blow, and I feel it deeply. So many times this year, I tried to talk myself out of feeling jealous over photos of Callum with another woman. I tried to tell myself it wasn't what it appeared. That he was still mine.

"When's the last time you saw a headline about me?" Rafe demands. "Maybe you're just upset that your prince and I aren't so different after all," Rafe says. "Perhaps neither of us are the men you think we are."

Apparently not. Because I'm realizing that as charming as Rafe can be with his words, he's just as skilled at cutting to the quick.

Before I can lose control of my emotions any more, the way I always seem to do around Rafe, I yank myself from his grasp. And when I accidentally stomp on his foot in my haste, I feel a brief sense of triumph.

CHAPTER ELEVEN

Serafina

Blinded by my tears, I make my way down a darkened hallway until the sounds of the ball fade behind me. A few guards are posted, but they clearly know me, as they hardly budge. I'm sure The Dane is shadowing me from a distance, but otherwise, I'm blessedly alone.

Finding an unlocked door, I slip inside a darkened room where I can fall apart in private. I don't bother turning on any lights. I don't want to be discovered, and if someone does come in, at least the darkness will hide my tears.

My eyes adjust, through the tears and moonlight, until I make out a few seating areas. I grab the back of a brocade sofa for support, bending to lean my forehead against it. Hopefully the material is hardy enough not to be stained by tears, because I'm currently a waterfall of them.

I'm not only heartbroken, I'm angry. Furious.

Not at any one particular person but at everyone, really—

myself included. I'm angry with monarchies. With royals and with commoners alike. With binding contracts and laws and expectations, with the need to be proper and keep everything contained.

I'm furious with the way the media heralds Rafe's and Callum's gorgeous dates and how they find fault with Mum's ankles or my lack of significant relationships.

I'm angry with Callum's parents and my own for setting all this in motion with their arrangement. Angry with myself for not being honest with Callum about my feelings or anything else. Angry that I thought things would magically work out between us.

I'm disgusted that I considered letting Callum kiss me when he has Brit, disgusted that he almost tried.

I'm furious with Rafe for sweeping in to rescue me, then wounding me with his words, which weren't even so far from the truth.

I'm angry that he makes me feel things, when all I want is to be numb.

I'm angry with my stupid heart for being so soft, so easily wrecked.

I'm angry with Brit for her very existence, and especially angry with her for asking me to wear this horrific, heat-trapping dress.

The harder I sob, the hotter I become. The heat is trapped beneath the heavy drapery fabric and makes me feel like I'm on the verge of detonating. With shaking hands, I untie the cord around the high waist and fan the skirt out, trying to get air to circulate inside. It's no use. I'm wearing a sweat box.

After what could be two or twenty minutes of falling apart, I feel … not better, but spent. Completely undone and emptied in a way that's incredibly satisfying. Between the tears and the perspiration, I feel like I've been wrung out.

When was the last time I cried? Oh, right. This morning.

But when did I last allow myself to let loose?

When have I ever really let myself FEEL like this?

It's incredibly freeing, even if it hurts. The lessons on being a proper princess, on presenting the perfect image, may have struck too deep. I've caged myself, more than the rules and stipulations ever have. Even in private, even amongst those I trust.

I really have been an Ice Princess. Like Elsa from the movie, I've made *conceal don't feel* my motto. And I'm sick of it!

Yanking up the dress, I gather the material of the skirt around my waist to leave my legs bare. Perching precariously on the back of the sofa I just cried on like it was my best friend, I kick off my shoes and let my legs swing free. For a few moments, I just let myself breathe.

Beyond my role as a princess, beyond the expectations, I am a *person*. A person sitting in a dark parlor with her skirt above her knees, contemplating deep thoughts about life.

A laugh bubbles out of me, and at first I slap a hand over my mouth, hearing the echo in this large space. But no—I don't need to stifle myself. When I let go, I laugh for several long moments, awkward, ugly snort-laughs that would have embarrassed me anywhere else.

Now, they feel like the truest sounds I've ever made.

This feels like the best kind of therapy.

That is, until a voice and movement from the shadows makes whatever's left of my heart stop beating. I gasp.

"Feel better?"

Rafe. Recognizing his voice doesn't stop me from reacting in a panic. I jolt, losing my balance, and find myself tumbling heels over head off the sofa backwards. I land bum-first with a crash and a crunch on what is—or *was*—probably an antique coffee table covered in expensive trinkets. Based on the pain radiating from my nether regions, what feels like broken glass or wood splinters are now embedded in my arse.

"You … you … you *scoundrel!*" I yell, trying to disentangle myself from the broken bits of table.

Painful sensations accompany even the slightest movements, confirming my worst fears: whatever breakable things broke are now stabbing my bottom.

Oh, HEEL no.

Rafe's dark chuckle matches his dark shadow, looming over me. "I wanted to have an effect on you," he says. "Just not this kind. Here, let me help."

The last thing I want is help from this man.

"You're like a vampire," I spit, "always lurking about in dark shadows, emerging only to frighten innocent young women."

"I've been called worse," Rafe says. "Take my hand, Angel."

I refuse, slapping him away. The pain in my arse has removed any sense of decorum or patience. It feels like a burning porcupine has quilled me in the butt. And I don't want to even think about what I've broken. Everything in the palace is either some kind of historical artifact or an heirloom: priceless, irreplaceable.

Painful.

"How did you even get by The Dane?" I'd incorrectly assumed he would keep people out.

"You don't want to know. But it involved potted plants, crawling on my belly, and a bit of bribery. Isn't he Swedish?"

"That's why it's funny. Kat gave him the nickname years ago, and he hated it so much, we decided to keep it."

Rafe shakes his head, biting back a smile. "Oh … kay."

"If you want to actually be useful, why don't you find the lights?"

I wish I hadn't asked, because when the lights come on, it reveals an even bigger mess than I thought. The table is splintered almost beyond recognition, and there are bits of blue and white porcelain in shards, along with some clear, cut glass. No, not glass—*crystal*. As long as I don't move, I can almost pretend as many of the pieces aren't in my bum as are scattered on the expensive rug.

I shoot daggers at Rafe with my eyes, while it feels like a million tiny daggers are stabbing my bottom. The least this stupid dress could have done with its thick fabric is protect me from the broken glass. I wince, as a shard digs into my bare foot. Why did I take off my shoes?

Rafe, of course, looks every bit as composed as he did earlier. Though I still see amusement in the tilt of his lips, there's concern in his eyes.

"Are you hurt, Angel?"

"Stop calling me that. I'm no angel!"

He clears his throat. "Serafina, let me help you. Please."

Something about hearing my full name on his lips makes me obey. Or maybe it's the please. Possibly just the fact that I actually *do* need help.

I let him grasp one of my arms in two of his. I can't hold back a hiss of pain, and Rafe's brows lower. He pulls me to my feet, and as he does, I feel a slight tug, hear a rip, and suddenly I'm falling into Rafe's arms, feeling much lighter than I was moments ago.

We both freeze, eyes locked and faces inches from each other. His hands are warm on my lower back, and I'm clutching his—for the record, very nice—biceps. Cool air touches my skin in far too many places.

I close my eyes and speak first. "My dress is gone, isn't it?"

His eyes flick down and then immediately back up. "Yes."

"Could this day get any worse?"

"Should I be offended, considering our current position?" His lips twitch in a smile.

"This is all your fault."

"I think we could blame Brit for being such a terrible designer. Or perhaps the king and queen, for not having sturdier furnishings. I plan to leave the palace a strongly worded two-star review."

A laugh bursts out of me, and I rest my forehead on Rafe's shoulder while my shoulders shake. But even this movement makes me more aware of the painful splinters.

Careful to keep the rest of me as still as I can, I lift my head. "You're insufferable."

"Thank you."

"Not a compliment."

He shrugs. "And not the worst insult I've received either. In that same vein of positivity, you're now free of that horrible dress."

"Now *I'm* insulted."

His voice drops an octave. "I'm only commenting on the dress, Seraf. Even in something so obviously a travesty of so-called fashion, you still look beautiful."

Oh.

"Don't look so suspicious of my compliment."

"Who said I'm suspicious?"

"I can read you better than you think."

"What am I thinking now?" I ask.

A beat goes by in which he studies my face. I tell myself that I'm letting Rafe continue to hold me close because the moment I jerk away, he'll see the ridiculous undergarments

I'm wearing, and I'll never hear the end of it. But it's surprisingly nice being in Rafe's arms.

His smile widens, and his voice is soft. "You're thinking that the moment I let my guard down, you're going to kick me in my crown jewels."

He's remarkably accurate, and I stifle another laugh. "Well done, Rafe. Maybe you do know me better than I thought. Now. Why did you come here?"

"Not to get you out of your dress," he says, and then his eyes take on a devilish twinkle. "At least, not like this."

"Rafe," I hiss.

His expression gentles into something more sincere, and his hands flex on my back. "I came to apologize."

Not at all what I was expecting. Perhaps because I'm not sure how to take sincerity from the duke, I keep my tone light. "For which thing?"

"Well, now I'm amassing a list. I truly didn't mean to scare you or to make you fall through a table. But I came to apologize for hurting you with my words about Callum. I know you've been hurting, and I didn't mean to hurt you even more. I just hoped you'd see for once …"

I'm almost desperate to hear the words he doesn't say. "See what?"

He shakes his head and meets my eyes. "It doesn't matter. I know you're hurting, and I twisted the knife even more. Forgive me?"

"Why do you care if I do?"

"I care more than you know," he says, those chocolatey eyes warm and soft. "Hurting you is the last thing I want to do."

As with the food service he brought to my room and the way he swooped in to rescue me from Callum and Brit earlier, this kindness shows a different side to Rafe. Maybe

143

not a different side—maybe I'm seeing a different man than the one I thought I knew. Really, other than scandalous headlines and Callum's continued warnings, what do I know of him? The question is unsettling.

I make Rafe wait another moment, which seems only fitting, despite the new way I'm starting to see him. "I forgive you."

His shoulders slump with relief. "Thank you." He looks thoughtful for a long moment, maybe even a little sad. "You really love Callum, don't you?"

I drop my gaze to his shoulder and the deep black of his suit. "I suppose I always have."

It's the best answer I can give. Though honestly, my emotions are too all over the place to say how I feel *now*. I've always thought I loved Callum. As a friend, as more. But can you really love someone when that love isn't returned? When I think back over my conversations with Callum since I arrived, I'm also beginning to question how well I truly know Callum, or if he even knows me. My "love" in hindsight now seems … thin. More like a fairy tale, a childish dream, than anything substantial.

"That's what I thought," Rafe says, and I should correct him. I find that I *want* to, but when he starts to ease me back, out of close range, out of his arms, I gasp in pain. The skin-tight spandex encasing my butt and upper thighs seems to be tugging at all the little pieces when I move, forcing them deeper.

Concern replaces what looked like sadness in his eyes. "What is it?"

"When you frightened me and I went through the table, some glass and things broke. And pieces are … *in* me."

"Let me see."

Rafe starts to turn me. I shake my head. "No! No. You can't."

"Why not?"

"Because, um …" I blink up at him, clinging to his muscular biceps lest he decide to see for himself. "I'm not dressed."

"You're in nothing worse than a bathing suit. Probably a little more coverage, actually."

He's right, though there's something far more embarrassing about being exposed in my shapewear. It feels more intimate somehow, even if the one-piece undergarment has more fabric than a bikini.

My cheeks are positively flaming. No man has seen me in *any* undergarments. Ever. And this is Rafe … who has likely seen countless women in much less. Things that were sexy, for show, not meant to smooth over any imperfections.

I laugh, and it sounds more than a little bitter. "Honestly, this is probably more than you're used to seeing women wearing."

His brows furrow. "Seraf—"

"No. Just—let me think." I grip his arms even harder. "I honestly think I'm going to need a physician."

"Is it that bad? I'm so sorry, Seraf. Why didn't you say something sooner?"

Probably because I got caught up in bantering—*flirting?*— with Rafe. A fact that makes me feel even more intensely embarrassed.

"Please. Tell me what I can do to help you. The last thing I want is to see you hurt. Especially at my hand."

There is no artifice in his words, none of the usual charm oozing from his pores. I'm seeing the Rafe behind the mask. And it's so much harder to resist than his charm. I can resist flirtation and see it for what it is. This? A man who honestly cares enough to seek me out when I'm nursing a broken heart? It's enough to shatter my defenses completely.

Except I'm supposed to be winning Callum, not falling for Rafe.

And it's not like Rafe is even interested in me. He's being a friend, at best. This is what friends do for one another.

Or … maybe not. Maybe I'm just being bewitched. *Watch out for Rafe,* Callum told me earlier. *He's up to something.*

No more. I swallow thickly, the emotions of the last twenty-four hours threatening to overwhelm me.

"Would you be able to see about finding the palace physician?"

"Of course," Rafe says. "Anything else?"

I shake my head and attempt a small smile. "Who is this serious, responsible guy, and what did he do with the playboy devil?"

Rafe's grin is slow, and it makes my stomach flip. "Aw, Angel. Did you make the mistake of typecasting me into just one role? You should know I can play many parts."

"I guess I'm starting to see you in a new way. I'm not sure who you are."

Rafe leans closer, and for just this moment, his breath on my cheek makes me forget all about my pain, my undergarments, and Callum.

"I'll be anyone you want me to be, Angel."

Before he can move away, I move up on tiptoes to be closer to his ear, despite the twinges of pain. I'm not sure what makes me do it, other than an urge to see if I can throw Rafe off the same way he's done to me.

"Right now," I tell him, smelling the woodsy spice of his cologne, "I need you to be the man who calls the royal physician to help pull shards of glass and wood from my bum."

He begins to chuckle, and it's at that very moment when

Callum bursts through the door, a royal guard in tow, The Dane looking sheepish. I gasp, realizing at once how compromising this position looks, Rafe and I in each other's arms, me in only my undergarments.

And Rafe, of course, with a smirk like he planned this very thing from the beginning.

CHAPTER TWELVE

Serafina

Possibly the only thing worse than falling through a coffee table and getting splinters and shards of porcelain and crystal in your bum is having a physician cut off your shapewear, then remove the pieces one by one with a pair of tweezers.

It's been thirty minutes, and I swear the man will never finish. I guess it's true that I don't do things by halves. Kat watches from a chair in the corner like I'm the evening's entertainment, eating some kind of crisps she procured from who knows where. If she were a gif, she'd be the one of Michael Jackson throwing popcorn in his mouth, grinning.

At least the royal physician had the decency to hang a makeshift curtain over my lower half, so Kat can only see the front of me. I'm propped up on my elbows on this uncomfortable medical table. My cleavage keeps trying to escape the loose top of the hospital-style gown, which is only slightly better than being totally nude.

In short, I only thought I'd been thoroughly humiliated earlier when I had to parade in front of photographers in the curtain dress. But no, the full extent of my embarrassment is having the dress ripped off and having a doctor pull splinters out of my bare bum. At least I know the physician has, like the staff is required to both here and in Viore, signed nondisclosures and other agreements. He won't be selling this story or anything he hears.

"You don't need to look like you're enjoying this so much," I grumble to Kat, wincing as the physician gets another piece. I hear the *plink* as he drops it into a metal tray. It's just like in the medical dramas I've enjoyed bingeing in the past.

I'm not sure I'll ever see them the same way again.

Ow. Plink!

"This is honestly the weirdest, most exciting thing to happen to me in months," Kat says. "Sorry."

"Shouldn't you be off snogging with the viscount?"

Kat rolls her eyes. "It's just snogging. You don't snog *with* someone."

"Semantics. Point being: why aren't you with the viscount?"

Kat shrugs, wrinkling her nose a bit. "He was too easy. There was no challenge. He was too into me."

Ah, to have that problem.

"I need a man who gives me a challenge. Someone … different than my norm."

Someone like Claudius? Before I can even think about uttering his name, Kat continues.

"Speaking of, how is *your* man situation going? Operation RTC. Let's start from the beginning. I want to hear it all."

Plink!

I focus laser eyes on her. "There's not much to tell, honestly."

"I beg to differ. I saw you and Callum enjoy a dance together, one where you seemed very into each other. Then there was the American invasion, you danced with Rafe, and then you ran off. You were found in a compromising position with the Duke of Devilishness himself. Now you're getting splinters removed from your bum. Want to fill in some of those blanks for me?"

Plink!

Yes, let's fill in those blanks.

It should be easy to recount my evening. Only ... I myself am a little confused as to the particulars. Or how I *feel* about them. I had an emotional breakdown, broke a table, then had Callum burst in on a moment that looked far more intimate than it was. Callum and Rafe almost came to blows, pulled apart only by The Dane, who was then pulled off by Callum's personal protection officer. (At least, Callum's PPO *attempted* to pull The Dane off. I'm pretty sure The Dane *let* himself be removed as he's got a good foot in height and girth on Callum's man.)

"It was all Rafe's fault," I finally tell Kat. A simplification, yes, but not untrue.

"It looked like he played the hero tonight."

"More like the villain." The response comes easily, but I'm not altogether sure it's true.

Kat studies me for a long moment. "I'm not so sure if we haven't confused the leading men's roles."

A knock at the door saves me from having to dignify that remark, which is ... surprisingly accurate.

Then again: there's no one else I want in here right now. I'm sure my face goes pale. We're tucked away in a set of medical rooms I saw after the swan attack. That's two times too many, if you ask me.

"See who it is!" I hiss at Kat. "But under no circumstances are you to let anyone inside this room!"

There may be a curtain hiding my backside, but there's no hiding the rest of me. She opens the door a tiny crack.

"What do *you* want?"

I assume by Kat's tone of voice that she's speaking to Rafe and I drop my head into my hands.

"Just let him in," I say.

But it's a golden-blond head of hair that peeks through the door. I swallow, and a whole host of nerves zip through me. Kat steps aside to let Callum walk inside. He gives me a shy smile, his eyes flashing concern.

I try to signal with my eyes for Kat to leave, but she resumes her position in the chair, munching away on her crisps with an amused expression. Meanwhile, I do my best to hide the assets I'm displaying by crossing my arms awkwardly over my chest. I'm pretty sure that just makes the situation worse.

"Are you all right?" Callum asks.

Plink! I wince, and Callum does too, eyeing the curtain.

"I'll be fine. Just have a few more splinters to remove from my, er … self."

"Probably a few *dozen* more, Your Highness," the physician calls from behind the curtain.

Lovely. "Thanks for the update, *doctor*."

Callum gives me a sympathetic look and runs a hand through his hair. He's still wearing his tux, without the jacket. He has his sleeves rolled up, revealing his tanned forearms, which normally I'd be ogling. Now, it's more of a clinical appreciation. It must be the weight of the day finally hitting me.

The crown prince has great forearms. Whoop-de-do.

They don't compare to Rafe's biceps.

That thought jolts me, and I almost drop my hold on the front of the gown.

I clear my throat *and* all thoughts of arms from my mind. "Dare I ask what the damage is? I'm not even sure what I broke."

Callum bites his lip, trying to hold back a smile. "Nothing of great importance."

"Callum."

"Just an antique table that's two hundred years old."

I groan, dropping my head to the table. "What else?"

"Only a few small trinkets, really."

"Such as? How small? What's their worth?"

When he doesn't answer right away, I lift my eyes to glare at him. He's wearing what is normally one of my favorite expressions on him, a boyish look that implies mischief. I've seen it dozens of times over the years, but at the moment, I'm just irritated.

"Hard to say what they're worth, exactly. A few cut crystal glasses broke."

"And?"

"A ceramic tea set from the King of Spain that was a gift for my nana's wedding. No worries."

"I broke an irreplaceable wedding gift from the now-dead Spanish king? But, sure. I won't worry."

Callum chuckles. "Nana said she never did have much use for the king or his leaky tea set." He makes a face. "I do believe she was making some kind of euphemism, but I don't want to know."

Kat laughs, and both Callum and I glance at her. I'm pretty sure we'd both forgotten she was there.

"Don't mind me," she says. "Carry on."

Callum turns back to me and leans his hip against the table. He's so close that I can smell his cologne. A bit too much, to be honest. Or maybe it's the way it's mixing with the antiseptic.

With a casual tone that sounds a little forced, Callum says, "I have to ask—what were you doing with Rafe? It looked rather … cozy."

Plink!

"It wasn't what it looked like."

"What, exactly did it look like?" Kat asks. "Just a quick visual, if you don't mind me asking."

Callum and I both ignore her this time.

"I fell through the table. Rafe helped me up."

Callum's eyes drop down, taking in the bare skin on display. Every exposed inch breaks out into goose bumps at his gaze. His cheeks turn pink and his lips tighten as he meets my eyes again.

Kat is grinning in the corner.

"And what happened to your dress?" he asks.

"When I fell, the fabric caught on broken pieces of the table. It sort of ripped off when I stood."

"Hm," Callum says, and it's clear from his tone and the hard expression in his eyes that he's still imagining some totally different scenario. Considering the sheer number of items being removed from my bum, the idea of something romantic going on is ridiculous.

It's ridiculous anyway. There's no way Rafe is actually interested. Despite his flattering words.

I could explain this. I should. But seeing Callum look possessive—*or even jealous?*—should be a good thing for me. Isn't it?

The memory from earlier sweeps over me: how freeing it felt to let all my emotions out. Kat—who's still noshing on

154

crisps in the corner like we're a real, live reality TV show—had a point about not holding back. Maybe it is time to tell Callum the truth. If he knows how I feel, all arrangements aside, he can make his choice freely.

Only ... I'm no longer certain how I feel. Earlier, when Rafe asked if I loved Callum, there was a tiny whispered voice that felt a lot like truth. And it said *no*.

For the second time that night, a door flies open, interrupting a moment. Rafe, looking disheveled and distraught bursts inside the small exam room. The Dane and Callum's PPO are right on his heels, looking like they want to kill each other as much as Rafe. The room is hardly large enough for all these men or all the testosterone.

Kat grins delightedly, and the physician frowns from around the curtain. "You can't all be in here," he says.

"Remove him," Callum says to his protection officer.

"He stays," I say, and The Dane and Callum's man face off.

"Fine," Callum says after a beat. "Both of you, back out. And how about you do your jobs and keep anyone else from entering?"

"I'm the patient here!" I protest. "I should decide. But yes, do keep anyone else out."

The Dane gives me a nod of his square jaw, and he follows the other officer out. The moment they've gone, Rafe removes his jacket, draping it over my shoulders as he gives me the strangest embrace of my life.

It's hard to be hugged when you're lying on a table, trying to hold a thin gown over your otherwise naked body while a man behind a curtain is pulling Spanish royal porcelain from your derrière.

Still, I appreciate the coverage of Rafe's jacket, and the warmth of his embrace. His lips find my ear and I almost squeal. My eyes are probably like saucers, and Callum's look like he could start a world war with the anger brewing in his.

"Just go along with it," Rafe whispers.

And then he brushes his lips over mine in the quickest, most shocking, and somehow hottest kiss of my life.

If I weren't still holding my gown and now his jacket in place, I would have grabbed Rafe by his shirt front and pulled him back for another.

Because you can't just kiss someone like that!

And you can't just STOP kissing someone like that!

What does it mean?

And how did he manage to put so much tenderness, yet so much scorching heat into a kiss that was over almost as soon as it began?

Sorcery, I tell you. The man is a sorcerer.

And what was that about going along with something?

My brain is such utter mush at the moment, I'd go along with Rafe if he asked me to join a traveling circus.

I try to regain some semblance of control, but it's nearly impossible. My cheeks are flaming red, my breath short, and my lips are aching for more contact.

My eyes meet Callum's, and if I wondered if he looked jealous before, I have no doubt now. His gaze is heated enough to start a fire as he turns to glare at Rafe. Kat leans forward in her chair, and I can almost hear her chanting, *Fight! Fight! Fight!*

Now that my brain has resumed almost normal function, I have so many questions. I know Rafe said to go along with it, but I'm the kind of person who needs to define the *it* first. "Rafe, what—"

"I'm so sorry," he says, tracing a fingertip over my cheek. "Are you all right? I've been so worried. I would have been here sooner, but they wouldn't let me back to see you."

"That's twice you've gotten by The Dane. Perhaps I need to up my security."

"Perhaps when it comes to you, I won't let anything hold me back." Rafe's words aren't teasing, not like mine were. If anything, his tone and his eyes are intensely serious.

But … he can't be serious, can he? As usual, I have no idea which end is up.

Callum interrupts my racing thoughts. "More like, when it comes to getting what you want, you'll stop at nothing. No matter who gets hurt in the process. Look where we are."

"It wasn't Rafe's fault," I protest, unsure why I'm defending him. Technically, it *was* his fault, even if it were an accident.

"Try to hold still," the doctor says from behind the curtain. "I've got one or two more shards that are very close to your gluteal cleft."

Plink!

I squeeze my eyes closed. Why is this official term somehow so much worse than if the physician had simply said my butt crack? No, that sounds bad too. It's all bad.

Please, someone kill me now.

"Thank you, doctor, for that most thorough update," Rafe says, and I can hear the smile in his voice even before I glare up at him. "And for taking such good care of my Seraf."

My Seraf.

It shouldn't thrill me to hear him say that. This is all some kind of elaborate game or prank. I'm just not sure who's winning, who's losing, and who's being pranked.

"Rafe," I say through gritted teeth.

Callum begins backing away. "I suppose I'll go. It seems like you've got everything you need here."

Kat raises her brows at me, and I know this is the place where I should ask him to stay. And yet … I don't.

157

"I'll take care of her from here," Rafe says. He holds out a hand to Callum, as if to say, *no hard feelings, old buddy, old pal.*

Callum practically sneers at Rafe's extended hand, glances at me one more time with an inscrutable look, and leaves the room. The door slams behind him.

"Bravo!" Kat says, clapping as Rafe bows.

"And ... *scene*," Rafe says. "Convincing, no?"

My stomach dips. These last few minutes—which I guess were some kind of performance—almost had *me* convinced.

"What are the two of you going on about?"

"Did you see Callum's face?" Kat interrupts. "Priceless! Just perfect! Well done, Rafe."

"Thank you, Lady Kat." Rafe squeezes my shoulder. I bat his hand away.

"Will someone please explain?"

Rafe grins. "If you didn't notice, Callum is burning up with jealousy."

"Practically a molten lava river of jealousy," Kat agrees.

I scoff. "Callum's just angry because he hates you."

A few days ago, I hated Rafe too. That feels like a much simpler time and a much simpler emotion than the conflicted tangle of things I feel for the man whose jacket is still draped over my shoulders.

"It's true," Rafe agrees. "He can't stand me, and he most especially can't stand the idea of *you* with me."

"Yes, but—"

"Seraf, I may be your best bet to help you win your prince. That's what you want, isn't it?"

Isn't it?

For reasons I cannot fully fathom, Rafe's question sits like a cement block in my stomach. My lips are still buzzing from his kiss. Which was ... just for show? I definitely bought it. No wonder Callum did.

And Rafe did and said all this because he thinks I want Callum.

What if I don't want Callum?

What if I want someone else?

"Is that what *you* want?" I'm not sure where the question came from, but it sounds strangled and hangs in the air like a spectre.

Rafe's mouth opens, then closes. His brown eyes glow with an intensity I feel echoed in the very center of my chest. His jaw tightens, as though he's straining to hold back his words, or maybe to compose them. I watch as his Adam's apple bobs.

Plink!

The telltale sound of a latex glove snapping ends the moment. Rafe drops his gaze and steps back, leaning against the wall with that cool grace he always possesses.

The physician crosses the curtain, looking weary. "I'm happy to report your posterior is as good as new." He grimaces. "Well—as good as it's ever going to get, I suppose."

Kat snorts, and I pull Rafe's jacket completely over my head to hide my red cheeks.

When will this horrendously long and terrible day end?

CHAPTER THIRTEEN

Rafe

As I stride away from the medical rooms in the palace, I find myself tugging roughly at the buttons of my shirt. I just need … air. Space. *Something*.

Everything feels too tight, from my suit to my skull. It's like a set of walls are slowly and almost imperceptibly closing in on me. I make a beeline for double doors leading to one of the many terraces and push outside, taking deep breaths of early summer air.

What did I just do?

Did I really just kiss Seraf—and then make it seem like I was only trying to help stir Callum's jealousy?

"You really are a Royal Rogue."

I say the words out loud, because I need to hear them. I'm a verbal processor, and with few people in my life I could trust until my therapist, I've got years' worth of bottled-up feelings to let out. Which apparently translates into talking to myself on palace terraces nearing midnight.

I walk to the very edge and the low wall overlooking an expanse of lawn below. With my palms flat against the wall, I lean over, trying to steady my breathing. My therapist suggested finding a focus object when breathing exercises or visualizing a safe place weren't as helpful. Somehow, imagining your happy place doesn't really work when you don't *have* a happy place.

Usually, that object is the ring I always keep in my pocket. But it was my mother's wedding ring, and right now, I'm not sure I could handle the reminders it brings.

Instead, I zero all my focus on the rough stone wall beneath my palms. It's warm, though the sun has long since dipped below the mountains. The grit of it against my skin is like sandpaper, and I rub my hands back and forth over its surface, letting myself catalogue the sensations.

The stone is solid. It's immovable and rough. When I slide my palms over it, I can hear the quiet rasp of it, like a gentle whisper. If I press harder, there is a tiny bite of pain.

Breathe, you big idiot. Breathe.

Within a few minutes, the hot coil of panic in my chest has loosened, and I no longer feel like I'm about to burst out of my skin.

Emotions are healthy—at least, that's what my therapist says. But an argument could be made that a numb existence is better than trying to manage panic attacks.

What exactly set me off just now?

There are so many good choices. Was it seeing Seraf dancing with Callum and the look of dumb love on her face? Or when I got to hold her in my arms, pretending for a few moments that she was mine? Perhaps it was when she all but admitted to still loving the clueless prince. Or feeling her lips on mine—which really was such a gutsy and stupid and probably terrible move.

No—those moments may have factored in, but I think it was when I made it seem like my true feelings were an act, cheapening all my words and making them seem like pretense.

And when Seraf called me on it, asking me what *I* wanted, I froze. That was my moment, and I choked.

I know why.

It's because no matter what happens here, my uncle has already poisoned it all with his *favor*. If I win Seraf over, it aligns with his goals, whatever they are. That can't be good. And what if she found out and thought that's why I pursued her?

The other option is what I told her—that I'd help her win Callum. I'm not sure what makes my stomach churn more. Especially because I know Seraf would probably be better off with the prince than me.

"Are you out here gloating?"

Callum's voice brings a fraction of the tightness back to my chest. I drag my palms over the stone again, reminding myself to focus, before I turn around.

Those few seconds are necessary to remind myself of the part I'm supposed to play, the role everyone expects of me. I slip back into *that* Rafe, familiar and easy like my favorite pair of jeans worn to fit me just right.

"Don't be such a sore loser, Cal."

I slide my hands into my pockets as I turn to face him, leaning against the wall and brushing my fingers over my mother's ring.

Callum stands a few feet off, looking ever like the Golden

Boy, even in the moonlight. He's the royal version of Captain America with all the blond hair and the square jaw and all those things that women seem to not just love but *admire*.

I'm not sure admiration is an emotion anyone has ever held for me. Not for anything more than my physical appearance, anyway.

The reality is that down to his Disney prince heart, Callum is the real catch. No matter how much I want to hate him for being the one Seraf loves.

"Serafina isn't a competition, Rafe."

He's right, of course, and it's clear my words have just confirmed what he thinks about me—that I'm trying to make Serafina's affections into some kind of game, treating her as less than a person.

I shrug, giving him an easy grin that I know will drive him mad. "Okay."

He steps closer, crossing his arms over his chest. The anger and jealousy practically leak out of his pores. I hate it because it reveals the depths of his feelings for Seraf. But what kind of feelings? That's what I don't know.

For years, I've wondered if he was in love with Seraf, the same way she clearly is with him. How could he *not* love her?

I fell for her the first time I met her, when we were just children. Within moments, she'd grabbed my heart straight out of my chest.

Metaphorically, obviously, and she's held it ever since. She has no idea, of course. That's the thing about her. She's winsome and charismatic, like a star burning so bright you can't NOT stare. But too humble to see herself that way.

Seraf is as angelic as her name. Gorgeous, with the kind of beauty that shines through from somewhere deep inside.

Yeah, I know. That sounds like straight out of a cheesy love story. The thing is, it's true.

She's also a little goofier than she lets on, has a sharp wit I've only just started to see her unleash, and has managed public humiliation with the kind of poise that would assure even the royal haters that she'll make an amazing queen.

And maybe I know all these things only from afar, since she's never let me get close. But every moment I do spend with her only confirms my theories and deepens the feelings I have for her.

Why can't Callum see any of that? He doesn't seem to. And yet, he won't let anyone else have her. Least of all, me.

"You can't play with her," Callum continues. "She isn't one of your conquests."

"And you'd know about conquests, wouldn't you? Seems you've been having your own this past year. Quite a change for the Golden Boy."

"It's not like I've done anything awful. Those women knew what they were getting—a prince for a night or maybe two."

Hearing him talk makes my gut lurch. Is that how I used to sound? Is that really how I lived?

Because being here, in such close radius to Serafina, all of that seems like such a cheap imitation, so incomparable with what she has to offer. I'd rather take my chance and lose than settle for something less.

And yet, the best man for her is still Callum. He's the one she wants. I have no illusions about either of those things.

Despite his callous words, he's not living so differently to most men our age. No matter what he says, it doesn't seem like Callum. My best guess—and maybe this is the therapy talking—is that something triggered his own streak of playboy behavior.

He'll settle. And when he does, he'll finally see what's

right in front of him. I just need to help nudge him in the right direction.

Not because the dummy deserves it, but because it's what's best for Seraf.

Isn't that love? Wanting what's best for the other person, even if it breaks your heart?

Plus, there's the fact that Uncle wants me to break them apart. And anything that's good for him is bad for me. Bad for everyone, really. His text from a few hours ago flashes through my mind: *Hope you've made some headway with the princess. Remember what's at stake for you.*

Ugh. Even thinking of Uncle has my gut churning.

So, despite what I really want, I'll don my Team Callum shirt and help the woman I love get the man she deserves. I'll be the good guy, the hero, while casting myself as the villain.

I raise my eyebrows. "Now you've brought home an American to meet the king and queen—interesting choice."

Callum takes a step closer. "Don't talk about Brit."

"You actually care about her, then? I wasn't sure. Not with the way you were looking at Seraf earlier."

The punch isn't wholly unexpected, yet it still knocks me off-balance.

Callum certainly is in shape, maybe more than in our last scuffle where we were pretty evenly matched. I'm sure we still would be—if I planned to fight back. Which I don't. I'm sure his protection officer or another guard is watching from somewhere and would pull us apart if things got out of hand.

I groan, straightening up and rubbing my jaw. "Nice one. I'm sure Seraf would be impressed."

He points a finger at me. "Don't you call her that."

"I can't talk about Brit. I can't say Seraf's name. Any other women you need to claim just so I can't? You're the one who just told me this wasn't a competition. Yet you're

166

acting like that's exactly what it is. Maybe the rumors aren't true about the arranged marriage between you and Seraf."

His whole body goes still, coiled like a snake.

"Stop calling her that," he growls.

"Is that a no? Or did one of you change your minds?"

Callum's fists are balled tight, and I watch him carefully in case I need to block the next blow. I suspect it will be harder than the first.

"I will never be forced into an arranged marriage." Each of his words is spoken with a fierce conviction.

I tilt my head. "Even when it's Serafina?"

"*Especially* when it's Fi." His lips curl. "I wouldn't ruin our friendship with some farce of a wedding our parents chose for us. But just because I'm not marrying her, that doesn't mean you can step in. My warning still holds—stay away from her."

"You still think I'm that bad?"

"All my judgments of you come from experience."

True. What Callum knows of me from school is a spoiled brat, someone who cared little for others and rested on his titles and privilege rather than trying to live up to those things and possibly deserve them.

Sure, maybe a lot of my behavior over the years is due to losing my family and my uncle's poisoning influence. I was a mess masquerading as a guy who had it all together without a care in the world.

But whatever my reasons, whatever my baggage, I take responsibility. I still made choices—many wrong choices. Can I blame Callum or anyone else for seeing only my past?

I could try to tell Callum how I've changed—about my breakdown, my therapy, the changes I've made in the past two years. I haven't just turned over a new leaf. I uprooted the whole plant before starting from a new seed.

He wouldn't believe it though. Callum is going to believe what he wants. Which serves my purposes just fine. He believes I'm still a rogue and I'll force him to face his feelings about Serafina. She'll get her happily-ever-after, and I'll … well.

I don't know. I would disappear to my duchy, but if I don't perform for Uncle, I won't have that for long. He'll find a way to turn the conservatorship into ownership. Of that, I have no doubt.

"You're really not going to marry her?"

"I don't need to explain my actions to you," Callum says.

"You might want to explain them to Seraf. She seemed pretty surprised about Brit at the tennis match. Perhaps a little disappointed."

That's putting it mildly. I saw her heartbreak, even if Callum didn't notice.

Maybe I'm wrong. Maybe this big dolt standing in front of me isn't what's best for her.

But he's still what she wants. She told you so.

I swallow down my bitterness and disappointment. At least Callum has the decency to look pained.

"I never wanted to hurt her."

"And yet that's exactly what you've done. So, I'm here to sweep up the pieces."

Callum explodes, his shouts echoing off the walls of the palace, making me glad we're on the non-residential side, because likely no one can hear this argument. I hope.

"I've told you before—stay away from her! Don't say her name! Don't touch her! Don't look at her! Don't fill her head with your lies!"

He is right in front of me now, his finger poking me in the chest. Everything in me wants to rise to this occasion, to

168

return shout for shout, to curl my hands into fists the way I would have—and did—in the past.

Instead, I turn the ring over and over in my pocket, trying to keep my focus there, to keep myself grounded in the moment, to remember who I am and who I'm pretending to be.

"You. Don't. Care. About. Her." Callum pokes me once more in the chest, then steps back. "You only care about yourself."

I walk up to a hornet's nest and take a swing. "And what if I'm not lying? What if I actually do care about her?"

A sense of calm seems to wash over him suddenly, and Callum steps back, pacing away from me, dragging his hands through his hair before striding back to me, keeping a bit more of a distance now, as though he doesn't trust himself to be close.

"It won't matter," Callum says, his voice so low and quiet I can hardly hear him. "She knows who you are. And you could never be the kind of man who deserves her."

He's right, of course. Even if she wanted me, I'm probably not the man Seraf deserves. A man here on his uncle's bidding, even if I'm working against him, not for him. A man who has been so cowardly as to love someone from a distance and never tell her.

But is Callum really so much better?

Callum stands there, breathing heavily, looking exhausted. My heart seems to be fighting its way out of my chest and right up my throat. I slide Mother's ring up to the knuckle on my finger, feeling the way circulation stops. I wait a few moments, then slide it off and pull my hands from my pockets.

I head back toward the palace, bumping Callum's shoulder lightly with my own as I pass him.

"It seems that the decision is really up to Seraf, isn't it?"

I just need her to make the right choice. As much as it kills me, it should be Callum.

He says nothing, and I push open the door back into the palace, wishing I could believe that if it came down to it, Seraf would choose me.

CHAPTER FOURTEEN

Serafina

"Come on," Kat whines. "Let's emerge from our dark cave of despair and have a proper breakfast downstairs."

"No, thank you. I rather like my cave of despair. Just me and my donut."

Not a real donut, mind you, which would have been preferable, but my donut pillow. It's something the physician gave me to provide a little relief for my sore bum. Probably by tomorrow, I'll be fine, but today, every movement brings with it pinpricks of pain across my posterior.

Then there's the matter of my heart, which is just as prickly. Too bad they don't make some kind of ergonomic donut pillow to cradle your heart.

Kat flops back down on my bed dramatically. "You can't just hide up here."

"Sure I can. Look at me! Hiding is the new black. Plus, I'm not hiding. I'm working."

This isn't even a lie. I'm toggling between several different windows—a spreadsheet filled with data, existing policies, and a draft of my coronation speech. Nothing helps me unwind like ... work.

Does this make me a nerd? Probably.

Do I care? No.

"You should go though. You're dressed too nicely to stay in my cave."

Kat smooths a hand over her black dress, which is just long enough to avoid being scandalous. It's quite a lot for not-yet noon. I narrow my eyes, looking at the diamond studs in her ears, the subtle makeup, and the high heels she kicked off a bit ago. Definitely not brunch attire. Before I can ask her about it, she hits me with a question I'd like to avoid.

"We aren't going to talk about it?"

"Talk about what?"

I keep my voice even, but my heart is anything but steady. There are several things *it* could mean.

Callum's jealousy.

Rafe's all-too-convincing performance to instigate afore-mentioned jealousy. Emphasis on *performance*.

Or ... THE K-I-S-S.

That one has to be spelled out lest the word take root in my mind, causing replay after replay of the k-i-s-s. I mean, not to say I haven't thought about it. A lot.

But it could be worse!

I could have stayed up ALL night, not just most of the night. Shifting in my bed, trying to find a comfortable position that didn't hurt my bum, thinking of Rafe's lips over and over again. Feeling the memory of them and the way my lips tingled at his touch, how hungry they were for more.

When I wasn't reliving that moment, I was replaying his words in my mind, trying to make sense of them. Was it all an act? Why? As always, Rafe leaves me disconcerted and uncomfortable.

Kat's laugh pulls my mind away from the k-i-you-know-what. I spin to face her.

"What?"

"You're imagining it, aren't you? Replaying the moment his lips—"

I slap my hands over my ears and begin singing the least sexy song I can think of in a hurry, which is "It's a Small World." I don't know all the verses—does it have actual verses?—so after a few repeats of the same two lines I know and a lot of humming, I glance up at Kat, who looks like, well, the Kat who ate the canary.

I remove my hands from my ears.

"Feel better?" she asks.

"Surprisingly, yes."

"Rafe kissed you, and it was short but HOT."

Before I can cover my ears and start singing that horrible song again, Kat leaps off the bed and grabs my wrists. "Deep breaths, Sera. Stay with me. It's okay. We can talk about this."

I try to wrest my arms from her grip, but Kat used to do Krav Maga, whatever that is, and I don't stand a chance against her tiny, muscled arms.

"Let's just talk about it."

"Let's not."

She rolls her eyes. "We *need* to talk about it."

"We absolutely do *not*. Let me go."

"Not until you—"

"DANE!"

It seems weird to add the *the* when I'm directly addressing my protection officer. Maybe this is when I should use his name (which is Anders), but I use it so infrequently that he probably wouldn't come.

The door flies open as Kat narrows her eyes at me. "Low blow, Princess," she says, releasing me and stepping back.

The Dane lets out a very rough sigh and raises one white-blond eyebrow at me. He's a man of few words—twenty-seven that I've heard him utter this year by last count—but I've learned to read those eyebrows. This look says, *Really? You called me in here for this?*

"False alarm," I say cheerfully, and that brow lifts incrementally higher. *I've had enough of your shenanigans*, it says.

He turns it on Kat next. To her, there's a slight shift, which I take to mean, *You should know better.*

"Sorry." When he turns to head back to his post outside, she adds in a whisper, "*Mostly.*"

Another sigh escapes him, one that says he wishes we didn't pay him so well so he could take another job. The moment the door closes behind him, Kat and I burst out laughing. I slide out of my chair, puddling on the floor like I'm suddenly made of gelatin.

"Ouch!"

I momentarily forgot about my stupid bum, and must roll over on my side to avoid the stinging ache.

Kat flops down beside me, and the moment our eyes meet, the laughter starts again, until tears are rolling down our faces. I almost expect The Dane to come back in to see if we are okay.

This feels almost as good as—no, maybe better than—crying last night. While tears have their place, I haven't laughed nearly enough this year. Worries about my course-work, about Callum, and about my coronation hung over me like fog.

Laughing with Kat makes the mist start to dissipate, even if my circumstances are more pressing than ever before.

"I have an offer for you," Kat says, when our laughter has finally slowed and my belly is aching.

"Is it one I can't refuse?"

She props herself up on one elbow, her dark hair falling over one cheek. "You tell me. I'll drop the whole—"

"K-i-s-s."

"Yes, that. I'll drop it in exchange for ... the dossier."

I haven't given the dossier a bit of thought since my parents sent it over with the marriage contract and the Vioran charter yesterday. I don't particularly want to look through what my parents dug up about potential suitors.

But do I want to look at that more than I want to discuss the k-i-s-s with Rafe?

"Deal."

———

"Fish eggs? He takes baths in *fish eggs*? To what end?"

Kat's voice keeps pitching higher and higher. The windows in our room might shatter if she keeps going. I agree with the sentiment, if not her decibel level. Caviar baths are ... well, I'm honestly not sure the best word for them. Other than: NO.

"It isn't for the smell, that's for sure."

Kat tosses her tablet down on the chaise where she's made her home for the past hour while we pored over my parents' dossier on the potential husbands for me.

I will sum up by saying: they weren't wrong to rule these prospects out.

"When he arrives at the ball, I'm going to find him and shake his hand," Kat says, speaking of the Marquess of Tarrytown, who apparently takes nightly baths in caviar. "I need to know if his skin is softer."

175

"The cost alone would bankrupt Viore! Can you imagine?"

I wish caviar baths were the strangest thing we've found. I expected the dossier to be a collection of basic bios. What I got instead are deep dives into every dark secret along with my parents' commentary, which was fairly scathing and often humorous.

Apparently, they dug much deeper, probably with the help of private investigators. Or psychic detectives? I have no idea how they've gleaned the information in these documents, but it's probably criminal.

I wish I could unread some of the things we've read tonight. But there is no going back. I know whose parents were actually second cousins, who has secret children (quite a lot more than you'd expect, honestly), and who has bizarre habits, tastes, and—dare I say it?—fetishes.

SHUDDER.

There are gambling addictions (the most savory of addictions on the list), secret mistresses, and one particularly handsome baron who was born with a tail. A TAIL. It's been surgically removed, but that didn't remove the DNA. Call me shallow, but I don't want to consider having babies with tails. Especially after I saw the photograph.

"Seems like you've dodged a lot of bullets," Kat says. "But there's one more on the list."

I throw my arm over my eyes as she picks up the tablet again. "I'm not sure I can take any more! I know too much!"

Kat clears her throat. "It's Rafe."

The words settle heavy and cool on my skin like I'm suddenly buried in a snowdrift. After a moment, I sit up and face Kat. "What does it say?"

Kat scoots over, handing me the tablet. "I didn't read it."

I try to give the tablet back, but she hops off the bed and

locates her shoes, a strappy pair of black heels that make her legs go on for miles.

"Here. Let's finish up."

She waves me off, checking her phone. "I have somewhere to be."

"That sounds suspiciously like a date. Did you change your mind about the viscount?"

"Ugh! No. And after looking at that, the last thing I'd want is a man with a title. No offense."

"None taken ... mostly."

"Plus, I think you should look at that one on your own," Kat says. "IF you look at it."

"If."

"Maybe some things are better left unknown," she says. "We weren't meant to learn everyone's secrets."

She's right, and I feel a pang of guilt. Then I think of caviar baths and don't allow myself to feel bad. Given my position, some things I do need to know. This isn't a typical situation, and I'm not considering typical men to date. I need a man with a title I can marry in two months. There is no time for surprises. Especially not tails.

"And before you protest or cover your ears, I have to say something else."

"Okaaay."

"I'm not sure what your parents have dug up on him, but I think Rafe is a surprisingly decent man. I've seen the way he looks at you, and despite what he said, I don't think it's an act or a game. I think he has feelings for you."

The thought makes a thrill zip through me.

"But he made it sound like it was all for show. To make Callum jealous. Which doesn't even make any sense. Why would he want to help me with Callum?"

"I can't answer that, but I agree—his words and actions don't line up. He wants you."

"But—"

Kat swipes a hand through the air. "No more buts. Read his file ... or don't. But I hope either way, you'll consider that Callum may not be your only—or even your *best*—choice."

I cannot find a single word to respond to that.

"If I see either of them, do you want me to send them up? I could say you need help rubbing antibiotic cream on your bum." Her eyes twinkle.

"Absolutely not! I'm happy to rub my own bum." Kat laughs, and I fumble for words. "I mean, with the antibiotic cream, that is."

Kat laughs as she opens the door. "I'll just tell anyone who asks that you're up here, rubbing your own bum."

I grab a wooden paperweight shaped like an apple from the bedside table and toss it at her, but she slips out. The paperweight lands harmlessly on the rug. I should pick it up, but instead, I move to the desk.

In the quiet of the room, there is just me and the tablet. It feels as heavy as a loaded rifle in my hand.

Do I look? Do I not look?

How might it change things if I do? Can Rafe's secrets really be so much worse than a tail or a secret relationship with a blood relative? And maybe most important of all, if I find something that is a dealbreaker, how disappointed will I be?

Unable to resist my curiosity, I swipe to the next page of the tablet, where my heart does a little dance at the sight of Rafe's smoldering eyes in an older photograph, probably from a few years before. His hair is shorter, his stubble a little less pronounced, but his eyes have that same intensity as they do now.

I realize I'm tracing his lips in the photo, like a total creeper. Maybe reading his file will help me not keep replaying that k-i-s-s over and over. If there's something incriminating in here, maybe I'll stop feeling all these swooping things in my belly that I refuse to call butterflies. It's INDIGESTION. And this file could be like my antacid to settle me once and for all.

Taking a breath, I begin to read.

CHAPTER FIFTEEN

Serafina

There's a knock at the door, and I drop the tablet, frantically wiping my eyes. The Dane wouldn't let anyone so much as approach my door if they weren't someone I approved of, but there is still no one I want to see right now. Not after what I just read.

I sniff, and my voice wavers as I call, "Yes?"

"It's the big bad wolf. Do I need to huff and puff to blow the door in?"

Rafe. I bite my lip, squeezing my eyes closed. Can I face him right now? Though the information on his file wasn't remotely incriminating, it tilted my world on its axis, or maybe tilted my heart. If my feelings for the duke were confusing before, they're even more so now.

One thing reading it did NOT do was remove the swooping, winged creatures in my belly. Or the way I'm instantly more aware of my lips at the sound of his voice.

"Come in." I turn the tablet off, then straighten the laptop, left open from hours ago. The figures swim in front of me on the spreadsheet, even more than they did before.

Even with my back to Rafe, I can *sense* him approaching. I turn to face him, wincing as I do. Even with the donut pillow, I keep forgetting my injuries—at least, until I move.

"Angel," he says by way of greeting.

"Devil."

I need to pretend like everything is normal. Like he didn't kiss me last night and then basically take it back. Like I don't know things about his past I shouldn't know.

My performance must be convincing, because he chuckles, and I blush as his eyes rove over my face.

My pretzel of a stomach twists into another knot and instantly, parts of my body I wasn't aware of moments ago decide to make themselves known. My hairline prickles as though the wispy, baby hairs I'm always trying to tame have all stood on end. There is the slightest ringing in my ears, and my cuticles are tingling.

Perhaps I'm developing an ear infection and am overdue for a manicure. I'm sure these physiological reactions have nothing to do with the man standing in the center of my bedroom, hands clasped behind his back. He looks, as always, handsome, and also, as always, like there's a private joke I'm not privy to.

Underneath all the things I'm feeling at the sight of Rafe, there's an understanding that wasn't there before. And guilt, because I know things I shouldn't know about this man.

"I like you in glasses," Rafe says.

I forgot I had on my blue-light glasses I wear when on my laptop. Immediately, I rip them off and toss them on the desk as though they're covered in spiders. Rafe opens his mouth to say something, but I hold up a finger.

"Don't you dare say a word about a sexy librarian."

"Sexy librarian?" He tilts his head to the side. "I guess I can see that. I was thinking more along the lines of sexy statistician."

"What?"

Rafe closes the distance between us and puts a hand on the back of my chair. Instinctively, I turn to face my computer. Even through the fabric of my shirt, I can feel the heat from his fingertips. He leans in closer, staring over my shoulder at the spreadsheet.

"Is this about the royal guard?"

I slam the laptop shut. "It's nothing."

Rafe could move now that the laptop is closed. He should move. But he doesn't. He is right up in my space, caging me in with a hand on the back of my chair and one on the desk.

I could also move, but somehow that feels like it would be giving in or giving up, so I don't. Standing my ground seems of the utmost importance. Maybe I like playing with fire a little more than I thought? Being this close to Rafe certainly is like standing near an incinerator.

Being this close means I also notice what appears to be bruising around his jaw. "Did you get into a fight?"

"It's nothing."

It's not nothing, but before I can continue in my line of questioning, he continues.

"I'd love to hear your thoughts," he says, and if that statement weren't enough to distract me from the bruise he doesn't want to talk about, his breath warm on my cheek does the trick.

"Oh. How do you know I have thoughts?"

Rafe chuckles, pushing off the desk to move away. Does it mean my brain is broken that I immediately miss his close proximity? Probably. Brain damage from spreadsheets. Or from Rafe's presence. Having him near me is like putting a magnet next to a compass. My needle has completely lost true north.

I don't turn to see what he's doing but keep my eyes firmly trained on my closed laptop. I really hope he's not getting in my bed again. It took the maids washing the sheets for me to rid them of his scent.

"The spreadsheets were a clue. But I know you have thoughts because you're brilliant."

My cheeks warm with his praise.

"I bet you've been thinking about this all through uni. Your majors, French literature aside, were directly related to hot-button issues for Viore. I'd be willing to hedge my bets that you took some environmental science courses as well. Ones that maybe gave you food for thought on how to handle the sustainability and environmental standards of Viore's copper mining."

How does he know that?

I spin in my seat, ignoring the pain in my bum. Rafe is not in my bed, but leaning casually against it, long legs crossed in front of him, hands in his pockets.

"How did you *know* all that? My parents don't even know."

He tilts his head, narrowing his eyes. "Why not?"

Because they wouldn't believe I have something to offer, for one. My parents do love me, but they have a very firm set of expectations for me which are, at best, limiting. At worst? They're sexist and patronizing.

Even if I spoke with them about the policies I've drafted and what I'm planning to include in my coronation speech, my position is far from theirs. My dad pooh-poohs the idea of anything environmental, writing it off as nonsense. And as for my ideas of how to modernize Viore, how to rebrand the

monarchy in ways that would shut up the royal haters, well
—Mum would be horrified.

"They'll hear my ideas soon enough," I say, sounding defensive to my own ears.

"I'd love to hear them now," Rafe says. "Consider me a test subject. Hit me."

I stare at the man who confuses me more each time I speak with him. He's like what I've seen of fun houses in the movies. Each time I'm with Rafe, it's like stepping through another door leading to a room filled with misshapen mirrors or false walls or a moving floor.

But then, given what I just learned, his layers and moving floors make more sense. I knew Rafe was orphaned, though I didn't know his mother was pregnant at the time. He lost his parents and an unborn sibling.

The uncle I've always disliked is truly a despicable human. The Baron de Silva has kept a squeaky-clean official record, but there have been allegations of psychological abuse over the years. Nothing proven, but from multiple sources. As for Rafe's discharge from the royal guard, it was for medical reasons. He had what was deemed a psychotic break and injured one of the officers during part of training. After spending a week or two in a private mental hospital, he was released. There is nothing for the last few years other than the name of his therapist.

Underneath the last paragraph, detailing the weekly therapy Rafe has undergone since the discharge, Mum had written *far too mentally unstable.*

I would disagree with her assessment. If anything, a man who has spent time in therapy, working through his known issues has to be better off than someone stuffing them down and ignoring them. But knowing all those things has changed how I see so much about Rafe. He has layers because he's complex. He's a survivor.

Whoever I thought Rafe was, I was wrong. I'm continually surprised, and I find that I want to know him more.

"You want to hear my ideas for Viore's future?" I ask carefully, not quite trusting to hope in his answer.

"I do. Quite a lot, actually."

He hops up on the bed, swinging his legs like an excited child. His interest in my political policies shouldn't have any impact on my attraction to the man. But I'm not sure there's a hotter picture than that of Rafe de Silva, eyes gleaming as he waits for me to talk nerdy to him.

"Fine—you twisted my arm." I grin, and he returns it, the force of his smile hitting me square in the chest.

Giving my head a little shake, I regain my focus. "First of all, I don't want to demilitarize fully, the way some council members are calling for, but I do want to cut back. There's no need to have such a large defense budget with the extent of our allies and the relative peace in Europe at the moment."

He nods. "Makes sense. And where would that money freed up in the budget go?"

"Toward developing our production of silicon. We have the resources, but not the factories needed to produce and refine it."

"That would be another excellent resource firming up your relationship with Elsinore. Smart." He pairs the compliment with a devastating smile.

"Exactly!" I get to my feet, feeling the blood humming in my veins the way it does when I get to talking about this. Only, I'm usually bouncing these ideas off Kat, who is half-heartedly listening while scrolling dating apps, or else is actively snoring.

"And like you guessed, I want to bring our copper mines

up to recommended environmental standards." I hold up a hand. "I know that's an unpopular opinion because of the economic factors, but I think if I spoke with Phillip, we could come to an understanding."

Rafe tilts his head. "Phillip? Not James or Callum?"

I'd rather not think about Callum at the moment. "King James would be opposed, I think. Like my father. They're set in their ways. I think Phillip would be able to convince him, and based on what I know, he and I are on the same page."

"The next generation of royals," Rafe says, sounding strangely proud.

"And the last big change, the one Mum will hate the most, is opening up the castle to tourism. I think the gardens should be free, but there could be minimal fees to view the inside. Free for schools and for educational purposes, naturally. This money could go to offset some of the costs for the programs I'm recommending so we don't need to increase taxes exponentially."

I realize I've been pacing, speaking faster and faster as I got excited, hardly taking a breath. I grimace, turning to face Rafe. "Sorry."

"Don't be sorry. Your passion is ... magnetic." Rafe's eyes are lit with a fire-like glow. "And your ideas? Fantastic. I was right."

"About what?"

"You're brilliant. And you'll do so much good for Viore."

Why do these words feel like the best compliments I've ever been paid?

They also come with the sudden reminder that if I don't figure out the whole husband situation, I may not get a chance to do good for my country. I'm not ready to think about that yet. And the way Rafe is looking at me threatens to melt me on the spot. I'm not ready to deal with that either.

So, I go back to the safe space of teasing. "I wouldn't have imagined you as such a good sounding board."

"Anything else you can't imagine me doing?"

The flirty tone in his voice has me imagining him doing a *lot* of things. None of which I have any business or good sense thinking about.

And so, I say the first thing that pops into my mind. "I'll admit, I have a hard time picturing you in the royal guard."

I immediately want to take the words back, especially considering what I know now of his discharge. But Rafe doesn't seem bothered by my words.

Instead he lifts one dark brow in challenge. "Is that idea so preposterous?"

"You don't seem like the sort to follow orders. Anyone's orders."

"Typecasting me again, Princess? You can't picture me as a soldier?"

He stands and stretches lazily, ever reminding me of the Cheshire cat, and then walks over to the window, turning his back to me.

Oh I can picture it. The dark jacket stretching over his broad shoulders. The medals on his lapels. The jaunty little cap and the fitted pants ...

"Seraf?"

Clearing my throat, I join him at the window. I follow Rafe's gaze out to the gardens. A few men in brown coveralls are trimming hedges. Rafe eyes me without turning his head fully. I feel exposed under his gaze, even when it's not direct. "Sorry. What did you ask?"

"If it was really so hard to imagine me as a soldier."

I tilt my head, squinting dramatically at him, all while

trying not to imagine him in uniform. "I guess I could see it. Maybe."

Rafe spins on his heels suddenly, facing me but in the position of a soldier. Shoulders back, heels together, chin up, and eyes narrowed on some point just over my shoulder. He gives me a salute, a little different than that of Viore's royal guard, with three fingers extended rather than all five.

Even without the uniform, this is a good look on him. Too good. I take a step or two back, needing the space. And yet ... I don't want too much space. I'm drawn to this version of Rafe, one more facet to his personality that is surprising. One more layer, peeled back.

"At ease, soldier," I tell him.

Without breaking his gaze or his position, he barks out a reply. "Awaiting orders, sir."

I bite my lip, but it does nothing to stop my slow smile. *He wants an order? I can do that.*

"Make my bed, soldier."

"Yes, sir!"

Okay, maybe I should have thought about this more. I know that just a few moments before, Rafe was sitting on my bed, but seeing him in official soldier mode, tucking in the corners of my sheets makes me break out in a full-body shiver.

Yes. This was definitely a very bad idea.

When my bed is made to perfection, Rafe marches—and I do mean *marches*—back over to me, still with that same straight-backed position, not making eye contact.

Even in soldier mode, he still somehow oozes a bad-boy vibe. Is it his stubble? I swear, there must be a setting on his electric razor called rogue o'clock shadow to keep the hair on his jaw just the right length.

Maybe it's his mouth? Even when he's most serious, it's like the ghost of a smirk exists on his full lips.

No—that's an actual smirk. Rafe breaks character, running a hand through his dark hair as he grins down at me.

"Not bad, eh?"

I need a break from his intensity, so I walk over and inspect my bed. "Actually, I think you missed a bit of lint here."

Rafe follows me, examining the bedspread, and now we're standing close again but also next to my bed. This is not helping my mind stay out of places it shouldn't go. He smooths his palms over the white comforter, which is definitely lint-free. And now I'm imagining his hands sliding over my pale skin the same way.

"I'm sorry I accused you of defecting," I say, taking a few steps back.

His eyes seem wary. "It's okay."

I hope maybe he'll open up, telling me the truth, but I guess we aren't at that point yet. Which makes it all the more awkward I know this about him.

He smiles and changes the subject. "Have you had breakfast? Or lunch? Maybe we could sneak some food out of the kitchen and have a bit of a picnic. I thought we should talk about last night."

Yes, we definitely need to talk. But talking to Rafe, spending time around him—it all seems to be knocking me off-kilter.

Rafe reaches the door before me and swings it open, holding it as I walk through. The Dane eyes us both with a blank look from across the hall.

"Did you forget something?" Rafe asks.

I touch my hair and smooth my hands down my trousers. I'm dressed, though casually, and I'm in the habit of doing my hair and makeup first thing just in case. I never know what might be thrown my way. My cell phone is in my pocket, and I need little else.

"I don't think so."

With a wicked grin, Rafe ducks back inside the room and comes out with my donut pillow. I debate on whether or not I should run back in my room and lock the door.

"Can't have you going around with your bum unprotected," Rafe says. "It's precious cargo."

My blush is instant, and if I'm not mistaken, The Dane gives a low growl.

"Shut up about my cargo."

Rafe chuckles. I start off down the hall, which unfortunately leaves him trailing behind me, my cargo in full view.

I come to a stop, then spin to face him. "Why don't you go on ahead?"

Rafe grins as though he knows exactly why I'm asking him to do so. He strides ahead laughing. "Feel free to check out my cargo, Angel. I don't mind."

"You wouldn't," I mutter.

In a voice so quiet I might have imagined it, The Dane mutters, "I mind."

CHAPTER SIXTEEN

Serafina

This is not a date. This is not a date. This is not a date.

Maybe repeating things three times only works if you've got ruby slippers on. Because no matter what I try to tell myself with the logical part of my brain, this FEELS like a date.

The day could not be more glorious with fat, puffy clouds lazing across the deep blue sky. Birds are singing. Nearby, roses are in bloom, their fragrance lightly teasing the air. Rafe and I are seated on a picnic blanket (which might actually be Brit's dress returned to its original purpose), a basket Rafe had waiting in the kitchen with all my favorite things, and the man himself, whose sheer presence makes it IMPOS-SIBLE to not have date feelings.

Especially after the you-know-what from last night. I've had to switch from spelling it out to using a vague reference. Spelling wasn't enough considering the lips that you-knowwhatted me are right THERE. Plump, delicious, and currently closing around a strawberry.

I watch him take the lush red fruit between his teeth. A little juice makes its way down his chin as though trying to touch as much of his skin as possible. It's slowed by Rafe's perfect stubble, and he manages to wipe it away with his fingers before it trails a path down his neck.

All this moment needs is the right mood music and I could sell copies online for thousands of euros. It is perhaps the sexiest thing I have ever seen.

THIS IS NOT A DATE!

I clear my throat and look away from Rafe's sexy strawberry mouth. "So, what's your endgame here?"

My question startles a snorting laugh out of Rafe, who almost pours hot tea on his trousers. He sets down his cup, rattling against the saucer and pins me with his molten chocolate eyes.

"Why do you ask?"

I sweep my arm over the picture-perfect picnic. "All this. You showed up in my room and said we should talk like it was spontaneous. But you already had all this planned."

When we left my room, Rafe knocked twice on the door and a stout, pink-cheeked woman with graying hair emerged with the basket and blanket, giggling up at Rafe. It was almost like the sight of him transported her back to her school days. Is it weird that I felt the slightest bit possessive when he kissed one of her lined cheeks? Or maybe it was the way she swatted his bum with a dish towel while giving him flirty eyes.

ANYWAY.

Rafe chuckles and finishes refilling his teacup. "You got me there. I did plan this. But do you think me doing something nice means I have an agenda?"

"The thought did occur to me."

Rafe eyes me curiously. "I'm curious what kind of people you're surrounding yourself with if you're assuming everyone wants something from you."

"Not everyone does." It's a lie, but not a huge lie. Mostly because I limit the circle of people around me. "I'm speaking particularly of *you*."

"Moi?"

He blinks rapidly, feigning affront, and I don't get distracted at all by his thick, dark lashes as they flutter. They're like one of those tricks of nature—the way some moths have a fake eye on their wing to scare off predators. Only Rafe's physical features are all designed to draw women in—to their doom and detriment. Knowing this doesn't keep me from falling for it.

"Don't pull the innocent card with me. If nothing else, I'd think you're trying to fatten me up."

His smile turns positively wicked, and I remember what he said when he knocked at my door earlier. Now, he's the wolf in the grandmother's bed, wearing her cap and night-gown, smiling with those white, white teeth.

"Maybe I'm already planning ahead for this year's Christmas feast." He tosses me an apple. "Put this in your mouth, would you? Just for curiosity's sake."

I toss the apple right back, but a little too hard. Rafe ducks, and the apple disappears into a bush. With a chit-tering squawk, a squirrel dashes for the closest tree, shouting what sound like squirrel obscenities at us both.

"You're definitely trying to fatten me up."

I pat my belly, full of a chocolate croissant, a slice of buttered bread, and several small tea sandwiches. Not to mention more than one cup of tea with sugar and heavy cream. I'm desperately in need of a nap to rest my growing food baby.

"You're welcome. If only food were the way to a woman's heart."

Who's to say it isn't?

Honestly, this is working a little too well for me. Not that I'm falling for Rafe, but after the you-know-what and the dossier, I'm seeing him differently. Maybe Kat's words planted something in my brain. She said Rafe might be a better choice than Callum. Could she possibly mean that?

Days ago, I couldn't have imagined sharing a picnic with Rafe de Silva, the Royal Rogue. Now? I can't stop thinking about his lips, the kind words he's said, and—oh yeah, the fact that he said he was my best bet to win Callum.

Rafe sets his cup down in the saucer and pushes them both to the side, scooting closer to me. It can be awkward to sit properly and comfortably on the ground, especially because of my donut pillow. Needless to say, I can't exactly wiggle away when Rafe's thigh presses against mine.

"Let's talk about my proposition from last night."

"You propositioned me last night?" I raise my brows, then shrug. "Must not have been memorable."

Rafe leans closer for just a moment, but it's long enough to have my body's internal alarms ringing.

"If I were to proposition you, I promise you it's something you would never forget."

I give his shoulder a light shove, needing space, and he settles back again, allowing me to breathe.

"Back to last night. What exactly are you offering?"

A breeze sends my hair blowing in Rafe's direction. He's sitting close enough that the strands brush against his cheek. With a soft smile, he tugs a strand, curling it around his finger before letting go. It's such an intimate movement, and maybe I should be wary, but I love everything about his touch.

"I meant when I proposed to help you win Callum," he says.

Right. Callum. Just his name makes a sour feeling expand inside me, and I wish I had eaten a little less of the picnic fare.

"Assuming I *want* to win Callum over, how exactly could you help?"

Rafe's smile dips into an unfamiliar frown. "Don't you want to win him over?"

I pick up a leaf that's blown into my lap, turning it over in my palm and tracing the thin veins with my finger. "How much do you know about Viore's charter?"

"We didn't exactly study it in school."

"Right." I sigh and toss the leaf into the wind, letting it blow away. "Like Elsinore, our king and queen are exactly what their titles say—not a consort, not a prince or princess. A full king or queen, even by marriage. But when the monarch who is from the lineage turns fifty-five, they both must step down for the heir."

"And your father's fifty-fifth birthday is in two months."

I nod. "Yes. That's pretty common knowledge. There is a clause that is less well-known, mostly because it hasn't been a potential issue until now. At the time the ruling monarchs step down from the throne, the heir must be married. And not just married, but wed to someone with a title."

Rafe blinks in surprise at this, and I continue.

"If not, the Council of the People may call a vote to abolish the monarchy."

I let that sink in, and Rafe nods a few moments later. "So, you need to marry someone with a title in two months."

"Yes."

He's quiet again and I tilt my head back, letting the sun hit my cheeks. But when Rafe speaks, the sun is suddenly too warm, and I let my chin fall to my chest.

"How do you feel about that?"

No one has asked me how I feel about this. As with so many things in my life, I don't get to feel. I simply accept my duty as what it is. I don't even know how to answer that question, so I take my time.

"I feel our laws could be modernized in a way that doesn't feel so arbitrary."

Rafe touches my hand, and I stare down where his fingers rest on my pale skin. "No, Seraf. How do you feel about this for *you*?"

I shouldn't be blinking back tears. But the surprising insight in Rafe's question cuts me deeply. A few days ago, I would have called the duke a stranger. Maybe an enemy. Now, he's the only other person besides Kat who is truly and actively checking in on me. And the concern in his voice is no act.

Rafe cares.

But this. Is. Not. A. Date.

I consider pulling my hand away, but I don't. Call me selfish, but I will take any bit of tenderness and care he's offering. Even if it's not romantic.

"How I feel doesn't matter. I have a duty to do."

Rafe's fingers curl around my hand and squeeze. "It matters how you feel."

A single tear drips down my cheek, thankfully on the side of my face not near Rafe. Does it matter? I'm supposed to be strong for my people, to do what's right for them.

"I *feel* like I need to find someone to marry me in two months."

"And until this week, you thought that person would be Callum."

I sigh. "That's what my parents led me to believe. Apparently, the only one not on board with this plan was Callum. It's ridiculous, isn't it?"

"No." His hand squeezes mine again.

For a moment, I allow myself to imagine that this is a date. That Rafe is interested in *me*, not in getting me together with Callum.

But this is just a fantasy. One I like rather a lot more than I probably should. Which means I need a subject change and *quickly*.

"So, this plan." I carefully avoid the word *proposition*. "What did you have in mind?"

Rafe drops my hand to run it through his hair. He looks off toward where the squirrel is still cursing at us. He's gotten a friend on board and now there are several squirrels heckling us. Seems fitting somehow.

"The plan is simple. You pretend to date me. Callum gets jealous and realizes what he's missing out on. You and I break up so you can have your happily-ever-after with the man you really want."

That doesn't sound like a fairy tale. It's more like the kind of romance novel that Kat's always reading—fictional. It definitely does not sound like real life. Or even a good idea.

It also sounds desperate on my part and vastly unfair to Rafe. Does he think he can only play the secondary character? Does he not know that he has Leading Man written all over him?

"No."

Rafe blinks at me for a moment, then tosses his head back, roaring with laughter.

"This is what I love about you, Seraf. You fight me at every turn."

He likes that? Honestly, I guess I enjoy our back-and-forth too. A little too much. Especially considering the little shiver that went through me when he said *what I love about you, Seraf.* He doesn't love me. He loves something *about* me. Not even remotely the same.

"Tell me your objections," he demands when his laughter has faded. His eyes still sparkle with amusement. "I'm too handsome. Is that it? You don't think you could possibly resist me if we pretended to date?"

He's hitting a little too close to home. I can hardly resist him now, and we're not dating or even pretending to date. Having all of Rafe's charm and attention lavished fully on me might wreck me forever. Hasn't he already? I went from considering him a mortal enemy to staying up all night dreaming about his lips. And that's the last thing Rafe needs to know.

"I'm not sure I could pretend to like you convincingly."

Rafe picks up a silver fork and pretends to stab himself in the chest, rolling his eyes back in his head before flopping over as though dead. I give him a nice shove, and he rolls away, laughing, and nearly ends up on a platter of pastries.

"You are ridiculous."

He doesn't even argue but sits back up with a smile. "You know, I don't think I get insulted enough. It's quite refreshing, constantly having you put me in my place. Perhaps you should make a spreadsheet with an extensive list of my faults. You know, just to keep my ego in check."

"I'm not sure anything could keep your ego in check. I'm also not sure my computer has enough memory for a spreadsheet quite that large."

Despite being full, I pick up a strawberry, taking a dainty

bite. It's every bit as sweet and juicy as it looked when Rafe ate it, but still somehow disappointing.

"I think you're missing the big picture here," he says. "Last night, you didn't have to pretend at all. I did all the work, and Callum almost climbed out of his skin with jealousy. We're talking about a week of me flirting and adoring you."

GULP. There is absolutely no way I can survive a week of Rafe flirting and adoring me. Not when that tiny, almost-insignificant-in-the-grand-scheme-of-things kiss has occupied my mind ever since last night.

"I don't know."

"How about this—we don't pretend we're a couple. Be my date to the Centennial Ball. I'd wager if Callum hears about that, he'd break up with Brit and come running after you before we even get to the ball."

The clock is ticking. I can't forget that. Some women have a biological clock. The ticking of my get-engaged-to-save-the-monarchy clock is more like a doomsday timer.

"What, exactly, would this entail? IF I went along with your plan, that is."

Rafe's smile is practically feral, immediately making me regret the question. "Oh, you know. I'd flirt shamelessly. Whisper sweet *somethings* in your ear. Give you gifts to woo you and be the best date you've ever had on the night of the ball. A regular Duke Charming."

I can't help but laugh. "You don't do anything by halves, do you?"

"I prefer going all in when it's something I want."

The statement thrills me, though it shouldn't. *He doesn't want me.* But that begs another question. What DOES he want?

"What do you get out of it?"

I hadn't meant to ask the question, and Rafe seems surprised I asked it. Something flashes across his face before his smile slides into the familiar smirk. "Helping a friend," he says simply.

I snort. "We aren't exactly friends."

"I don't usually picnic with strangers."

"Do you picnic with friends? Or is it reserved for women you're trying to woo?"

"I've never had a picnic before."

The serious tilt to Rafe's voice is a hangnail, a bothersome little pain I can't ignore. "You mean, with a woman?"

He shakes his head, then runs a hand through his hair. "This is my first."

"Oh."

Hearing that Rafe hasn't ever enjoyed something as simple as a picnic makes my heart hurt. Selfishly, strangely, I like being the first woman he's had a picnic with. Even if THIS IS NOT A DATE. But it makes me remember the loss of his parents, and effectively, his childhood.

It's not as though I've spent my life picnicking or something, but I've had some with my parents on the lawn behind the castle as a child. Kat and I even spread out a blanket and ordered take-away Indian back at uni, Kat soaking up whatever sun she could in a barely there bikini, me in khaki shorts and a loose blouse.

"I'm sorry."

The light mood has fled. It's impossible to ignore the shift. He nods, seeming to understand that my apology is for something bigger and deeper than his lack of picnics. I take Rafe's hand, giving it a gentle squeeze. Tempted to hold it for longer, I force myself to let go.

Rafe reaches for his endless supply of easy smiles, like

202

he's just the cavalier, casual man I've always thought him to be. Now, though, I'm able to see past the mask.

"I'm enjoying my first picnic very much," he says, popping another strawberry into his mouth. It's almost obscene the way his lips wrap around the piece of fruit, and I glance away as his tongue darts out to catch the juice.

I am no longer enjoying my picnic. Because I am enjoying it way too much, and I do not WANT to enjoy it too much. I need space from this man who is overwhelming me.

Adjusting my donut pillow, I sit up a little straighter, trying to inch away from Rafe without it being noticeable. Only, it's hard to move without wincing. I'll scoot another inch while he's looking down. But now he's going for another strawberry!

Nope. No more sexy strawberry eating.

With a little gasp, I grab the bowl and toss its contents over my shoulder. The unhappy squirrels stop cursing us and scamper down the tree to feast.

Rafe quirks an eyebrow, and I give a small, fake laugh that makes me sound like a cartoon version of myself.

"Sorry. I thought I saw a spider in the strawberry bowl." I clear my throat. "Anyway. Back to my question of what's in this for you. Besides picnics, obviously. Is it part of your rivalry with Callum?"

"No. It's definitely not about that."

I wish I could believe him. But knowing how their history is, I'm sure that has to be at least part of it.

"Why can't I just be doing this to help you out of the goodness of my heart?" Rafe places a hand over his heart, drawing my attention to the fact that a few buttons of his crisp, white shirt are undone.

Were they undone this whole time? I think I would have

noticed that swath of olive skin and the tempting line of muscle barely visible through the opening.

Has Rafe been undoing them in slow increments just as I'm slowly trying to scoot away? If so, that makes this the slowest game of chase perhaps ever.

"Maybe I'm just charitable."

I snort. "Right. Rafe de Silva, Duke of Weldon—the picture of charity."

Rafe *tsks*. "Maybe you don't know me half as well as you'd like to think. I'm guessing you've gotten most of your information about me from a combination of the tabloids and your favorite prince, who is no fan of mine."

Right on both counts, not that I'll admit it. "I've also seen evidence of your wicked ways with my own eyes."

Rafe grins. "Am I so wicked, Angel?"

"I won't deign to answer. In any case, this plan has no visible benefits I can see." When he raises a sexy eyebrow at me, I poke him in the shoulder. "Also, it should be noted that if I agree, this will not be a *with benefits* kind of arrangement."

He feigns shock. "How could you suggest such a thing? Though …" He taps a finger on his lips, and I do my best not to look. "I will say that kiss last night was very effective in making Callum jealous. Just think about what a slower, longer kiss might do."

My heart is a drumbeat in my ears, and I feel drugged by Rafe's words, by the image they invoke, by the possibility of what a slower, longer kiss with him might be like.

Don't look at his mouth.

Do not think about kissing.

Do not even glance at his—

My gaze falls to Rafe's lips. Like his full eyelashes, his mouth seems far too generous, and without the strong line of his jaw and that blasted stubble, it would be almost too soft.

The man does have a point. If anything could, a kiss *would* make Callum jealous. I should absolutely consider it.

I mean, if I'm really all in on this idea of winning Callum, I should do whatever it takes. Right?

The only problem—or one of several I'm currently facing—is that I'm more excited about the prospect of kissing Rafe than winning Callum. And now that I've started thinking about it, I can't seem to stop.

The few other kisses I've shared have been bumbling attempts that had me wanting to run away rather than go deeper. I know it would be different with Rafe. Right now, his lips probably still taste of strawberries, the sweet a contrast to the scrape of his stubble on my cheek—

I turn away, shutting down the part of my brain that has been lost to desire. I focus on the clouds misting over the top of the mountains in the distance, counting caterpillars until my heart slows down.

My next words are ones I pick carefully, regaining the control I'm usually so famous for, the control that seems to go missing whenever Rafe is around.

"My biggest objection is this: I don't want to be wanted just because Callum is jealous, or because he doesn't want me with *you*. If he wants me, it needs to be for *me*. No other reason."

"I think I understand. You want to be loved for *you*."

Rafe's voice has a faraway quality, and I can't bring myself to look at the face that accompanies the sound of it. He sounds almost sad, like he understands this sentiment all too well.

"Doesn't seem like too much to ask, does it? Except, perhaps, in this case."

"It's not too much to ask. Ever. Especially not in your case."

There he goes again, with those flirty words, which probably mean nothing to him, but mean everything to me. Or they would, if he meant them.

Does he mean them?

I close my eyes, trying to imagine Callum's mouth forming the same sentences. I simply can't picture it.

"Does Callum know?" Rafe asks.

"Know what?" *That I've been in love with him since we were children?*

I'd prefer not to admit that to Callum or Rafe, though it seems as though all my secrets have been dumped out before Rafe and he's picked through them all.

"Does he know that you'll lose the monarchy if you're not married to someone with a title by your father's fifty-fifth birthday?"

The words hit me with a sudden, bitter dose of reality, like the candy coating of aspirin has worn off, leaving only the medicine taste underneath.

My smile is tight. "We haven't discussed it, though I'm sure our parents have. I'd rather him not know. You won't tell him, will you? I'd hate to think you're some kind of spy."

I try to keep my words playful, to drag this heavy conversation back to flirtatious picnic conversation. Too bad I tossed the strawberries to the squirrels. They'd really come in handy about now.

"Not that I tell Callum things, anyway, but I'll definitely keep this between us. You can trust me. It's why my hair is so big," Rafe continues with a cheeky grin, giving his dark head of hair a toss. "It's full of secrets."

I study his hair. I won't tell him I think it's rather lovely— such a nice, glossy black. Is he sensitive about his hair?

"Your hair isn't so big."

Rafe's mouth drops open, and he snaps it closed again, studying me. "You … don't know what that's from?"

"What *what's* from?"

Shaking his head, he says, "Never mind. So, Callum doesn't know that you have to marry someone titled in two months' time. And you don't want him to know. Because you want him to want you for you, not because he's jealous or he wants to swoop in and save you."

I tap my nose twice. "Exactly. If I'm to have love, it needs to be for real."

"And if you can't find love?"

My stomach is a pit of nerves, thinking of Valdonia. "Then I'll marry for duty. For my country and its people."

Rafe is titled. The thought comes out of nowhere. And while it's not the first time I've thought of it—hello, dossier full of secrets—I want to laugh. If Callum, who grew up as a prince, who is already a working royal, doesn't want to be caged in with this kind of life, there is no way Rafe would be willing to sacrifice his choices, his freedoms.

Rafe tilts his head to the side. "You want to be loved for love's sake, but you'd marry someone you didn't love out of duty?"

"I don't expect you to understand."

Rafe gazes off into the distance, and when he speaks, his voice is almost lost underneath the sounds of hedge trimmers nearby, which would certainly ruin the mood of our date, but this is NOT a date.

"Perhaps I understand more than you know."

If his voice is almost lost, the next one I hear is shrill enough to make us both wince.

"Princess Serafina! How lovely to see you again!"

I suppress a groan, glancing up to see Brit and Callum approaching. They're hand in hand, though Brit seems to be dragging Callum. The two of them could not appear more different. Her eyes—ignoring the purple bruising starting to fade to an ugly green—are bright and shining with pleasure and her steps are quick as she approaches, hair bouncing.

Callum hangs back, serious and subdued. Rafe wasn't wrong about the jealousy. It's painted in broad strokes from the tightness in his jaw to the stubborn set of his shoulders. I want this to mean something to me, but I can't find it in me to hope for it to be significant.

I want someone to love me for me, I remind myself. *Not simply because he's jealous.*

Yet the sight of Callum's jealousy does spark something in me. It's a satisfying feeling. But an ugly one too, I think, as Brit beams at me. It feels more like winning, a selfish kind of satisfaction, than love.

"So, it is true!" Brit says, clapping her hands with glee before sitting down on the picnic blanket uninvited.

Today, her outfit is a little more toned down. And by that, I mean it's flesh-toned. All of it. It is some kind of bodysuit that's form-fitting in some areas, loose in others. Overall, she looks mostly nude, but with the dirty bits blurred out. Like a Barbie doll, all tan skin with no blemishes or—gasp! —nipples.

I wonder what side of Americana this outfit represents or if this is simply an unfortunately chosen bodysuit.

Rafe has his chin tucked to his chest and looks like he's trying to hide his laughter. Some help he is.

"Sorry—I didn't follow. What's true?"

Brit points between the two of us. Callum is a gargoyle, utterly still and menacing behind her.

"You two! A couple! I love it!"

All the laughter is gone from Rafe's eyes as he glances at

me, and for one long moment, the enormity of my next words seems to hang in the air.

Rafe tilts his head, and I can almost hear him saying, *Your choice, Angel.* I can only blink at him. He raises his eyebrows, one corner of his mouth twitching as though working to hold back a smile. *Cat got your tongue?*

Why am I now hearing Rafe in my head?

But indeed, the cat has my tongue.

Until I look up at Callum. His eyes bore into me with an intensity that I've never seen. Strangely, I feel almost nothing at all.

That's when the cat returns my tongue, and I manage to smile sweetly, locating the part of me that I always call on when I need to become the Ice Princess everyone expects me to be publicly, as I reach for Rafe's hand.

It's warm in mine, and he squeezes my fingers. A sigh falls from my lips, and I realize how much tension my shoulders held when they loosen. Rafe hides his surprise well, but I see a flash of it there before he grins widely at me.

I look back up at Callum, giving him my own smile before I face Brit. "We're not exclusive *per se.*"

"Yet," Rafe adds, piercing me with a stare that reaches some deep recesses of me that feel like they're just waking.

I force my gaze away, looking back at Brit's wide blue eyes and bouncing curls. "But I did agree to be his date to the ball."

"How wonderful!" Brit says.

Rafe lifts our joined hands, bringing my knuckles to his lips. I'm not sure what's hotter—the look he sears me with or the burn of his lips on my skin. I'm thinking of his kiss from last night and the strawberries between his lips today.

"I'm hoping for more, but the princess plays hard to get."

I can almost believe that he means it, that he wants more.

But of course, Rafe doesn't want more. Not with me. Not when I come with a whole kingdom and he would lose his freedom and any choices he still has. This is nothing more than a game to him, a way to best Callum probably, and it's my whole future to me.

"I'm so happy for you!" Brit squeals.

"I'm so happy too," Rafe says, pressing his lips to my skin again, and I ignore the warning sensation in my belly that somehow, all of this will end badly for me.

CHAPTER SEVENTEEN

Serafina

The following morning, I stand outside two double doors, taking the deepest of breaths and counting eight caterpillars. Pasting on a smile, I walk into what could be the dressing area of an exclusive fashion boutique. Apparently, I'm the first to arrive at this dress fitting.

If I weren't royal, with Kat acting as my fashion consultant, I'd completely dress myself from the internet or one of those monthly subscription services. I absolutely hate shopping and even more, I hate trying things on. Especially with others. There is something so vulnerable about it. I'd rather look at spreadsheets for sure.

The plush red carpet is broken only by a strip of wood flooring stretching out like a catwalk toward three massive mirrors, angled to give full views from every side. White sofas and a few chairs form a semicircle opposite the mirror, near a small raised platform in the center. A few curtained dressing rooms are off to the side and one wall is lined with a hanging rack full of dresses.

Kat would be squealing and sprinting over there to check labels and sizes and run her hands over all the fabric. I'd rather turn and run back out the door.

I stay because this morning's event isn't about me. It's about Callum's sisters making final choices on their dresses. And as much as I love the princesses, given the current situation, the idea of spending a few hours with them and their typical nosy questions has me wanting to run even more.

The room feels slightly stuffy, perhaps because there are no windows, and I try to recall if I've ever been in here before. Yes—I have a sudden memory of hiding in one of the dressing areas from Callum in a game of hide-and-seek. He never did find me—have I mentioned the Elsinorian palace is rather massive?—and I ended up finding *him* in the kitchen eating ice cream.

"Serafina!"

"Fi!"

Henri and Juliet practically maul me as I turn toward the door, and we fall laughing in a tangle on the sofa. Which is unfortunately less comfortable than it looks. I almost wish for my donut pillow. Almost.

"Ouch! What is this made of? Cement?"

Juliet laughs as Henri calls, "Mum! This sofa is rubbish!"

Mum?! How did I miss that the queen is coming?

But she's not only coming, she's here with the queen mother on her arm and a flurry of servants flanking her carrying drinks and a cart of food. This is not a low-key dress fitting with two girls who are like sisters to me, but an Event.

It feels a bit like an Ambush.

Suddenly the room is even stuffier. I'm like the filling of a sausage, being shoved inside a tight casing. Ew! Horrible image. Aren't the casings made from intestines or something? And the inside isn't much better, I'm sure. Strike that thought completely.

I'd thought when the girls invited me to come help them pick dresses that it was just going to be the three of us. Apparently, three's not a big enough crowd.

I should have run when I had the chance. Or perhaps hidden behind one of the changing curtains in a game of hide-and-seek no one else is playing.

"What a strange location for a concert," the queen mother says, looking frail in body but feisty in the eyes. "Do go on, then. I've heard you're a lovely soprano."

She waves a birdlike hand in my direction, and the princesses are no help, hiding laughter.

"I don't actually sing, Your Majesty."

"Oh, come now, Sera. Don't be shy," Henri says, a glint in her eye.

Juliet gives me a little push, and I grip the couch cushion. "We've all been waiting. Come on! Mustn't disappoint Gran."

Suzette is busy speaking to one of the servants in hushed tones, and my gaze lands on the queen mother when she begins to chuckle.

"Never fails to give me a good laugh," she says with a wide, dentured grin. "I know half the time my mind is muddy, so the other half, I get a kick out of pretending. Gets me out of a lot of awkward conversations. Or creates them."

I'll bet.

Suzette takes her seat next to the queen mother. "Are you being devious again?" she asks. Her smile is genuine, but there's a tiredness in her eyes.

"Better devious than dull."

"Debatable." Suzette smiles at the three of us, who are

still practically sitting on top of one another. "Now, that's a lovely picture. My girls."

Oh stars. I'd been so distracted by thoughts of losing Callum and the crown that I hadn't given enough thought to losing *this.* I give Suzette a weak smile, thankful for the distraction of the servants setting out dainty plates of tiny sandwiches and little dessert cakes. They hand out flutes of champagne before disappearing from the room.

"A toast," Suzette says. "To the future of our kingdoms." She lifts her glass high.

"And to luck!" we all respond, giving the traditional Elsinorian echo, my own voice sounding flat.

The bubbles go down easily, but I don't even taste it. Everything just feels so … off.

"Go on, girls," Suzette says, settling back in her seat. "Marta will be in soon in case we need measurements or alterations."

Henri and Juliet scramble for the dresses, which they've been eyeing since they walked in. I take another sip of the tasteless champagne.

"You as well, Serafina."

I set my glass down a little harder than I mean to, and the clink of it seems far too loud. "What?"

Suzette tilts her head, smiling. "I've chosen a selection of dresses for you as well. In Callum's favorite color."

She winks, and the bubbles in my empty stomach seem to hiss and riot. "Oh, no. I brought my own dress." Also in Callum's favorite color—a sapphire blue. "I couldn't possibly—"

"You could, you can, and most importantly, you WILL."

Well, then.

"Thank you."

I stand, relieved to walk away from the intensity of Suzette's gaze.

I haven't been sure after my disastrous first day here where the king and queen stood in terms of the arrangement. In terms of ME. Does this mean they still hope to see me and Callum together?

Her thoughtfulness, though forceful, should warm my heart, and in a small way it does. I've always—until this week, really—felt I belonged with their family.

And yet, as I look through the exquisite dresses, I can't shake the feeling of discomfort. The very same one I had when talking with Rafe about the idea of trying to make Callum jealous. None of this feels *right*.

Brit is Callum's girlfriend, and she should be the one here, trying on dresses in Callum's favorite colors with his family. And, despite knowing that Rafe and I simply made an arrangement, I feel disloyal to him being here with Callum's family.

An arrangement—like the one you had with Callum?

THAT is a thought I'd like to squash immediately.

Juliet and Henri have already disappeared behind the curtain by the time I've chosen a few dresses. All blue, all gorgeous.

Though I know it's a question best left unasked, I can't help it from coming up. "Will Brit be joining us?"

Suzette's lips twist. "No." The single word has the weight of a boulder.

The queen mother clucks her tongue. "I'm sure she's already got a dress. Probably made out of an American flag."

From behind their dressing curtains, Henri and Juliet giggle, and I hate feeling mean. I hesitate, a few hangers in my hand.

"I like the one with the lace sleeves," Suzette says,

arching a dark blonde brow in a formidable way that has me scurrying for the dressing room.

Behind the curtain, I can't meet my own eyes in the mirror as I slip out of my clothes and into the dress with the lace sleeves. The zipper is in the side seam, so I'm able to get in without help. The dress fits as though made for me, and I wonder if Marta has already made adjustments to these dresses so they're not just in my size, but literally fitted to me.

When I step out, everyone *oohs* and *aahs*. The princesses look gorgeous in their own gowns, but they practically leap out of the way, encouraging me to walk toward the mirrors at the end of the little wooden walkway. Marta has appeared with a tape measure and her little leather sewing case, a deep frown creasing her face.

I walk toward my reflection on legs as unsteady as a newborn foal who has also been hitting the bottle.

The dress is, without question, beautiful. Much better than the one Kat helped me pick out before we left uni. The sweetheart neckline and the long lace sleeves are beautiful and the whole thing hugs my curves without being too sexy or tight.

Henri and Juliet lay their heads on my shoulders, one on each side. Their thin arms curl around my waist and for a brief moment I feel more grounded than I have in days.

It pops like a bubble when Juliet whispers, "We hate Brit."

"She's the worst."

"We hate her."

"It should be you."

I cannot locate words, as they've completely left me. My throat has constricted so even if I could think of what to say, I couldn't speak.

I should be pleased, should feel triumphant. But I'm neither of those things. I love Henri and Juliet as sisters. I do. But I can't wish ill on someone so bright and shiny as Brit. Not in good conscience.

"You'd need your hair up to show off your gorgeous neck," Henri says, stepping back and twisting my hair up and holding it into some kind of loose updo shape. "See?"

I do see.

"I've got just the necklace for it," Suzette says. She has joined us all at the mirror, and the space seems to shrink as she unclasps her own necklace, a large diamond on a complicated gold chain, and loops it around my neck. "But this will give you an idea."

"It will be perfect," Juliet says. "I'd kill for your boobs."

"Juliet," her mum hisses as a flush begins to creep up my neck. "Though I can't disagree."

I bark out a short, awkward laugh, then step away from all of them, taking off the necklace, which feels like it's burning my skin. I hand it back to Suzette, unable to meet her eyes.

The next few dresses are pretty, but nothing quite like the first dress. Everyone gives me polite space, as though they can feel the impending panic that's spreading like a virus through me.

I need help zipping the last one, and Henri ducks inside when I ask. She must have chosen a dress because she's in the same designer jeans and blouse she was wearing when we arrived. I wonder if she chose quickly or my dragging heart is making the rest of me sluggish as well.

She meets my eyes in the mirror as she slides the zipper up. "You don't need to feel bad."

"I don't feel … bad, exactly. Just …" I shrug helplessly.

"You're a part of us." She gives my shoulder a squeeze.

"And my brother is just being stupid. He'll get over it, and things will go back to how they were. How they should be," she amends.

As she ducks out of the curtain, I realize with a deep prick of discomfort that I'm not sure I still agree.

I give myself another few moments before I emerge, only to find the room empty. The champagne flutes and plates of food are the only signs that anyone was ever here at all.

"Hello? Henri? Juliet?" I call as the door swings open.

As I turn, it's like my body is already aware of whose big frame is taking up the doorway.

"Not quite," Callum says. His smile is tight and his eyes look tired as he closes the door, leaning against it.

"Oh, hello." I hate the awkwardness that's the new norm when I speak to him.

His eyes drag over me, leaving a sticky, embarrassed heat behind. "Lovely dress," he says, shoving his hands deep into his pockets.

"Thanks. I was just here with your mum and sisters. Do you know—"

"I think this is a setup. Or, an attempt at one. Mum told me I was needed here, and I saw them practically sprinting down the hall, dragging Gran a moment ago."

"Ah. Yes. Well, that makes sense."

Embarrassment has liquefied my bones, but I manage to turn away. I walk toward the mirror to have something to do and somewhere to go that gives me some distance from Callum. It's this or duck behind the curtain of my dressing room. I'm uncomfortable, but I'm not at the point of hiding. Yet.

But when Callum slowly follows me down the walk, I wish I'd chosen the dressing room. He's careful not to step too close, and the message is as clear as the one his family gave off earlier.

"I know my family doesn't approve of Brit. And they definitely *are* a fan of you."

Most of his family, that is. Not the one person who really matters.

"We've got a lot of history," I say. It sounds lame, like I'm making an excuse, for his mum and sisters or myself, I'm not sure.

"We do. And that won't change just because we don't buy into our parents' plans for us."

I agree, at least in the political sense. The tie between our countries is strong, and I absolutely plan on upholding that. But in a personal sense, everything has already changed. Can't Callum see that? It's already changed, and despite Rafe's plan, I have to admit I don't see things going back to the way they were.

Would I even want them to? What felt like heartbreak days ago feels like a paragraph summary in a history textbook today.

"Anyway," Callum says, giving me a final appraisal. "Thanks for understanding."

Has he always been so full of assumptions? He just assumes I understand—why? Because I'm not kicking or screaming or arguing?

"Why are you with Rafe? Because I know why he's with you."

The words, dangled in front of me like bait disguising a sharp hook, make my mouth dry.

"It's none of your concern."

"I told you—"

I spin to face him, my hands on my hips. "You don't have the right to speak into my life. If you wanted that, you wouldn't have said no to this arrangement our parents planned. I'll do what I want with whom I very well please, *Cal.*"

I'm not sure if I'm defending Rafe or myself, or why I'm so angry, but being honest and raw with Callum feels incredibly freeing.

"You're right," he says simply, eyes cool. "I'll go."

He leaves as quickly as he came, and I stomp back to the dressing room, realizing only as soon as I get in there that I needed help from Henri zipping up the back. Hopefully getting the zipper down will be easier than getting it up.

It isn't. I can't reach the zipper, no matter how I bend my arms or twist my body. I'd need to be a member of the Cirque du Soleil to do so. I even try hooking the hanger through the zipper—carefully lest I rip what's probably a dress worth thousands—and end up still fully zipped, and now with a coat hanger hanging off the back of the dress, just as stuck as I am.

I could text Kat, but I didn't bring my phone or anything else down. I'll have to make a walk of shame back up to my room. Doing my best not to wrinkle the dress, I sit crosslegged on the floor, not unlike the way I did so many years ago, waiting for Callum to find me.

Just like then, I realize with no small amount of bitterness, he's not looking for me.

"Seraf?"

My head snaps up at the sound of Rafe's voice. I scramble to my feet and pop just my head out of the curtain, as though I'm naked, not just stuck in a dress I can't unzip.

"What—are you stalking me now?"

He grins. "But of course. It's a small palace."

"Huge, actually. You *are* stalking me."

"Knowing where you spend your time isn't stalking. It's … caring."

"Stalker." I drag aside the curtain and step out, avoiding Rafe's eyes as I turn my back. "While you're here, stalking me, could I trouble you for some help?"

The air seems to heat as he draws closer to me. "Ah, you want my opinion. I like it, though I think red is more your color. Is the hanger some kind of avant-garde fashion statement? Something from Brit, perhaps? I will say your cargo looks—"

"Don't even start with my cargo."

"Are you at least feeling better? I don't see the donut pillow anywhere."

"Rafe, enough."

"Well, how can I be of assistance?"

"I … can't reach the zipper." I stretch my arm around, trying again to do so.

I feel his breath on my bare shoulders before his warm hands land on my back, sliding over my skin before reaching the zipper. This was a bad, bad idea.

"Actually—"

"Relax, Angel," he murmurs, but I stiffen instead, because I swear I could almost feel his lips on my shoulder. His hands brush my skin again, and my eyes flutter closed.

"Rafe," I warn as he begins to drag the zipper down. Slowly, slowly, one metal tooth at a time.

"Seraf."

"*Rafe.*"

His hands pause. "You asked for my help. Do you not want it now?"

I reach, hoping he's pulled it down enough that I can do it myself. But I just end up grabbing his hands. I drop mine back to my sides. "Just—hurry."

He doesn't. I'm not sure a zipper has ever been unzipped with such painstaking slowness. The sound of it is like a groan of frustration—or no, that's me.

I'm groaning. Only it doesn't sound like frustration. It sounds a lot more like desire that has clawed its way to the surface after being buried alive.

Rafe's hands finally reach the center of my back, and I can feel the brush of air on my exposed skin. Or maybe that's Rafe's breath? Either way, I'm sure I can get it the rest of the way. I practically dive behind the curtain.

"Thank you!" I call, my voice high and tight.

"I'm always here." His low voice travels through me like a lit fuse. "Anything you need, Angel. Especially if it involves zippers."

SIX YEARS AGO

Rafe

This isn't the first time I've seen the inside of the headmaster's office, and unless Callum decides to leave me alone or I change schools, I doubt it will be the last. I do wish the headmaster would do something about the smell though. It looks as though it should smell of leather and books, but instead has this stale-cigar, sour-sock funk going on.

Headmaster Bland glares at the two of us over his half-rimmed glasses, then tosses them on his desk and rubs his temples, as though fighting off a headache. The motion makes the loose skin of his forehead crease and then relax, reminding me of those wrinkly dogs.

What's the breed again? Shar-pei?

Normally, the comparison would make me laugh. But I suspect laughing would hurt not only my jaw but my ribs. Callum got a few good kicks in before we were pulled apart by teachers in the dining hall. He's strong and agile, I'll give him that.

"There are no winners here," Headmaster Bland says.

Very true. We both look horrible, and I'm pretty sure nothing was resolved.

Callum says I need to stay away from Serafina when she comes to our lacrosse game this week. Oh, and also, *forever*.

Because I cannot resist pushing his buttons, I told him that I planned to make her mine by the end of the weekend.

Yeah, a terrible thing to say.

Cocky, proprietary, very ... alpha-hole. Is that the right term?

I don't mean it, at least, not in the way I made him *think* I did, like Serafina is some conquest. Far from it.

Callum has no idea that I've had a crush on her from afar since the moment I met her, hiding in a dark hallway of the palace. He doesn't even know I *did* meet her. Serafina might not even remember. I like to think she does, but it's unlikely.

It's also unlikely that what I feel is JUST a crush, or that she would ever return my feelings.

The point is: Callum is under the impression I'm interested in Serafina only because of his friendship with her.

Like this whole world revolves around him.

Like Serafina *belongs* to him.

It's not like he wants to date her. He made it very clear that he views her with overprotective-older-brother vibes. How he could see her as a sister is beyond me.

Maybe it's the way he seems to feel he *owns* her, which made me say something to set him off. I really should have kept my mouth shut. Now he'll probably poison her against me in some way.

Real smooth, Rafe. Way to ruin your chances before you even begin.

Headmaster Bland leans forward, going for intimidation, but it just gives him a double chin. "You two might think that your names, your money, your titles will protect you. But those things all mean that you're called to a higher standard than others."

His frown deepens, and I concentrate on lounging in my chair, looking like I'm about to fall asleep. One eye is already swollen closed, so I'm halfway there.

"And because you're called to higher standards, your consequences will be higher as well. You'll both lose the ability to attend the fall festival, though you will help the janitorial staff to clean up the grounds afterward. And for the next month, you'll share meals at the same table. Maybe that will help ease whatever tension is here and help you work through it in a conversational way rather than physical."

Not likely. Callum and I are way beyond working out whatever this is. I'm not even sure how or why this rivalry started, only that it never seems to end in my favor.

Look, Callum isn't a terrible guy. I know this. His jerky behavior seems to extend only to me. I'm sure it stems from the fact that my uncle, a power-hungry baron, has been a loud voice in calling for an end to the monarchy. I hate my uncle too, but I can't help being associated with him. At least, for now.

Sitting up straight, Callum says, "I think Rafe and I worked out our differences, sir."

Not even a little bit, but whatever.

"I'm very sorry for the trouble we caused. And for losing my temper," he finishes, and I can hear the sincerity in his voice.

It would be easier to hate Callum if he were awful. But he's just not. The Golden Boy nickname he's already earned in the media is, well, *earned.*

"Callum, your father is very disappointed. He's waiting

for you to call him. You're dismissed to use the phone in the main office. Jean will connect your call."

That's it?

Callum is the one who took the first swing, but sure—let him go because his title is bigger than my title. Because he doesn't get in trouble whereas I am more familiar with the cigar and sock smell than I want to be.

"Yes, sir." Callum gets to his feet, heading for the door.

He's the perfect prince. I'm the screw-up. The orphan who should have learned to deal with his loss instead of letting my bitterness at the hand I've been dealt fester into something uglier.

The door closes behind Callum and the headmaster raises his bristly white eyebrows at me. "Your uncle is on his way. He wanted to handle things in person."

I clench my jaw, trying to ignore the way my stomach roils.

If I had known that this would bring Uncle here, I would have made more of an effort to deescalate the situation rather than riling Callum up. The back of my neck starts to heat, and sweat prickles along my spine and beneath my arms.

What can he do to me here, though? There are too many witnesses.

Most importantly, there's no tiny cupboard under the stairs for him to lock me in.

"… understand?"

I shouldn't have thought about the cupboard. My mind spun off to dark places, dark and tiny places where the walls press in on me. I've missed what Headmaster Bland has said.

"Yes, sir," I tell him, assuming that will about cover whatever he said. I shift in my seat.

There's a knock at the door, and my lungs feel like they're shrinking. I don't turn around, and I don't need to.

"Charles."

That voice haunts my dreams. Even here, even when I'm so far away from his reach.

I guess I'm never really *that* far. He loves to remind me of that, popping in from time to time. Always at the worst times. For another two years, he's my legal guardian. And then … I hope I'll never have to see his face again.

Uncle and the headmaster make small talk while I try to keep my breathing steady. I hate that Uncle can still make me feel this way. I'm taller than he is now. I could probably take him in a fight.

But he would find a way to make me suffer even more if I did.

It doesn't have to be that bad, I tell myself. *Just turn off your mind, do what he says. Don't let him touch your emotions. Wall them up. It will be fine. You will be fine.*

You're a survivor.

Uncle has me stand, apologizing to Headmaster Bland. I do so, already feeling my walls slide into place, the ones that keep Uncle's words and his punishments from reaching me.

We pass Callum in the office, no longer on the phone with his father, but charming Jean, the headmaster's secretary. She shoots me a narrow-eyed look, the one people reserve for the problem child.

Uncle stops and narrows his gaze on me. "Have something you want to say?"

Not really. But I know what's expected of me.

"I'm sorry, Prince Callum." I give him the best formal bow I can when my spine feels like each vertebra is coming unattached.

He smirks. "I forgive you."

I can't even bring myself to feel indignant that he's the

one who started it and I'm the one apologizing. I feel nothing. I will be okay. Uncle heads for the door, and I follow.

I don't ask where we're going. It's better when I don't speak. I'll get this over with, whatever *this* is. Then, this weekend, I'll see Serafina at the lacrosse game.

Focus on that. Focus on her face, the sound of her voice.

I watch every interview, read every article. I can tell when she's cut her hair. Sometimes, I can even tell when her smile is genuine rather than just the formal smile I'm sure she's been trained to use. There's a certain light in her eyes.

Think of that light, her light.

Uncle leads me to a building on the edge of campus, used as a hospital in one of the wars, then turned into a dorm. Now it's used for storage, I think.

At the door, Uncle pulls a set of unfamiliar keys from his pocket. His eyes glow with that look he always gets before one of my punishments.

Ignore. Ignore. Ignore. He doesn't have the power to hurt you.

Our steps echo through the hallway of the building, which is shadowy and cobwebbed, something out of a horror movie.

Uncle is the monster.

No, not a monster. That's what he wants to be. I don't have to let him. *Uncle Italian MoleNeck*, I think to myself, repeating the name I invented as a kid when these punishments were so much worse.

He might want to be a monster, consider himself the evil mastermind, but he's a clown. A nobody. He's the emperor with no clothes, and one day, I'll expose him for what he is and what he's done.

I imagine Uncle in a clown's costume, the too-big shoes, a green puffy wig, and a nose that honks if you squeeze it.

He wants to be a villain, inspiring terror in me. But he is a fool. A silly clown.

We stop in front of a door in the middle of the hallway. It's small and looks like it leads to a closet of some kind.

A closet, not a cupboard, I remind myself. *You'll be all right.*

"In," he says, stepping aside so I can see the darkness.

Despite myself, I tremble a little.

The night is darkest just before the dawn. Serafina's words. Well, Harvey Dent's words from the *The Dark Knight*. Which were paraphrased from a book written in 1650 by historian Thomas Fuller. Still, whatever their origin, to me, they are Serafina's words, said at the perfect time when I needed them most. I've held on to them ever since.

They remind me of hope. They make me remember Serafina as she was the night I met her. I say them to myself, picturing her as I've seen her more recently in photos and videos, smiling that joyful smile. Saying these words to me.

Hope.

"Your father would be ashamed," Uncle says. "You don't deserve to even bear his name."

My father wouldn't be ashamed. The older I get, the more sure I am of that.

"It's your fault they're dead."

No. It isn't.

"To think, if your mother knew how much of a trouble-maker you've become. You're a disappointment."

My memories of Mother are hazy, but I only remember sweet smiles. Kindness. She told me stories at bedtime, scratching my back, telling me she loved me. I pull those memories to the front of my mind, blocking out Uncle's words.

He closes the door, and the darkness of the small space blankets me. I close my eyes. Feeling my way forward, I find a solid back wall and turn, leaning against it. If I open my eyes, there's a thin strip of light under the door.

Hope.

I clench my hands to keep them from trembling. I hate being almost a grown man and fearing the dark, fearing closed spaces. I've gotten better at handling this, and now that I'm away at school, it happens less and less.

I hear the door to the building slam, and I clear my throat.

A few years ago, I started trying something new to go along with repeating truths to myself, combating Uncle's lies. It's like imagining my uncle dressed in a clown suit.

With a warbling voice that I know is off-key, I begin to sing the first lines of ABBA's "Dancing Queen." When I finish the last chorus, I switch to "Livin' on a Prayer." Then it's One Direction's "What Makes You Beautiful" and Justin Bieber's "Baby."

The poppier, the happier, the cheesier the song, the better. Because how can this moment be frightening, how can I think about monsters and darkness and fear with this kind of soundtrack, even sung off-key?

So, picturing Serafina's face, the light in her eyes and her smile, I belt out my version of terrible closet karaoke, hanging on with white knuckles to hope.

CHAPTER EIGHTEEN

Serafina

I am holding—not just holding but *using*—a power drill, and it's the most powerful and most accomplished I've ever felt in my whole life. Not even bothering to hide a huge smile, I send the next screw into place, securing the final hinge on this cabinet door.

"Well done," Rafe says, and his compliment feels like a caress.

Our eyes meet as he swings the completed door closed. And for a moment, all the air in the room seems to be laced with a humming tension. Then I remember where we are, what we're doing, and why this is a bad, terrible, no-good idea, and I take a big step back.

Where we are is in a small cottage in the village directly surrounding the Elsinorian palace. It's Working Day, a time when royals and the peerage convene on nearby towns to help with large and small work projects. I've never been in

Elsinore for it, though I've always wanted to go. I'm even more thankful that I'm getting a firsthand look now, as I'd like to start our own Working Day in Viore.

It also doesn't hurt that I've spent the day working alongside Rafe.

This year, because of the Centennial celebration, it's on a much grander scale. And while critics would say this event is about optics, making the royals look in some ways accessible, as though we care about the common problems, the reality is that we do care. At least, those I know do care.

The surprising thing is how much Rafe seems to care. If I hadn't spent the day with him, I wouldn't have believed it.

"I told you," Rafe says, as I pick up another screw. "I knew you could do it."

"I knew I could too," I fire back.

"Of course you did." Rafe smirks.

In truth, it took him several minutes for Rafe to convince me I should take over with the drill.

Why, exactly, is that? Why was I so hesitant?

Probably years of my parents both reinforcing what they think is proper princess work, which will blossom into proper queen work. That kind of work does not include wielding power tools. More like … wielding tea sandwiches and a solid set of manners.

As much as I've been working to counter that and as much as I plan to continue fighting my way out of the box they've tried to build for me, I guess sometimes I still doubt my own abilities.

And this isn't even that hard! I got it right the very first try, despite being terrified I'd ruin the whole kitchen somehow. I could put together a house now, from the studs up, just me and my trusty drill.

Studs—is that the right terminology?

I think that's what I've heard on the few home renovation shows I've watched. Now I wish I'd paid more attention. I also wish I had one of those cool belts, the soft leather kind, so I could tuck the drill in, just like a holster at my waist. I imagine the weight there, and I like the idea.

There are only a few more doors left and we'll be done upgrading the dented and faded cabinets in this cramped kitchen. Honestly, I'm disappointed.

Rafe has been a great partner, cracking jokes and making conversation and charming the families we've helped from the grandmothers to the children. Most especially the children, which surprised me to no end.

One dog tried to bite him, but it was blind and also bit the leg of a ladder, so I'm not sure that was a judgment on Rafe's character.

"A little more," Rafe says, holding the next new door in place as I work on the hinge. "You want it flush."

"I don't need you mansplaining," I say, though I totally wouldn't have known how to make this flush without him taking the time to teach me earlier.

"I'd never dare mansplain to you, Angel. Talking is simply my way of trying to feel useful. You're doing all the hard work. I'm not even sure you need me. Someone else could just as easily hold this door. Actually, Farrah," Rafe calls to the little girl sitting at the kitchen table, watching us with rapt attention.

"Yes?"

"I need your help if you're up for it."

She is next to us in a flash, and I smile down at the girl with crooked braids to match her crooked front teeth. A spray of freckles across her cheeks completes the look, which is utterly adorable. Rafe crouches to be eye level with her.

He bites his lip, and I try not to track the movement. "Do you think you're strong enough to hold this door in place?"

She giggles, ducking her head shyly. But then she stands a bit straighter and flexes her biceps, showing off her muscles. Rafe stumbles back, falling onto his butt on the dusty, scarred wood floors.

"Whoa!" he says, putting one hand to his chest. "Why didn't you show me those earlier? Now, how about you come take over my job? I think you're better suited for it."

Farrah giggles, her cheeks turning pink, and I try to keep my heart from exploding.

I would never have imagined Rafe as the kind of man who would be a natural with children, but he absolutely is. For a brief flash, I see him as a father, swinging his own children around, laughing and relaxed. I press a free hand to my chest, like my palm can possibly hold back the flood of warm and gooey things I don't want to be feeling.

Not when it isn't real.

Rafe nods at me, and I pretend I'm not inwardly swooning over him right now. While I open the next cabinet door, he lifts Farrah, setting her on the counter while still keeping a protective hand behind her. From the other side of the kitchen, Farrah's mother, a woman whose weariness seems to seep from her pores, blinks back tears and takes a photo with her phone.

"Thank you for offering to help," I tell Farrah. "If you'll simply hold the door straight, I'm going to replace this hinge, using the drill."

She nods seriously, her blue eyes gleaming as she takes hold of the cabinet door firmly. Over her shoulder, Rafe's eyes meet mine, and a little firework of excitement goes off in my belly.

It's been like this between us all week, and because of

this, I've done my best to avoid Rafe whenever possible, though he keeps finding me. In my room, in the gardens, hiding in some far-off wing of the palace. I'm beginning to wonder if he has a tracker hidden somewhere on my body.

Today, it's been worse. Or better? I still can't decide if how I feel around him is exquisite or exquisite torture. Claudius handed me our list of tasks earlier today and told me to have fun. He never says things like that, so I'm beginning to think he hand-picked our jobs, which have all been fairly straightforward tasks with wonderful families. I saw Callum earlier, looking sweaty and frustrated and carrying bags of garbage, so I'm thinking Claudius definitely gave us the cushy jobs.

We've done everything from help touch up paint on fences, scrubbing floors, patching holes in a barn, and now putting new, working hinges on cabinet doors.

Honestly, this has been one of the happiest days I remember. Rafe and I work seamlessly together, as if we've been doing it for years, not as if before this week we were barely strangers. As he's done all week, he's shown me a different side to the man formerly known as the Royal Rogue.

There is nothing roguish about the man who has involved this little girl, making her feel like she's strong, she has purpose. He does the same for me. Even when he explained how to use the drill, how to hold it and get the screws in flush, it was humble. I only teased him about mansplaining because it's so far from the truth.

He spent the day teasing, playing, and generally letting me take on any job I wanted or felt like I could handle. And, as with the drill, challenging me to try ones I might not have thought I could handle.

I smile and have to look away when Rafe winks at me.

"Okay, Farrah. Here goes," Rafe says. "Are you ready?"

"Born ready."

She's completely serious, so I do my best to hide my smile. I can see Rafe doing the same, and I focus on the job at hand.

And while this darling girl holds the cabinet steady with a fierce look of determination, I finish replacing the hinges. Rafe helps move her to the next cabinet, making sure her bare feet have solid footing on the counter and acting as a spotter without making her feel coddled.

There's suddenly a flurry of activity from the front of the house, and Farrah's mother disappears from the kitchen as a familiar, deep voice sends awareness rushing through me, as well as a prickle of something else. Not desire, but something much more uncomfortable.

Rafe's gaze collides with mine again over Farrah's thin shoulder, and I can only meet his eyes for a moment before looking away.

Callum strides in, and the first thought I have is that Brit isn't here, followed shortly by the realization that this small kitchen is not nearly big enough for these two men. The air is fraught with tension almost immediately, and it's like the equivalent of someone turning on all the burners of a gas stove, letting the room fill with the pressure.

I suck in a breath. "Hello, Callum."

"Fi," he says warmly, then gives a stiff nod to Rafe.

"Your Highness," Rafe responds in a flat tone.

"You're Prince Callum," Farrah says in an awed voice, and Rafe lifts her stiffly from the counter, placing her on the floor in front of Callum, who immediately crouches down to her level.

She gives him a perfect curtsy that makes my heart squeeze, and when I glance over, I see a similar look on her mother's face as well.

Callum bows to her in an exaggerated motion, grinning before ruffling her hair. She giggles, her cheeks going red and her hands twisting with visible nerves.

Rafe has retreated to the corner of the room like a shadow, leaning with faux casualness against the wall, watching this whole exchange with the ghost of a smile.

"What were you doing up on the counter?" Callum asks, and I hate the dismissiveness of the question, and the censure clearly meant for Rafe, but read by the little girl as though she's done something wrong.

"Oh," Farrah says, taking a small step back. Then, bless her, she juts her chin out and shows her muscles again, like she did for Rafe. "I'm strong enough to help," she says, and I see Rafe smile for real this time.

"Of course you are," Callum says, as though he hadn't just questioned her.

His eyes flit to me and then his brow furrows before lifting in surprise. He smiles, and it feels patronizing before he even speaks. "And someone must be slacking in his job," he says, giving Rafe a heavy dose of side-eye, "if the princess is using power tools. Here."

Callum holds out his hand to take the drill, but I mirror Farrah and lift my own chin. Before I can answer him, the little girl takes a tiny step forward again.

"Princesses can use power tools," she says, her small fists on her hips.

I want to wrap her up in a hug or perhaps have Rafe lift her on his shoulders to parade her around like a champion. She glances back at me, and I hold out my hand for a fist bump. With the most adorable smile I've ever seen, she grins at me.

"I've got this," I tell Callum.

"Okay, then," he says with a chuckle, brushing his blond hair back off his face.

As he steps forward to hold the cabinet door, a photographer manages to make it inside the kitchen, which is growing smaller by the moment. The man with the camera is followed by a woman I recognize from the palace as one of the PR and press secretaries. She whispers something to the photographer, who starts clicking away.

Farrah's mother gets edged out of her own kitchen, clearly uncomfortable with the crush of strangers. Or maybe with the fact that her dim, fairly dingy kitchen is being photographed. The nice, white new cabinet fronts help lighten up the room, but it's a quick fix. I consider saying something about the appropriateness of this gesture, but it's not my home and not my country. Not my PR.

Farrah looks lost until Rafe pulls out a chair for her at the wobbly kitchen table, taking the seat beside her. He pushes a salt shaker toward her, keeping the pepper for himself and angling it toward the salt shaker. Bending low, I can hear his silly voice as he makes the pepper shaker like a little person. Farrah giggles, emulating him as they begin to play.

The sight of it stirs something in me, and I forget Callum and the drill in my hand until he clears his throat. The smile immediately slips from my face.

"If you aren't going to use that," he starts, and I know he's probably eager to do more than hold a door in place, especially now that the cameras are here.

"Right. You hold this one and then we can switch off at the next?" That's rather diplomatic. But I don't miss the hint of irritation in his eyes.

I lift the drill as I've been doing for the past few cabinets, and maybe it's because of the extra bodies in the room, but it's suddenly sweltering in this small room, hot and hard to breathe. I keep getting the angle wrong, and it takes me four times to get one screw in the small hinge. My hands begin to cramp, then tremble. I can see Callum watching me carefully, biting his tongue, and I refuse to make eye contact.

The drill bit slips off the head of the screw altogether, and I almost gouge a hole in the wood next to it. Callum clears his throat again and says quietly, "Need a break?"

I nod, hating the pity on his face, hating the way I feel so useless. Gone is my power trip and the high of feeling like I could build a house myself. I switch places with Callum, holding the door while he expertly finishes both hinges faster than I did one screw, as though this is the easiest job in the world.

"We make a good team," he says with a smile, and my thoughts stutter to a stop, because that's the last thing I'm thinking.

No, *Rafe and I* made a good team.

I glance at the table, realizing that both he and Farrah have slipped away without me noticing. Right—the plan. He's probably giving me alone time with Callum since Brit isn't here. But the joy has been sucked out of the room, and my heart feels sluggish and slow. The salt shaker is tipped on its side, a thin spray of salt dusting the tabletop.

"Looks good, doesn't it?" Callum says, closing the cabinet and giving it a fist bump.

"Sure."

He brushes his hair back from his forehead, indicating that I should move to the next cabinet. We shuffled down a few steps, and I hold the door steady while he removes the screws, then hold the new one in place while he drills in each screw perfectly. Every so often, I hear the camera crew's shutters snapping.

Meanwhile, my mind is on Rafe, and how soon I can get

out of here and back to him. "How has your morning been?" Callum asks, then squinches up his nose.

"Great. Rafe and I work well together."

Callum's mouth tightens, and the drill makes a loud, obnoxious noise as he pushes the screw in too far. "Sorry," he mutters, reversing the direction of the bit and drawing it out so it's level.

I step back, wiping my brow and taking a sip from the glass of water Farrah's mother was kind enough to offer. I couldn't remember the last time I drank water from a tap, but it tastes surprisingly fresh.

"I still don't understand you and him—what you're doing."

"I don't need to explain myself to you, Cal." The nick-name—one I've certainly never used for him—slips out, making his eyes narrow.

"He's rubbing off on you."

"That wouldn't be such a bad thing." Callum rears back, eyebrows ratcheting up his face, but before he can say anything to ruffle me further, I continue. "You seem to be the only one who hasn't left the boyish competition behind. Frankly, I'm over it."

Callum leans his hips back on the counter, gripping the edge with white knuckles. Somehow, despite the dust on his cheek and the visible shine of sweat on his forehead, he manages to look like a model.

"You think this isn't a game to Rafe? You think him paying you attention isn't just his way of messing with me?"

I set my water glass down on the table and cross my arms. My mouth is burning with the desire to tell Callum that he's wrong about Rafe, but I've had the same fears myself.

That's not what this is.

240

Then what IS it?

Because I'm standing here with Callum, the man I'm supposed to be making jealous with Rafe. And … I don't care. I don't care if Callum gets jealous. I'm not sure I care about Callum.

"You don't know him the way you think."

"And you do? After a week's time? I spent years with him at school, Fi. Years. I didn't think you'd fall under the same trap as all the girls he strung along, making them think they were different, or that he had changed for them."

Callum shakes his head, then picks up the drill again and nods to the final door. "Come on, then. Let's finish up."

I want to strike back, to defend, but my eyes feel stung and swollen, my lungs tight and overworked. There's a lot of truth in Callum's words. I do barely know Rafe, and I suddenly remember the way I felt about the darkly handsome duke just over a week ago. The thin sliver of doubt in me doubles, then grows into a ream of paper.

I am standing just feet from the prince I've always dreamed of—my best friend, my assumed fiancé. And I don't feel warmth or flutters or any of the things I used to, the things I should.

When I think of Rafe, who has disappeared, presumably to give me a chance to be alone with Callum, I definitely feel something. There's a lifting of my heart, followed by a quick crash as I consider Callum's words and the doubt they've planted.

We're silent as we finish attaching the last new door. When the photographer asks Callum to pose for a photo with Farrah's mum, I step away, sweeping the spilled salt from the table into my palm and tossing it over my shoulder. Then I make my way out of the cottage, alone.

CHAPTER NINETEEN

Serafina

It doesn't take long to find Rafe, who is holding Farrah's hand as she balances on the edge of a barely dripping fountain. The sight of his wide smile aimed at Farrah, has something in me singing.

When he sees me coming, his eyes widen a little in surprise before crinkling with a smile. He bends, whispering something to Farrah, who nods and jumps down. She runs straight to me in her bare feet and braids swinging.

Giving me a little curtsy, she says, "Princess Serafina, the Duke of Weldon would like you to accompany him on a walk. Will you accept his invitation?"

She is simply adorable. Rafe hangs back by the fountain, hands in his pockets and scuffing a toe along the cobblestones. There is a boyish look to him right now, shy even, so far from the smug, sauntering duke I'd grown used to seeing.

Kneeling so Farrah and I are on the same level, I say,

"Would you be so kind as to tell the duke I would love to take a walk with him?"

Farrah turns and shouts, "She said yes! That's five euros!"

I can't help but laugh as I stand. Rafe counts out the euros and sets them in her palm. With a wave and a mischievous grin, she runs back toward home, bare feet seemingly unaffected by the bare cobblestones.

Rafe approaches, and my pulse stutters. Shy is a good look on him. Is there a bad look on the man? Highly unlikely.

I put my hands on my hips. "So, this is what it's come to? You're paying underage matchmakers?"

Rafe laughs, shaking his head as he reaches me. We begin walking side by side, making our way back to the center of the village. The workday is almost done, to be followed immediately by a feast and dancing in the town square.

"Let's call it a finder's fee," Rafe says. "Sounds less desperate, yeah?"

"Slightly. But only five euros?"

"I offered one, and she negotiated up to five. Enterprising head on that little one."

I raise an eyebrow. "One euro? That's where you started? I'm trying not to be offended."

Rafe leans close, his shoulder bumping mine. "You are a treasure beyond value. Priceless."

His words hit me like fizzy champagne bubbles, effervescent and light in my bloodstream. The problem is that I never know how seriously to take Rafe. He's flirtatious and teasing so much of the time, and he seems serious now, but isn't he trying to help me win Callum? Wasn't this supposed to be pretend?

I wish it weren't pretend.

The thought startles me, though it shouldn't, as I've been thinking around it for days now. I stumble a little on an uneven stone, and Rafe's hand finds my elbow, steadying me. When it drops away, I long to have it back.

"You're good with children," I say, desperate to turn the conversation in a direction far from my thoughts.

"I enjoy them."

The answer seems too simple, too easy. So, I press. "Do you want a big family?"

I realize, too late of course, that this might be a painful question for Rafe, given his family history. I desperately wish I could take it back.

But he answers earnestly. "I do. It's something I didn't get to have."

I consider saying *I'm sorry*, but it seems like the wrong thing, and I have nothing else to offer.

"How about you?" Rafe asks, a smile pulling at his lips. "This seems like such a second- or third-date question—not that I've been on many of those—but do you want kids?"

I can't help but laugh at his phrasing. Has Rafe been on second or third dates? I'm not about to ask. Also, maybe it shouldn't do funny things to my insides that he wants a big family, but it does.

"I'd like a big family. It's just me, and sometimes that gets lonely. My parents had trouble getting pregnant."

"That's why you're in this position now," he says, and I hate the reminder that the reason he and I are together has something to do with the requirements that I find a husband of a certain stature within the allotted time.

"That and I went to university. It's about the only thing I've fought for with my parents. They saw it as a waste of time."

"And how do you see it?"

"As preparation for the job I'm to do."

We're quiet for half a block, walking slow.

"How did the rest of the kitchen go?" he asks.

I know what Rafe probably means: Did I make any headway with Callum?

The question I'm asking myself: Do I WANT to make any headway with Callum?

No, and also no.

"The kitchen is done. Looks lovely."

Giving me a sideways glance, he asks, "That's it?"

"Yeah. Callum hung the rest of the cabinets, they took some photos, and … yeah."

"*Callum* finished the cabinets?"

"Yep."

Rafe makes a little humming noise in his throat. "I'm surprised he got you to part ways with the power tool."

I don't want to admit to Rafe that I lost my confidence. Or that Callum made me feel small. Honestly, I'd rather not talk about or think about Callum at all.

Callum? Who's Callum?

I would rather pretend that Rafe and I are not spending time together as a means to an end—an end I'm no longer sure I want. Maybe just for now, I can simply pretend that we are a normal couple—whatever normal means—on a normal date. No strings. No monarchy. No pressure.

Rafe's hand brushes mine, just an accidental touch, but I grab it, twining my fingers through his. This touch produces two equal and opposite reactions in me, and I'm not even sure how that works. A part of me eases, like a sigh, feeling steadied by his hand in mine, the way I did when he grasped my elbow moments before.

But where our skin meets, heat and excitement builds, spreading slowly through me. It's like that scene in *The Return of the King* when the signal fires are lit, one by one by one from peak to peak. I feel the light in my hand, then my elbow, my shoulder, my neck, then down my spine.

There, there, there, there—until I'm all aflame with excitement, with desire.

Cool it, Serafina. You're not supposed to feel this way about Rafe. He certainly doesn't feel this way about you.

Or does he? He is holding my hand at this very moment. He has done and said so many sweet things to me over the past few days.

But no. He *can't* like me. Because his goal is to set me up with another man. For reasons that still don't seem clear to me.

The more I think of Callum and the dismissive way he took the drill from me, the way he's made me feel foolish and small this week, I'm beginning to wonder if the man I thought I loved was no more than the IDEA of Callum. Not the actuality. What I do know and feel sure of, is that I do not love Callum now.

Even so, Rafe isn't my boyfriend, nor does he want to be. I'd do well to remember that flirting is his natural default, even if I'm not used to it being aimed in my direction.

I start to let go of Rafe's hand, but he squeezes, trapping my hand in his. His smirking smile returns.

"Not so fast," he says. "I rather like this new development. It's nice holding your hand."

Trying to ignore the veritable swarm of butterflies dive-bombing my belly, I offer him a teasing grin. "Have you never held hands with a woman before?"

"I—" He pauses, then goes quiet.

I study his profile, wondering at the serious expression. He meets my gaze, then looks away.

"No, I don't guess that I have," Rafe says, all too seriously. "Not like this."

I'm incredulous. "You? How could you not—*oh*."

My neck and cheeks feel hot as realization hits me.

It's not for lack of experience, but Rafe hasn't held hands with a woman because he was always moving much faster, toward a different goal.

Hand-holding must seem so … *juvenile* to him. Not for the first time around Rafe, I feel self-conscious about my lack of experience. My first instinct is to pull away again, but he said he liked holding my hand. Drawing in a deep breath, I choose to take him at his word.

Because I like it too. Quite a lot, actually.

Straightening my shoulders, I take a breath. "Well, I'm happy to be your tour guide, introducing you to the wondrous world of holding hands." I squeeze his fingers and he squeezes back. "Any questions so far?"

"Does it usually feel this … nice?" He makes a face. "Nice is such a *nice* word."

"The *nicest*."

Rafe laughs, and then his thumb begins to stroke softly over the back of my hand. The movement is slight, but its impact on me is not, just like the featherlight kiss from a few nights ago. My tongue seems cemented to the roof of my mouth, my heart is having some kind of event, and my left knee just wobbled.

Holding his hand is way more than *nice*.

Villagers are all out and about, watching, smiling as we pass by. We smile back but continue on our way. It's a little surprising that no one is trying to get photographs or fawning over royalty. Not that Rafe and I are as important as Callum or Phillip or even Henri and Juliet, but still. I wonder if that's how this village simply is, or if, for this particular day out of the year, there's a sort of unspoken agreement to let us be somewhat normal. Other than the security guards who have been keeping a watchful eye from a distance. I prefer to pretend they aren't there. It's hard to ignore The Dane, and I swear he's garnering more stares than we are.

"Do you usually come to Working Day?"

"Every year," Rafe says.

"I never could have pictured you at something like this," I confess.

"Of course not. You had me pegged as something else, as someone else."

And now that I have the information from the dossier, I realize how inadequate my assessment of him was. Not incorrect necessarily, but definitely incomplete. I turn over Kat's warning in my mind that I didn't need to look at the files on Rafe.

We weren't meant to learn everyone's secrets, she said. Something to that effect. And now, walking through the streets of the village holding his hand, I'm more aware of this knowledge than ever.

"Was I completely wrong?" I ask gently, needing to know who this man is. The Royal Rogue? Something else entirely? Both?

He takes a moment before answering, staring down at the cobbled street where we're walking. "Two years ago, I was exactly who you thought me to be."

He grips my hand tighter, almost painfully so. I wonder suddenly if this conversation is too much, especially considering the boundaries of our friendship. Relationship? I'm not sure where we are in terms of the real, the fake. I think we're coloring outside of the lines at this point.

"You heard that two years ago, I was discharged from the royal guard," Rafe says.

"Right. For medical reasons. Are you ... okay now?"

"I am, thank you." His thumb changes from making little

lines on my hand to small circles, and my skin prickles with awareness. He clears his throat. "While technically, the discharge was for medical reasons, I was suffering with mental health issues, not physical ones."

He pauses, as though to give this a moment to sink in. I hate that I already know this and have to pretend that I don't. *Dang my parents and their stupid dossier!* And let's not forget my curiosity, which made me look.

It still takes a moment to process, even coming from him.

Rafe de Silva, having a mental health crisis? I shouldn't be so surprised. The theme of the week seems to be that I have seen him as more of a two-dimensional character than a fully formed, complicated, kind of amazing human. I'm blown away as much by the fact that he's admitting this than the fact that he struggled—struggles?—with it.

Though the topic of mental health has become more commonplace, carrying much more public sympathy and understanding, it's still fairly taboo, especially for those of us holding important positions.

And, to be a little sexist, especially with men. Most guys wouldn't want to admit that they can't get the lid off a jar, much less that they're struggling with mental health. I want to know more—I want to know everything, really—but I wait, letting Rafe unspool his story one thread at a time.

I do step a little closer, hopefully letting him know by my proximity that I am here. And maybe he gets that, because he continues.

"During one of our training exercises, we were in a closed-up bunker. Confined, dark spaces are ... hard for me."

I squeeze his hand, and feeling like that's not enough, stretch my other arm across to rest on his bicep. It makes walking a little more awkward, but Rafe slows our already languid pace to practically a crawl. I don't mind in the least.

"I had what is considered a mental breakdown. Honestly, I don't remember much, but I apparently injured one of the officers. He was okay, but I spent a week in the mental ward of the hospital."

"I'm so sorry, Rafe."

"It's fine. Honestly, this was the impetus I needed to make a change. A lot of changes, actually. I spent time in therapy, a particular kind called EMDR, which deals with— I'm sorry. Am I boring you? This doesn't matter."

"No! You're not boring me at all. Please go on. What's EDM?"

Rafe laughs. "Not EDM—that's like club music."

"Oh, right. Probably not so helpful for therapy."

"Not any I've heard of, but you never know. Anyway, EMDR stands for Eye Movement Desensitization and Reprocessing. It uses physical stimulation such as eye movement and tapping to help process anxiety and post-traumatic stress. The goal is to focus on the tie between the physical and the mental and emotional, helping to process through trauma."

I hate Rafe's uncle so much I can practically taste the bitterness on my tongue. What did he do to Rafe? I know losing his parents was traumatic, but somehow, I just know that this was not simply about the car accident that orphaned him. I think of those reports, the ones which could never be substantiated. I want justice for him so badly I might be willing to kill for it.

"Fascinating," I tell him, somehow hiding the homicidal rage I'm currently fighting against. He raises one dark brow, tilting his head to glance my way. "I mean it. I haven't heard of this kind of therapy before. Did it help?"

"It did. I mean, I also did a lot of talking—so much talking—through things. But anyway, that's the short version of why I might seem different from the man you thought you knew."

I feel relieved now that he's told me himself, even if he didn't give all the details. Neither did the report—it just held some educated guesses. If Rafe was willing to tell me, I don't mind so much that I already knew bits and pieces.

"I should have known better than to judge you based on headlines."

"I'm grateful none of this made it into the headlines. Not that I'm ashamed—I'm rather proud, actually. But if I ever share this story, it will be on my terms. Not some money-hungry paparazzi."

"I hope you do share sometime. I mean, if you're willing. It could make a big difference. Perhaps help lessen the stigmas around mental health."

"I'd like to do that sometime, absolutely. For now, I'm working on keeping my head down and getting my life back."

"Your life back?"

He's quiet for a moment. I study the angle of his jaw from the corner of my eye. His raven hair gleams in the fading sunlight and his dark eyes are fixed somewhere ahead of us.

"My uncle used this as an excuse to take control of my assets."

"What?"

"It's a conservatorship. You know," he says in a teasing tone that sounds a little forced. "Think: Free Britney."

I haven't paid too much attention to celebrity gossip over the years, but I know one of Kat's classes discussed the legal battle between pop star Britney Spears and her father over conservatorship. Rafe's uncle has something similar? This was not in my parents' dossier, and I can't help but wonder how they missed it. Something legal like this should be public record, shouldn't it? I'm furious at the idea that Rafe's uncle would take advantage of his vulnerable state to wrest control of it.

I'm sure if I speak to Kat, she'd know—

"Hey. I see the wheels spinning. Don't take on this problem. I'll handle my uncle."

"But—"

He shakes his head, cutting me off. "I do appreciate that you care. More than you know. But it will be fine."

We'll see.

"Angel? Promise me, you'll let this go. I didn't tell you this so you'd try to fix it."

"Fine." Though I agree, I cross the fingers of my free hand where Rafe can't see. I have a feeling this might fall under the category of things I can't let go. But at least for right now, I will.

We've reached the edge of the main square, just as the strings of light hanging over the park at the center flicker on. Sunset won't be for at least another hour or two, but here, with the surrounding three- and four-story buildings and storefronts, the shadows are starting to stretch long. Flowers bloom everywhere, in bright window boxes and in garlands strung from the lamp posts. The effect is nothing short of magical, and the square is starting to fill with people.

Rafe stops, pulling me into a little alley next to a restaurant which smells of tomatoes and garlic. My stomach rumbles, and Rafe grins at me.

"Are you ever *not* hungry, Angel?"

"It's a theme with you," I say, and then blush when his grin turns flirtatious.

"I make you hungry?"

"For *food.*"

I shove him lightly, and he dramatically flops back against the brick wall, tugging me by our still-joined hands. Giggling,

I stumble forward into him. This brings us chest to chest, and as I meet his eyes, I realize we are intimately close. I should step back, but I don't.

"Thank you for listening, Seraf." His eyes skate over my face.

"Thank you for sharing." Choosing my words carefully, I add, "And if and when you want to tell me more, you can trust me."

"I hope you know that the same goes for you. I'm here for you. Whatever you need."

The air shimmers with the tension between us, as heavy as a tree laden down with snow in a Vioran winter. But I feel anything but cold, my chest brushing against Rafe's, our hands still clasped as though they're now fused together.

Sorry, hand, you are now part of a pair.

Hand: I have to say, I don't mind even a little bit …

I shake my head a little, trying to dislodge the conversation I'm having WITH MY OWN HAND.

And then, Rafe ruins it—my mental conversation and the hand-holding.

He pulls away, sliding both his hands into his pockets, a picture of casual ease. *Did I imagine the whole moment between us?*

"You should go talk to him."

"Who?"

"Callum."

It's as though I've been tossed in the Glacée, the always freezing river running near the palace, fed from melting snow in the mountains. My bones snap tight, and I fight off a shudder.

Rafe just opened up to me … and now he's trying to shove me at Callum again?

I stare across the square. Henri and Juliet are in one

254

corner near a flower shop. Nearby, an older man is explaining something with wild gestures, while Callum feigns interest—and not too believably. The man is none the wiser and continues his story. Callum sees me watching, glares at Rafe, and gives me a little wave.

"See?" Rafe says. "A perfect opportunity."

As always, Rafe has that way of tossing me off my feet when I'm feeling steady. I had started to feel like maybe he and I were building something—trust, or maybe even sliding from something fake to something real.

Or not. I mean, this was the plan, wasn't it? Rafe is supposed to help me win Callum. I'm not supposed to be falling for Rafe.

Maybe I'm not on board with the plan anymore.

Without another word, I start across the square, trying not to be hurt by the way he pulled the plug on the sweet moment I thought we just shared. But I don't head for Callum. Instead, I make my way to his sisters.

"Sera!"

Henri and Juliet grin and link their arms through mine, and I let them steady me.

"Did I see you and Rafe holding hands?" Henri asks, leaning close.

"He's so handsome," Juliet sighs. "How does he kiss?"

"Juliet!" I scold.

"Yeah, Jules," Henri agrees. "You can't just ask like that. You have to be a little more subtle. Example." She turns to face me, blinking up with faux-innocent eyes. "Are the rumors about Rafe's prowess true?"

"That's even worse!" I tell her. Also, I don't want to think about Rafe and rumors of his prowess. Not even a little bit. "Both of you, ease up!"

We locate a little park bench under a flowering tree and

sit. From here, I have a perfect view of Rafe and Phillip, who look to be having a serious discussion. Really, does Phillip have any other kind?

Juliet sighs. "You can't blame us for being curious. If you're not going to marry our brother like we hoped, Rafe is a nice consolation prize."

He's anything but a consolation prize.

My eyes catch on Callum, who is now flanked by three women, vying for his attention with their hair tossing and their bosom heaving. Based on Callum's smile, these moves could be added to a biology textbook as effective mating rituals of human beings.

One breaks off and heads toward Rafe, and I find my chest tightening.

"Rafe's reputation leaves something to be desired," Henri says, also watching.

My focus zeroes in on Rafe. The woman tosses her blonde hair and tries to angle herself into Rafe's conversation. I'm glad Henri and Juliet still have their arms linked through mine. Otherwise ...

Rafe gives the woman a polite nod and smile, then turns back to Phillip in such a way that she's cut out of the conversation. The tightness in my chest loosens, and I sigh. The woman heads back to Callum, who's all too happy to speak with the three women. They all laugh at something he says.

He's not that funny, ladies.

"Rafe isn't the only one with a reputation," Juliet says. "Our brother has become something of a manwhore."

"Jules!" I give her arm a squeeze. "That's not appropriate to say of anyone. Much less your brother."

"Fine. He's been *indiscriminate*," Juliet says. "Is that better? Careless? Thoughtless? He's played the field, dated around, taken the car for a test drive—"

"Juliet! Gross." Henri fights off a shudder.

"You both would do well to pay less attention to rumors. Especially concerning your brother."

Juliet snorts. "Even when we see them confirmed right in front of us?"

Callum has picked flowers from the garlands nearby, decorations someone here probably spent hours making. He tucks one behind the ear of each woman, earning him bright smiles and pink cheeks.

And I am not jealous in the least.

And yet ... I felt anxious just moments ago when the one woman tried to talk to Rafe. This makes me feel fickle. Didn't I think I loved Callum just days ago? Wasn't I feeling possessive, jealous, and even crushed by his relationship with Brit and by him with other women this year?

How can I change so quickly to having any kind of feelings for Rafe?

Though ... Rafe is titled. You could marry him instead of Callum.

That thought is errant and wild as a thistle. Donning mental gardening gloves, I pull it up straight from the root.

I need to get myself sorted. Maybe just get a good night's sleep. My parents will be arriving tomorrow, and as much as that makes my stomach fill with dread, they'll slap some sense into me.

"Where is Brit, by the way?"

I'm sure she would mind the attention Callum is paying to the three women. They look about ready to drag him off to a cottage for a pre-dinner appetizer.

"She and *Callie* had a fight," Juliet says, making a fake pouty face. "We'll see if they last until the ball. I'm betting no."

"I'm with you. Sera? For or against?"

257

"I'm not betting on relationships and neither should you."

The women have disappeared as we've been talking, and Phillip has been swept up in a conversation with a man walking a pig on a leash. The look on Phillip's face is priceless, almost as hilarious as the looks on Rafe's and Callum's faces as they stand next to one another.

It's probably too much to hope that they would patch things up one day, get past whatever is between them. Maybe even be friends.

"Well, if you don't end up with our brother, I wholly support you and Rafe," Henri says.

"You'd have gorgeous children," Juliet says.

Henri scoffs. "Why are you jumping right into children? Women can do more than just bear children like some kind of baby factory. We don't even know if Serafina wants to have children."

"I do." An image of Rafe with Farrah comes to mind, giving my heart a soft little squeeze. He wants a big family. So do I. "But not yet. I have a lot of work to do first."

"That's the spirit!" Henri cheers.

She's loud enough that both Callum and Rafe turn toward us, their sour expressions shifting. They each raise a hand to wave, like mirror images of one another, or maybe more like negatives of a film strip, seeing as they're so different.

The three of us wave back, my smile tentative as I feel the weight of both of their gazes fixed on me. And suddenly, it feels like the game isn't between the two of them, but with the three of us. I'm the one moving the chess pieces on the board, but I don't know which team I'm rooting for, black or white.

CHAPTER TWENTY

Serafina

My parents arrive the next afternoon, bringing with them an icy wind. Not a literal one. Just the kind that has my whole Rafe-induced confusion morphing into something more like numb, abject terror. I swear I can feel their presence in the palace even before Claudius comes to fetch me in the afternoon before dinner.

I am not at all surprised to find Kat arriving with Claudius, though she pretends this is simply coincidence. Not buying it. I did happen to notice Claudius's absence from Working Day the same way I noticed Kat's.

They have got to be the strangest pairing ever, but I am here for it.

After spending yesterday with Rafe, falling into an abyss of confusion over him, I've spent the morning hiding out in my room. I drafted up proposals, looked over more spreadsheets, and also worried like it's my job.

Though I'm totally trying to avoid Rafe, I can't keep my mind off him. His warm chocolate and caramel eyes, his wicked smile, his surprising kindness.

I can't remember the last time I laughed as much as I did last night at the festival. At least, once Rafe seemed to realize I wasn't going after Callum, and returned to my side.

I even allowed myself to be dragged into dancing—only because Farrah begged me, and I'm a sucker, even when I know Rafe put her up to it. Farrah's bright eyes and Rafe's hand on my waist made dancing not so dreadful. And I didn't step on Rafe's feet once. Winning!

Kat sweeps into the room, ignoring my questioning look, while Claudius stands ramrod straight by the doorway. I'll have to pump one or both of them for information later. Kat seems oddly hesitant to say anything, which makes me wonder if she has actually fallen for a man for once. She'd be hard-pressed to find someone better—or more opposite to her—than Claudius.

He tries to pretend he's not listening while Kat gives me a little pep talk that doesn't quite do its job.

"It's go-time. You've got this. Start with one truth," she says, holding up a finger. "One true thing. Like that 'two truths and a lie' game, but maybe with two pleasantries and a truth. Tell your mum she looks lovely and ask your dad if he's lost weight. Then—BAM! Tell them you're planning to update the environmental standards for the mining industry. Or that you're going to the ball with Rafe."

Or that I'm falling for Rafe. Hard.

And I have no interest in Callum, contractually or otherwise.

"Just one truth." Kat holds up a finger.

"Right."

"Do we need to play 'Eye of the Tiger' before you go?"

From the doorway, Claudius snorts. "My apologies," he says, turning it into a fake cough. "Are you ready, Your Royal Highness? Your parents are waiting."

Kat gives my cheeks a pat that borders on a slap, and I follow Claudius out into the empty hallway. The burgundy carpets mute our footsteps as we walk, and my thoughts tangle on the worries plaguing me.

The last time we spoke, Mum told me to win Callum at whatever cost, to get him to honor the contract. Now ... I'm not sure of that plan at all. Maybe I'm a little sure, actually. Sure that I do NOT want to marry Callum.

Then there's the little matter of attending the Centennial Ball with Rafe. And the feelings I have for him, which keep growing. They're like mushrooms, popping up where they're unwanted, despite the lack of light or fertilizer.

Fine, this is a terrible analogy. Why do I always have the worst analogies? First sausage, now mushrooms. Rafe is nothing like a fungus. He's actually a wonderful man, not one to be compared to a mushroom. He's a man deserving of both light and fertilizer—there I go again.

The point is: I don't know how my parents will feel about this sudden shift.

My guess? Not great.

What I should do is simply tell them. The way I should also tell them about my plans to open up the palace and bring the copper mining up to environmental codes.

The same way I should have told Callum how I felt years ago to save myself from the embarrassment of this week.

When Claudius speaks in a low tone, it sounds obscenely loud.

"If I may, Your Royal Highness ..."

"You may. Always. I value your opinion, Claudius."

His smile is so fast I almost miss it. "Thank you. I

261

thought I'd ask if you'd like me to have an extra place set at the table this evening."

"An extra place?"

"For the Duke of Weldon."

Why does my heart suddenly race thinking of Rafe? It's as stupid a question as asking why birds suddenly appear whenever someone is near.

"Was he not invited?" I have barely glanced at the itinerary Claudius gave me a few days ago.

"Tonight is simply your parents, the royal family, and one or two extra guests."

How cozy. And awkward.

He clears his throat, and I feel as though he's sending me secret signals. He must mean Brit will be attending. How awkward, considering the negotiations after!

Of course, saying yes will add an extra layer of tension to everything. Why not? The more tension the merrier—isn't that how the old adage goes?

"Please do. And if you're able, I'd love to add Kat as well." I'll take all the moral support I can. With Rafe and Kat, I should be properly bolstered before I have to endure whatever the negotiations are. "Unless the two of you have plans …"

I give Claudius a teasing glance as we reach the doors to my parents' suite. "I don't know Lady Kat's plans, but I'm sure she would be amenable to a special dinner with the royal family."

"Queen Suzette won't mind?" I ask.

Claudius doesn't smile, but his eyes twinkle. "I think a few extra guests will be the least of her worries this evening."

This makes my stomach roll a little, and I press a hand to it. There is no way around it—tonight will be wholly unpleasant. But now I'll have two people firmly in my corner.

"Thank you, Claudius. I know I've asked before, but any chance I could steal you away to work in Viore?"

As he knocks on the door, he gives me the faintest hint of a smile. "Perhaps I could be convinced."

Thank you, Kat.

"We'll revisit this conversation at a later date."

When Mum opens the door of her suite, my lips part, ready to let go of all the truths I've been hoarding like sweets. Then her arms come around me in a hug that's more like a frontal assault, squeezing all the air and motivation out of me.

"Hello, darling." Mum air kisses both of my cheeks and pulls back, studying me with a scrutiny that makes me squirm.

Can she see straight into my soul? Sometimes it feels that way.

I escape her hold. "Hi, Mum."

"Sera!" Dad says, striding over to wrap me in a hug. He's soft and warm and so comforting that I almost start to cry.

When I was six and fell out of a tree in the gardens, I managed not to cry. The wound in my side (a result of a broken-off limb catching me on the way down) ended up needing five stitches, but I kept myself composed all the way until I reached my father and had to tell him what happened. Something about his presence makes me feel safe enough to lose control. At least a little bit.

"Don't worry, Sera," he says, squeezing me tighter. "We'll get all this sorted."

I cling to him until I'm sure I won't become a bubbling mess, then pull back and give him a smile. "Of course we will."

"You look lovely," Mum says. "Callum would be out of his mind to choose that American tart over you."

"She's actually quite nice. Not a tart, just a little … effusive."

Mum sniffs. "And if Callum's parents think they're getting out of this contract unscathed—"

"Mum. Can we forget the contract for a moment?"

She raises her eyebrows. They've been overplucked to the point that now they're like twin punctuation marks. At this moment, they look like angry, misplaced parentheses.

Dad clears his throat. "I'm afraid there's too much on the line for that, Sera."

Mum's eyebrows lower into something like concern, though I think it's more of an attempt to placate me. "Oh, darling. Sit, sit. Let's get some tea and discuss this reasonably."

Which really means … sit down and shut up while we tell you how things are going to be.

Kat told me I need to stop hiding my feelings and stand up for myself, to be honest.

It sounds so much easier than it is, now that I'm trapped in this suite with my parents. The room feels small, though their suite is more than double the size of mine, with a large living area and two bedrooms. Mum and Dad sleep separately because Dad's snores could be heard from a space station.

I take a seat on the sofa across from my parents. A tea service has been set out on the low coffee table between us. I smile, picking up a tiny sandwich, thinking of my picnic with Rafe.

My smile immediately evaporates. Because I still don't know how or what I should tell my parents about Rafe. The cover story—he's my date to the ball? The actual story—he's pretending to be interested in me to make Callum jealous?

Or the unfolding story—I'm developing feelings for the man I couldn't stand just a week ago?

For now, we'll just pretend he doesn't exist. That seems like the best course of action.

"We're meeting with the king and queen in an hour, and I'd like to be prepared," Mum says.

"It's really simple," Dad says. "They're either going to honor the contract or not. Callum will propose or not."

I set my unfinished sandwich down on a plate and take a sip of tea. It's too hot and scalds my tongue. I keep hold of the cup because I need something to do with my hands.

"We can wait a little while on final decisions. Can't we?"

According to Rafe, his plan will make Callum so jealous that he'll dump Brit before then and come running after me. Despite Callum's obvious jealousy, I still question this outcome—whether it will happen at all, and whether this is how I want to have Callum. Oh, and the little matter of DO I EVEN WANT CALLUM?

"Sera, darling, I've been planning your marriage to whatever proper groom for two months from now. Which means we'll need to announce your engagement beforehand, with enough time in between for a few events and interviews."

I'm choosing to ignore how much I hate the way my wedding, which should be a bride's happiest day of their life, feels more like a bullet point on someone else's agenda. And I am not so unlike a game piece on a board, where Mum can simply move me around to the next spot where I need to go.

Is it surprising? No.

Do I hate it? Yes.

Am I really certain my parents' micromanaging will all stop the moment I'm crowned? No.

"Interviews?"

Viore doesn't treat its royals the way many countries do.

We've always been closed off, the castle and its grounds sealed off from public visits. That's one of the first things I intend to change for many reasons, and something I haven't mentioned to my parents, who will surely disapprove. Mum and Dad do the bare minimum as far as public appearances, choosing to treat their jobs as, well, jobs. Ones that don't need public interviews and media darlings.

Which is why Mum can plan a wedding for me and no one will care. I'm no Kate and William. I've only become a topic of gossip since starting uni in London, as the paparazzi were happy and hungry for even a lowly royal like me.

Mum picks up her teacup and blows in it before taking a tiny sip. Never one to burn her tongue on hot tea.

"Yes, interviews. We thought this would be good in light of the somewhat … unflattering press you've received during your time at uni."

The Ice Princess thing. Right. I could point out that my press could have been much, much worse. I could have dated so many men I was labeled a slut. Or worse. This kind of press never hurts men, who are celebrated.

Anyway, I didn't date. I'm sure if I had, I'd have been the Impure Princess or some other rubbish.

Can women win? Sometimes, it doesn't seem as though we can. We're tarts, or we're frigid. Weak or overbearing.

"You know none of those articles are true."

"Of course not," Dad says. "We simply need to reclaim the narrative."

"Wow. I've never heard you talk about the public narrative before," I tell him, raising a brow.

He grumbles, stuffing another small sandwich in his mouth. "It's the blasted PR training we've been going through."

PR training? That's … different. What other things have

my parents been cooking up without telling me? It's on the tip of my tongue to ask, but for the moment, I'd rather not know.

"Right. To go along with this idea of your image, we'd like to paint a happy picture of you and your groom. Which will be much easier if it's Callum."

"As opposed to the Prince of Valdonia."

Or Rafe.

"Yes, exactly. You understand."

"I don't want to marry him. He's an old man." *Who smells of Wensleydale.*

Mum gives me a tight smile. "Right. It's not ideal. But this is the crown we're talking about. The monarchy. The future of our country and kingdom. You did read our dossier?"

I swallow hard and nod.

"So let's hope this dinner goes well."

I'm not holding my breath.

CHAPTER TWENTY-ONE

Rafe

It's clear from the moment I step into the dining room that I'm walking in on some kind of chess match. The kings and queens are at either side of the long table, with the pawns—aka the children and a few other dignitaries or royals like me—in the center.

I'm also clearly not very welcome. Not a surprise given things between me and Callum. The disappointment lies in the fact that Seraf gets a pinched look about her face when she sees me. Immediately, her eyes dart to her parents.

Ah. So she didn't tell them about me. Splendid.

Feigning the confidence that used to be like my second skin, I saunter into the room, formally greeting the king and queen, then Phillip and Callum, who has Brit plastered to his side tonight. At least she gives me a genuine smile. It's easy to smile back because I appreciate the lack of pretense. Also, she's wearing some kind of formal dress made of what looks like bandanas and denim.

I've got to give the woman points for commitment to her point of view, fashion-wise. Even if it's dreadful.

I move next to Seraf's parents, bowing deeply. "Your esteemed Royal Highnesses."

"Rafael." The king gives a curt nod, using my full name, which I hate. It's what my uncle also calls me, and why I started going by Rafe with a hard A, to distance myself as much as possible from my given name.

The king seems to know this too, or maybe I'm misreading the twist of his lips and the hardness in his eyes when he looks at me. Probably not.

It's just as well that Seraf is only faking it with me. Her parents would never approve.

Seraf gives me a tentative smile and seems relieved that I've read the room well enough not to make mention of whatever we are. What are we, exactly? I have no idea.

She looks beautiful tonight, but then I've never seen her look anything less than. If only she knew the way seeing her makes my whole torso practically vibrate with nerves. She probably would never believe it. I'm not sure if that's because she still sees me as the playboy I admittedly was, or because no one has assured her of her beauty. If only this were real, I wouldn't stop telling her.

Might as well start now.

"Princess, you look radiant. As always."

Her parents exchange a look, but I don't let myself linger, only glancing at Seraf quickly enough to see her cheeks turn pink. Good. It's as much as I can do at the moment.

Once again, I'm seated across from her, though not directly. Kat is next to me and a giant floral arrangement all but blocks Seraf from view. There's an empty seat beside her, and if it weren't breaking all kinds of proper protocols and wouldn't get her in trouble, I would steal across the table or even climb underneath it and take the seat.

"Rafe," Kat says through bared teeth. "How lovely to see you."

I eye her, wondering at the change. Just yesterday she looked at me appreciatively. Now it's more like the way a wolf appreciates a lamb.

"Kitty Kat, you seem ... a little murdery tonight."

"I might be. It depends on you and what you do to Seraf."

I feel something hard press into my ribs and realize Kat is threatening me with a butter knife. Good thing they haven't given out steak knives at the table. I raise an eyebrow.

"If you hurt her, so help me—I'll filet you and feed your innards to the sharks."

The knife jabs harder. While it may not be sharp, I will likely bruise from this. "Even without the threat, which I take seriously despite being sorely landlocked, I would never hurt her. Ow!"

The knife jabs harder. "Maybe not on purpose. But she's all sweet and innocent and you're like a predator coming in for the kill. I'll hold you to your words. With force as necessary."

I manage to snatch the knife from Kat, placing it next to her plate but keeping my hand over it for a moment. "You've got nothing to worry about, Kitty Kat. I want to do whatever's best for *her*."

Kat studies me for a moment and seems satisfied enough that I let go of the knife. If the blade weren't dull, though, I'd never have handed it back. Kat would certainly use it if she felt the need.

"Oh, brother," Kat mutters. "If you mean what you said, Sera's going to need your help in just a moment."

One of the servants leads in an older gentleman with a belly drooping over his belt and his hair combed over the top of his balding head in a similar fashion. He's given the seat right beside Seraf.

Even from around the plant, I can see the way she immediately stiffens. Even more when he turns to her with a smile that's decidedly smarmy. His eyes almost immediately dip to her cleavage and I'm ready to throw the floral arrangement at his head.

He looks vaguely familiar, but I can't place him.

"The Prince of Valdonia is our guest this week," King Louis announces. "He's a special friend to our daughter."

Special friend? Seems more like … oh. *No.* They wouldn't … *would* they?

It seems like this prince, who has at least twenty years on Seraf must be her parents' answer to Callum not honoring his end of the contract.

Which means that Seraf is having dinner with the man she loves (who is with someone else), the man she's (sort of) pretending to date (who is secretly in love with her), and the old man her parents are planning to set her up with (who deserves a few rounds with my fists).

There definitely isn't enough wine. I'm not even sure there's enough scotch in the palace for this dinner.

If I didn't care about Serafina, I'd find this whole thing amusing. I'd sit back and watch this play out the way Kat did the night Seraf had the splinters taken out of her bum. But I do care, which means I need to fix this somehow, to ease things for Seraf's sake. The only question is *how*.

I glance over to find Callum looking furious, which seems to be his new resting face. Guess I'm not the only one putting the pieces together. I want to give him a good shake.

He can't not claim Seraf yet not want her claimed by anyone else.

How can he *not* claim her? I'll never understand Callum.

"You need to do something," Kat hisses, jabbing me with the tines of a fork this time. It's a lot more painful than the butter knife, and when I try to snatch it from her, she deftly tucks her hand away.

"Give me a minute to think," I mutter. "Seraf didn't tell her parents about me. She didn't seem to want anyone to know about us."

Whatever us is.

"Plans change."

Yes, but how do I know what she wants? How can I help right now, when there's some ridiculous bush of flowers hiding her from me so I can't even read her expression?

This isn't school where I could toss a note her way, asking: *Do you want me to challenge this geriatric prince to a duel for your hand? Check yes or no.*

Being a royal and attending an all-boys prep school, I never got the chance to pass notes. I'm almost sad to miss the opportunity now.

But tossed notes won't work. I need to attempt to at least *see* Seraf. I read her well when I walked in. Maybe I can do so again now.

"Excuse me," I say, grabbing the arm of a passing servant. I fake a sneeze. "I'm so sorry. My pollen allergy"—fake sneeze—"is being bothered by these arrangements. Would you mind terribly taking them away?"

Sneeze.

"God bless you," the servant says. His eyes shift to the queen. "But I'm not, um, sure ..."

"I'll take care of it right away." Claudius, who is one of the palace staff but definitely not one who should be dealing with floral arrangements, appears, and with a snap of his fingers, has a small team of servants removing all the centerpieces.

Kat looks like she's about to burst out of her seat, and if I'm not mistaken, Claudius winks at her before disappearing in a cloud of flower petals. Queen Suzette looks shocked and confused, opening her mouth to argue when I distract her by raising my hand.

"Sorry—this is my fault."

I fake another sneeze, and beside me, Kat coughs to hide a giggle. She makes an entertaining—if not helpful—sidekick. I can understand why she's Seraf's best friend.

"I'm allergic to—" I stop mid-sentence, realizing I have no idea what kind of flowers these are.

"Hard work?" Callum supplies, with a grin. Brit elbows him.

Good for the American!

"Peonies," Seraf interjects loudly. "And lilies."

Heads swivel in her direction, and I shoot her a wide grin. No one speaks, as though this whole exchange is somehow suspect.

"Pollen, really," I say.

"And those flowers are particularly high in pollen counts."

Seraf smiles back at me, and I don't think I could overstate the excitement I'm feeling at our camaraderie, our shared secret across the table in this room crowded with people.

"Well," Queen Suzette says, her smile relaxing a bit, "I'm sorry. I had no idea."

I shrug. "I don't exactly advertise my allergies."

"Just your conquests," Callum mutters, and Brit appears to kick him under the table.

I could say the same to him, but I prefer not to engage.

No reason I need to stoop to his level. He's only making himself look bad, at least to those within earshot.

I raise my brows at Seraf now that I can see her, tipping my head slightly toward the prince seated across from me. He's using his cloth napkin to shine his silverware, examining his reflection in their surfaces before placing each one back down on the table and lining them up evenly.

Seraf grimaces, then closes her eyes briefly, shaking her head. It gives me time to study her face, the way her long lashes rest on her high cheekbones, the way her mouth looks when it's pursed.

Completely kissable. That's how it looks. And the one kiss I've had was not nearly enough to have tested this theory.

Her wide blue eyes flick open, catching me staring openly. I don't even flinch. Let her know that I'm studying her, let her know how I feel through the way my gaze heats. Her cheeks turn pink again, and I have a new favorite color.

I raise my brows again, lifting my chin in invitation. *Well?*

She bites her lip, and I imagine her saying, *I don't know what to do.*

I run a hand over my jaw, then let it fall to the center of my chest, tapping once. I then tilt my head slightly toward her parents. *You could tell them about me.*

Her brows furrow, and her expression falters. She didn't miss the way her parents looked at me, then. Like I'm the mold ruining an otherwise perfectly good pastry.

I try not to feel disappointed. Of course, her parents wouldn't approve of me if she told them.

I sniff, angling my chin slightly toward the prince. He's moved on from the silverware to fussing with his napkin. Not fussing—he's folding it. Into the shape of a crane, actually. He holds it out to Seraf, who hesitantly takes it.

I've got to hand it to the man. A folded napkin crane is actually kind of sweet. And if he weren't so much older and if Seraf didn't look so off-put by him, maybe the gesture would be romantic. Instead, Seraf forces a smile at him, which seems to give him a shot of boldness, as he lifts her hand to his lips and gives her a dry kiss on the knuckles. His eyes are one hundred percent focused on staring down the front of her dress.

Though I know Seraf didn't want or invite the gesture, hot jealousy rolls through me. I want to take a page out of Kat's book and use my fork as a weapon.

Seraf practically jerks her arm out of the socket pulling it back, trying to regain her composure. The prince doesn't even seem to notice.

At least this has the effect of making Seraf come to her senses. Her wide, pleading eyes meet mine. *Help! S.O.S.!*

I bow my head and lift one hand, palm up. *At your service, Princess.*

Seraf seems to think for a moment, and I watch her carefully, curious as to where she's going to go with this.

Before she can say a word, though, her father clears his throat. "Before dinner, we wanted to make an announcement. A private one, which shall be made public shortly." He glances at Seraf, then nods at the prince, whose crocodile grin widens, revealing a rather large gold tooth.

Right now? Seraf's father is going to announce this right now?

It definitely doesn't look like he has Seraf's approval or even that she's been told. She didn't hide her shock quickly enough. I wonder if his game plan isn't so unlike mine—make Callum jealous and force him to man up.

And just when it seems like her father is about to

announce an imminent engagement, Seraf leaps to her feet and interrupts him.

"This week I agreed to be Rafe's date to the Centennial Ball." The room quiets, but the announcement doesn't seem to have the power she hoped it would. I give her a small shrug.

Her mother openly glares at me while her father just heaves a sigh, like she's wasting his time, and opens his mouth to get on with his announcement.

"And I've also agreed to marry him."

Well, that escalated quickly.

That's when the shouting truly begins.

CHAPTER TWENTY-TWO

Serafina

I'm surprised at the speed with which the insults begin flying.

"This is all because your son can't keep it in his pants!"

That's Mum, ever the beacon of decorum. I drop my head in my hands, but I don't miss the way Brit's cheeks flame. I truly do feel sorry for her now.

Welcome to the royal family! Where we're just as messed up as every regular family. But with crowns and countries at our disposal.

"Perhaps if you'd done a better job managing your own country, you wouldn't be feeling this pressure now," Suzette snaps.

Under the table, a foot finds mine, and I'm about to jerk away when I glance over and see Rafe giving me a look. He's slid down low in his seat, probably so he can reach me. I put my other foot on top of his and give him a watery smile, then shrug, mouthing, *Sorry.*

I just dragged him into this without even asking. Maybe this touch means he doesn't totally hate me. But if he doesn't, he probably will if this continues to escalate.

The queen mother takes all this distraction as a way of procuring a glass of what looks like scotch from a server. I'm not about to cut down on her fun. When I'm that age, if I haven't died of embarrassment first, I hope to be enjoying life's pleasures wherever I can. Even if they come from a bottle and aren't good for my liver.

I'm startled when the Prince of Valdonia stands from beside me, tossing his napkin down on his plate. I realize that the most disappointing part of all of this is that the fight started before we even got to dessert. The stench of Camembert wafts off him.

"I thought we had an agreement," he shouts at my father, then looks down at me. Or, should I say, down my dress. "And you're going to let her marry this fool!"

That's my last straw. I get to my feet, sorry to lose Rafe's touch but needing to—finally—say something. If not for myself, then Rafe. Or both of us.

"At least he looks at my face when I speak, not my breasts!"

Okay. Perhaps this wasn't the best lead-in.

"Hear, hear!" the queen mother says, lifting her glass. "To lovely breasts."

Silence blankets the table. Juliet and Henri stifle giggles in their napkins. My father's face looks like a roasted tomato, ready to burst. Valdonia doesn't look nearly apologetic enough.

This is ridiculous. All of it.

"We can do better than this," I find myself saying. "We *are* better than this."

Phillip stands. "I agree. Serafina, Callum—I'd like both of

280

you to join me for a discussion. As for the rest of you, I would recommend returning to your rooms before you say or do anything else you regret in the morning."

The tone in Phillip's voice doesn't allow for argument, and no one does. Which is odd, because he's not the king. His father sits silent, staring down at his hands. Our mothers are glaring daggers at one another. I'm warding off dark stares from both Callum and the Valdonian prince.

But hey! He's looking at my face, so maybe my little outburst had some impact. His gaze drops to the front of my dress.

I spoke too soon! He learned nothing.

Callum follows Phillip, though he looks as though he'd rather be going to the dungeon. Oh my goodness—Phillip isn't taking us to the dungeon, is he? Yes, Elsinore actually does have a dungeon below the palace. It's more of a dusty, unused historic relic, but still.

I glance at Rafe, who has a dazed look on his face. My stomach dips. I didn't mean to drag him into the middle of this with me. I'm sure the last thing he wants is to be my fiancé, real or fake. Volunteering to help me make Callum jealous as my date to the ball isn't the same as becoming my fake fiancé. Kat told me to tell one truth today, one small truth, and instead I told a massive lie. One that I think is going to wreak massive havoc on not only my life, but Rafe's.

I'd rather drag him from the room and apologize profusely, but Phillip is waiting.

Kat gives me a subtle thumbs-up, which isn't nearly as subtle as she thinks, and I hurry to the door, where Phillip stands, waiting. No sooner has the door closed behind us than shouting resumes.

Phillip sighs deeply and gestures for me to go ahead. "We'll convene in my office," he says.

"I have a better idea," Callum says. "Follow me."

Phillip looks as though he'll argue, but instead, his shoulders dip in resignation and both of us follow his brother. I quickly realize where he's headed, and my chest squeezes with nostalgia even before we exit through a low doorway at the top of a thin staircase.

Callum has led us to the top of the palace wall, an area near the front gates where he and I used to play knights. We once dumped boiling tar over the side—it was actually a bowl full of chocolate sauce—and hit one of the guards posted below, which got us in heaps of trouble.

Unlike earlier in the week, where it was painful to walk in the garden with Callum, saying goodbye to all our memories, I don't feel sad thinking of this. So much has changed in a matter of days.

"Do you think the stains came out of that guard's uniform?" Callum asks, like he's reading my thoughts. Or, at least, sharing the same memory.

"They did not," Phillip says, looking unamused. "Chocolate doesn't easily wash out."

Callum's grin fades and he leans back against the waist-high stone wall, crossing his arms over his chest. "Well, then? Get on with the lecture, big brother."

I feel suddenly out of place, and like I'm walking into a familiar pattern or argument. The tension is thick between these two. How did I not notice it before now? The two of them have never been close, but something else is happening now. What am I missing?

Phillip ignores Callum and turns his attention fully on me. "Father is ill. Liver failure. He may have some time; he may not."

Those words instantly make tears form in my eyes and I press my hands to my cheeks.

"Way to soften the blow, genius," Callum says.

Phillip clears his throat. "I—um. Sorry. I should have worded that better."

"The only way to word it better is to have not said it at all," I say in a strangled voice. I turn away from them both, staring at the jagged line of the mountains, black against the golden pink of the sky where the sun had dropped out of sight.

Liver failure? King James?

Squeezing my eyes closed, I think back to him this week. His wife taking away his drink. Him getting out of breath from shouting. He doesn't look yellow, but then his skin tone did seem darker. I thought it was from sun, but early jaundice doesn't look yellow so much as a change in pigment.

He could die.

Which means ... Phillip and I will both be crowned within the same year. Assuming I get married and Viore can't vote to abolish the monarchy. Young, new rulers of two connected countries. Navigating this could be tricky ... or it could be easy. It also means the line of succession has grown very close to Callum.

I turn back to Phillip. "I'm so sorry."

He nods. "Thank you."

I look at Callum, who won't meet my gaze. I can recognize by the tightness in his jaw that he's hurting, and I wonder how much of his recklessness this year has to do with this knowledge. How long have they known?

"So, the arrangement wouldn't have worked anyway, then?" I can't bring myself to say more, to mention James dying or hinting that Phillip could as well.

Phillip follows my train of thought. "Considering the lines of succession, it wouldn't be prudent. Though not impossible. Our countries—and more than that, our families—have had a close relationship for years. I'm in no mind to see that change. To be clear, the two of you are not planning on honoring the contract and marrying each other?"

Callum meets my eyes, then looks quickly away. "I won't be forced into an arranged marriage."

It doesn't hurt now, when it would have a few days ago. It feels like the period at the end of a sentence. Honestly, it's a relief.

"No," I agree.

Phillip nods. "And ... Rafe?" Phillip raises a dark blond eyebrow. "You'll marry him by your father's birthday?"

Unlikely.

I'm sure Rafe isn't planning on marrying me any more than I planned to announce our engagement tonight. I feel frantic with the need to find Rafe and clear things up. I need to apologize for dragging him into this, to see how we can extricate ourselves from my lie without causing a bigger scandal or any more harm. Unfortunately, this conversation needs to take precedence.

Callum watches me with fire in his gaze. But he doesn't get to react. He doesn't get to care when he made it clear he doesn't want me.

"Don't worry about me," I tell Phillip. "I'll take care of things on that front."

I hope. Honestly, I'm not sure how. I wanted to get out of my father announcing an engagement to the Valdonian prince, not force Rafe into a marriage with me. If Callum feels claustrophobic thinking about taking on a role as King of Viore, of marrying for duty, I can't hold out any hope that Rafe would do so. With us, it's all pretend.

Isn't it?

There's always the option of what Kat said—winning over the people. As the three of us stand there, bathed in awkward tension, sadness, and the falling evening, an idea begins to form.

I straighten my shoulders and imagine Kat or Rafe, cheering me on. "Phillip, I would like to see the relationship between our two countries solidified more officially."

"As would I," Phillip says. "What do you have in mind?"

"If you're amenable, I would like to discuss some changes I plan to enact, and talk about how we can continue to work together in this period of transition."

Callum looks broody, staring over the wall with a clenched jaw, but I have Phillip's full attention. "I'd love to hear it."

With a deep breath and a silent hope that Phillip and I can get on the same page, I share my plan to modernize the copper industry and utilize the barely touched silicon deposits, creating a new line of trade between Viore and Elsinore in the interim.

When I'm finished, the sun has finally dropped so far below the ridge of mountains that it's even harder to read Phillip's expression than usual. The walkway has some inlaid solar lights, but they are dim, mostly to help lead the way out, not show whether the crown prince approves of my idea.

"Do you have something written up to this effect?" Phillip asks.

"Yes." I'm glad I spent the morning working on it while avoiding Rafe.

"Then let's head down to my office and see if we can get something official drawn up tonight. With all the drama, I'd feel better having something solid in place. It's not public knowledge, but I've been sworn in to act and sign on my father's behalf. And though you have a few months to go, I'll consider this a good faith agreement. I'll get our legal team in there as well."

"Thank you," I whisper, feeling a hot joy burst in my heart. It's one thing to have Kat and Rafe tell me my ideas have merit, but to know that Phillip—serious, kingly Phillip —is willing to sign a good faith agreement about this, is more than I could have hoped for.

My parents will be furious that I went around them. Or maybe, just maybe, they'll be proud I'm standing on my own two feet. They wanted me to honor a marriage contract to keep the peace with Elsinore; I have to think this is far better and more practical.

"I also have one more kind of odd request. But an important one regarding legal conservatorship over a particular dukedom."

Callum wears a blank look, but Phillip seems to understand exactly what I'm referring to. He gives me a quick nod.

"Right. It will be a long night. Let's go." With long, sure strides, Phillip heads back for the door.

Callum hangs back, falling into step beside me. "You've changed, Fi."

Maybe. Or maybe you never knew me at all.

I'm not sure he means it as a compliment, but I say "thank you" nonetheless, following Phillip and leaving Callum behind.

CHAPTER TWENTY-THREE

Rafe

I really should have checked my phone screen before answering. I'll blame the mad rush of adrenaline after the whole SURPRISE! YOU'RE ENGAGED TO YOUR DREAM GIRL (who really wants to marry someone else) moment that just happened.

Yes. That really just happened.

I'm pacing the hallway, waiting for Seraf after essentially getting kicked out of the room so the more royal royals can yell at each other.

"I hear congratulations are in order."

Uncle's voice is oil, slick and dark, seeping into the smallest corners and cracks of me. Usually I'm prepared for conversations with him, mentally and emotionally shored up to be impenetrable. Not today.

Today, I'm completely vulnerable, my emotions far too

close to the surface. The barely contained glee in his voice burns through me.

I'm suddenly concrete tossed into the sea, sinking hard and sinking fast. Pressure builds in my chest as I go down, and darkness threatens to overwhelm. I'm striding down the hall without purpose, needing somewhere dark, somewhere private.

I could just hang up, but given everything that's just happened, I won't be able to put him off for long.

"How did you know?"

It's a dumb question, but right now, that's the extent of my brain function.

Uncle always knows *everything*. Seraf has teased me about knowing so many things and it's true, I do, but only because information is currency with Uncle. And the more I'm armed with on my own, the less he can hold things over me, something important when he already holds so much.

"This little thing called the internet."

My gut twists. "It's already out in front of the public?"

"We can thank one of the Elsinorian princesses. Leave it to teens. They can't keep their mouths shut. Tell one high schooler and suddenly, the whole world knows."

I've made my way back to my room on autopilot, and I lock the door behind me, falling into an armchair that is nowhere near as comfortable as it looks, and it doesn't look comfortable.

I wonder if they know yet. If the room full of shouting and accusations, kings and queens whose rooks and bishops and knights aren't behaving have paused long enough to check their phones. Maybe they've gotten alerts on their phones, or perhaps their PR person is busting in to tell them that all this got a little more—okay, a LOT more complicated.

I had been prepared to wait for Seraf to come out so we

could talk about how to extricate ourselves from her lie. I mean, for ME, marrying Seraf is what I wanted. But this is not how I wanted it to happen, being surprised and announcing it in the middle of a dinner party with two royal families who have a vested interest in her marrying someone else. I also would kind of like an engagement with the woman I love to be real and not fake.

You know, *small things*.

Then there's the matter of my uncle, who poisons everything he touches. And his hands are all over this, all over me.

Right now, he thinks I'm doing what he's asked of me, being the obedient little boy he tried to make me into through force and manipulation.

But that's not what happened. I never planned to go along with what he wanted me to do. It just so happens that Seraf announcing our engagement is the exact thing most likely to please Uncle.

My desire *happens* to align with his goals.

And that's exactly why I need to get out of this fake engagement as soon as possible.

"When I get in tomorrow, you'll have to tell me how you pulled this off. I'll be honest—I didn't think you could. But I'm so pleased. The princess must be a much bigger fool than I even thought."

My fists clench and all my muscles tighten with the need to defend Seraf. But I know better than to engage in a war with my uncle.

I have to tell Seraf. I have to stop this. But now that our "engagement" is public knowledge, it's going to be far more complicated to get UN-engaged.

"It's not what you think," I tell Uncle.

"Frankly, I don't really care what it is. You've managed to keep her from solidifying the union with Elsinore. That's step one. Whether you marry her or walk away the minute before the time expires so she'll lose the monarchy, I'm pleased. Just a few more months of the ruse ..."

I hang up the phone, powering it off before I throw it against the wall. It thuds against the plaster, but it's not even satisfying because I know it didn't break. I have one of those almost indestructible cases.

I want someone to love me for me, she'd said.

Thinking about those words right now guts me. The thing is—I do love Seraf for Seraf. But she'll never believe me. Not now.

I'd hoped to speak with her about this, to untangle this thing that got a whole lot more complicated the moment she made her grand announcement. And God, for a few seconds, I let myself pretend, to imagine what it would be like to be engaged to Seraf, to be the one she chose.

I shoved all thoughts of Uncle to the back of my mind and just focused on her—beautiful, brilliant Seraf. But she could never love me, not really. I've known for years that it was stupid to hope. Even if she did, I'm not the kind of man who deserves her.

And with thoughts just like that, my brief moment of imagining ended. Because I'm not a part of her fairy-tale ending. I'm just the stand-in for the man she really wants, or maybe just a shield from the man whom she doesn't.

But what if? What if I could be the kind of man worthy of standing by Seraf's side, of sharing her bed? I'm not a little orphaned boy, shamed by his uncle. I'm not a failure or a playboy. The things I've done in my past, the mistakes I've made don't need to define me. Isn't that what the last two years of therapy have helped me understand?

I could be worthy of her. I would give up everything for her. If she really needed me to marry her to keep the crown and to prevent her from marrying the lecherous Prince of Valdonia, I would.

I would do anything for her. Including marrying her when she sees it as duty. I'd have a lifetime to convince her it's love. To win her over.

Only two glaring problems with this: first, this engagement isn't real. And second, I need to somehow untangle myself from my uncle's plans once and for all.

CHAPTER TWENTY-FOUR

Serafina

"I'm so SO sorry, Rafe."

I don't mind not being able to look in his eyes while apologizing—I'm not sure I could stand it—but having him pressed up against me isn't helping. I'm much too aware of his warm, solid chest pressed to my back as a photographer snaps away.

Because the morning after announcing a fake engagement, the obvious thing to do is take engagement photographs, right?

My mother said—after consulting the new PR firm she and Dad hired—that we won't officially confirm or deny the rumors started by Juliet last night. But we will take engagement photos.

"Tilt your head a little bit more to the right," the photographer orders.

I shift slightly, which only puts my cheek closer to Rafe's

body. I try to hold my breath because he smells so dang good. And every hit I take of his woodsy scent, my brain seems to get more and more scrambled.

The photographer clicks away. "Good."

No, it's bad. All of it. Very, very, VERY bad.

The worst part? I'm not sure how I'm going to get me—and more importantly, Rafe—out of this mess I've made. The Duke of Weldon has been nothing but kind and helpful—and, okay, yes, flirtatious—this week, and what did I do? I took our little ruse and turned it into some full-on con job.

Rafe: Be my date and I'll pretend to like you to make Callum jealous.

Me: I'm not sure … but I guess we can try it?

Also me: And now let's pretend we're getting MARRIED!

Perhaps this is some kind of mental break. I feel like there must be a condition, like royal insanity. Kat didn't seem to think so when I asked her, and when I forced her to google it, she found nothing. I think maybe we could find information on the dark web? I told her to ask Claudius, and she only rolled her eyes.

I've spent the night pacing and agonizing, which makes this early morning engagement photo shoot far from ideal. Especially considering I wasn't able to find Rafe last night to speak with him about all of this.

After I got through being shouted at by my parents and listened to them shouting back and forth with Callum's family, Rafe had simply vanished. Claudius, after arriving to give me an updated itinerary of the next few days—which now includes things like engagement photo shoots and wedding planning business—told me where Rafe was staying. Only, he wasn't there. Or anywhere.

And given the fact that Rafe and I never exchanged phone numbers, I showed up this morning, half expecting Rafe to have already vacated Elsinore completely. I mean, that seems like it would fit his modus operandi. He's never settled for more than five minutes with a woman. Getting engaged to me wasn't part of his plan.

Especially now that my parents, unhappy as they are, seem fully committed to making this happen for real. I'm not sure if it's some kind of passive-aggressive punishment, if they think this will make Callum jealous enough to break it off with Brit, or if they're simply desperate enough to accept a man they don't even like because I need a groom.

But when I walked out to the gardens, where the photographer had set everything up in the gorgeous, glowy morning light, Rafe was already here, looking even more handsome than usual in a dark suit, white shirt, and tie the royal blue of Viore's flag and the exact color of my dress.

He broke into a smile, and for a moment I could almost *believe* the way he was looking at me—like none of this was pretend at all. It made my heart trip over itself, which happened right before I actually tripped. If Rafe hadn't caught me with those big, strong hands currently on my waist, I would be taking photos with skinned knees and palms.

Rafe chuckles, and I feel the vibration of it deeply, as though the sound has gone straight to my bones. If he weren't behind me, stabilizing me, I'd liquify into a puddle. Then again, it's the mere fact that he's standing so close and seems to somehow be all around me, even taking up the tiny air molecules I'm breathing in, that I am feeling liquified at all.

"No need for apologies, Angel."

"Are you kidding? I've dragged you into this and made a huge mess of things."

"I wouldn't say dragged," Rafe says, and he's leaning so close that his breath is a caress on my cheek.

My eyelids flutter closed.

"Eyes open, please!" the photographer barks.

The man is hard to take seriously, though he clearly takes himself this way. He looks like a snowman, round and dressed all in white, and with an inexplicably orangey-red tint to his nose—which also is long and thin and a little carrot-like. Rafe whispered earlier, "He looks like Frosty the Snowman." With his dark, beady eyes, and black hat, I can't unsee this image.

The man has also been incredibly cold almost to the point of rudeness, which only makes me more uncomfortable.

"Don't apologize, Angel. You don't want our engagement photos to scream, 'They're actually in the middle of an argument,' do you?"

Rafe is teasing. The slight tickle of his fingers at my waist confirms this, though I could tell from his tone.

This isn't an argument, but I almost wish it were. Rafe has been far too accommodating about all this. And by *all of this*, I mean the ridiculousness of the last twelve hours, when I convinced my mum and dad that Rafe and I are, in fact, engaged.

Which, to be clear, we are not. Despite the hard reality of taking wedding photos.

"Could you angle your bodies just slightly to the right?" the photographer asks, waving a hand.

Angle your bodies.

It should sound like a simple direction from a photographer. But the command has me wanting to do a whole other kind of angling. One I have zero experience in.

Rafe's hands tighten on my waist, flooding me with an unwanted heat. His breath on my cheek only makes it worse.

I'm sweating almost as much underneath this dress as I did with the curtain dress.

That feels like *ages* ago. The day I talked with Callum and part of my heart shriveled up and died. Dancing with him, then dancing with Rafe. Falling through the table. The k-i-s-s. Starting this whole charade that somehow turned from flirtation and a date to the ball to … this.

That was a different Serafina, I realize, because thinking back on the events with Callum this last week, there's no trace of the ache. Have I been pushed into numbness by the overwhelm of recent events, or do I actually not care anymore? The thought is jarring.

"Better. Just hold it."

The photographer clicks away, the camera shutter obscenely loud as I realize I have no idea what expression I'm wearing. I seem to have lost my ability to control my face. Or control *anything* for that matter.

This isn't how I imagined my engagement playing out. Not just the how, but the *who*. Or whom? Whatever. Proper grammar can go hang itself.

Rafe's fingertips flutter on my waist, rising just slightly to my ribs. My breath hitches, and the photographer clicks away.

"Rafe," I warn, using my elbows to keep his hands from rising any higher while still trying to maintain our happy-couple pose.

"Darling," he replies, nuzzling my neck.

I jerk away, and Frosty's sigh is bone-weary, like we're his errant children. Emphasis on the errant.

"Sorry," Rafe says, looking anything but contrite.

"Let's try a few poses on the pathway," Frosty orders, gesturing to where he wants us. "Holding hands and walking toward me, looking at each other."

We comply, Rafe slipping his hand casually in mine, but Frosty complains about our expressions. Too surly—me, and too smug—Rafe.

"We're rubbish at this," Rafe mutters to me with a look that, if anything, is more smug. He doesn't seem to mind in the least.

I think we're pretty much on par for two people pretending to be engaged and in love.

"Speak for yourself." I shoot him a smile, and the smugness softens into something sweeter.

Click click click click.

"Not terrible," Frosty says.

Rafe raises his brows and mutters through a smile, "Did you hear that? We've upgraded to *not terrible*."

Frosty studies our surroundings for a moment before his gaze lands back on us. "Let's try over there, by the climbing vines." He talks us through the next pose, which is more formal, standing side by side, my hand resting in the crook of Rafe's arm.

The pose might be stiff, but Rafe keeps flexing his bicep, tapping out a rhythm on the back of my hand, clearly trying to get a laugh out of me.

"You're incorrigible," I tell him through my best fake smile.

"Gesundheit."

I barely stifle a giggle, which has Frosty grumbling again. But I realize that Rafe's flirtations have helped me relax. At least, a little. It doesn't do anything to help solve the looming problem in front of us though.

Before this, it was like he and Callum were playing a game where I felt like a bystander unsure who to cheer for. Or maybe I was more like the ball or the prize or something.

Now, Rafe and I are playing a game, and I don't know the rules, only that I'm losing.

Losing control, losing focus, and maybe losing a piece of myself.

Despite Callum's warnings over the years and recently and even with my own misgivings, Rafe seems to be chipping away at my resistance. The fact that I don't mind the way I should sets off warning bells.

And now, because of my big mouth and my unwillingness to be paired with the Prince of Valdonia, who was so angry he flew home last night with one last sneery/leery look at me, now I can't get the space I need from Rafe to clear my head.

A giant yawn overtakes me, and the photographer sighs, pulling the camera down to glance back through the photos on the screen. Rafe steps back, giving me the room I was just craving. Only, I miss his touch, his closeness, his warmth.

"Sorry," I mumble.

The ridiculously early morning light is perfect for photographs in the rose garden, but I have been stifling yawns in between shots. Probably in some of them as well.

Rafe chuckles and moves closer. His mouth is far too close to my ear, and I shiver. In response, he seems to drag me even closer. We yawn in unison, then both laugh.

It was a late night. But not for the reasons the photographer—or anyone else—might think. After my rash pronouncement, dinner dissolved into what can only be described as proper chaos. My parents, trying to save face in front of not only the Valdonian prince but also Callum's parents, did their best to pretend like they were thrilled about this.

James and Suzette, who still seem to be somewhere between wanting Callum to comply and not wanting to seem like they're breaking the contract, made a series of passive-aggressive comments which led to an out-and-out shouting match with my parents about feudal laws.

Clearly, no one cares about feudal laws.

What they care about is preserving the monarchy and the tenuous relationship between our two countries.

In a panic, realizing what Dad was about to announce—namely, that they were selling me off to Valdonia—I had done the only thing I could think to do. It was not a well-thought-out (or at-ALL-thought-out) plan. Which leaves me wondering what exactly my exit strategy is. At this point, I'm in a nose-diving plane, realizing there are no parachutes.

"Smile like you mean it, Angel. Not like you're having your teeth pulled." Rafe's nose brushes my hair, making me shiver.

His squeezing hand at my waist becomes more of a tickle, and I can't hold back my laughter.

Click. Click click click.

"Rafe," I sputter, spinning a little in his arms to glare.

But it's hard to be mad when he's beaming down at me, his eyes holding an affection that looks a little too genuine. He spins me the rest of the way, turning me in his arms like I'm simply putty. Maybe I am. Because I'm having a hard time right now drawing a line between what's real and what's fake.

Especially now that we're ENGAGED.

Rafe, being the good sport that he apparently is, has gone along with this completely. TOO completely? He hasn't asked so much as a question. Not that there's been time for it. There was a flurry of activity—and a good bit of shouting—and now, the next morning, we're having official photographs taken.

Which ... is making this seem a lot more permanent than

I had ever planned for it to be. Again, not that I planned any of this.

I bite my lip, trying to hold back the flood of emotion that's currently trying to work its way from my chest up through my face.

"That's better," Rafe murmurs, lifting one hand to stroke my cheek.

Click click click.

"What are we doing?" I ask while maintaining a semblance of a smile.

"We're taking engagement photos. This is something customary when announcing an engagement, royal or otherwise."

"Typically, fake engagements don't require photos."

Rafe's smile falters for a moment. "I wouldn't know. I've never been engaged."

"*Fake* engaged."

"A mere matter of semantics, Angel."

Despite my strict instructions for my heart to beat at normal speed, it goes off the rails like a runaway freight train. Panic? Excitement? I'm not even sure.

"Rafe," I protest, but he silences me with a look, as though his eyes carry paralyzing darts, leaving me unable to move.

He leans close, his lips brushing my cheek and sending a flurry of tremors through my limbs.

Click click click.

"Relax, Seraf."

"How can I relax?! I forced you into this without even asking you, and now my parents and the whole world think it's real! We're getting flipping engagement photos taken, Rafe."

He chuckles again, the sound making goose bumps appear on my bare arms. "I am aware of what we're doing."

"Less talking! More smiling!" Frosty says.

I'd love to do less smiling and more glaring at the man, but I manage to pull my face together. Somewhat.

"How can you be so calm? We have to talk about this! We have to make a plan! We need to figure out—"

"Shh."

It's not the sound that makes my lips stop moving, but the way Rafe nuzzles my cheek that renders my vocal cords incapable of movement.

"Normally, I would think it rude to interrupt a woman speaking her mind," Rafe says, and he leans so close his lips brush my temple. "Especially a princess. But I want you to take a breath. Can you do that?"

I manage to nod.

"Would you like to talk right now?" he asks, and I nod again.

Frosty makes a noise somewhere between grunt and a growl. "If you two are going to waste my time by being all over each other—"

"Excuse me," Rafe snaps, and I can feel the way his whole body stiffens. I'm imagining solider Rafe again. I rather liked that look on him, and I like the version in front of me right now.

"Show some respect," he snaps. "I think you're forgetting that you are speaking to the Princess of Viore. Now, why don't you give us a moment, and take that time to think very carefully about how you speak to my fiancée. I won't tolerate this disrespect again."

Frosty melts a little under Rafe's rebuke, which, to be honest, really did something for me. When he called me his fiancée, a little shudder of desire went through me.

Which I need to quell immediately. Because Rafe is not my actual fiancé but a fake one. He's a friend. A flirty friend. One who seems to have a disastrous impact on my body, but I don't have to let my body rule me. I'm the Ice Princess.

It's just … Rafe's heat seems to have melted the Ice Princess away. I'm not sure what's left of me underneath.

I'm not the kind of person who wants to be rescued—talk about princess clichés!—but that display hit me like a heat wave.

"Now," Rafe says, after Frosty mumbles an apology and wanders off, messing with his camera settings, "we have at least a few minutes. Let's talk."

His hands tighten on my waist, his eyes skimming over my face, as though trying to read my thoughts before they hit my lips. I wish him luck, because I seem to have lost the ability to think altogether.

"Angel?"

I stare into his eyes. They are warm, melted caramel. I swallow. "It was wrong of me to drag you into this. My dad seemed ready to marry me off to that Valdonian prince—"

"Not happening," Rafe says, a firm set to his jaw. He's got that same look from moments ago, where he's all fierce and unyielding. I wish I could fan my face without being obvious about it.

Relief washes over me at his words. I get the sense that he really would do whatever necessary to keep me from being forced into a marriage.

Including marrying me? I shove that thought away.

"I can't marry that man. I just panicked and didn't think this through. I'm so sorry I used you, that you're stuck in this with me. I'll figure something out."

Tears fill my eyes, and I tilt my head back, blinking up at the sky in hopes they won't spill over and ruin my makeup.

Rafe's strong hands are impossibly gentle on my cheeks. He guides my face, tilting it down until we're almost nose to nose. My heart, which is too stupid to realize the serious nature of our conversation, takes off like a wild horse.

"Do you still want Callum?"

The words are ice water, poured over top of me, drenching and icy.

This was not a question I was expecting. And I'm startled into silence when I realize that my gut reaction was a resounding *no*. I've seen a different side of Callum this week, just as I have with Rafe. To be honest, I've also seen a different side of myself, or maybe I'm finally seeing myself through a clear lens.

When I'm with Callum, I'm embarrassed at how starry-eyed I become, how soft, how willing to follow him around like a puppy, to let him set the tone. I disappear like I'm his shadow, not a singular person on my own standing beside him.

With Rafe, I have no trouble speaking my mind, having opinions—strong ones, and voicing them unapologetically. We fight, we tease, we talk without inhibitions. Being around him is like I've been taken off mute and instead dialed up to a ten. With Rafe, I am Serafina at full volume.

I'm brighter, stronger, *more*. And he helps draw that out of me by giving me the space to be unapologetically ME. I never had that with Callum, not even close. I was too worried about winning him over, about what he wanted, what he thought.

Oh my stars—I think I'm falling in love with Rafe.

The realization makes my cheeks flame hot and my breath lodges somewhere behind my ribs. I study Rafe's face, seeing him in a whole new light.

But as I'm watching, his expression shifts. The warmth

fades, and he blinks a few times, clearing his throat. His hands fall from my cheeks and instantly I want them back. I want to grab his hands, to thank him for giving me room to be myself, for being my anchor in the midst of this stormy week. But the words are stuck in my throat.

Hurt flashes across Rafe's face, fast and intense as lightning—there and gone so fast I wonder if I really saw it.

"Rafe, I ..." My words fade because this is all too big, it's all too much, too uncertain.

"I understand," he says, with a smile that is completely humorless.

He doesn't, but I can't manage to even protest. How can I explain it to him, when I can hardly understand what I'm feeling myself?

Frosty returns with the worst timing ever and has a modicum more politeness in his tone. "Let's move over in front of the rosebushes," he says, and Rafe strides away, not waiting for me. His turned back speaks volumes and makes regret rise like bile in my throat.

But why should Rafe be hurt? This hasn't ever been about me or his interest in me. What man interested in a woman tries to help play matchmaker with another man?

Actually, the idea sounds a lot like the plot of a movie Kat and I watched a few months ago. Which only cements the fact that it cannot be real. Rafe isn't hurt because he doesn't feel that way for me.

Does he?

Maybe it's unfair, but the tiny whisper of a question in my mind makes me want to know how Rafe feels. I may not be willing or ready to put out my own feelings yet, but maybe if I knew his for sure ...

Frosty comes and arranges us in a different pose, facing each other this time. I'm pretty sure he's copying the exact poses and setups that William and Kate and Harry and Megan used. If I'm right, next up, Frosty will ask Rafe to sit down on a stone wall or step and have me sit in front of him, elbow on Rafe's thigh, our heads tilted together.

Oh—because I'm a princess I can't be just as obsessed with the British royals' lives? Ha!

We're stiffer than we were before our conversation, and Rafe seems to be holding himself back from me. We're touching, hands on one another's forearms, my cheek almost pressed into his chest, but it's like a veil hangs between us. I can tell by Frosty's heavy sighs that he isn't happy. They're our photos, but I suppose he'll get credit for taking them, so it won't look good for him either if we look like we actually are faking our fake engagement.

"You were all over each other. Now you're both a bit stiff. I'm not reading any emotion in your body language. How about we sweeten things with a kiss?"

"What?" Rafe practically chokes out that single syllable, his eyes cutting to me and then quickly away. "I don't, um …"

I can hardly believe it, but Rafe's cheeks have flushed, and there's something about his reaction that emboldens me. The photographer's suggestion planted a seed of an idea in my brain and Rafe's unexpected reaction dumped a bucket of fertilizer on it. Now there's a full-on beanstalk shooting up into the clouds.

I'm transfixed by the upward tilt of Rafe's mouth, the tiny white scar threaded upward near the top of that perfect cupid's bow lip. I'm suddenly ravenous for knowledge. Where did the scar come from? When did he get it? What would his lips feel like on mine?

He clears his throat, breaking through what I realize is my own hazy, heated gaze. "Seraf? Are you with me?"

How could I be anywhere else? The idea is absurd. I nod slowly, feeling a flush steadily rising like a thermometer up my body, starting at my chest, up over my collarbone, my neck, and finally hitting my face full force in a way that I know Rafe can't miss.

"We, um, don't need to do something just because someone else says—"

I silence Rafe by rising on my toes and pressing my lips to his.

I'm driven by need: a need to know how his lips feel on mine for longer than a second, a need to know how he will respond to me, a need to know if there is any chance that this could somehow all be real.

But the moment our mouths meet, panic overwhelms me.

What am I doing?

I pull back, even as my blood rushes through me like a tide crashing toward Rafe. His hands on my arms tighten, like he's going to hold me there against his mouth, but then release.

The rising flush of my desire has cooled into extreme embarrassment. I'm sure it's immediately obvious that I have zero experience in the kissing—or *anything*—department. It was clumsy, my lips barely brushing over Rafe's full bottom lip. I think my teeth may have grazed him too.

That lame kiss probably reminded him of the kinds of women he dates. Ones with loads of confidence and the experience I lack so thoroughly. If he had any feelings for me, I'm sure they just shriveled up and died.

What was I thinking?

And that's the problem—I wasn't thinking. I was *feeling*. I've let myself be taken over by Rafe.

Didn't I tell myself days ago that I wouldn't succumb to

his charms the way so many other women have? I was so foolish to think that this could be something huge like *love*.

Only, when I dare glance up at Rafe to see his reaction, hoping for anything but one of his smirking, Cheshire grins, I'm stunned by his expression.

His face is completely slack, lips parted, his cheeks flushed a color that probably rivals my own. He's blinking as though trying to clear something from his vision, his gaze darting between my lips and my eyes, finally settling on the latter.

"Seraf," he whispers. "You kissed me."

"I'm sorry."

"*Why?* Why on earth would you feel the need to apologize?"

"Because I shouldn't have, and it was so … I'm so …"

"Gloriously perfect," he says, and my mouth snaps shut.

Click click click click.

Oh, stars. The photographer probably caught this awkward kiss. I'll have to ask Kat to take a croquet mallet to his camera.

Rafe is still staring at me with a wonder that doesn't make sense. It was hardly a kiss, more like a fumbling brush with the real thing. And yet, I felt something too, before the panic overtook me. It's hard to put into words what I felt as our mouths met, even imperfectly as they did. It was like something turned a key in a door or maybe in the starter of a car.

Something opened, something clicked, something began.

No, no, no. Mustn't romanticize something when I have so little experience. Rafe might look stunned, but probably because this is all supposed to be fake.

The look of wonder turns to desire, and suddenly, it's as

though an invisible force is tugging us back together. I'm helpless to stop it. I wouldn't want to even if I could.

Rafe bends to meet me, his lips parted, eyes no longer a warm caramel but a roaring fire of hot, dark coal. It ignites something in me, heating my blood until it's boiling, yearning, reaching. My eyes droop closed, and Rafe's breath is featherlight on my lips. I'm about to explode from wanting, about to grab him by the lapels of his jacket and—

"What's going on here?"

Mum's voice is a bucket of ice dumped over my head, and I try to leap away from Rafe like a teenager who's been caught by her parents. Which, I guess I have. Minus the teenaged part. I'm doing nothing wrong but can't help the hot embarrassment or the way I stiffen in Mum's presence, pulling away from Rafe.

She glares, and I remind myself that I'm an adult. And that, as far as she knows, Rafe is my fiancé.

"We're taking the engagement photos, Mum."

As scheduled, which Claudius let me know about last night. Apparently, he had a whole new agenda drawn up and delivered by eleven p.m. last night. He's very good. I wonder if I could steal him and bring him to Viore with me to handle my schedule there?

"Your engagement photos," Mum says, as though she's trying to get herself to believe the reality clearly in front of her.

At least, if we're going with the story that Rafe is actually my fiancé. Is he? Fake or real?

What do I want to be the true story?

Last night, I fell asleep thinking of Rafe. I woke this morning with his face in my mind. Rafe is the one I want.

Not Callum.

I'm not interested in making Callum jealous, of winning him from Brit.

Yes, there's the smallest pinch when I think of all our history, our friendship, and the hopes I once had. But I don't have regrets. I feel no sadness, no sense of loss. Maybe a misty nostalgia, but nothing more.

Mum is practically invading our space by the time I remember she's there. With a firm hand, she guides me and Rafe apart. He humbly nods, letting her separate us.

"Now," Mum says, eyeing us both with the kind of look I've seen her give the terrors, "let's remember that this is a royal engagement photo shoot. Not some kind of spread for *People* magazine."

She scoffs at that idea, then rearranges us. And maybe because I'm still completely in shock from my terrible kiss attempt and the resulting half-finished conversation, I let her arrange us in more formal poses for the kinds of photographs expected of the Ice Princess, despite the fact that I'm becoming totally thawed out.

CHAPTER TWENTY-FIVE

Rafe

I don't need to be nervous. Why am I nervous? I've spent all week with Seraf. She's not just some date, not just some woman I've been dating or am attracted to or am trying to win over. She's become a friend.

And maybe therein lies the nervous rub.

Because I have no idea what I'm doing or how to do it. My uncle wants me to win Seraf over for reasons yet unknown. I've told Seraf I'm helping her win Callum, all while trying to show her why I'm a viable option as well, even if not the better choice. I'm the choice I wish she'd make.

I turn the ring over in my fingers.

THE ring. My mother's ring.

She never took it off. When Uncle gave it to me, I think he intended it to hurt, and hurt it did.

"I thought you might want to have this," he said, dropping the ring in my palm like it was some trinket, something insignificant.

They'd been gone a year by that point, and he should have given it to me sooner. But he didn't. I know it was intentional. A way to pick at the half-healed wound I was so desperately trying to let heal. My fingers closed around it, protecting it from him, but also protecting me from it. I shoved it in the back of a drawer—not the underwear drawer, which is always the place robbers look first. I kept it there for years, and when my therapist suggested keeping a grounding object with me, it's the first thing that came to mind.

It's not like I thought I'd be getting engaged to Seraf, real or fake. But when she stood up at the dinner and announced our engagement, my hand slid into my pocket, touching the stone. I've been wanting to give it to her ever since.

And now, I'm going to.

I should have done it right away. But things were so crazy immediately after. I planned to when we took our photographs, but she looked so beautiful when she arrived that I was momentarily stunned and forgot. Then she kissed me, and it wasn't until a few hours later I even remembered my own name, much less the ring in my pocket.

Tonight feels riskier now, because it's THE moment. The ball.

I know she was supposed to get engaged tonight, or at least make that announcement of an engagement with Callum. And no matter what she says about not caring, I know this all has weighed on her. All of it. Her parents' expectations, the strife between the kingdoms, and Callum parading Brit around in front of her, even while he's a bonfire of jealousy at the sight of Seraf with me.

What if he does want her? What if she still wants him? One moment, I think the attraction is mutual. Seraf looks at me in a way that no other woman ever has. She looks at me the way I've always wanted her to. And the next ... she can't tell me if she still wants Callum.

I close my eyes for a moment, pressing the pad of my thumb into the sapphire stone. If she still wants him and he's finally come to his senses, I'll walk away.

Yes, I'd be miserable--hating myself, hating him, but if that's what Seraf wants, it's what she'll have. I'll not stand in the way of her happiness if she wants to have it with Callum.

As much as I can't stand the man, do I really think I'm better? That I'm worthy of her?

If this week is all I'll have of Seraf, it's been a good week. The best of my life. I've seen her smile. I've *made* her smile, even laugh this week. If nothing else, I know she no longer sees me as the insufferable Royal Rogue she saw me as before. It almost makes me believe I could be something more. She sees the man I want to be, the man I'm trying to be. And if Seraf sees it, maybe I can too.

I slide my finger through the ring, feeling the smooth inside of the platinum band. Is it possible that I've won her over, or that I still could?

I'd love to think so. I'd love to think I have a chance.

"Ready for your big night?"

The tiny hairs at the nape of my neck stiffen in alert like guard dogs as my uncle's voice reaches me. I turn, and there he is, in my private room, leaning against the wall.

"How did you get in here?"

"I go where I please," he says, that snake smile spreading over his lips.

It would make sense, now that I'm older, to be able to look him in the eyes. Two years' worth of therapy should have at least left me with the boldness, the confidence, the surety that I don't need to cower around my uncle.

And yet.

Two years of therapy can't simply override more than ten years of systemic emotional abuse and gaslighting. His voice, his eyes, his smell make me revert back to the scared, grieving little boy I was when my parents died and I was left in his care.

It's a struggle even now to remind myself of the true things. Uncle is an abuser, even if he never left physical scars. He can't hurt me any longer. Even though he still wields so much authority over certain aspects of my life.

He doesn't have power over me, I remind myself.

"I'd like you to leave."

He sits down in the nearest chair, crossing his legs and raising one eyebrow. "And I'd like your duchy. Oh! That's right. I already control it."

Yes, but you don't control me.

I slide my hands into my pockets, finding the ring and pressing gently, a reminder grounding me in the truth.

"I need to go."

"What's the rush? The ball isn't for a few hours. I thought we could hang out. Chat. Catch up, for old times' sake. Discuss your recent engagement and the next stage of our plan."

I'm not about to tell him there is no more plan, or at least, that I'm not on board. Getting him up in arms before a public event would end badly, I'm sure.

"No, thanks." I head for the door.

I pause in the doorway, holding the frame for support. Turning back to him, I ask, "Is there even a reason why you're doing this?"

The smile he gives me is the one that used to haunt me. Now, it just makes me angry. "Is this the part where you expect the villain to do the whole monologuing bit, explaining the whys and hows of his devious plan?"

No. Because he's not the villain opposite the hero. He's just a sad, lonely man.

I shrug.

"Maybe I just like seeing people suffer."

That, I can believe. Maybe there's more to his involvement. It wouldn't surprise me if there's some financial reason he wants to weaken the relationship between Elsinore and Viore. But he might simply enjoy stirring the pot, setting chaos in motion. Or, as he said, watching people suffer.

I nod. "Feel free to enjoy the room and let yourself out whenever you like. There's nothing here to snoop through, I'm afraid. Nothing that would interest you, anyway."

The hunger in his eyes intensifies, and I know that he'll take the bait and spend the next bit of time in my room, scouring through my things, looking for anything important.

And he'll find things, small clues I've left. Half-written notes, scratched out and balled up in the rubbish bin. A map I printed out, along with a spreadsheet I created with just numbers and abbreviations that mean absolutely nothing. I felt a little silly doing all of it. Now, it seems like time well spent.

I didn't know when he would arrive, only that he would, and I wanted to have a fake game of clue to leave him. A room full of red herrings. It's hard to keep the smile off my face as I imagine him trying to make sense of it all.

"I'll see you at the ball," he says, trying to sound casual. I imagine that the moment he hears my footsteps disappear down the hall, he'll be turning everything upside down.

But the important thing, I think as I stride down the hall, is that he'll be preoccupied for at least an hour or two. Long enough for me to do what I need to before seeing Seraf.

Nothing says Strong, Confident Man like standing outside a room, not knocking for five minutes while sweating profusely. It shouldn't be difficult to knock on Phillip's office door. It's just a door. He's just a crown prince whose younger brother (and my own past reputation) has probably poisoned him against me. Knocking is a simple act, the rapping of knuckles against a wooden surface. Children can do it. I can do it.

"You can do it," I whisper to myself, lifting my hand.

"I wouldn't be too sure if I were you."

Callum. In my head, his name is said like a curse word, or like the way they always said *Newman!* in the reruns of that American show, *Seinfeld.*

I force a grin as Callum steps forward, edging me back, and raps his knuckles twice on Phillip's office door. He gives me a gloating look as he begins to turn the knob.

"See? It's really not so hard. Maybe with a little practice, you can learn to knock on doors."

Really, I don't know how Seraf tolerates this man. Not just tolerates but WANTS this man. Or ... wanted? I'm hoping it's that. Her kiss today, though brief, seemed to tell me one thing. Her silence when I asked how she felt about Callum, told me another.

I really don't want to talk to Phillip with an audience, especially not THIS audience, but as Callum strides through the doorway, he hooks a thumb over his shoulder at me. "I found this riffraff hanging around outside. I think he was eavesdropping."

Phillip is wearing a pair of glasses I've never seen and drops them onto his desk, rubbing his temples before giving us a stern look.

"Come in, both of you. And close the door."

Now I'm stuck. I can't exactly run back out the door saying, "Just kidding! I was only popping in to say hi!" But I'm not willing to say what I need to say in front of Callum. It will be hard enough confessing to Phillip.

"Drink?" Phillip asks, getting up to pour himself a bourbon.

"Yes, please," Callum says, but I shake my head.

Casually crossing my hands over one another in my lap, I let my fingers start to tap out a melody. This isn't exactly the method my therapist recommended, but it's less likely to be noticed than if I crossed my arms and tapped my shoulders. I take several slow breaths while the princes take sips of their drinks.

"Well," Phillip says. "Who's going to start? We only have a few hours before the ball. I'd prefer not to spend any more of those hours in this office."

I wave a hand for Callum to start, but being the good sport he is, he waves right back to me. "You first," he says. "I insist."

"You outrank me. Why don't you go ahead? I'll wait."

"Nonsense. I can't wait to hear what this is about."

Callum seems sure there's some secret here, something that he might use to ruin me. And, of course, he's right.

My thoughts tangle. I meet Phillip's gaze across the desk, and I'm not sure what he sees there, but he turns to Callum.

"Why don't you give us a few minutes?"

"That's okay. I don't mind." Callum lounges back in the chair, crossing one foot over his other knee.

Phillip sighs. "I mind. I'll send for you when we're done."

Callum looks indignant, but seems to know Phillip isn't mucking about. He gets to his feet, sloshing a little of his drink on me in the process. "Fine," he says, practically stomping from the room.

Such a man-child.

When the door closes, I dive right in, afraid I'll freeze like I did outside the door moments ago. "I need to speak with you about my uncle."

"The Baron de Silva?"

My smile is tight. "That's the one. I'm trusting you with this in confidence and hoping that if needed, speaking up will grant me favor. I'm going to need it."

"Go on." Phillip steeples his fingers together, leaning forward on the desk with flinty eyes. The man is like a stone, completely firm and unreadable.

Taking one last deep breath, I uncross my hands and settle into my seat. This is going to take longer than a few minutes, and I only hope Callum isn't listening outside the door. Not that any of this will be a secret for long, which is the point, really, but he's the last person I could trust with this.

There isn't a good starting place, so I simply dive right into the meat of it. "My uncle means to ruin the relationship between Elsinore and Viore by any means necessary. I'm not fully sure why—other than him being a terrible person who enjoys playing with people like they're toys in a sandbox."

Phillip blinks, his gray eyes still unreadable. "Go on."

Will he believe me? Will he hate me?

Will Seraf?

I remember the words of Uncle's latest text, telling me I'd outdone myself getting engaged to the princess.

He told me I must have learned something from him after all.

The thought makes me sick, even now. Even knowing it's so far from the truth.

The engagement may be fake, but it's not because I'm falling in line or because I'm like my uncle. I went along with it for Seraf's sake, and because secretly, I want it to be true. I'd like to make it true.

Which means I need to start telling the truth.

"And right now, the way he's been trying to do this is through me."

CHAPTER TWENTY-SIX

Serafina

Every so often, my life feels like a cliché. Tonight, being a princess getting ready for a ball, is one of those nights. But I have so far avoided a pumpkin carriage, a glass slipper, and any little birds and mice who offer to help me get ready.

Instead, I've got Kat, who's been chatting my ear off about Claudius while fixing my hair and makeup. Apparently, the very boring Claudius is actually the most interesting man she's ever met. I wonder if this is because he's actually interesting, or if it's because he's the first man with whom Kat is interested in having more than a casual fling.

Which means that now both Kat and I know his shoe size (thirteen), his favorite football team (Manchester United), and his greatest fear (clowns on motorbikes).

"It's quite specific, though, isn't it? Not just clowns, but clowns on motorbikes. Would he be okay if they were on foot? Or in a car?"

Kat pins up a last lock of my hair. "Totally fine. It's something about the clown-motorbike combination. Isn't that daft? He's simply fascinating, isn't he?"

"Yes." *To her.*

But I don't mind the chatter, because it keeps my brain's wild roaring to a minimum. And roar it is. I'm a veritable buffet of emotions, and the reasonable part of my brain is trying to pick through them, as though trying to decide which of the appetizers will leave me with indigestion.

Tonight is the Centennial Ball.

The night I always thought I'd be announcing an engagement to my best friend and childhood crush, Prince Callum of Elsinore.

Yes, CRUSH. Not love.

It took this week with Rafe to know the difference.

I could never have predicted how differently things would turn out. Not in a million years. To be honest, I still don't know how this will all end. And THAT is why my stomach feels both tight and fluttery, like it can't even decide how to process my nerves.

"You're all set," Kat says. "And looking gorgeous, if I do say so myself, darling. Come on, let's have a look at you." She pulls me by the hand toward the full-length mirror in my room. "See? Gorgeous."

"And you would know, being gorgeous yourself," I tell her.

Kat, who usually sticks to blacks or other deep, dark colors has gone with an effervescent white, setting off her dark bob, which she's done in beachy waves with light makeup and a dramatic pink lip.

"Claudius is going to drop his clipboard when he sees you."

"Mmm. I do *love* his clipboard."

I don't want to know.

"Now—what do you think about this look?" Kat asks. "Not too much, is it?"

"No."

Kat spent so long working on my face—and refusing to let me see—that I half-expected something clownish or Kardashian. I trust Kat, of course, but it did seem to take forever. Instead of dramatic, my makeup is the kind that almost looks like I'm not wearing any. The most noticeable bit is a light cat-eye swoop she's drawn in liquid liner, which makes my eyes look enormous. My cheeks have a rosy flush and there's a slight sparkle on my lids, with my lips a pale, natural pink. My hair is mostly pinned up into a loose knot, with wavy tendrils hanging down, framing my face perfectly.

"You've outdone yourself, Kat."

"And the dress! It's spectacular!"

It's the one with the lace sleeves and sweetheart neckline, the one Suzette, Henri, and Juliet loved. The one in Callum's color.

"Are you sure? The sleeves feel …" I wiggle my arms, expecting the dress to feel constricted, but the fabric is actually kind of perfect, flexing with me.

Kat frowns. "It's ridiculously perfect."

"The color doesn't make me look washed out?"

Kat laughs. "No! Trust me. You look like a feast in this. I know that you're going to make Callum's jaw hit the floor." Her lips tilt and her eyes sparkle. "Oh, sorry. Rafe's jaw will hit the floor. I forget—who are you marrying?"

I know she's teasing—I've told Kat about my feelings for Rafe and my realizations about Callum. Still, it hits a little too close to home. I know I'm not marrying Callum. But I don't know where things stand with Rafe. Our engagement is still fake. Officially, anyway. Unofficially, I'd like it to be real. My feelings certainly are.

"You need to tell him how you feel," Kat says gently. "Not repeat mistakes of the past and all that."

"I know. It's just complicated."

"Don't tell me there's still a debate raging inside your head about which eligible royal you want—the prince or the duke?"

"There is no debate," I say firmly, feeling slightly queasy as I do. "I just don't know what Rafe wants. And how can I know? I dragged him into this engagement."

Rafe's words pop into my head. *I wouldn't say dragged.*

"I'm pretty sure Rafe de Silva never does anything he doesn't want to do. Newsflash: he wants *you*. It's time to tell him you want him back."

I flex my fingers, shaking out my hands. Kat makes it sound so easy. In truth, I'm terrified.

I hardly know Rafe. Before this week, he was an almost stranger I didn't care to know. Callum was the one I wanted. Is it really possible that a switch flipped in my heart, redirecting its affections like a train sent on a new track?

My parents hate Rafe. His reputation won't win any favors with the people of Viore. He is, as my father said, a PR nightmare. I know this is why my parents didn't want to officially confirm yet. They're still probably hoping the arrangement with Callum will work.

I check the clock on the wall. Rafe will be here in ten minutes. Why does a sudden jolt of emotion zoom through me at the thought? It's how it feels the moment a roller coaster crests the top of the first big hill and begins to plummet.

I remember from the first and only time my parents took me to an amusement park. They shut the whole thing down for us, which was a bit of a bummer, as the absence of screams and laughter and other people made it seem like a haunted park. I remember clutching my father's hand as he led me to the first car on the biggest coaster there. I remember the way my stomach rose and flipped as we began the plunge down.

And I remember throwing up the second we hit the bottom.

I don't feel so different now.

"So, you'll talk to Rafe?" Kat says, her voice uncharacteristically hesitant.

"Must we discuss this to death?" I blot a little of my lipstick, but I've already blotted it into oblivion and now I need to reapply. Then it's too bright, so I begin the blotting game again.

I'm so distracted by the tube of Persimmon Pink that it takes a moment to realize that Kat's gone silent. I slide the cap on my lipstick. Kat's face wears an earnestness so rare that I wonder if I should call the physician.

"What? Are you all right?"

"This is a big decision," Kat says. "The biggest."

"I know it is," I say, perhaps a little snippily.

"Even if I ever get married"—she makes a gagging face —"it won't be as big a decision as this is for you."

"Way to make me feel better about it," I mutter. "No pressure at all!"

"I can't help it." Kat kicks off her nude heels and begins to pace. "If I weren't a true friend, if I didn't care so much, I'd just smile, smack you on that deliciously plump bum of yours, and tell you best of luck."

Her words are piercing, slipping straight through my ribs to my heart. Swallowing a lump in my throat I turn, making a show of examining my backside over my shoulder.

"Deliciously plump, you say?"

Kat gives a frustrated little scream, tugging on her hair. "Sera, listen. Don't start doubting this decision based on *oughts*."

"Oughts?"

"Who you think you *ought* to love. Who you think you *ought* to be with. Who your parents or anyone else's parents or the press think you *ought* to be with. I know once you say those vows, that's it for you. And not just because of the crown. It's your sense of loyalty and honor and duty to your country and to the man you pledge yourself to. But in order to serve your country best, tonight, do what serves *you*."

"That sounds so selfish."

"It's not selfish. It's like what they say about parents putting on their oxygen masks before putting on their child's."

I make a face. "I'd rather not think about my plane crashing right now. It feels a little too close to home."

"Forget about that. The point of the analogy," she says, "is that sometimes you have to put yourself first before you can serve others well. With a kingdom to serve, this matters even more." Kat takes my arm, gently but with a grip that commands my attention. "You are going to do great things for the people of Viore. But you need an equally great man beside you."

"And you think that man is Rafe?"

"Before this week, I might have doubted it. But I've seen the impact he's had on you. Callum made you shrink. Rafe makes you soar."

The words settle into me, solid and warm. Rafe *does* make me soar. Unexpectedly so. I still feel unbalanced around him, which in large part is due to the attraction I've been trying to deny. But it's also because he challenges me. He's exactly the kind of man I need beside me as king.

I just have to convince him, my parents, and the people of Viore.

There's a knock at the door, and Claudius pops his head in. "Lady Kat," he says, his bright eyes taking on a new glow as he looks at her. "It's time."

Kat nods, gives me a quick hug, and says, "Time to soar, Sera," before ducking out into the hall. Claudius steps out only to walk back in a moment later, lugging a box that's clearly heavy. It's wrapped in pink and gold paper, and he places it on the bed.

"A gift," he says, starting to leave again.

"From whom?"

"The Duke of Weldon."

My stomach flips. Before the door is even closed, I'm tearing into the paper, not caring about the mess. Inside a box is another box, this one pink and made of some kind of tough, weatherproof material.

A card sits on top, *Angel* written in a messy scrawl.

With shaking hands, I carefully edge my nails under the envelope's perfect seal, pull out a single thick, cream card, and read the few lines there

To the woman who already has everything—remember that you can DO anything.

-R

The wordplay is just like Rafe, and my cheeks hurt from smiling.

I find latches on the handle of the pink box and unclasp

them, my fervor for opening quickly dulled to a snail's slow drag. Inside is a brand-new set of power tools, the same pink as the box.

When I pull the drill from its slot, turning it over in my hand, a single tear falls near the side, where in gold letters the words "Avenging Angel" have been engraved.

I'm not sure how long I stand there, turning over Rafe's gift in my hands. But it isn't long before it feels like too weighty of a thing for me to hold.

With a snap, I close the box, lugging it to the wardrobe and hiding it underneath the skirts of my dresses, leaning against the closed wooden doors when I'm done, as though I'm holding back the boogeyman.

My heart beats against the cage of my ribs, and I bite the inside of my cheek so hard I taste blood. I catch my reflection in the mirror, the perfect makeup, the perfect hair, the perfect dress. It suddenly feels all wrong.

Opening the wardrobe again, I flip frantically through the dresses on the rack until I find exactly what I'm looking for.

TWELVE YEARS AGO

Rafe

That will be the last time. The very last time.

A lie, but repeating it over and over seems to be the only way to help me cool down after one of Uncle's "conversations." I repeat the words over and over and over again in my head, even whispering them sometimes, knowing that in this back hallway of the Elisinorian palace, no one is likely to hear me.

Sometimes it helps thinking of the mole on Uncle's neck, ugly and huge and shaped like Italy. I told him that once, and he put me in the closet for seven hours. Uncle *hates* Italy. Maybe more than I hate the closet. No idea why, but now, whenever he's going off on me about something or other I've screwed up, I can sometimes get through it focusing my gaze on that mole.

Uncle Moleneck, I'll think. *Uncle Italian Moleneck.*

A giggle escapes me, sounding half-mad, threatening to break into a sob.

On days like today, when it's really bad, and I'm left feeling burned and hollowed out, I need time to come back to myself. Eventually, my breathing slows and I stop hearing the whoosh of blood in my ears. The wild feeling threading through me starts to subside, and I don't know if it's been two minutes or twenty.

What's important is that I cool down before reappearing at the dinner. Uncle will expect it. And I know what happens all too well when I don't meet Uncle's expectations. The closet ... or worse.

I didn't even realize I'd missed some social cue or other tonight until I saw that tight-lipped look and the flash in his eyes that always sends dread tumbling through my stomach. I'm still not even sure what I did. Used the wrong fork? The wrong title for someone? Didn't smile at the right time? Tonight, he didn't specify. I'm sure if I don't figure it out by bedtime, there will be some new punishment awaiting me.

There are so many rules, all running together in my head like a map full of roads, crisscrossing one another and circling back, none of them with names.

"How could you be this stupid?" he said after pulling me into another room. I don't mind being called stupid. I know he's wrong about that. I have high marks at school, even if I struggle to remember all the things Uncle wants me to. His rules are ever-changing, his expectations endless.

"Your father would be ashamed to call you his."

That one always hits the mark, and probably always will. He knows how to press his thumbs into my grief like a bruise. Even as he tells me that it's been a few years, that I should be over it. I'm a pansy for missing them, for still being sad.

But I am still gutted. And I'm not ashamed of it. I loved them, my father and my mother, who was pregnant with a little brother I'll never know. Whenever I think of them, grief is a steel-toed boot kicking me in the gut.

I don't *think* Father would be ashamed of me, at least not for the reasons Uncle says he would. Then again, I'm a coward, hiding in a back hallway, curled into a ball.

Coward.

Dad wouldn't be ashamed of me. That's just Uncle's voice. And Uncle is ... not well. That's the excuse I give myself for the way he treats me, the things he says. Maybe he's grieving too?

I know he must be wrong. My parents loved me. They wouldn't be ashamed.

Would they?

Even as the grief doesn't fade, my memories of them are growing fuzzy and unfocused. I can't remember the sound of Father's voice anymore. I only hear Uncle, telling me again and again what a disappointment I am, how my parents would have disowned me. That sending me to boarding school was their way of getting rid of me.

Could it be true? I don't think so. I think my uncle is a liar and a selfish, cruel man. I have to keep telling myself that, even though he shows me his cruelty daily. I'm the only one who seems to see behind the mask. At least, I assume no one else sees. Otherwise, he wouldn't have a position of power. His eye is on being prime minister, and I hope he never gets that much power.

I know this, know he's a horrible human, and yet ... the more he talks, the harder it is to get his voice out of my head. I wish he'd hit me. Then, at least, I'd have some marks, some proof of his cruelty. Maybe then I could tell someone and they'd take me out of his care. But the only marks he leaves are invisible, with the whip of his words. These are the worst of all, like they take root in my brain and I can't get them out.

I don't realize I'm slapping the sides of my head until I hear the sound of footsteps. I clench my fists in my lap and sit up, sinking back a little into the shadows.

But when a girl rounds the corner, there's no way to hide.

"Oh, hello," she says in a voice that's like music. I realize with a start that it reminds me of my mother's voice, the sound of which I was forgetting.

Immediately, I want to know this girl. I want to hear her talk, to hear her laugh, to remember my mom.

Which is stupid. I need to move on, as Uncle says. They're gone.

But still ...

The girl hesitates, and I realize I've made it awkward. Splendid.

"Hi." At least I didn't stammer as I sometimes do. My voice didn't wobble on that one sturdy syllable.

She doesn't seem put off by my stupid greeting. I don't talk much to girls. Especially pretty ones. They make me tense up, and this one is especially pretty, her hair loose and shiny brown, her smile wide and genuine. My spine is as straight as a metal rod.

"May I join you? This is a good hiding spot," she says, and my throat goes dry when she sits down beside me, smoothing her dress over her legs.

"I'm not hiding," I say, my voice sounding creaky and dumb. She doesn't seem to notice.

"I am," she whispers, nudging me with her shoulder. "Hiding, that is."

Something rises up in me, a feeling I haven't felt before. A protectiveness, maybe? I don't want someone to hurt this girl the way Uncle hurts me. How would I even ask that?

"Hiding from someone?"

"Oh, from all of them. From all of this." She waves her hands around, and I'm relieved that no one is hurting her. "It's exhausting, isn't it?"

I nod, because being at these events really is overwhelming. But even though this girl is seated beside me on the floor, she seems so prim and proper—surely it's not hard for her? Maybe she means something completely different to what tires me out.

"I'm Sara," she says, holding out a hand.

Am I supposed to shake it? She's a girl—maybe I'm supposed to kiss it? That thought makes me hot and shaky. This feels like a test, and I'm blanking out on the right response, meanwhile, her hand is just hanging there.

You're so stupid. Your father would be ashamed.

I shove Uncle's voice from my head and finally grasp the girl's hand in mine. Her palm is smooth and cool. I'd like to hold it forever. Her smile widens as she gives my hand a firm squeeze and a shake.

"Lovely to meet you," she says, then raises her brows. I realize she's waiting for my name.

But my throat feels like it's closing at the feel of her soft skin on mine. I don't want to let go, and so I squeeze her hand back, maybe a little too hard because she winces slightly, and I let go immediately, making fists again.

"Thanks for letting me share your spot."

"It's not mine."

She smiles, and it feels like something is tumbling down inside my chest. "It's ours, then. Yeah?"

"Yeah."

Tipping her head back against the wall, she sighs heavily, like she's bone-weary. I try to study her face, trying not to look obvious about it. I don't spend much time looking at girls. I could look at her forever, if it wasn't creepy to do so. But I'm drawn to something more than her pretty face. There's a sweetness about her, a light. Having her next to me has lifted the heavy shroud left from Uncle.

I almost want to thank her, but it wouldn't make much sense if I tried.

Clearing my throat, I'm about to ask her where she's from when a voice calls out from nearby.

"Fi!" It's a boy, maybe around our age, slightly familiar, but I can't place it. "Fi, where are you?"

She smiles at me again. "That's me."

Fi? I thought she said her name was Sara? Must be some kind of nickname. Disappointment sits like a stone on my chest.

"I guess duty calls," she says, getting to her feet.

She gives me a little curtsy when she does so, which is silly, since I'm only a duke, a nobody really. That's one thing Uncle makes sure I know. I have some land, a title, and money I can't really touch.

But I know Uncle says that because he's jealous. Mum married into being a duchess, and I know she and Uncle were once poor. He can't access all my money, even though he's my guardian. Most of it's tied up in a trust I'll be able to access when I'm eighteen.

And then: no more Uncle. I'll be free, and I won't look back.

"Lovely to meet you," Sara says, even as the voice calls again. A boyfriend? A brother?

I hope it's a brother.

She starts off down the hall again before I can find words, and then turns just before she falls out of sight.

"And hey—maybe you don't need to hear this tonight, but it's something my mum always tells me. 'The night is darkest

334

before the dawn.' It's a quote from someone famous," she adds, then drops her voice to a whisper, eyes sparkling. "But I think Mum got it from a Batman movie."

With a giggle, Sara disappears around the corner, and I swear, a little piece of me goes with her. It's ridiculous, really, but my heart is leaping up into my throat and everything in me is practically screaming for me to follow her.

Before she can get too far, I leap up and dart after her, sticking my head around the corner to watch as she walks away. My throat tightens as I see who she's walking next to: Crown Prince Callum of Elsinore.

I didn't like Callum from the moment we met at school, even though he's probably not a bad guy. And that's part of it. He's all easy smiles and sunshine. Well-liked and the guy everyone wants to be around.

Jealousy gripped me like a hot fist at the sight of his whole family moving him into the dormitories: Mom, Dad, older brother, and two younger sisters. It was so easy to see how much they cared for each other, that it wasn't just an act they put on. I'll never have anything like that again, and at times, the unfairness of it practically chokes me. That very first week of school, I made a snide remark—fine, multiple snide remarks—which jumpstarted our whole stupid rivalry. All because I wanted what he had.

I have another reason now to be envious. He also has *her*.

There's an easiness between him and Sara. They walk with their heads tilted toward one another. Callum slows his stride slightly so she can keep up. Their laughter bubbles back toward me before they turn a corner.

I realize with sudden clarity who she is. She said her name was Sara, and I assumed the normal spelling. But it's Sera, short for Serafina, the Princess of Viore.

It's a small country I only know about because Uncle

talks often (and bitterly) about the fairly recent discovery of copper in some of their mountainous regions. Viore and Elsinore have a close relationship, the copper now helping with something to do with Elsinore's technology and blah blah blah.

The important part, at least to me in this moment, is that Callum and Serafina are close friends. And maybe even—*no.* We'll stick with friends.

Friends is something I can work with. I don't know if and when I'll see her again, but I'm sure I will. And maybe then I can make a better impression than some weird boy hiding in a secret hallway.

CHAPTER TWENTY-SEVEN

Serafina

The only problem with finding the dress I'm looking for is the little matter of zipping it up. I would need to be a contortionist to get this thing closed. I could wait until Rafe arrives … but I fear we might not leave the room if I open the door in a half-zipped dress.

There's always The Dane, but—no. Not him.

When the knock comes at the door, I panic. Hopping around, I flail my arms over my shoulders, desperate to grasp the stupid zipper. "Just a moment!"

There's a beat of silence, then a most unexpected voice calls, "Princess Serafina, it's Brit."

I pause, my arms at odd angles behind me. Brit?

When I open the door, holding the dress up by its front. I almost don't recognize Brit in jeans and a simple white blouse, no bizarre Americana fashion in sight. I'd forgotten how naturally pretty she is with her blonde curls and big eyes, a much more vibrant blue than my own.

The Dane lifts a single brow, and I nod, trying to angle myself behind the door so he doesn't get an eyeful of me half-dressed.

"Come in."

Brit barely enters the room, standing stiffly with her hands in front of her. When I close the door and make my way to her, she gives my dress the once over, her eyes going wide.

"That's beautiful," she says. "What a statement!"

Brit calling my dress a statement isn't the best endorsement, and I'm wondering if I should put back on the blue dress with the sleeves in Callum's color.

"I was thinking of changing," I say, giving the top another good yank up.

Her eyes go wide. "No! It's perfect. The color is dramatic, but the rest is understated. Classic. It makes *you* shine. Can I help with the zipper?"

I turn around, feeling suddenly shy as Brit's cool hands find the zipper and tug it up, doing what I couldn't for myself.

In the mirror, I have to concede that Brit is right—the dress is classically beautiful, and I've never looked better. "Thank you." I offer her a small smile in the reflection.

"Of course."

I turn back to Brit, realizing I haven't asked why she's here. With a hopeful smile, she clasps her hands in front of her again, looking younger and more like the kind of person you can't hate even if you want to.

"You're probably wondering why I'm here."

"A little."

"I wanted to apologize," she says. "I had no idea about

338

your history with Callie—sorry, Callum—or the fact that there was some kind of arrangement between y'all. I feel like I walked in and stepped in the middle of everything."

I wave off her concern. "That's really not necessary. Things were complicated and now they're … well, they're not anymore."

"Is it my fault?" Her eyes fill with tears, and how is it that I feel like comforting her?

Remember—she made you wear the curtain dress.

The urge to hug her passes.

"Really, I think it's all for the best. Please, don't trouble yourself. But why aren't you dressed?"

"I'm not going to the ball. I'm going home," she says. "Callum and I are done."

They're done? This is what I wanted, isn't it? A week ago, which now seems like a lifetime, I wanted Brit gone so Callum would be free. Now, the thought simply makes me sad. I'm not sure if it's for her or for him. But it's definitely not for me.

"I knew he didn't love me. And I don't know what might happen between the two of you now, but I wanted to apologize and say that if he wants you, I think he'd make some woman very happy one day. And if it were you, I would be glad."

I'm not even sure what to say, but Brit removes the need for words with a sudden hug that feels more like someone desperately clutching to a raft after her boat capsized.

"Well, thank you. I appreciate it. Truly. And I do wish you the best."

When she lets me go, I take a deep, almost gasping breath now that my lungs aren't being constricted. And with a last, wavering smile, Brit leaves, only seconds before there's

339

another knock at the door. I've barely had time to process her words.

But what's to process? I already think I know what—or *whom*—I want.

"Hang on a moment." I stuff the blue dress into the wardrobe, right next to Rafe's gift. "Sorry to you both," I mutter, then slam the wooden doors shut.

With a quick glance in the mirror, just to make sure all my bits are properly tucked in, I make my way to the door.

"You haven't changed your mind, have you, Angel?" Rafe's voice sounds very close and a little muffled, as though he has his cheek pressed to the door.

I place my palms flat on the wood, trying to rein in my jackhammering heart. "About which part? Being your date? Or being your fiancée?"

His chuckle rolls through me like thunder. "Either." He pauses, and his voice sounds more tentative when he speaks again. "Or even being my friend."

Only because I've grown to know Rafe this week do I pick up on the edge of vulnerability in his voice. I used to think him so proud. And while Rafe can at times display an admirably large dose of cockiness, I've seen past that now, and know there is also a large part of Rafe that is soft and easily wounded. A side which may struggle not to believe what the headlines and even more, what his uncle, may have said about him.

Slowly, I turn the knob and open the door, holding my breath and counting caterpillars as though my life depends on it.

Rafe stands a few feet back, looking devilishly handsome in a dark tux expertly tailored to fit his broad frame. His jawline has been shaved closer than I've ever seen it, and I can't help but stare at his smooth skin. I want to put my hands all over it but instead clench them at my sides.

"Wow," I breathe. "You look—"

"Gorgeous."

Rafe's voice sounds as equally breathless as mine, and I'm not sure he even heard me at all. My gaze travels up and over his cut cheekbones to his eyes, which are wide, and pinging all over me.

I bite my lip. This dress was the right choice.

With a more plunging neckline than I usually go for, it's strapless and fitted—it has to be for me to wear it. There is no chance I'd risk some kind of wardrobe malfunction, which means I can scarcely take a deep breath. Totally worth it for Rafe's reaction. TOTALLY.

"I thought you were wearing blue," he says, eyes still trailing over me in a way that makes me feel hotly desired and powerful.

"Someone told me I'd look good in red."

His eyes fly right to mine and pin me in place. We stand there, locked in some kind of eye battle. I'm not sure what we're fighting for, or who's winning or losing, only that the tension between us has ramped up exponentially. The air is saturated with it. I'm surprised I can't see the waves of it, rippling like a mirage.

"Shall we go?" I ask.

Shaking his head a little, Rafe clears his throat. "Yes. Sorry."

He holds out his arm and I step forward, curling my hand through the crook of his elbow. My whole body seems to ease in a sigh at the contact. Rafe looks down at me, studying my face with a tilt of his lips.

"Have I told you that you look simply beautiful, fiancée?"

A tremor moves through me when he says fiancée. "I think the word you used was gorgeous."

"You're both. Beautiful. Gorgeous. Hot. Perfect."

He punctuates that last word by brushing his lips in a sweet kiss on my temple that ends much too soon. I find myself gravitating toward him, becoming sucked into his orbit.

As he begins to walk, guiding me down these familiar halls, we're silent. I'm lost in my own thoughts and I'm not sure where he is. I could ask, but I'm not sure I want to. I'm still not sure what I want.

I'm wearing the red dress, not the blue.

I'm on Rafe's arm, not Callum's, and it's exactly where I want to be.

There is this energy between us, and understanding that is so new, so fragile.

And yet, Callum broke up with Brit just as Rafe predicted. Callum has been jealous, which means … something. There's still time for us, for the arrangement. Both of our parents still want that match.

But do I?

Rafe stops suddenly, nearing the end of the hallway, where I can hear the sound of voices and distant music. He pulls me into a little alcove and spins to face me, taking both my hands lightly in his.

"Before we join the throng," he starts, then pauses. I can visibly see him swallow, like it takes effort. He seems nervous. Does Rafe de Silva get nervous?

His hands are trembling, and I give him a reassuring squeeze, my stomach dropping as his nerves ignite my nerves. "Rafe? What is it?"

He removes one of his hands, sliding it into his pocket. "Seraf. I have something for you."

342

And then, Rafe drops to one knee.

My ears are ringing, and the beating of my heart is like a distant drum. "What are you doing?" I whisper.

He opens his palm to reveal a ring. A gorgeous blue stone, sapphire maybe, ringed in tiny diamonds.

"It was my mother's," he says in a quiet voice.

I'm already shaking my head. "No, Rafe. I can't wear your mother's ring. Not when—" I swallow, my eyes pricking with tears. Happy or sad? I don't even know. "Not when all of this has been … fake."

Rafe blinks up at me, expression guarded, and I tug at his wrist, careful not to knock the ring loose. He lets me pull him to his feet. We're standing inches apart, the hand with the ring still between us, a lot of unspoken things between us.

Taking my left hand, Rafe holds the ring carefully, poised over my fourth finger.

"This can be as real as you want it to be, Seraf."

As real as I want it to be.

The ring is right at my fingertip, cool and smooth, and solid.

"It's always been real for me."

I search his eyes, which are as serious as I've ever seen them. My mind rolls back over this past week with Rafe—his words, his touches, his actions. And yet … I'm astounded, shocked into utter silence by the idea that this could possibly be true.

Me? Rafe wants me?

Rafe shifts, and it feels like a moment has passed, a window shut.

"I know that the plan was to make Callum jealous, to help him see what he should have seen—what I've seen—right in front of him."

343

I can't help but stiffen at the mention of Callum and the plan, which seems so stupid, so small, so insignificant in light of the conversation we're now having.

Callum? Who's Callum?

Just some prince I used to know.

"He's the better choice for you, Seraf." I start to shake my head in protest, but Rafe doesn't give me a chance to speak. "The alliance of your families, the history you share—all of it. Plus, his reputation, even after this year, is still better than mine. As much as I'm loath to admit it, he's a decent man. An idiot for not snatching you up though."

Callum doesn't want me. He said as much to Phillip and me. His words play back through my mind.

No, he didn't say he didn't want YOU. He said he didn't want an arranged marriage.

Which is basically the same … isn't it?

I'm not sure why I'm even letting these thoughts play out, as I don't want Callum, the man perhaps I *ought* to want. I want the man in front of me.

This is all just so much to take in. I feel as though I've lived a lifetime in the last week.

"It's your choice, Angel. I know you don't get many of those, so know that this is completely up to you. You can choose Callum, if he gets his head out of wherever he's stuck it, or you can choose me."

Rafe is offering so much more than himself. He's offering up his freedom in order to give me a choice.

But a part of me is still stuck in disbelief. "Are you really asking me to marry you? This is for real?"

Rafe nods slowly, his caramel eyes soft. "But you can just wear the ring as part of the ruse if you want to keep it as that. You can wear it now, and decide on a real engagement later. Whatever you decide, Seraf."

"But you would marry me?"

"Yes."

No hesitation. No question. No arguments.

And, perhaps most shocking of all, no hint of teasing.

I'm wax on a summer day, melting into a puddle and losing all my shape.

What am I to do with these words? With this response? With this man?

I want to scream out yes, to throw my arms around him and slide his mother's ring on my finger. Something stops me, something holds me back, and I'm not sure if it's just my normal default to question things, to make big decisions with careful thought, or if there's still a part of me hung up on Callum.

A little over a week ago, I wanted to marry the prince. Now, I'm considering marrying another man, a man I thought I despised.

The man I thought I despised isn't the man standing before me.

I know this, like I know how badly I want to say yes and let Rafe slide the ring on my finger.

Yet everything is happening too quickly and in a strange, tangled order. Are Rafe's feelings true? Are mine? How much of the pretense of our relationship was that —pretense?

Is it even fair to Rafe if I say yes?

His life has been so free. As a duke, he can go where he pleases, do what he wants. Once he's free from his uncle's conservatorship, something Phillip promised me he'd take care of, Rafe will have everything restored.

If he marries me, he'll be King of Viore. It's the opposite life from what he's had, from what it seems like he's wanted. He would lose all his freedoms. Like me, his choices would be limited. Everything would change for him.

He's sacrificing his own choice, yet offering me one. It hardly seems fair.

"Ruling Viore—is that even something you want?"

Rafe doesn't flinch. "I want you, Seraf. And whatever comes along with you, I'm willing to bear."

Willing, but not eager. To *bear*, not to embrace.

I can't help thinking it might kill Rafe to be trapped in such a position, to go from a life with all the benefits of having a title to one with all the responsibilities of a king. I imagine the light I love so much dying from his eyes, his shoulders stooped with responsibility, the familiar smirk absent forever.

Now, I feel like I have another choice before me. One that doesn't involve what's best for me or Viore, but what's best for Rafe.

"Seraf," he says gently. "For now, wear the ring. I won't take it as a yes. It will simply answer questions for people, hold up the engagement they believe to be true. And when you have an answer, give it to me. Your choice."

Again, that word. *Choice*. The antithesis of duty. An indulgent word, one I'm rarely able to have. One I'll be taking away from Rafe if I say yes to his proposal.

"I need to think," I tell Rafe, not missing the quick flash of disappointment in his eyes, replaced immediately by understanding. "But I'll wear the ring for now. For tonight. If you're sure."

"I'm sure."

Rafe smiles, then slides the ring on my finger. It fits almost perfectly, and he stares down at it, holding my hand gently in his. I think of his mother wearing this ring, of his loss, and tears burn my eyes. I do my best to blink them away.

"No pressure, Seraf. I know I don't have as much to offer—"

I touch his cheek, and he covers my hand with his, the ring which once belonged to his mother between us. "Stop. Don't say that. Any woman would be lucky to have you at her side."

I truly believe that, though I hate even the idea of another woman anywhere near him. I want it to be me. I want to say yes, to make this real and official.

But something is still holding me back, and I'm not sure what the hesitation is. Only that I need to feel SURE before I can wear the ring for real.

"My mother would have loved you," Rafe says, emotion coloring his voice.

"I wish I could have met her, met both of them."

"Me too," he says, and when he glances back up at me, his eyes glisten with unshed tears.

I lean up to press a kiss to his smoothly shaven jaw. He blinks in surprise, and my cheeks flush. I smile. "I needed to know how it felt without your ever present five o'clock shadow. I hope that's okay."

"More than okay," he says, those caramel eyes darkening. "In fact, if you're amenable, I'd like you to know what a kiss from me is like. A *real* kiss."

If our two brief kisses are anything to go on, I have a pretty good idea what a real kiss would be like. Honestly, I'm not sure I can handle it. "Trying to sway my decision?"

Doesn't stop me from wanting to find out.

His smile moves millimeter by millimeter over his face, and if I ever thought it was wicked before, it's nothing compared to now. "Simply making sure you have all the facts."

"Facts, hm? Is that really playing fair?"

"Oh, Angel, I never promised I'd play fair."

My heart is beating so fast I think it might actually have stopped.

Rafe touches my lips with a finger, not closing them, but it halts my response nevertheless. I think my breath has stopped too.

"May I?" he whispers.

I think I nod, but the functions in my body seem to have shifted all attention to the main priority now, and that priority is my lips. Rafe traces their outline with his finger, dragging slowly between them as they part.

Already, this is the most sensual, romantic encounter I've ever had. If I weren't so desperate for his mouth on mine, I'd be embarrassed by the flush in my cheeks, my jagged breaths, and the look of need I know he sees in my eyes.

Rafe doesn't make me wait long, yet there is nothing rushed when his lips meet mine.

There is no hesitation, no holding back, but he lets the kiss unfurl slowly, like turning down the sheets on a bed.

The press of his lips is softer and sweeter than anything I could have imagined. There's no fear he'll pull away like he did in the physician's room, nothing of the clumsiness of my kiss during our photo shoot. My lips now seem to know exactly what to do as Rafe's mouth begins to move over mine, coaxing me to follow where he leads.

I'd follow those lips over a cliff, dying happily on the rocks below.

I mean, hopefully, it won't come to that.

GET BACK IN THE MOMENT, SERA.

Right. The best kiss of my life. Turning back off overactive brain ...

I close my eyes tighter, shut off the overthinking part of my brain and let the physical sensations blanket me. My nerves hum to life and then begin to sing as his hands shift, one cupping my face and the other splaying over the small of my back, tugging me closer until I'm flush against him, his body heat like a furnace roaring to life and burning me right along with it.

His head tilts and mine tips the other way, allowing our kiss to dive deeper. He's soft and slow, languid kisses that shift in pressure, surprising me with lightness, then more firm. Teasing, then consuming. He kisses the way he flirts, all intensity wrapped in a kind of playfulness. But there's something like reverence too, and his mouth is echoing all the promises he's made to me.

It's all I can do to hold on, and I realize that I am holding on—literally—to the lapels of his suit.

But I want more. Rafe's kiss has woken me up, and I feel greedy and needy and desperate for more of him. I let go of his suit and slide both hands up his chest, feeling and hearing a deep rumble as my hands skim over his shoulders, finding his neck. One hand rests on the hot skin there and the other moves through his hair.

For a moment, I almost lose myself in a moment of indecision and vulnerability. Is this okay? Is this what I'm supposed to do? Does he like it?

He must, because another rumble escapes him, and his kisses begin to match my desperation. The pace of his lips picks up, more urgent now, more passionate. His body shifts and suddenly I realize he's backed me into the wall. I'm grateful for its sturdiness along my spine, which otherwise feels like it's going to slide right out of the back of my body and pool in the floor, useless and limp as a noodle.

"Seraf." Rafe murmurs my name even as he kisses me, which is a skill I don't possess at the moment.

I can't speak. I can hardly breathe, hardly move other

than to keep pace with him, to continue to let my hands explore Rafe's neck and drag through his hair over his scalp.

His breath is mint and intoxication.

His grip on me is steady, a promise of safety, of security.

The heat between us? *Explosive.*

Even as I think this, Rafe presses another closemouthed kiss to my lips, then another, and I can sense him closing this door.

It's the last thing I want. Forget the ball. Forget everything. I'd like to move into this alcove permanently and spend the rest of my days just exploring Rafe's mouth with mine.

We've only just started to map this out—I have so much more I want to see! Taste! Explore! I want his mouth on my neck, my cheek, my collarbone. I want my hands beneath his suit jacket, his shirt even, and feel the muscles there. I want so much more than this kiss, things I've never had, and never wanted so badly.

A sad, embarrassing whimper of a sound escapes me as he pulls his mouth from mine, leaning forward so his forehead is on the wall beside me, his breath coming in pants and ghosting over my bare shoulders.

"Rafe," I breathe.

The hand cupping my cheek moves, his fingertips skating over my face, down along my jaw and trailing down my arm. Goose bumps erupt over every surface of my skin.

"You are everything, Seraf. Everything. That was … wow."

It pleases me to no end that I've made him feel this way. Even with all my inexperience, my dumb thoughts of leaping off cliffs mid-kiss, and my ignorance of what to do with my hands—Rafe is affected by *me.*

"Can we just stay in this alcove forever?" I ask.

He chuckles. "I don't see any reason why not."

"It's a plan, then. I'm sure Claudius could have some furniture moved in here within the hour. Storage might be an issue …"

Rafe rumbles a nonsensical response and tilts his head, brushing his lips across my neck. It feels as good as I imagined it would, and I lean into him before he pulls away, taking two steps backward until his hips rest on the wall across from me. Maybe he needs the steadiness of something else too.

I focus on my breaths, slowing them, trying not to throw myself across this space at the man who just turned my world upside down in more than one way. And though I don't feel like the kiss should have been life-altering for him, Rafe looks just as stunned and disheveled as I do. I love that I'm not the only one affected. That someone so inexperienced as me could make someone like Rafe need to step back.

"You still have a choice, Angel." Then Rafe smirks, and the look that has infuriated me so many times now makes my stomach clench with want. "But I wanted to make sure you knew what was on the table."

He's taking us back to the safety of teasing, as Rafe knows me well enough to be sure I wouldn't make this decision based on a kiss. But he underestimates the power of it. It must be the drugging influence of his lips, but his words bring an image in my mind—me laid out on a table, Rafe hovering over me, sweeping down to kiss me again.

"We should probably head down to the ball," he says.

"Do we have to?"

His eyes flame to life. "I wish we didn't, but yes. I think we'd both be in a royal amount of trouble if we were missed. But … I need a minute."

351

He needs a minute? I need a lifetime—not to recover, but I think I need a lifetime with him.

The moment we step out of the alcove, we're facing off with The Dane. I swear, for a giant, he's easy to forget sometimes. Probably because when he wants to, he's good at disappearing into the background. Other times, like right now, he wants to make his presence known.

And he likely just watched my alcove makeout session with Rafe.

"Oh, hello." I smooth a hand down my dress. When he lowers his chin, giving me a look of disapproval, I glare right back. "You're not my father."

"But he pays my salary."

I huff out a breath of irritation, but Rafe, keeping one hand on my lower back, stretches the other out toward The Dane.

This could go south very quickly.

After staring coldly at Rafe for a few seconds, The Dane's giant paw envelopes Rafe's hand. I swear, I hear bones crunching.

"Anders," Rafe says.

He knows The Dane's real name?

The Dane—*Anders*—only grunts, but he does loosen his grip and step back, giving Rafe the tiniest nod of something that might be approval. Or might just be a silent agreement that he's not going to kill him.

Right now, anyway.

CHAPTER TWENTY-EIGHT

Serafina

While a ball might sound romantic in all the stories and movies, there is a lot more mingling and politicking than romancing at an actual ball. I should be thankful, as I'm not sure being in Rafe's arms, dancing, would help clear my head. Not after that kiss.

And my head is anything but clear. It's fog on a mountaintop, and it feels as though any step I take might result in falling from a precipice. Then again, falling isn't so bad. I'm rather enjoying the falling I'm doing with Rafe.

And there is no question now. I'm thankful he didn't try to kiss me days ago, as it would have clouded my mind even more than it is. I have a big decision to make, a *choice*, and I shouldn't make it in a haze.

Marrying Rafe. It's an idea I can hardly wrap my brain around, and the idea of it has me giddy, smiling too widely at people, half listening. That, in and of itself, should be my answer. But I'm still concerned about Rafe.

"Did you follow any of that?" Rafe asks as a baron from Germany finally walks away, finally done boring us about his favorite pastime. Which, apparently, is hunting chamois, a subject he can wax on about for longer than one might expect or hope.

"I don't even know what a chamois is. I kept thinking of those rags used for cleaning—a shammy? Is that the name?"

Rafe barks out a laugh. "I think you're referring to the Sham-wow. It was some American product. I saw videos on YouTube."

I giggle. "Right. Somehow I don't think that's what he's hunting."

"Chamois are like a goat-antelope. I'm sure we could ask him to show us photos. Let's go see if he has some on his phone." Rafe starts to walk after the baron and I grab his arm, pulling him back.

"Please, no! I can't take any more."

"How about a drink? Or a bite to eat? I must keep you fed for Christmas dinner."

I give him a flirty smile and bump him with my hip, enjoying the sound of his laughter. The song changes, and I smooth a hand down his lapel. "What about a dance?"

A grin breaks out over his face. "You want to dance with me? I thought you hated dancing."

Again, there's that vulnerability shining in his eyes. Women are always going on about wanting strong, alpha-type men. While I admire strength and want someone to have a backbone, there is something beautiful when I see this softness in Rafe. Maybe because it's a secret, something hidden and kept just for me. I feel honored to be someone who gets to see it.

"I do. But any woman at this ball would want to dance with you. Probably even the queen mother."

Rafe's nose scrunches, and it's an adorable look on him. His eyes dart around the room. "Did I tell you she was playing footsie with me the other night at dinner?"

I can't help but laugh at this. "No, but I believe it."

He turns amused eyes on me. "And you're willing to take her on—over me?"

"I'd take on anyone in this room for you."

My heart picks up as I realize what I've said. Teasing slid right into truth so easily.

Rafe studies my face for a moment, one side of his mouth hooking upward in a half smile that makes my stomach flip. "I'm honored, my little fighter." His hand finds mine, and the contact sends nerves skittering up my arm. "And I'm pleased to have you with me, wearing my ring. Even if it's only temporary."

His voice drops for this last part, making sure no one around us can hear his words. I'm floating as he leads me by the hand out onto the floor in the center of the ballroom with its grand, coffered ceilings and crystal chandeliers.

I expect Rafe to pull me close, but he keeps a more formal position, our hands clasped while his other is on my waist, mine on his shoulder. We fall into a waltz, and I'm grateful for my training, for years of dance that allow my muscle memory to take over. Rafe is a great dancer, which helps. I try to relax into his sturdy arms, losing myself in the steps and music.

"Oof!"

I lost myself a little too much and stomped on his foot. "Oh, sorry! Dancing isn't my greatest strength. You should know that up front."

"I wish I'd known that earlier," Rafe teases as I relax,

letting him lead me. He's more than competent, with the grace of a big cat, like a panther.

"Would you take back your offer?"

"You mean my proposal?"

Even though I was there for it and I'm now wearing his ring, simply the word proposal makes me giddy. "Yes. That."

"I would have asked you sooner. I've been looking for a woman who doesn't see dancing as her greatest strength. It's on my list."

"Oh, you've got a list?"

His expression shifts from teasing to something inscrutable. "Something like that."

"Did you actually write it down?"

"It's just in my head."

"What else is on it? Besides not being a great dancer, I mean. Is it a long list?"

He doesn't answer for a moment, and the air changes between us. Almost imperceptibly, I feel a shift in him. It's in the way his hand rests on my waist, his fingers curling into me, sliding down a little on my hip.

He draws me closer until we're moving like liquid through the crowd even with my clumsiness. Rafe leans in until his lips find my ear. My eyes flutter closed even as the rest of my body sparks with awareness.

"Do you remember when we first met?" Rafe asks.

I roll back through my memories, finally landing on one that makes me smile. "The lacrosse game. I came to watch Callum. The two of you got into a fight."

His head shakes next to mine. "That wasn't the first time we met. Think again."

I do, scrolling and scanning and trying to place Rafe in my memories. He must sense that I'm unsuccessful, because he whispers again in my ear.

"'The night is darkest before the dawn,'" he says, and I almost gasp as the memory hurtles to the front of my mind, vague at first, then sharpening into something real, as though I'm there now.

There's a boy in a shadowy hallway, and the sight of him immediately makes my heart swell with camaraderie. He's hiding the way I want to be. The event is some boring state dinner Mum and Dad made me attend. Horrible conversations, horrible food. Callum's been ignoring me, and I got my feelings hurt, escaping down a side hall until I found quiet. And this boy with the raven hair and big, sad eyes.

Rafe.

"I'd forgotten," I say. "That was you—the boy in the hallway."

"I never forgot you."

"But we hardly spoke!"

"You said enough that I could see who you were. Even then. That's the day I started making my list."

"Your list? What could you possibly have taken away from that encounter?"

I want to see Rafe's face, but he's holding me too close.

"My list is one word. And it's not a character trait. It's a name."

My breath catches, and I stumble. Rafe tightens his hands on me, gently leading us to the side of the floor, where he stops. I think he's going to look at me, but he keeps me close.

Somewhere, I can almost feel my mother having a coronary about our inappropriate behavior. She'll show up any moment to interrupt us and remind me of decorum. Hopefully, she's otherwise engaged and won't be able to extricate herself.

I need Rafe to finish, I need him to tell me—

"Serafina." My full name gusts from his lips like a plea

and a declaration. I was hoping, and yet I'm still shocked and pull back to stare at him. With his smooth cheeks and vulnerable eyes, he's that little boy in the hallway again. Looking hurt, looking lonely, looking for someone to sit beside him.

"But that was so long ago," I protest. "And you never acted like, well—you never flirted with me. You were always with other women."

Rafe's mouth dips down. "It was always you I wanted. But I hardly saw you, and when I did, I didn't know how to behave. I didn't think I was worthy of you."

"Rafe. You can't think that way."

"I've been working on that, Angel. But anyway, you also had Callum guarding you. Lording over you like you were his property."

"What?" My fingers tighten where they're still gripping his shoulder and his hand.

"He warned me off you so many times, told me I wasn't worthy to even speak to you, that I needed to leave you alone."

Callum did—*what?!*

It's one thing for him to tell me to be careful of Rafe. For him to actively tell Rafe—or anyone—that they needed to stay away from me is outrageously overstepping.

I scan the room, furious and wanting to give him a few words of my own. The idea that Callum didn't want to claim me, even now, even with the arrangement, and yet would tell Rafe he couldn't date me. Was it just Rafe or were there others?

"Angel." Rafe takes my hand and brings it up to his lips for a kiss. My anger dims, replaced with a different kind of heat, one that makes me want to grab Rafe and drag him back up to our alcove. "What's past is past. We're here now. I need you to know that I've always—"

"There's my nephew." A hand grasps Rafe's shoulder, uncomfortably tight based on his wince, and Rafe steps back from me as his uncle steps forward.

I try to even my features out. The Baron de Silva has always made my skin crawl with his cold eyes and that mole shaped like Italy. It's not his fault he has an ugly mole that's massive on his neck. Really, it isn't. But paired together with his personality—or lack thereof—and what I know of him from Rafe and from the dossier, the mole just seems like a manifestation of his inner ugliness.

"Princess Serafina." He gives me a little bow, and though I'm usually not one to really notice or care if people are doing it correctly, he seems to not quite bow as much as he ought.

It's a power play, and yes, it bothers me.

It bothers Rafe too. I can see it in the clenching of his jaw and the fire in his eyes. "What do you want, Uncle?"

"I just wanted to congratulate the happy couple," he says, and I can tell that's not really what he means. He's not happy for us. And he doesn't want congratulations. He wants something else. I don't like it.

I want to step closer to Rafe, to face this man together, but Rafe seems to be distancing himself from me. Maybe he's trying to draw his uncle away, but I'd rather just face him together. Rafe can't meet my eyes.

I manage a smile. "Well, thank you. Now if you'll—"

"Has my nephew talked to you about the particulars of his estate?"

Not to be dismissive, but I don't care about the particulars of Rafe's duchy. I'm about to be the queen. And even if I weren't, that's the last thing that matters to me. No one, not even Callum, would be bringing something equal to the table in terms of a marriage.

"We have many things yet to discuss," I say, hoping he'll read into my words and the dismissiveness there. *Yes, I know you've stolen his duchy from him. At least until Phillip reinstates it. I don't want to discuss any of it with YOU.*

He glances between me and Rafe, who's burning a hole in the floor with his gaze. "Clearly there are many things my nephew hasn't made you privy to. We'll have to correct that —and soon."

The way he's speaking, and the way Rafe is practically shrinking, assures me there is some kind of secret, horrible thing the baron is holding over Rafe to reveal in his own time. Rafe knows it.

And I'm left in the dark, feeling suddenly vulnerable without Rafe's strength and his assurances. I hate how quickly I'm filled with doubt.

"Can I borrow you for a moment?" The baron tugs at Rafe.

I want to step in, but Rafe doesn't seem to want me to. I clench my left hand, feeling the solidness of Rafe's mother's ring on my finger. It's some small comfort, but not enough.

"Fi. I've been hoping to steal you for a dance." Callum is suddenly there, exactly where I don't want him to be, his hand on my elbow. "May I?"

Callum directs the question to Rafe, but his uncle is the one who answers, as though Rafe has been struck dumb. "We're stepping away for a moment. The princess is all yours."

I wait for Rafe to say something. Callum frowns, as though expecting the same resistance. Rafe looks up, shooting his uncle a look that doesn't so much as pierce his smug look. It's then I realize Rafe has never really been smug. Because seeing his uncle, there's simply no comparison. Rafe's was only an act, a covering over insecurities.

I should step in—I sense that Rafe needs me. Even if he's undergone therapy, it's clear his uncle has a hold on him. I realize he reminds me of that boy, the one I found in the hallway all those years ago and had forgotten until tonight.

He needs me, I think, but he lets his uncle pull him to the hallway. Feeling sick, knowing it's the very wrong thing, I allow Callum to lead me to the dance floor.

Just like I always do with Callum, I let him take control. I turn, watching Rafe and his uncle disappear through a doorway.

Callum holds me too closely, and I lean back, establishing more space between us. Everything about his hands on me feels wrong. Last week, when we danced, I had been all starry-eyed and hopeful, even through my heartbreak. Now, when I look at him, I'm more detached. He's my friend, Callum. The man I want, the man I love, the man I should be with right now just walked out the door.

Callum smiles. "Are you having a good time with your fiancé?"

The edge in his voice has me rolling my eyes. "Yes, actually, until we were interrupted. How are you doing since the breakup with Brit?"

It could be polite conversation, but maybe I mean it as a dig. Maybe I'm being a little passive aggressive. Maybe I just want to walk away, go find Rafe and tell his uncle to scram, then find another alcove.

"Brit was a mistake, Fi."

Well, that's certainly not going to win Callum any awards.

"I'm so, so sorry," he continues. His eyes plead with me. For what? What could he possibly want right now?

My eyes track to the door Rafe just left through. Where

did they go? Will they come back? What is his uncle holding over him now? This feels somehow bigger than just the duchy.

"You don't owe me an apology," I tell Callum, hardly paying attention to my own words.

"I do, actually, and I wish you'd let me make it."

"Fine." If I let him say his piece, then I can go.

Callum's face changes to something earnest and I can already see where this is going.

Oh no.

"Fi, I made a lot of mistakes this year. The biggest one was making you think I don't want to marry you."

"But you don't want to marry me. You've said so. More than once."

"That's not exactly true. I was just confused. It wasn't you, but the idea of being forced."

"And now you're not confused? I think you actually said you didn't want marriage, *especially* to me."

"You're twisting my words."

"Maybe. But I think you're twisting up your feelings. I'm sorry, Callum, I don't want you to think that you can just patch this up with a few words and apologies. I've had a lot of time to think about this over the past week. I had a crush on you. One which was unrequited. It was girlish and stupid and probably had as much to do with me trying to agree with the course my parents had mapped out."

"Before you say anything else," Callum interrupts, "I need you to have all the facts."

How did I not see before the way that Callum practically runs over me? He interrupts and thinks he can just tell me what to do or think, who I can and can't talk to, because he somehow magically knows better.

"Before you give me all the facts that you *think* I need to know, I need you to know this—I don't love you. And I'm going to marry Rafe."

Callum's face goes ashen, and he stops moving, so we're not dancing anymore but just standing in the middle of the floor.

"That's what I needed to tell you. I spoke with Phillip earlier. Rafe's uncle sent him here for the express purpose of driving a wedge between us—between Elsinore and Viore, between you and me. He wants to see the relationship between Elsinore and Viore crumble, so he asked Rafe to step in and drive a wedge."

I go cold, even before the next words leave Callum's mouth. I already know what he'll say.

"Fi, Rafe didn't want to marry you. He just needed you *not* to marry me."

My heart doesn't break. It doesn't even crack.

But it does squeeze painfully because I know, even without confirmation, that what Callum has said—at least some version of it—is true. Rafe's reaction to his uncle, his uncle's smarmy smile. But this isn't the full truth, and I know that just as strongly.

What's more painful than what Callum said is the smile on his face when he thinks he's bested Rafe … at *my* expense.

"I warned you," Callum says. "I told you he'd break your heart, Fi."

Trying to extricate myself from Callum's arms without making a scene, I take two steps away from him. His touch, his smell, the sight of him makes me feel nauseated.

"You did warn me. But the ironic thing, Cal, the most heartbreaking thing is how much *joy* you're taking in this situation. If I believed what you're telling me without any explanation from Rafe, it might be painful. Crushing, even. But what's worse is knowing you'd rather be right—you'd rather *win*—even if it means seeing me crushed in the process."

I take no pleasure in the shocked look on his face, or the guilt when he realizes I'm right.

"Fi, I didn't mean that. I only—"

I hold up a hand. "Enough. We'll always be friends. But I'm sorry I wasted so many years fancying myself to be in love with someone who only cares about himself."

"And you'll get that with *Rafe*?" His look of contrition from moments earlier has vanished, replaced only by anger and disbelief.

"Do you know what he told me about you earlier? I'm sure you'll never guess. Rafe told me that you deserved me more than he did. He told me that given a choice, I should probably choose you. But he's wrong. Completely wrong—in his estimation of himself and definitely about you."

"Fi, I didn't—"

"I'm choosing him, and I'm choosing to believe him. To at least give him a chance to account for this. He deserves that. And I deserve better than this."

I leave Callum gobsmacked in the center of the ballroom floor, and hurry through the doors Rafe and his uncle left by earlier. They're nowhere in sight, so I return to the ballroom, looking for Phillip.

I trust when I speak to Rafe, he'll clear all this up with the full story. Not whatever Callum has pieced together. What I *know* is this: Rafe's uncle is a dirty liar, a manipulator, and likely an abuser. Not that it matters, but he also has the ugliest mole I've ever seen, which is a perfect physical manifestation of his ugly, shriveled heart.

Maybe breaking apart Callum and me was his plan—for reasons I still don't fully understand—but I believe what Rafe said to me earlier.

He loves me, and he wants to marry me.

I finally locate Phillip, who seems more than happy to let me pull him away from the pouting socialite looking at him like he's her meal ticket.

"I'm sorry," I say, not sounding the least bit sincere.

"Thank you," Phillip mutters.

When we've moved away to relative privacy, I take a breath. "Callum said Rafe spoke with you earlier about his uncle?"

Phillip looks uncomfortable, which at least confirms what Callum said. Some version of the story about the baron is true. I won't allow myself to think it's *all* true. I won't.

"He's somewhere with Rafe and, well ..."

"He's here at the palace? At the ball?"

I nod. "Of course. Why?"

"Because security was supposed to locate him for me, to keep him out. He must have arrived earlier or slipped by someone."

"He is slippery."

Phillip is immediately in motion, briefly touching my elbow to make sure I follow. He motions to one of the guards in his service, who discreetly flanks us as we exit the ballroom, pulling another two guards along with him.

"We'll handle his uncle," Phillip says. He shakes his head.

"Thank you. I have one more favor to ask. If possible, I'd love to make use of the press."

"Tonight?"

"Tonight. I have a few things I need to say, and I hope you'll stand with me. As a partner. As allies."

"And it must be now?"

I meet his gaze. "Yes."

I know Phillip well enough to understand that the blank look in his eyes means the wheels are turning behind them.

He's considering what I've said, weighing possibilities. Usually, I'd respect this about him. It's what will make him a great king one day, and his father's stand-in while it's needed. This is no small favor. I've asked to essentially hold a press conference during the middle of his country's Centennial Ball.

Still, I do think he could consider a little bit more quickly.

Because I'm over here holding my breath like my life isn't hanging in the balance. *NBD, Phillip. TAKE YOUR FLIPPING TIME.*

After a moment, he nods and I release a long, slow breath.

"Meet me in my office so you can lay out the details. There's one thing I need to attend to, and then I'll have the press alerted to meet us."

I hope this grand gesture I'm about to make is enough to convince not only a man, but my whole country.

CHAPTER TWENTY-NINE

Rafe

The last thing I want is Uncle pulling me away from Seraf, or getting anywhere near her. It's made worse by the fact that I know she's dancing with Callum. The thought makes my teeth grind. I need to get this conversation over with.

I need to pull my uncle out of my life, but he's been like a tick. Extraction isn't as easy as giving a solid yank.

A start would be for me to stop acting like a big baby who can't look Uncle in the eye. My therapist has said facing Uncle and confronting him could make things worse and isn't necessary for me to work through this.

Still, it feels important to *me*. It feels necessary to *me*.

Taking a breath, I straighten my back and square my shoulders, finally lifting my chin to face the beast, as it were. His eyes are the stuff of many nightmares: cold, expression-less, compassion-less.

But as I stare him down, there's slight hesitation there as

he sees something different in me, something that's come through the past two years of talking this out, working through it. I won't downplay Seraf's role either. Simply experiencing her bravery, her kindness, and her love has given me a gift that I call on now.

When Uncle glances away, unable to hold my gaze, I mentally award myself a trophy and then look at his mole. *Uncle Italian Moleneck.*

"What are you smiling about?" he snaps.

I cross my arms, leaning casually against the wall. "I have many reasons to smile, Uncle. Shall I list them for you?"

He sneers. "If you think this means I'll reconsider the conservatorship—"

"That's the least of my concerns. When I'm living in Viore, some paltry duchy won't matter. And you won't be able to pull my strings anymore."

"So you actually plan to marry her? And you think you'll be able to use her—"

"Stop. I will not be *using* Princess Serafina for anything. I love her. The money, the title, all of it means nothing to me. I want her. I've always wanted *her.*"

Even before I knew who she was. Even before I was the kind of man who might be worthy of her consideration.

This silences him for a moment, and I can almost see the gears turning in his head. Uncle hates being out of the loop, not having all the facts, and I know he's trying to see how he can use this turn of events to do whatever he's trying to do.

I don't quite know what's in this for him. It could be a kickback from someone who wants to pull strings on a large scale, maybe one of the anti-royal groups. This could be a part of something bigger. Or, it could just be that Uncle has always hated King James and Queen Suzette. Hatred or jealousy would be enough to motivate him to ruin lives and hurt people.

"Once the princess knows the truth—"

I don't let him finish. "You can't tell her without exposing yourself, which I know you'd never willingly do. But what's more, I've already spoken about your plans. She'll know the truth soon enough, and she'll hear it from me."

I can only hope that when she hears it from me, Seraf will believe me. That she won't think for a moment that anything between us had to do with my uncle or a duchy.

"Nothing I've done with Seraf had to do with you. And nothing I do in the future will have to do with you either. I'm done."

"If you ever want to see so much as a euro—"

"Keep it. The duchy too. They're meaningless to me, and I won't let you use them to make me dance like your puppet."

I've heard the expression *blood draining from someone's face* but didn't understand it until now. Uncle looks like the color of paste. It only makes his mole stand out more.

"Who did you tell?"

"Crown Prince Phillip of Elsinore."

The human body is an amazing thing. In seconds, Uncle's face has gone from pasty white to the purple of canned beets, something his chef tried for years to force me to eat. I've never liked them—until now.

Uncle shakes his fist at me, but I don't so much as flinch. He's never hit me, and he never will. He's a coward, and now that he knows his words and his manipulations and machinations can't make me dance like his puppet, he has nothing left.

"Don't think I won't take you down with me! Don't think I won't—"

369

"Baron de Silva—a word, please."

The voice from behind me is smooth and even but commands attention and carries power. Suddenly, Phillip is beside me, along with two imposing guards. Both of whom have necks like tree trunks. I'm surprised to see Anders step up beside them. His nod to me is almost imperceptible, and it gives me a sliver of hope.

Uncle's posture straightens as though he's been pulled taut by a string. And he has. A string of fear. He begins to bow, but Phillip holds up a hand.

"Enough with the formalities. Let's go. My father wishes to have a word with you."

Uncle's eyes flick to me, and in the past, I would have felt a shiver of fear at the look in them. After all, rats are dangerous when backed into a corner.

"No need to bring Rafe into this," Phillip adds. "He and I have spoken at length. Come on. I'd like to make quick work of this matter and continue with our celebration."

The two guards flank Uncle, but Anders edges one of them out with simply a look, taking the spot on Uncle's right. Anders towers over him, and the rage rolling off him is barely restrained. I know Seraf's father pays his salary, but I wonder if I could somehow add a bonus. Once I can control my finances, that is. I'm sure Uncle wouldn't approve the expense.

Phillip pauses for a moment, waving Anders and his men on. When they're out of earshot, the Crown Prince studies me.

"Thank you for your honesty about this matter and for coming to me with this. I'm sorry for what you've suffered. I hope to offer your uncle a position that's suited to him."

I tilt my head, glancing at my uncle's retreating back.

"You're offering him a position? As what—scullery maid? Refuse worker?"

Phillip actually chuckles. I didn't think he had it in him. "Hopefully, something worse. Something that will keep him busy and far away. Some kind of position with our people in Italy, perhaps?"

It's my turn to laugh. I shouldn't be surprised that Phillip has learned the country Uncle seems to hate even more than Elsinore. "Brilliant. Yes."

"Again, thank you. I hope that—whatever happens—this is the start of a relationship built on trust."

Whatever happens.

I know he means with Seraf, and the relationship between Elsinore and Viore. And in truth, I have no idea what will happen. She's wearing my mother's ring. I think she loves me.

But you basically told her to choose another man, you dolt.

Phillip starts off, then pauses. "Also, two more things. First, your uncle's conservatorship has been dissolved. He's been removed from any and all accounts and titles."

I can only blink for a moment. "How?"

"Having the title I do affords me some exceptional power I can use in extenuating circumstances. Consider it done."

And just like that, the tick has been removed. Uncle has no power over me. It's a relief, but I realize that I already knew that. The duchy and my bank accounts were just things. Big things, but still. He lost his power when I refused to fall in line, when I told him I wouldn't be his puppet. That said, this feels like a triumph.

"Thank you."

Phillip's gaze shifts away from me, and I don't think I'm going to like this second thing nearly as much as the first. *Way to lead with the good news first, buddy.*

371

"I had to loop my brother in when I told Father about all this earlier. I just wanted you to know that Callum is aware of what your uncle was trying to do."

Now the blood feels like it's draining from my face. Maybe my whole body. For years, Callum has done nothing but try to turn Seraf against me. All the progress I've made in gaining her trust may be wiped out before I even have a chance to explain. I'd love to think she would believe me over Callum, but in reality, he's had her ear for their whole lives. I've had a week.

"Do you know where Seraf is?"

At a quick glance in the doorway of the ballroom, I see neither Serafina nor Callum, which shouldn't make my gut wrench with dread, but still does.

"Actually, yes. She's gathering for a press conference right now. You can follow me to the press room."

A press conference?

"To announce *what*?"

Phillip looks at the watch on his wrist. "We need to be there now."

As we walk, my mind feels like it's been taken over by a surly mob of football hooligans. Why a press conference now? What did Callum tell her? WHAT IS SHE ANNOUNCING?

There is no world in which I can honestly believe that Seraf would be announcing an engagement to me. Not without telling me first. Not when Callum is the last person she talked to.

I also want to believe with all the belief I have that she's not announcing an engagement to Callum.

I swallow down the emotion in my throat as I follow Phillip through a maze of hallways, wishing I could feel like I'm walking toward something other than the gallows.

CHAPTER THIRTY

Rafe

Phillip leads me to the press room. I slump against the back wall, trying to be invisible, which is fairly easy considering the way the press is intensely focused on the front of the room. I'd like to ignore the worries and fears steadily crawling up my spine, but it's not so easy. The buzz of excitement among the press only feeds the rising noise in my head.

I'm fighting off a loop of statements in my mind, planted from Uncle, and even myself.

I'm not worthy.

I'm a failure.

My parents would be ashamed.

No one would want to be with me—especially not someone like Seraf, who deserves someone good and wholesome. Someone like Callum.

I reach in my pocket for my mother's ring, remembering

only as I do that it's on her finger. At least, I *hope* it's still on her finger.

Breathing deeply, I cross my arms casually over my chest, tapping out a rhythm with my fingers. It's another technique I learned, one that's supposed to help regulate and rebalance my nervous system. Simple movement, complex function.

It seems impossible that anything could calm me now, but when the door at the front of the room opens, my thoughts have quieted.

Phillip strides into the room, his presence as commanding as I've ever seen it. Serafina follows, looking as regal as I've ever seen her. I instantly straighten, dragging a hand through my hair.

Seraf changed from the red dress into a more demure black suit jacket and skirt, but looks every bit as breathtaking as she did earlier. She could draw my gaze wearing a potato sack, a theory I'd like to test later—if given the chance.

I can't read anything on her face, and I can't see her hand to see if she's wearing the ring.

I will her eyes to find me over the heads of the paparazzi who are now in a frenzy. But Seraf doesn't see me—or perhaps doesn't *want* to see me.

The conversations of the press halt, even as the tension in the room mounts. I find myself standing straighter, waiting for Seraf to see me. But her eyes sweep the front row of the press and then move back to Phillip.

If only she'd look at me, I would know. I would know how she feels about me, what she may have decided that she's announcing now.

Phillip has been kind and decent to me, especially today. Would he bring me here only to be heartbroken and humiliated? No. Callum would. Not Phillip.

I cross my arms again as Phillip holds up a hand, instantly settling the journalists.

"Thank you for gathering here," he says. "I know this is quite unprecedented during the middle of the Centennial Ball. But I have the support of my father, His Highness King James, and would like to extend the floor to Her Royal Highness, Princess Serafina of Viore."

With a sweeping motion of his hand, Phillip steps aside, but not back, as Seraf steps before the microphone with a confidence that only makes her more beautiful. Phillip's stance, standing shoulder-to-shoulder with Seraf, is a display of solidarity and support of whatever she's about to say.

But Seraf hardly needs it. As she opens her mouth to speak, she comes alive. My chest glows with pride.

"Thank you, Prince Phillip. Thank you, members of the press. Though I am speaking from the palace of Elsinore, this message is as much to my own people of Viore. I appreciate your time and your consideration."

She pauses for effect, and the whole room hangs on her silence. "To the world, I have been known as the Ice Princess."

Seraf smiles, amusement lighting her eyes, and there are a few chuckles. I've never liked the nickname, perhaps because I've never seen anything cold in her. But now, she's using it to her advantage, and it's brilliant.

"Sometimes, at the expense of seeming human, I've made the choice to be proper and poised. Maybe, at times, even cold and aloof. The nickname has been fitting for the persona I've shown you, but not for the princess—and the person I am. Or the queen I'm to become. Starting now, I plan to be more open and more forthcoming, especially with matters of national import, but also matters of the heart."

Her eyes briefly find mine when she says the word *heart*,

and her gaze slams into me with the force of a battering ram. Hope is a tiny, flickering flame beginning to glow brighter in my chest.

And then she meets my eye and winks.

Winks!

I cannot restrain the wild grin that breaks out over my face.

Seraf continues, "Citizens of Elsinore, my people of Viore —as you may know, I must be married by my father's fifty-fifth birthday, according to our Vioran charter. If I am not, the Council of the People may call for a vote to abolish the monarchy. I know for many of you, that seems like a viable or even good option."

She stares confidently out at the press, who I feel are just waiting like vultures to pick apart her bones. Seraf has never looked more royal, never more beautiful.

"As for my wedding plans, I know you've heard uncon-firmed rumors of an engagement to The Duke of Weldon."

My heart leapfrogs up into my throat. The press begins to murmur until she holds up her hand—her left hand, which flashes my mother's ring like a neon sign. The murmurs increase in volume at the sight as the journalists jostle each other for a better photograph. When Seraf meets my eyes, then gestures to me, the noise becomes more of a roar.

"Would you be so kind as to join me?"

Normally, the press doesn't make me nervous. Nor do spotlights. But I've always been playing a part for them. Now, I'm only me, and it has my heart racing.

With my eyes firmly on Serafina, I make my way to the front of the room, ignoring the clicks of shutters and the chatter around me. I'm unsure what she'll say.

But whatever Seraf asks of me, my answer will be yes. I only hope that's what this means.

I hesitate a moment too long, wondering what the appropriate greeting is for taking the stage at a surprise press conference with your possibly fake but possibly real fiancée. Seraf turns and grabs my hand, tugging me to stand so she's flanked by Phillip on one side, me on the other.

I don't look at the members of the press. I only look at *her*.

"I would like to introduce my fiancé, the Duke of Weldon, Rafe de Silva. I believe you may know him by another name, which is a bit more unflattering than the one you've given me and one which in no way accurately portrays the man standing beside me."

Though I'm having to fight back feelings of being unworthy to stand here, by her side, there is nowhere I'd rather be. Clearing my throat, I lean in a little toward the microphone, wearing a smirk.

"At times, the Royal Rogue might have been just a little bit accurate."

Seraf laughs, and even Phillip makes a sound that's almost a chuckle.

"But it's not who I am," I say, all traces of my smile gone. "It's not how I wish to be known, and I will be doing my best to prove that over time to you."

I turn to Seraf as I say *to you*, squeezing her hand as I do so. Her eyes, a few shades lighter than my mother's sapphire, are bright and happy.

Addressing the press again, Seraf says, "While I am a supporter of free speech, I do hope that in the future, my fiancé and I both might earn new nicknames, even if that takes some time. As long as you avoid any weird couple names, that is."

I bite my lip to keep from laughing. The press don't know what to do with this glimpse they're getting of the real Seraf

—honest, a little goofy, and incredibly charismatic, drawing respect even as she talks about couple names. But they're gobbling it up.

I realize Kat, Claudius, and Anders are now standing at the back of the room. Kat's face splits in a smile and the other two look—well, about as expressionless as they normally do, but they're *here*, which is a show of support with or without smiles.

Phillip clears his throat, clearly indicating that he's ready to move on with things.

"Right," Seraf says. "Nicknames aside, I would like to ask a favor. Be patient with me. With the both of us. Give us a chance to prove ourselves to you, to prove the monarchy has a place in Viore."

She glances at me, then Phillip. I trace my thumb over the back of her hand, hoping she understands my reassurance: *I'm here. You're doing great. I love you.*

"This week, I have written up a preliminary agreement signed by King James, who is, I hope, enjoying the festivities rather than this dull press conference." Seraf smiles at the laughter in the room, then continues. "Prince Phillip stands in his stead as a show of support of this agreement, which will extend our trade agreement to include silicon. In the meantime, I plan to see the Vioran copper mining industry come into accord with the recommended environmental standards. This will better protect our people and our resources, with as little impact on our economy as possible. This agreement strengthens our relationship with Elsinore, and is a sign of good faith that I—that *Rafe* and I—will listen to the people and serve you well." With a smile, she turns to the prince. "Phillip?"

He gives her an approving look, then gazes out at the journalists. "Any questions?"

The room erupts with shouts, but I lean toward the microphone again, even as I pin Seraf with a look.

"I have a question for the princess. I've asked before, but just need an official confirmation. Seraf, will you marry me?"

"Officially and unofficially, my answer is yes."

The sound of shouted questions and cameras clicking is drowned out when Seraf wraps her hand around the back of my neck and presses her lips to mine.

———

Seraf

Phillip allows more questions than I thought he would, and I feel dead on my feet by the time he closes things down. From the back of the room, Kat gives me two thumbs up and blows me a kiss, while Claudius simply nods, which feels like I've won a trophy.

I'm unsure whether it's been fifteen minutes or five hours when we escape into a back hallway, trailed by The Dane, who seems surlier than ever.

"Thank you," I tell Phillip, smiling as he and Rafe shake hands.

"Of course. Now, if you'll excuse me, I promised my father I'd dance with seven women tonight. I have three more to go."

He looks about as excited about that prospect as I was about wearing Brit's curtain dress. The moment he's gone, Rafe slides his arms around my waist and pulls me close, burying his nose in my hair. We stand like this for a few minutes, long enough that The Dane walks away, giving us our space.

"Seraf, I need to tell you something. A lot of *somethings*, actually. Things I should have said much, much earlier."

His whispered words brush over my skin, making me want to do anything other than talk. But this is a conversation we've put off for too many hours already. And once we talk …

"Would you care to take a walk in the garden? I'd like to hear your side of things, listen to you grovel and beg for forgiveness, and then perhaps make out beside the rosebushes. Does this sound agreeable?"

The earnestness in his eyes is hard to resist. "I'd love to start with the apology. Seraf—"

"Nope." I lean back and place my whole hand over his mouth, smiling when his lips move over my palm in a sweet kiss. "You need to squirm a bit. It's healthy. And I rather enjoy knowing you're squirming. Seems only fitting."

I move my hand. Mostly because now my thoughts are having a hard time leaving his lips.

"As you wish."

"Don't even try with *The Princess Bride* quotes! Real princesses need a bit more than that. If you're going to tell me you love me, just say it."

"I love you, Seraf."

I grin. "You're making this far too easy!"

"I think things have been hard enough on you." He tucks a piece of hair behind my ear, his fingertips trailing over my jaw in a way that makes my stomach tilt.

"Do you have something you'd like to say back to me?" He raises his brows.

"We'll see how your groveling goes."

Compared to the volume in the press room, the garden is like a tomb. But in a good way—not a creepy way—as Rafe and I stroll through Queen Suzette's roses. It's quite beautiful in the stillness and darkness, and exactly what I need to settle the adrenaline still coursing through me.

Though Rafe's touch and his proximity have a whole different kind of excitement building.

We cover all the biggest, most important things first, like his uncle's manipulations and how it was never part of Rafe's motivation for pursuing me.

"Of course not," I tell him. "You said you fell in love with me at first sight. And you practically tried to give me away to Callum. You should have seen his face when I told him that."

"You told Callum that?"

I lean my head against Rafe's shoulder. "I did. Right when I told him that you were the better man. The one who would have sacrificed for me, rather than sacrificing *me* in order to be right."

Rafe goes quiet. "I missed a lot tonight."

"You were around for the most important bits."

We stop near a fountain with a few stone benches bathed in moonlight. Rafe sits and draws me into his lap, curling his arms around my waist and setting his chin on top of my head. I draw in a deep breath, enjoying his woodsy scent.

"As long as I don't miss the part where we make out in the rosebushes."

"I'm not sure it's possible for you to miss that."

"And I don't want to miss whenever you decide to tell me you love me—even if that's not tonight but in a month."

"Or two?"

He chuckles. "Or two."

"How about six?"

With a sigh, he presses a kiss to my hair. "I'm a patient man."

"I love you, Rafe." I squeeze my arms around his broad back, loving the feel of his warm, solid body against mine.

"Are you sure you want to do this? To take me on? To take on ruling a kingdom with me?"

He pulls back enough I can see the smirk on his face. "Would this be before or after the making out in the rose bushes?"

I tilt my head. "Solid question. I'd have to say ... both."

"Should we get started, then?"

"Absolutely."

My heart kicks into high gear as Rafe leans in, his breath warm and his lips soft and inviting. I'm more than ready for round two of the alcove. This will be sweeter, because in a few hours' time, we've gone from unsure to solid.

But when his lips are just millimeters away from mine, a sound makes us both freeze. It's two people, singing completely off-key. And incorrect lyrics to boot.

" ... your eyes—the knife, the meat. Your eyes—admit defeat ..."

"Is that ..."

"The sound of Kat and Claudius falling in love whilst butchering a Peter Gabriel song? Yes. Yes, it is."

Our kiss is put on hold for long moments of laughter, but I don't mind, because Rafe and I have the rest of our lives to kiss in alcoves and rose gardens and hopefully dozens of other locations from here to Viore and back again.

Preferably, without the terrible singing as mood music.

EPILOGUE - THE ROYAL WEDDING

Serafina

I hope the start of my wedding day is not a sign of things to come. It comes bright and early, by way of Leonidas—the lone female terror—humping my leg.

"Leo! Have some common decency! At least wait until my alarm next time!"

I try to dislodge her with gentle kicks, just as said alarm starts going off. Though there's something wrong with my phone—it's not my normal soft chiming alarm. I'm so distracted that I accidentally give Leo the boot right off the bed. Thankfully, she lands on her feet like a cat, and trots out of the room to find more unwilling partners.

I stare down at my phone, confused. I hear Rafe's voice. Is he calling? No—he must have recorded a message and set it to play on a loop as my alarm.

"Wake up, sleepyhead," recorded Rafe says. "Today is our big day. I love you, Angel. I can't wait to see you, to wed you, and to—"

You don't need the rest of the alarm to get the point. He's looking forward to today. As am I.

Rafe's voice keeps playing as I stare down at the lock-screen photo, which is from our fake engagement shoot in Elsinore. We ended up scheduling another, real shoot once we left Elsinore for Viore, where we've spent the last two months. And even though the new photos were much more real and were used in the official announcements and now hang in the portrait hall in a gold frame, I love these first photos by Frosty.

I remember how tentative everything felt, how desire was awakening, even as I tried to smother it. I remember the warm and also terrifying sensation of realizing I was falling in love with him.

In the photo I chose, I'm on the cusp of laughter, and I can see Rafe's fingers flexing as he tickles my waist. He's not looking at the camera at all, his gaze firmly pinned on me, a wide grin on his face. Not the roguish one, which I still rather like, but the *real* one. Not many people get to see it, which makes it a treasure all my own.

And as a princess soon to be queen, I don't get to keep a lot of things to myself. Including my wedding day.

"Good morning, darling," Mum says, flitting into the room. "Did Leo wake you?"

"Unpleasantly, yes. You let her in here?"

She ignores the question, giving me a quick kiss on the cheek that somehow says both, *I'm happy for you* and *I still haven't forgiven you for making this a public affair.*

"See you in a little while. Happy wedding day, dear." Mum passes Claudius in the doorway.

"By all means," I say, "everyone is welcome in my bedroom."

Claudius doesn't even look fazed. "You have ten minutes

until the beauty preparations begin. Then there will be photographs, a brief interview, and then one set of documents to sign …"

You know. Just a typical day in the life.

Kat bounds into the room, looking as tired as I feel, but with the kind of energy that can only come from a double shot of espresso. Maybe two. She pinches Claudius's bum as she passes by, but he keeps reading.

"Up up up!" she says, grabbing my hands and dragging me from the bed. "It's almost time to get beautiful."

"Impossible," Claudius says, forgetting the clipboard for a moment. "You're both already beautiful."

As I pass him on the way to the bathroom, I pat his shoulder. "Thank you. But I'm taken."

"Me too," he says with a slow smile, his eyes zeroed in on Kat.

———

The day is long, and my desire to see Rafe is the only thing keeping me on my feet by the time I'm in my dress, ready, and waiting to walk down the walkway in the garden. I haven't seen it yet, but I know it will be lit with candles and strewn with flowers as the sun settles down between the trees. Claudius timed it so the ceremony should end just as the sun finally dips below the horizon.

I stifle a yawn, and Kat gives my shoulders a little shake.

"Coffee? Tea?"

"I don't want bad breath or brown teeth. I'd probably spill it down the front of my dress anyway. A shot of adrenaline to the heart?"

She considers this a little too long. "I'm not sure I could arrange it in time."

"You shouldn't be able to arrange it at all."

"I think you're underestimating the power of Claudius."

I laugh and it turns into another yawn. "Too true."

With a last hug, Kat whispers, "You're beautiful. And the best man did win."

I couldn't agree more.

She heads out to take her place and Dad joins me, taking my arm. It may have taken a little more convincing than I'd like, but my parents are both fully supportive of my choice to marry Rafe. I think he's won Viore over completely now, just as he did me, through stubbornness and charm.

I'm covering a yawn with one gloved hand as Dad and I wait inside the back parlor for the moment. Somewhere outside the doors, Rafe is waiting. Along with family, friends, and a few thousand Vioran people on the sloping hills over-looking the garden path.

I won't lie; the nerves are fierce. Not about Rafe. I would have married him the week of the ball if possible. But having to do so in front of so many people makes my stomach dip. Even if it was my idea. It's not what's best for me. Me? I'd have taken a private ceremony. But having a lottery to win seats helped fund the first of what will be many updates to our mining practices. Totally worth it.

"You won't trip," Dad says, giving me a knowing smile.

I blink up at him. "How did you—"

The door swings open. "Mum! Aren't you supposed to be seated?"

"I couldn't without saying a few things first. Whilst I don't agree with all that you're doing, I appreciate that you're doing it. That you have ideas and are using your degree, harnessing your passions, and working to solve the problems you see. You're simply brilliant, Sera, and your father and I couldn't be prouder. Unless you were marrying Callum."

"Ugh! Mum. Way to ruin the sweet moment."

"I never was very sweet. Your father said he fell in love with my saltiness. And with my firm—"

Dad coughs.

"Mum!"

"Standards. I was going to say standards."

Claudius pokes his head inside. "Your Majesty, we really must—"

"Coming." Mum gives me a pat on the shoulder. "You look stunning, darling. You too, Sera."

Dad laughs, and I squeeze his arm. What seems like only seconds later, Claudius reappears. "It's time." He may not smile, but his eyes are warm as he ushers us down the silent hallway to the set of double doors.

I'm so ready that it's tempting to throw them open myself.

Time becomes as languid as the setting sun as the doors open and Dad walks me forward, carefully helping me down the short steps. The traditional Vioran processional is silent, which is both intense and beautiful.

Someone thought to have the gravel walk covered in fabric, which normally I'd consider a huge waste, but for a royal wedding, it simply is what it is.

The temptation as we move forward is to fix my eyes on Rafe, but he's barely visible at the end of the almost quarter-mile walk. Instead of squinting to make out my groom, I lift my eyes to my guests. We're moving slowly but there still isn't enough time to meet everyone's eyes. Still, I do my best.

I see you, I think, as my eyes move over the people lining the hills above. *I see you and you and you. You are my people, and I vow to serve you well.*

As we reach the invited guests, royalty and friends and family, I finally allow myself to look at Rafe.

387

He's standing still, but somehow it seems as though every cell in his body is vibrating with motion. His eyes gleam with joy, adoration, and tears, which he may try to deny later. I'll be sure to keep a few photographs to prove it happened. His hands are clasped in front of him, knuckles practically white. And his smile is wider than I've ever seen it, made more dramatic by the stubble I still call his rogue o'clock shadow.

Suddenly, I am right there, standing before him, and my father leans in to whisper something to Rafe.

I hope it's not a threat to behead him if Rafe treats me poorly. A sob catches in Rafe's throat, and despite the usual no-public-affection rule, he throws his arms around my father, who squeezes him right back.

I'm not crying; you're crying.

Actually, based on the sounds of sniffling, we are *all* crying.

And then, Dad steps back, leaving me alone with Rafe. Alone with a few thousand people, but it feels like just the two of us.

I don't remember reciting vows. I don't remember the message from the priest. I am only aware of Rafe's warm hands enveloping mine, and his eyes, which are aglow with love. He is all I need.

———

Rafe

The wedding could have been in Greek—or French, which I'm still learning—for as much as I heard and understood. Actually, come to think of it, some of it *was* in French. But

388

that's not why I don't remember what was said. My sole focus was my bride—Serafina is everything.

I nudge her gently awake as the horse-drawn carriage comes to a stop outside the front of the castle. After the ceremony, we fulfilled the Vioran tradition of taking a carriage ride through the main streets of the capital, where the people threw flower petals and the heels from bread loaves into the street. That second one I don't fully understand, but the birds will love it.

Speaking of birds, I hear wings flapping as we get out of the carriage. Seraf lets out a little gasp and clutches my arm. "What on earth are they doing here?"

I stare at the very large crate which contains several very large white swans. "I have a feeling this is a wedding gift."

"He wouldn't have." Seraf marches over to the crate, stopping just out of reach as several of the birds raise their wings and hiss.

A large note is pinned to the crate. It reads: *May your lives be as long as—but less bloodthirsty than—these birds. Many happy returns, Callum.*

I've just finished reading it when one of the swans snaps the paper up in its beak, tearing it to shreds.

"We'll have to get him back," Seraf says, and I groan, imagining the next twenty years of pranking back and forth with Elsinore. Then again, it's better than what I might have imagined my relationship with Callum to be like. Over a number of beers and a few nights at a hunting lodge, he and I made a kind of peace. We'll never be best friends, but we're no longer enemies.

And, I guess now we'll be pranking one another through eternity.

Seraf squeals when I pick her up, and begin walking up the castle stairs carrying her. She's light, but there are a lot of stairs, and perhaps it would have been better to wait until we reached the top to pick her up. Maybe if I get tired, I can tag-team Anders for a few dozen steps.

"Carrying the bride over the threshold isn't a Vioran custom!" she protests.

"It's not an Elsinorian one either," I grunt, my thighs aching. "But I thought it might be romantic."

"Actually," Seraf says, distracting me from the burning in my legs with a row of kisses moving up my neck, "the tradition is pretty unromantic. It signifies the woman's virtue. If the groom carries her, it allows her to retain the illusion that she would prefer to keep her chastity intact."

I pause, wondering if I should put her down, and not just because I'm sweating under my suit and my legs are shaking. Honestly, that's a horrendous tradition.

Seraf's kisses become slower, more sensuous. "But I'm very eager to hand over my virtue and my chastity to you tonight."

I'm hot now for an entirely different reason, and resume my trek up the stairs, now at a much faster pace. Aching muscles be damned!

Seraf laughs. "Rafe! I meant for you to put me down!"

"Can't have everyone in Viore knowing how much you're looking forward to handing over your chastity," I pant. "There isn't an actual belt, is there? If so, please know that I'm going to remove it with my teeth."

"Rafe!"

Seraf is still laughing as we reach the top of the stairs—finally—and I almost collapse as we near the large double doors.

Other than security, the castle staff has made themselves scarce for our return. So I'm surprised when a voice speaks from behind us. More surprised because it's Anders.

"Do you need me to carry you both over the threshold?"

Seraf gasps. "Dane! That's the longest sentence I've ever heard you utter!"

He grunts a response, and I hurry through the doorway, afraid he really might try to carry us both.

By the time we've made it up the rest of the stairs—which Seraf walked beside me—I'm a sweaty, shaking mess. Exactly what every groom wants to be on his wedding night.

Seraf is suddenly shy once we're in the room, and though I understand why, I plan to make tonight and every other night one in which she feels safe, comfortable, and completely revered by me.

Placing a gentle kiss on her lips, I use the last reserves of my strength to lift her up on the large bed in the center of the room.

"Darling," I say, kissing her again, long and slow and sweet. "After the unfortunate stair-carrying incident, I'm afraid I need to take a quick shower."

I intend to make tonight perfect for her, and that does not include being up close and personal with a man who smells like a freshly cut field of onions.

Seraf grins, and it turns quickly into a yawn. "Okay."

"I know you're exhausted, so if you'd rather sleep tonight—"

She grabs me by both jacket lapels, a sudden fire in her eyes. "I've waited long enough." And then she kisses me with such passion that it takes every shred of self-control I have to pull away. Her mouth is soft and hot and full of promises I can't wait to see fulfilled.

I step back quickly, and she pouts.

"A quick shower, Angel. Do not move!"

I strip out of my suit as I run to the bathroom, hearing Seraf's laughter as I almost trip over my pants. She stops

391

laughing and hums appreciatively when she gets an eyeful of my bare bum.

"Just a preview of things to come!" I promise, and her giggle is like music.

My shower is faster even than the ones I took in the royal guard, which is saying something. I fasten a towel around my hips, hesitating as I wonder if this is what Seraf would prefer, or if she'd rather I get dressed so she can undress me.

It's a moot point, because by the time I return to the bedroom, dried off with the towel tied low on my hips, Seraf is curled on her side in her puffy dress, snoring softly.

I'm not a creeper if the woman I spend at least an hour staring at while she's sleeping is my wife, right? Excellent. Because that's exactly what I do, and I'm not even apologetic about it.

Today, I fell in love even more with Seraf, knowing that she planned this whole day—her day—with her people in mind. I suspect in the coming years, I'll be the one who needs to remind her that she needs to remember herself, and I'll be the one who puts her first, because she'll put herself last, every time.

After I've tucked her in as well as I can in her dress, I snuggle up next to her slowly, hoping not to wake her. Though we've both been waiting and looking forward to tonight, I can't say that there is even an ounce of disappointment, because we have the rest of our lives for everything else.

So for now, feeling the kind of contentment I've never ever felt before, I fall asleep with Seraf's breath tickling my bare chest as my breathing matches up with her.

THE FAIRY TALE: HAPPILY EVER AFTER

Rafe

"And I've been putting your mum to sleep ever since," I finally finish.

Ava and I both giggle as Seraf lets out a sigh and a soft snore. "I'm not tired at all, Daddy."

I don't believe her for a second. She might have outlasted Seraf, but a few times, her lashes fluttered closed on her cheeks.

"Well, that's just too bad, my Ava-bird. It's definitely time for you to sleep."

"But, Dad!"

"No ifs, ands, buts, or coconuts," I tell her, earning me an eyeroll. It's a scary preview of what I know we'll have to look forward to in the years to come. These first five years passed by in a flash. I'm sure that the next five and then fifteen will as well. They say time flies when you're having fun, but I think I'd change that saying.

Time is bent when you're in love. The days are sometimes sweet and slow, and then gone in a flash, left only as memories. It doesn't just move forward, but you move through it, like wading through gelatin—in the best way possible, of course.

I slide out of bed, careful not to wake Seraf, and give Ava another kiss on the temple. Her lids are already drooping, and she tries to hide her yawn.

"Dad?"

"Yes, Ava-bird?"

"What happened to the other prince? The idiot one."

I grin. "Oh, that's actually your uncle Cal."

Her eyes go wide. "Uncle Cal was the idiot?"

I hold a finger to my lips. "We don't say idiot, darling. And don't tell your mum I told you."

"But wait! Mum almost married *Uncle Cal*? And he was awful!"

I didn't give her *all* the details in the story, just the edited-for-a-five-year-old version. And I made Uncle Cal look a lot better than how he actually behaved. Which was foolish. And idiotic. Definitely deserving of a moat full of dragons.

Not that I mind TOO much, since I got the girl in the end.

"Daddy, you forgot the best part of the story."

"What's that, Ava-bird?"

"They all lived happily ever after," she says.

I smile down at the two loves of my life, taking in the belly containing what will soon be another love who will elbow his or her way right into my heart.

"I didn't forget," I promise her, dropping one kiss on Ava's cheek, one on Seraf's forehead, and another on her belly. "I am living my happily-ever-after every single day."

ALSO BY EMMA ST. CLAIR

Sign up for email updates- http://emmastclair.com/romcomemails

Harper's Brothers

The Buy-In *(coming soon!)*

Love Clichés

Falling for Your Best Friend's Twin

Falling for Your Boss

Falling for Your Fake Fiancé

The Twelve Holidates

Falling for Your Best Friend

Falling for Your Enemy

Sweet Royal Romcom

Royally Rearranged

Hometown Heartthrob Series

Marrying Her Dream Groom

Forgiving Her First Love

Loving Her Cowboy

Trusting Her Cowboy Poet

Managing the Rock Star

Sandover Island Sweet Romance Series

Sandover Beach Memories

Sandover Beach Week

Sandover Beach Memories

Sandover Beach Christmas

Secrets Whispered from the Sea

ABOUT THE AUTHOR

Emma St. Clair is a *USA Today* bestselling author of over twenty books with an MFA in Fiction. She loves sweet love stories and characters with a lot of sass. Her stories have humor, heart, and closed door romance. She lives in Katy, Texas with her husband, five kids, and Great Dane, who doesn't make a very good babysitter.

You can find out more at http://emmastclair.com or join her reader group at https://www.facebook.com/groups/emmastclair/

If you're on Instagram, find her at: http://instagram.com/kikimojo

A NOTE FROM EMMA

It should come as no surprise that a book titled *Royally Rearranged* should have lots of surprises. Rearrangements, if you will.

I started writing this book in 2019, a full year before I started publishing rom-coms with the Love Clichés series. I had fallen in love with royal romances from authors like Aven Ellis, Melanie Summers, and Karina Halle. (Note: If you love closed-door romances, those are not closed door.) I dreamed of writing a book where the arranged marriage wasn't just an arrangement, but real, true love.

Which meant ... Callum was the intended love interest.

Rafe actually wasn't even a character when I started drafting, and I wrote the first fourth of the book without him. And then, suddenly, when I imagined Serafina crying over Callum in a darkened room, a man came out of nowhere, startling her—and me! She accused him of being a vampire in that first scene in my head, and despite her protests, Rafe became the shoulder she cried on.

The handsome shoulder.

In my mind, Callum would eventually come to his senses, showing up on Rafe and Serafina's wedding day to declare his love (and stupidity). Meanwhile Rafe, who was much more of a gentleman than his reputation made him out to be, let himself be the sacrificial lamb so to speak, allowing the press to think that he stood Seraf up and Callum saved the day.

And then Rafe, who had completely won over my heart at this point, would get a second book.

When I returned to write Royally Rearranged with that idea in mind, having simmered for over a year, I just couldn't stomach Serafina choosing Callum. Why did he wait so long? Why parade Brit in front of her? Why not choose Rafe, who was willing to give up his life of freedom and partying to take on a much more serious and binding royal role?

So, yeah. Rafe basically elbowed his way into the story and kicked the leading man to the curb.

I couldn't be happier about how it turned out.

I knew if I was falling in love with a side character, my readers would be too. I mean, I was feeling all the feels for Rafe right off the bat. You?

Anyway, that's the story of this story.

I'm still unsure at this point if there will be more royals. I considered writing books for Callum and for Phillip. Maybe even Henri and Juliet! But I'm not ready at this point to commit because another story of small-town Texas and a family of brothers and a single dad (Harper's family, if you read *Falling for Your Best Friend*) has taken over my mind and heart, just like Rafe did with this book.

Writing royals was harder than I thought, mostly because it involved a kind of modern world-building, plus doing more research than I usually like to do on things like titles, peerage, and the like. Even though I invented my own countries and systems, some things need to be similar to the existing monarchies. In any case, I think I enjoy reading royals more than I enjoy researching them!

But I hope you enjoyed this story, which did capture my heart, and if so, please check out my other books! If you enjoy rom-coms, you'll enjoy the Love Clichés, a completed series, and be on the lookout for the so-far-unnamed new series featuring the small Texas town and a poker theme. The first book, called *The Buy-In*, should be out before the end of 2021.

Oh, and one last note: I TOTALLY thought the song lyrics were "sewing machines of love" and that the song was about textile workers. It's a great song idea, right?

-Emma

ACKNOWLEDGMENTS

Thanks to Stephanie from Alt19 Creative for the epic cover!

Thanks so much to Laura Burton for reading the earliest, draftiest version of this and still loving it with all the enthusiasm she does everything. Thanks also for answering my dumb questions about what people in England call things. If you haven't read a Laura Burton book, you're missing a taste of happiness pie in book form. (They are closed-door rom-coms.)

Thanks to Aven Ellis for letting me ask you questions, for inspiring me, and also for the reminder that my people need PPOs. It's because of you that The Dane exists. I love The Dane. Readers, go read Aven's books! I love all of them, not just the royals.

A big thanks also to Patty Scott for reading the ugly first half AND for the note about peerage. Don't miss the Patty Scott books and be on the lookout for her romcom books under the name Savannah Scott.

Thanks to Jenny Proctor for introducing me to Marco Polo

and talking me off a lot of ledges. I love all Jenny's books and you should pick them up if you haven't!

Thanks to my beta readers, my arc readers, my faithful longtime readers, and the bookstagrammers who have basically made my life so much better. I never thought I'd love Instagram or find so many people who bring joy to me.

A huge thanks also to Rob, my hubby and inspiration for all the romance I write.

Thanks also to Alisa, the best PA in the west.

And to all the lovely readers who helped find typos and inconsistencies: Nicole, Heather, Lori, Catherine, Lisa, Vivian, Jillian, Marsha, Marti, Annie, Rita, Ruth, Teresa, Devon.

Made in United States
North Haven, CT
10 January 2024

47269497R00245